LAND

OF

FIRE

THE LAST OF THE ROMANS: III

DEREK BIRKS

DEREK BIRKS

This is a work of fiction.
Names, characters, places and incidents
are either the product of the author's imagination
or are used fictitiously, and any resemblance to any
persons living or dead is entirely coincidental.
Derek Birks asserts the moral right to be
identified as the author of this book.

LAND OF FIRE

Published by Derek Birks
Copyright © 2021 Derek Birks
Maps designed by Katie Birks, www.katiebirks.co.uk
Front cover courtesy of Sharpe Books
All rights reserved.
ISBN: 978-1-910944-53-0

Also by Derek Birks:

The Last of the Romans
Britannia: World's End
New Dawn – a novella
Death At the Feet of Venus – a short story

The Rebels and Brothers Series
    Feud
    A Traitor's Fate
    Kingdom of Rebels
    The Last Shroud

The Craft of Kings Series
    Scars from the Past
    The Blood of Princes
    Echoes of Treason
    Shadow of Doubt – a novella
    Crown of Fear [to be published in 2021]

For my warm-hearted sister-in-law Maggie who was a constant supporter and advocate of my writing and who is greatly missed by all her family.

Acknowledgements

As always, I would like to acknowledge the debt owed to my creative team for their constructive contributions and observations. I am fortunate to have an excellent graphic designer, Katie Birks, without whom the map would have remained as jumbled ideas in my head. My longsuffering wife, Janet has also, as ever been a great help.

Thanks are also due to Richard Foreman, of Sharpe Books, for his continuing support of my efforts to craft a credible story out of a very shadowy period of British history.

DEREK BIRKS

CONTENTS

Map South West Britain 455 AD 8-9

Glossary 10

The Players in Land of Fire 11

Part One: Iron Hill 13

Part Two: Vindocladia 53

Part Three: Kinfolk 132

Part Four: War 172

Part Five: Fate 253

A Note about Place Names 353

Historical Notes 354

About the Author 363

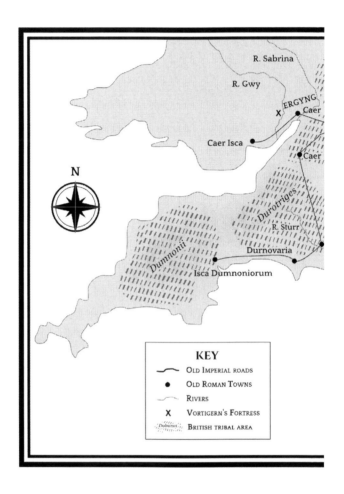

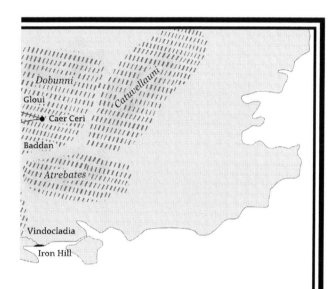

Dobunni

Gloui

Caer Ceri

Baddan

Catuvellauni

Atrebates

Vindocladia

Iron Hill

SOUTH WEST BRITAIN 455 AD

Glossary

apse: a semi-circular alcove seen in late Roman buildings and rooms

auxilia: support units in the late Roman army

bucellarii: a group of mounted soldiers personally loyal to an individual leader

burgus: a small fort of the late Roman Empire

cataphract: heavily-armoured horsemen

caupona: a fairly basic inn, or lodging house

dux: a high military office in the late Roman Empire

foederati: tribes who were bound by treaty to fight as allies of Rome

hard: a stretch of beach where a boat can be drawn up above the tide line.

navis lusoria: a small, shallow, military ship for use on rivers with oars and a sail

spatha: a long, straight, double-edged sword used widely in this period

villa: farm estate

wyrd: the Saxon concept roughly equivalent to fate

The Players in Land of Fire

The Aurelius Honorius family:
Ambrosius Aurelianus*, once Dux of an elite Roman bucellarii unit
    Honoria Florina, half-sister of Ambrosius
    Honoria Lucidia, sister of Ambrosius
    Inga, Ambrosius' lady, a young Saxon

The Bucellarii:
    Aurelius Varta, a Frank who is a long-time friend of Ambrosius
    Aurelius Marianus Onnophris (Onno), an Egyptian engineer from Alexandria
    Aurelius Maurus Rocca, a soldier from North Africa
    Aurelius Xallas, a soldier from Baetica in southern Spain
    Aurelius Molinus Caralla, a former cataphract (heavy cavalryman) from Britannia
    Flavius Silvius Germanus, a Burgundian soldier
    Lucius Artorius (Arturus), son of a Gallic soldier

The Britons:
    Vortigern*, High King of Britannia
    Pascent*, son of Vortigern
    Lurotriga, widowed queen of the Durotriges
    Marac, a British noblewoman
    Argetrus, a Durotriges soldier

King Erbin of Dumnonia*, ruler of south-west Britain

Cadrullan, magistrate of Caer Ceri

Carina, wife of Caralla

The Saxons:

Ulf, leader of a group of Saxons

Wynflaed, Ulf's wife

Ishild, Wynflaed's younger sister

The Scotti

Niall, leader of the Scotti raiders

Lugaid and Donnan, two brothers

Others:

Stavelus, a Roman officer from Verona

Father Gobban, a monk

Ferox, a war dog

NB. Those characters marked with * are actual historical figures.

Part One: Iron Hill

1

June 455 AD, on the south coast of Britannia

Ambrosius Aurelianus lay on the headland summit of Iron Hill with the midday sun warming his back. Looking down on the tired old port, nestled against the south side of the river estuary he wondered why anyone would want to raid it. It was a mere remnant of a once thriving settlement – a trading outpost now almost devoid of trade. Here and there a spiral of smoke drifted up to mingle lazily with the sea-borne haze while, below his vantage point several figures trudged stiff-legged up the winding hillside track. They were making for the smelting furnace over to his left where men and boys toiled each day to rake out a glowing ball of precious iron. No sooner was it out than the workers, their faces burnished by the heat, began hammering the ragged lump of white-hot metal into life. Watching the sparks fly was somehow entrancing – if only, thought Ambrosius the sins of men could be so easily beaten out.

Dragging his gaze from the iron workings, he looked to the west and was relieved to see a column of riders weaving a careful path through the marshy ground towards the twin earth banks. The latter, constructed by the ancients to protect the settlement from a land assault, were abandoned long before Rome's empire consumed Britannia. No-one now stood watch upon the crumbling rampart and only heath grass attempted to scale the earth banks. Soon his men would pass through the entrance and dismount to await his orders.

The previous day his new allies in Durnovaria had sent word - not for the first time - that a flotilla of small vessels had been sighted heading eastward along the coast. The people of Durnovaria and its hinterland knew all about Scotti raiders for in the past the barbarous seafarers had been known to ravage farms and settlements for many miles inland. But only a handful of local folk remembered those times now and Ambrosius found the recent reports scarcely credible.

Beside him his fair Saxon lady, Inga shifted uncomfortably.

"They should be here by now," she groaned. "These raiders… if they're coming at all…"

"You could have stayed behind at Vindocladia," he told her.

She pulled a face. "I see little enough of you, as it is."

Inga had every right to be annoyed for it was the third time he had raced south to patrol the coast without finding a single Scotti boat. Once again he had left his half-repaired Roman burgus at Vindocladia to intercept a non-existent foe and he was already regretting it. Yet what choice did he have?

His new alliance with King Erbin of Dumnonia – his only alliance – required him to answer any calls for help from Erbin's friends in Durnovaria. In return King Erbin had promised not to support the High King, Vortigern's vengeful pursuit of Ambrosius. Thus once again Ambrosius rode south with as many men as he could find mounts for - which meant about thirty. The rest of his company under the command of his loyal friend, Varta remained behind to carry on with the much needed repairs to the fort and to protect the nearby town of Vindocladia.

"So, here we are again," grumbled Inga, "and still… no Scotti. I begin to doubt these folk exist at all."

He stood up. "Come on," he said, offering his hand.

Taking it, she allowed him to pull her to her feet and then contrived to remain in his arms, pressing her breast against him. "There are better ways for Ambrosius Aurelianus to spend his time," she murmured, "don't you think?"

Beside her, the war dog Ferox gave a weary groan.

"Peace, Ferox," chided Inga.

"He always spoils the mood," said Ambrosius, laughing as he kept one arm around her waist while they sauntered along the headland. Several times he gazed seaward but a light haze obscured all save the high ground on the nearby isle which Romans called Vectis. If there were any boats offshore, he would not see them; especially as Scotti vessels were small, light craft – or so he was told – for he had never seen one himself. If the raiders hugged the coast they could remain out of sight until the moment they entered the harbour. But there were no raiders in the harbour yet and he reckoned there never would be.

"Your hair grows longer, Roman," observed Inga, idly twisting a rust-coloured lock around her finger.

"And not so Roman now, eh," he said, with a sheepish grin. For as the months passed, less and less remained of the outcast soldier from Rome's western empire. True, he still possessed the tools of his trade: spatha, helmet and shield, but little else; and here he was, arm in arm with a Saxon, trying to carve out a new life at the arse-end of the world.

"I think the mist is getting thicker," said Inga.

"It should be thinning by now," he grumbled, as they crossed back over the raised ground and returned to peer down once more upon the inner harbour. "But, as long as we can see down there, that's all that matters."

In the distance he surveyed once more the gravel hard where fishermen had drawn their small boats high up above the tideline. Close by, a rickety wooden jetty thrust a stubby finger out into the estuary channel and Ambrosius smiled to see children playing on the foreshore. But his grin of satisfaction froze, half-formed as a vessel emerged from the mist.

"What's that?" asked Inga, clutching his arm.

After a tense moment he chuckled with relief, for it was just a single ship and not a Scotti vessel either. If anything, it looked Roman in origin.

"A trader," ventured Inga.

"Could be," he said, but something about the ship irked him and, by the time Inga's grip tightened upon his arm he worked out why. The vessel was a navis lusoria, made for short, coastal journeys and river navigation; but its arrival here disturbed him far more than any Scotti incursion.

"That's… your ship," cried Inga. "Our ship…"

The previous year Ambrosius had brought them, against all odds to the shore of Britannia in just such a navis lusoria. Their ship was a supply craft built to patrol the Rhinus River but it was very like the one he saw below. This one could, of course have been any vessel... except that it certainly looked like the ship stolen from him at the onset of winter by his embittered half-sister.

Open-mouthed in shock, he stared as it lowered its sail and glided out of the mist into the harbour and there, at its prow like some carved image, stood Florina.

"No," he moaned, as if conjuring up a long dead spirit – except she looked far from dead. "How can she be here?"

"Because Frigg has delivered her into our hands," breathed Inga, a fire of revenge beginning to sparkle in her eyes.

"But last we heard she was still at Portus Adurni," he muttered. "That's far to the east."

"She could have come here to trade – for the iron goods," suggested Inga.

Ambrosius shook his head. "Florina, trade? She'd never sully her hands with buying and selling..."

Inga held his eyes. "Has she come for you?"

"I can't see how she could even know I'd be here..."

With the vessel scarcely fifty yards from the hard, a few rays of sunshine lighted upon it, glinting on burnished helmets and drawn swords.

"Christ's tomb, she's attacking the port!" he cried, seizing Inga's hand. "Come. We must get to the horses."

As they raced back along the headland Ambrosius looked in vain for his mounted comrades; but they must have stopped on the far side of the earth banks for he could not see them at all. As he and Inga hastily retrieved their mounts, they startled the iron workers at the furnace.

"The port's under attack," Ambrosius explained.

But when the bemused Britons peered down to where he pointed, they appeared to see nothing amiss.

"The ship!" he yelled at them.

"Aye, it's landing on the hard," observed one of the smelters cheerfully. "We could do with a ship coming in."

"Aye, I'm sure you could," said Ambrosius, as he helped Inga to mount. "But not that ship. You'd best stay up here."

He drove his mare down the slope at breakneck speed and only slowed a little when he glanced back to see Inga clinging, grim-faced to her horse's mane. Her horsemanship still left much to be desired, but he admired her determination to become an accomplished rider and, of course Inga would never admit defeat.

"Keep going," she urged. "I'll be alright."

But at the foot of Iron Hill, he pulled up to wait for her.

"What did you stop for?" she gasped, breathless as she wrestled her mount to a halt.

"Because I want you to ride across to the rampart and fetch the others," he told her.

"Where are you going then?"

"To the port," he said. "I need to slow Florina's men down a bit."

"Not on your own, you don't."

"Just get to the others quickly or the port will be lost," he insisted. "Now, ride."

Without looking back, he sped away towards the settlement. Since the track was little more than a stony gully worn into the hillside, his horse struggled to keep its footing on the loose surface, but the beast had heart and kept going.

At a sharp turn in the track Ambrosius heard the first shouts of outrage from the port. Poor beggars, desperate for trade they would have welcomed Florina's ship with open arms; but he was sure that, whatever Florina intended it had nothing to do with trade.

With luck the cries of alarm from the settlement would alert the rest of his company even before Inga arrived to stir them to action. If not then he would reach the port well ahead of them – on his own. He guessed that Florina would have at least a score of men aboard her ship - perhaps more - and some no doubt would be trained soldiers under the command of another former Roman officer, his erstwhile comrade the traitorous Stavelus.

On the outskirts of the settlement where the track levelled out, Ambrosius passed between two large roundhouses and was relieved to discover that the attackers had not yet swept right through the port. Then he glanced across towards the estuary and what he saw convinced him that Florina's arrival had not occurred by chance. Scattered across the water were scores of small vessels; it seemed that the elusive Scotti raiders had finally appeared.

More craft drifted into view, creeping through the narrow harbour entrance, each one with a slender, flimsy-looking mast and tattered fragment of sail. Sweet Christ, it was a wonder these folk had managed to cross the sea at all; but cross it they had. For the first time in years they were raiding the south coast but this time they appeared to have a powerful ally in his bitch of a half-sister. Even so, he could not imagine how such a unlikely alliance had been forged.

Thrusting all such questions from his mind, Ambrosius focussed on how best to delay the attack. Florina had far too many men for him to fight on his own but, if he waited for his comrades she would take the settlement almost unopposed. Perhaps if he stayed mounted and kept moving he could help some folk escape without getting himself killed. With luck, he might hold out until his men reached him. He prayed that God was with him – and perhaps Inga's goddess, Frigg too – for it couldn't hurt to have a little more divine assistance.

Some of the inhabitants were fleeing towards him, heading for the higher ground of the headland. They must have thought him mad as they scrambled aside to avoid his mount's pounding hooves - and of course they were right. But Ambrosius the soldier was drawn to a fight like a hammer to an anvil and, moments later the invaders felt his wrath. Taken unawares, looting soldiers fell to his spatha as he hacked right and left to scatter them like wildfowl.

The element of surprise was always a great advantage – until it ran out... The moment his opponents realised that they were only fighting one man, albeit a mounted one they lost no time in pressing in to surround him. He had scored a victory of sorts, he supposed for while the soldiers concentrated on him, many more of the port's residents took the chance to escape unmolested up the hill. But once he was cut off, it required only a handful of men to pen him in against one of the roundhouses, while the rest were free to plunder the port and harass its remaining inhabitants. Now they had him trapped, it would not be long before Florina and Stavelus arrived to gloat over their prize.

Cursing with frustration, Ambrosius darted his horse back and forth in an attempt to break out, only to be driven back each time by a wall of sharp spear points. A glance across to the hard told him that the Scotti were now landing in numbers. Easily identified by their lack of body armour, they carried simple but he imagined brutally effective weapons. While Florina's men contained the threat of Ambrosius, their savage allies - clearly well-practised in the art of pillage - proceeded to hunt down their prey or fire the houses.

Careless of the impact of their bloody handiwork, the Scotti moved on to from house to house in search of more plunder. Soon the roundhouse at Ambrosius' back was also put to the torch and smoke began to billow out from its damp timbers. He was trapped now, not only by his enemies but by swirling smoke and burgeoning flames. Eyes stinging, Ambrosius waited though his horse bucked under him in protest. With choking fumes filling his lungs he reckoned that neither he, nor his horse could endure for much longer.

2

Soon the pall of smoke was caught by the prevailing west wind which carried it into the squinting faces of Florina's men. In that moment, Ambrosius glimpsed a faint hope; but it would need patience and perfect timing. If he moved too soon, he would be hacked to the ground; but too late and he would burn alive. Though the fierce flames scorched his back and drove his brave horse to scream in fear, still he delayed a few more moments. Only when the fingers of smoke smothered his nearest opponents did he finally give his furious horse its head. Bursting through the half-circle of wheezing soldiers, the beast emerged largely unscathed and, though a spear narrowly missed Ambrosius' thigh he too escaped with only a few burns.

At once he darted away from his assailants and sped towards the hard, praying that his comrades were even now racing along the northern shore of the harbour. The Scotti raiders, he noticed were loading captured goods into their tiny craft, but his attention was drawn to the Roman ship – his ship - beached on the gravel hard. And there she was: the elegant, familiar figure of Florina, her once black hair tinged now with ragged lines of grey. Flanked by Stavelus, she was surrounded by at least half a dozen others and at her right hand stood a tall, almost white-haired Scot who Ambrosius guessed was in command of the raiders.

His half-sister looked magnificent as she strode towards him; but then, from a distance she always did. Her undoubted courage and determination might have been admirable if only he could forget the carnage she had wrought upon so many – not least her own family. But he could never forget - nor forgive - her betrayal and the murder of their half-brother. God's breath, to kill her own brother…

Several high-pitched shrieks sounded further along the shoreline where a group of children were being manhandled aboard several Scotti vessels. With a sigh of bitter resignation, Ambrosius turned his horse towards the struggling captives. Once he reached the shallows, he slid from his mount and waded in, spatha in hand. A bare-chested Scotti warrior greeted him with a spear thrust accompanied by a venomous, if incomprehensible roar.

With practised ease, Ambrosius turned the spear point aside and crashed the hilt of his weapon into his opponent's throat leaving him sprawling on his back in the water. Some of the other raiders, torn between wrestling their young prisoners aboard and meeting his attack, chose to the latter. Perhaps they realised that such a troublesome adversary would have to be overcome if they were to keep the goods and slaves they coveted. Thus a forest of spears soon confronted him.

A swift glance behind confirmed that Stavelus' Romans would also be upon him at any moment, but such was the soldier's lot. He faced the oncoming Scotti with a broad grin on his face knowing that he would perish, as he always intended in the savage blood heat of battle. Even above the yells of the Scotti, he could hear Florina shrieking at her own men to hack him down. But they would not find Ambrosius Aurelianus so easy to kill…

With every scrap of strength he could muster, he hurled himself at the Scotti spearmen, cracking aside the spears to slash hard at their bare, sweating torsos. Flesh was torn and bellies sliced open, clouding the water with their blood. Shocked by his relentless onslaught, his opponents almost broke ranks and only the tramp of Roman boots across gravel encouraged them. When they rallied and stood their ground, Ambrosius was forced to wade out into deeper water, almost up to his thighs.

Turning to meet yet more adversaries, he prayed he might hear the shouts of his approaching comrades, but still the shore echoed with the murderous voice of Florina. Then, abruptly the hellcat fell silent and another sound emerged. It was the thunder of hooves, growing ever louder that told him his bucellarii - his sworn men - were coming. Even before they stormed across the hard, Florina must have known that she was in trouble. Those beside her made no attempt to face the cantering horsemen and instead fled at once back to their ship and Florina, the queen of living to fight another day fled with them.

Hurtling past the jetty, Ambrosius' comrades slaughtered any men they found; Roman or Scotti, it made no difference to them. By the time Ambrosius waded ashore, his Scotti opponents had been swept aside in a dark smear of blood. Some of the Scotti did not lack for courage as they turned to fight… and die. Others, perhaps as many as a score or more fled the settlement to retreat across the narrow neck of land with the tall, white-haired leader at their head.

Ambrosius watched their progress until Inga, who had led the bucellarii to his aid enveloped him in an unrestrained embrace. But he knew it was no occasion for celebration just yet.

"Dux!" cried Arturus, an eager youth he brought with him from Gallia.

The young warrior brought Ambrosius his mount and then pointed along the hard to where Florina's crew were attempting to push their ship back into the water. Though the falling tide was hampering their efforts, fear was a powerful incentive and it drove them to haul the boat free.

"They mustn't get away," cried Ambrosius, hurrying across the gravel, but the ship was soon a dozen yards out into the estuary. "God damn her!" he roared.

But, to his surprise Florina's ship did not make for the harbour entrance; instead, it veered left to follow the river Sturr upstream.

"She's going, Dux," cried Arturus. "She's abandoned Stavelus and the others."

"Hah! That's no surprise," scoffed Ambrosius. "Florina was never burdened by loyalty; but she's lost half her men so I don't see why she would flee upriver."

"Perhaps she panicked," said Arturus.

Ambrosius was torn now: desperate to pursue her, but aware that there was still a battle to be won on the far side of the settlement. If Stavelus and the remaining Scotti were allowed to join forces they would make a formidable alliance.

"Arturus," he said, after a moment's thought, "take half a dozen riders and follow the ship up the river."

Before Arturus could set off, Inga said: "I'll go with them."

Though Ambrosius was at first inclined to protest, the sight of the indomitable Ferox beside her persuaded him to acquiesce. The ferocious war dog, bred from Molussian stock was more than a match for any warrior. It occurred to him also that she might well be a good deal safer with Arturus than staying at the port where there were still many enemies yet to be subdued.

"Very well," he told Arturus. "Inga will go with you, but just follow the ship. Do nothing more - then send me word where you are."

Arturus led out the small mounted party, back towards the great ditches seeking a safe track to follow alongside the river estuary. Ambrosius watched them go with a trembling heart but then, sucking in a lungful of smoky air he set off with his comrades to kill an old friend.

"Over here, Dux," The cry came from Flavius Silvius Germanus, who had served with Ambrosius since the old imperial days. There was no better man to have beside him when blood was being spilled than the blunt Burgundian; though at any other time he offered only grumbling dissent.

"It's Stavelus, Dux," explained Germanus. "He's hiding in one of the houses – like the feeble, faithless Roman dog he is."

Stavelus, outnumbered and desperate had been forced to take refuge in one of the houses but, in doing so he left himself no way out. Though his fellow Roman had betrayed him the previous winter when he first colluded with Florina, Ambrosius did not relish the outcome of their struggle. Stavelus had once been a loyal supporter and, without him they would all have perished long ago in the

26

mountains of northern Italia. For that at least, Ambrosius owed him a debt, though not perhaps a life…

"Come out, Stavelus!" he shouted. "And I promise that you'll have a swift, honourable death."

"Or you could just come in and get me, Dux," came the gruff reply from the hardened soldier within.

Aware that he still had the remainder of the Scotti to subdue Ambrosius could ill afford to delay long, lest more of the sea-borne raiders decided to return to aid their trapped comrades. Perhaps Stavelus was counting upon that and hoping that the Scotti would overwhelm Ambrosius' bucellarii. If so, his erstwhile ally was going to be bitterly disappointed.

Turning to his squat, North African comrade, Aurelius Maurus Rocca, Ambrosius ordered: "Fire it."

Moments later several burning brands were lobbed onto the roof of the hut and others placed against its walls so that in a very short time, the fire took hold. Ambrosius drew out his spatha in readiness and Stavelus did not keep him waiting. Wreathed in smoke, the Roman burst out of the entrance followed by a wedge of half a dozen snarling soldiers. Ambrosius, though he admired the Romans' courage, stood his ground and flanked by Germanus and Rocca, met their charge head on.

Stavelus hurled himself at Ambrosius with all his considerable muscle, but the fight was all too brief for his comrades were less-experienced warriors who were swiftly cut down. When Ambrosius wounded Stavelus in the shoulder, it was clear that he could not fight on. With the beleaguered Roman surrounded by blades, Germanus raised his axe to strike him down.

"Hold," ordered Ambrosius, for already the point of his spatha was resting against Stavelus' mail shirt. "Get after the Scotti," he ordered his bucellarii.

"But Dux," Germanus started to protest.

"Do as you're told." Ambrosius' rasping rebuke was spiked with anger and regret.

Rocca, judging his leader's mood rather better than his Burgundian comrade dragged him away before he could argue further.

When only the two of them remained, surrounded by a pile of bloodied bodies Ambrosius lowered his sword a little.

"You broke your oath to me, Stavelus," he said.

Stavelus nodded, weeping. "I know, Dux…"

"My half-sister used you," murmured Ambrosius, "but you knew that, my friend."

With a weary nod of the head, Stavelus agreed: "She's hard to resist, Dux…"

"But why is she here?" demanded Ambrosius. "Why are any of you here?"

"Why, for you Dux, of course," replied Stavelus. "What you managed against Vortigern last winter, she never expected. God's heart, your very survival was an affront to her. She wants your head, Dux and she won't rest until she has it."

Ambrosius sighed at the thought that of the very few kinfolk he had left in the world, one of them wanted him dead.

"I knew what I was doing, Dux…" confessed Stavelus.

"Aye," agreed Ambrosius and, without warning he swept his lethal spatha at Stavelus' neck with all his power.

Severed from its shoulders in the time it took a viper to strike, the traitor's head dropped to the ground and his lifeless body slumped forward, pumping out an ever-diminishing stream of Roman blood. Ambrosius had kept his promise of a swift execution, but the bitter taste of betrayal would not pass so quickly.

3

Ambrosius caught up with his bucellarii just below a dark-red ironstone outcrop in the lee of the headland. There the fleeing Scotti had been trapped but, despite their perilous situation, the lightly-armoured raiders seemed more than ready to defend their rock ledge. When he scanned the line of warriors, arrayed in good order with their weapons at the ready Ambrosius saw no hint of surrender. If he wanted to dislodge them from their refuge then he and his comrades would have to dismount and storm the ledge on foot. Doing so was not without its difficulties and Ambrosius, still reflecting upon his summary execution of Stavelus took his time to consider how to go about it.

Despite the eager impatience of some of his young Britons, he was not about to sacrifice lives to feed their lust for blood. He had known many such hot youths – indeed he had been one himself once. Young soldiers never expected to die but those who survived usually spent at least one moment on the dark cusp of death – and they never forgot the experience. For Ambrosius, it was his first taste of battle on a bloody, corpse-strewn field in Gallia. There, but for the cool head of his commander that day, Flavius Aetius he would certainly have perished in one last futile assault upon the retreating armies of Attila the Hun.

Amid the carnage that day, as men fell all around him Ambrosius had gained a powerful mentor; but he also learned a lesson. Now on Iron Hill his own young warriors wanted to slaughter every last one of the Scotti and paint their gleaming blades with the raiders' blood. But Ambrosius did not, for he was aware of other dangers. He observed that several of the Scotti kept darting glances down towards the harbour entrance – and he suspected he knew why. If the rest of the Scotti regrouped, they might yet come ashore again knowing he would be preoccupied with defeating their comrades. Thus, if Ambrosius committed all his men to the attack upon the ironstone ledge the remainder of the settlement would be defenceless.

Reason suggested that he should divide his force and send some men back to defend the port; but if he did it would make the task of crushing the determined Scotti on the bluff all the harder. Decisions, he reflected, always decisions; but it was the task of a commander to make the right choice – and make it fast.

"Germanus," he ordered, "choose five men to go back with you to the port."

"But the fight's up here, Dux," protested the Burgundian. "We shouldn't be wiping the arses of these local fools as well as fighting for them."

So soon after having executed a man whose loyalty he once valued highly, Ambrosius was in no mood to have his authority questioned yet again by Germanus.

"They're not fools because they must fish for a living, or hammer iron," he told the quarrelsome Germanus. "There'll be wounds to see to and fires to dampen – and you'll need to guard the landing place."

"Against who?" cried Germanus.

"Anyone who tries to take it," snarled Ambrosius. "So get your arse moving and do as you're told."

It was an argument Ambrosius could have done without but, for some of the younger men this was their first fight under his leadership and he needed them to understand what that meant; and to know that insubordination, even from one of his closest warriors could not be tolerated.

By the time a reluctant and far from penitent Germanus eventually rode off with his disgruntled chosen men, Ambrosius was discussing the impending assault with Ulf, who led a small Saxon contingent. Ulf had not come to Britannia with him as some others had, but joined him last winter when both had kinfolk abducted by the sons of the High King Vortigern. Together, Romans and Saxons had defeated the British king but at a high price. Not only had many of their men perished, but the escaping Vortigern had sworn to be revenged upon them both. In the months that followed, the Saxon – along with his fellows - had pledged his loyalty to Ambrosius and the latter came to value his advice highly.

"Getting the Scotti off that ridge isn't going to be easy," murmured Ambrosius.

"If they've a head for climbing, I reckon some could even make it down to the sea from there," observed Ulf, "if they got past the rock overhang."

"Aye," agreed Ambrosius. "So, you and your Saxons take the left flank and hold close to the cliff edge. If any Scotti try an escape that way, make sure they do so head first."

Ulf nodded with a fierce grin and then formed up his men while Ambrosius called Argetrus, the Briton to him. Argetrus reminded Ambrosius of himself only a few years earlier – a raw youth of scarcely twenty years of age eager to hone his skills as a warrior. Only a few months before, Argetrus had helped to rescue Ambrosius from a plot engendered by Vortigern. Afterwards Argetrus swore an oath of allegiance to Ambrosius and, where Argetrus led many more of his fellow Durotriges followed. Despite his youth the Briton was clearly much respected by his people.

"You'll command the right flank," he told Argetrus, "while Rocca and I lead in the centre."

The young Briton's smile was broad as he acknowledged the place of honour that Ambrosius was awarding him. "I won't fail you, lord," he said.

"Aye, but don't thank me too soon," said Ambrosius, stern-faced. "There's a price to pay, lad for leadership in battle - a price paid by the blood of those you lead…"

"Lord…"

"You must know when to press hard and when to hold your ground," said Ambrosius.

"Yes, lord," agreed Argetrus.

The youth's response was swift – too swift, thought Ambrosius, so he sent the young Briton on his way with a further warning. "Listen for my commands," he instructed. "And make sure you act upon them."

Ambrosius stared after Argetrus for a moment as he joined the battle-scarred African, Rocca in the front rank of his warriors.

"He's just a boy," observed Rocca.

Ambrosius nodded as the pair glared up at their waiting enemies.

"Are you ready, my friend," murmured Ambrosius. "Ready to test heart and muscle once again?"

In reply Rocca produced a wry grin. "Soldiers must fight, Dux, eh. Else they would be farmers…"

"Shields up!" shouted Ambrosius, drawing out his spatha and then raising his own shield.

His shout brought a roar of anticipation from his own men who, with shields lifted high prepared to advance up the slope. Provoked by his command, the Scotti too brandished their weapons in the air and began to emit wild, keening cries. For men with no breastplates and only a couple of mail shirts between them, Ambrosius thought they sounded worryingly confident. Well, he would be able to judge very soon the true mettle of his opponents.

Taking a deep breath, he bellowed: "Advance!" and walked forward with measured step to begin ascending the slope. Experience had taught him that there was little point in charging up a steep hill until he faced a hail of missiles. Soon enough, the lethal stones would fly for he had seen the slingers making ready but, for now he would save his strength. On his right flank however, the Britons under Argetrus surged forward as fast as they could, no doubt impatient to grapple with the Scotti who had plagued their tribe for so long - even if it was in the distant past.

On the left flank, Ulf looked across to Ambrosius for some sign that he should match the pace of the Britons.

Muttering a curse, Ambrosius grumbled: "By God, it's not a race…"

But since he did not want to attack in a ragged, ill-disciplined line, he waved Ulf forward and increased his own pace. His legs, still stiff from hours of squatting on the damp ground of the hilltop, responded only slowly but he was happy to let Rocca ease a little ahead of him.

At twenty yards distance the slingers let fly and only just in time did Ambrosius raise his shield an inch or two higher. Several stones rapped against it, the sheer force of their impact almost bringing him to a standstill. Others too were surprised and rocked back onto their heels, but some were less fortunate for the slingers were lethal at short range. Desperate to attack, several of the young Britons held their shields carelessly and were struck down or grievously wounded. Ambrosius, wondering if young Argetrus had noticed was pleased to hear his angry shout: 'Keep your shields up!"

All the while as Ambrosius' force continued to climb, the slingers plied their trade to devastating effect. Some gathered more stones from the rocky ground upon which they stood so they could heap even more misery upon their advancing enemies. Only when the gap closed to a few yards, were the slings discarded and the Scotti prepared to fend off their foes with spears and long knives. Breathing hard, Ambrosius and Rocca crashed into the Scotti ranks together, battering aside spear points with their shields and driving their spathas at the heavily-muscled, but unprotected bodies.

Eyes fixed only upon his immediate adversary, Ambrosius punched his spatha blade clean through a leather-clad shield and into the chest of its bearer. Without a moment's pause he wrenched out the blade, thrust his bleeding opponent aside and pressed forward once more. Though he hacked down another with his spatha, soon the two lines became so tightly entangled that there was no room to swing his weapon at all. In such a press of sweating, blood-smeared bodies the Scotti spears had a chance to blunt the keen edge of Ambrosius' assault. Lethal spear points began to discover narrow gaps between shields to slice into calves, thighs and even a few unsuspecting bellies.

But brave and bloody though their resistance was, the Scotti could not match the disciplined, relentless power of the bucellarii. Steadily the raiders were compelled to cede yard upon yard, leaving their dead and fallen wounded behind. Ambrosius, stepping over bodies rent by sword and axe picked out more than one pale young face lying still amid the blood and shit. As he butchered his way across the rocky ground, he knew that the Scotti defiance could not endure much longer.

Allowing Rocca to move ahead of him he studied his remaining opponents closely, seeking a weakness that might enable him to end the struggle swiftly. It was clear that the Scotti relied heavily upon two formidable fighters. One, the white-haired leader Ambrosius noticed earlier at Florina's side, handled his spatha like a seasoned Roman veteran. But there was another – thickly bearded and surely the very tallest of men – who wielded a spiked club to batter back any man who ventured near him.

The Scotti might be falling back, but these two warriors would continue to kill and maim as long as they had breath to do so. In the end they would be killed but, before they were he feared that the menacing pair would reap many more souls from among his company.

Abruptly he roared out a command to all his men: "Halt! Stand fast where you are."

His close comrades were far from surprised at his order and even took a pace back from the fray but others, unwilling to hold back when the Scotti appeared to be at their mercy cried out in dismay. Some of the young Britons continued to fight on until they were bawled at several times by Argetrus and finally, darting murderous looks at him they drew back. In the uneasy stand-off that followed, Ambrosius bellowed a challenge at the bewildered Scotti.

"Surrender - or you'll all die here on this ridge."

"We'll not yield to be your slaves," cried their white-haired commander.

"But you would live," replied Ambrosius, "and it's a better fate than you gave those folk at the port."

His opponent studied him for a moment before replying in a solemn voice: "Niall does not surrender – even to you, Ambrosius Aurelianus."

What Ambrosius would have given at that moment for a handful of Hun archers; for the alternative was going to be messy: costly in lives and utterly futile.

"Dux!" The warning cry came from Ulf on his left flank.

Glancing down to the harbour, Ambrosius could not see what Ulf was furiously pointing at, but he could guess. It was as he feared: the Scotti who had fled in their boats were returning

"Perhaps we're not quite as beaten as you think, Roman…" declared Niall, whose voice carried now a harder edge of steel.

Soon Ambrosius could see the boats for himself but he also marked how the sight of the tiny vessels creeping back to the shore lifted the spirits of the defenders. Where men were hunched in despair, they now straightened their backs and stood taller. Nothing stiffened a man's resolve better than hope. There would be no surrender now, nor did he have the luxury of time to wear his determined opponents down. He must cut them down or hurl them into the sea before their allies could scramble ashore and attack him from behind.

Staring at Niall with a look of cold fury, he cried: "So be it."

At once a deafening clamour arose from both lines of warriors but Ambrosius shut out all distractions as he roared the command to attack. Charging into the midst of the Scotti, he knew that Rocca would be close by him. With every step they took, they would carve a path through the opposing line. Sweeping his spatha at man after man while his shield deflected spears and knives, he drove on.

It was close, visceral work - close enough to smell his enemies' sweat and feel their blood as it splashed against his face. His savage onslaught carried him up to a patch of flatter ground near the top of the outcrop, where the two intransigent leaders would have to be overcome. The powerful Saxon Ulf, reaching the plateau at about the same time as Ambrosius grasped at once what was required and hacked his way towards the white-haired leader, Niall.

Sensing that the rest of the Scotti were on the brink of exhaustion, he shouted to his comrades: "Batter the devils off this cliff and into the sea."

Sucking in great lungfuls of breath, he bludgeoned his way forward through a press of Scotti bodies to hunt down the club-wielding giant. But the mighty warrior, with no hope of retreat advanced to meet him head on. Though Ambrosius was a tall man his opponent towered over him when the pair started trading shuddering blows. This was not some lumbering fool waiting to be outwitted; this was a warrior whose power and skill with his chosen weapon demanded absolute respect.

Struggling to counter each heavy blow arcing down at him, Ambrosius found his strength starting to ebb away, yet every lunge and feint he attempted was countered with apparent ease. Next moment his adversary's fearsome club splintered his shield and successive blows reduced it to a few strips of twisted wood clinging desperately to the iron boss. He was breathing hard even before the remnants of his shield disintegrated leaving him with only his spatha to defend himself – a spatha that felt ever heavier in his hand. The Scot, by contrast still showed little sign of tiring and only when Rocca despatched the fellow flanking his giant opponent did Ambrosius glimpse a slim chance of success.

Protected by Rocca's shield, he continued to batter the great warrior until at last he forced him to take a single step back. It was a tiny victory but that single step became the first of many while, a dozen feet away to the left a roar of triumph told him that Ulf's Saxons had broken through the Scotti ranks. On the right flank too Argetrus and his young Britons had mounted the slope and were hurrying to encircle the desperate defenders.

Niall tried to rally his comrades one last time but the exultant Saxons closed in upon him fast and two axes hacked the Scotti leader down. From that moment on Ambrosius saw only despair in the eyes of the remaining raiders as they looked to their one exceptional warrior who was still standing. But even he, Ambrosius thought looked downcast for the first time.

"Hold!" shouted Ambrosius, pulling back on Rocca's shoulder.

Though for the most part the assault came to stuttering halt, the vengeful youths under Argetrus continued to press forward, yearning to bathe their weapons in yet more blood.

"Hold, I said!" raged a furious Ambrosius, glaring across at his young captain.

"They deserve to die," cried Argetrus. "You've seen what they do – what they are."

"I see they are brave," replied Ambrosius, glowering at Argetrus until he put up his spatha and cast his rebellious look down to his boots. For a long moment Ambrosius remained silent, knowing that the eyes of all were upon him. Then he slowly turned his back upon the fuming Argetrus and faced the Scotti.

"You must yield now," he told them, aware of the rumbling dissent from others in his own ranks.

"Will we live?" asked his tall adversary, making no move to lower the barbed club.

"If you surrender now," Ambrosius replied, "you have my oath that you will not be killed."

While the Scot considered the offer, Ambrosius turned to face his own men, meeting any expression of dissent with a stern countenance. Head after head dipped in acknowledgement of his authority for no man dared challenge it. They had seen how even the mighty Germanus flinched at Ambrosius' rebuke.

Addressing the Scot once more, he said: "Well?"

Several more, tense moments passed before the battle-scarred Scot tossed his bloodied club at the feet of Ambrosius. The instant he did so, his despondent comrades hurried to discard their weapons and several sank to their knees in utter exhaustion.

Ambrosius, observing that Argetrus was stalking towards him could not resist a grin of appreciation for the youth certainly had no lack of courage. But before the Briton could utter a word, Ambrosius said: "See them all securely bound, Argetrus."

"We should just cut the throats of the savages," muttered the young Briton.

"Then we would be the savages," replied Ambrosius, who had seen more than enough slaughter for one day. "These men have surrendered to me, so you will bind them and see that their wounds are attended to. And Argetrus… make certain all your men understand: if anyone harms one of my prisoners, they'll pay with their own life – and so will you."

Without waiting for Argetrus to acknowledge the order, Ambrosius bellowed: "Ulf, bring your men."

Leaving Rocca to ensure that all was done as he had ordered, Ambrosius walked back down the corpse-strewn slope to where the horses were tethered. Mounting swiftly, he set off back to the port with Ulf and the Saxons in his wake. At the damaged, still-smouldering settlement he was relieved to find all was at peace. Several dead Scotti adorned the gravel hard, he noticed; so Germanus had found someone to fight after all.

Satisfied that any surviving raiders had fled, Ambrosius left the restoration of order in the hands of his closest comrades and took himself apart. Thus, while others continued to dress wounds or collect up discarded weapons, Ambrosius wandered along the shore trying to make sense of what had taken place that afternoon. The struggle on the bluff had used up most of the day and all too soon the sun would dip in the west. By then he needed to understand the significance of what had happened so that he could decide what to do next.

The Scotti had not raided this far to the east for decades - at the very least; yet today they had chosen to do so. On the very same day his half-sister, Florina had sailed her ship, crammed with fighting men from Portus Adurni in the east to the exact same place where the Scotti happened to land. It could not, of course be chance; it had to be the product of close collaboration. He had heard tell of barbarian alliances in the distant past, but they had surely been very rare.

He struggled to understand how someone like Florina had made contact with a horde of Scotti raiders who came from the far west; yet their leader, Niall had walked alongside her at the hard. In the battle he had addressed Ambrosius by name, so the Scot knew very well who he was. But, if the unlikely pair had made a pact to trap and kill him then it had been a calamitous failure. All it had achieved was a half-ruined British settlement and scores of dead men.

Yet...Ambrosius still worried that the slippery viper, Florina was remained at large and, as daylight slowly faded to a glimmer he became increasingly impatient for word from Arturus. When darkness fell and there was still no news, his fears began to grow.

4

Despite Ambrosius' valiant attempts during the winter to teach Inga to ride with more confidence, she still found that it required all her concentration. His advice had certainly helped but she had other, fonder memories of the hours spent with him when they took their horses out onto the uplands. There, unfettered for a time by the mortal fears that were such a constant companion in their early months together, they could almost relax. She smiled to recall how they would return, chafed by chill winds to the warmth of their chamber where for once it was her skills that outshone those of Ambrosius.

When spring came, she expected that they would build their lives there and was shocked when Ambrosius first confided that he intended to abandon the villa they had fought so hard to capture. Yet she remembered that at the very outset of their journey from Gallia he had made clear his desire to seek the kinfolk of his British mother, Clutoriga - if any still lived… Since all he knew was that she came from the town of Durnovaria in the west that was where Ambrosius decided to go.

Those who had sworn an oath to him were dumbfounded when he announced his decision but he offered to release them from their oaths if they preferred to remain at the hard-won Villa Magna. As it turned out, no-one chose to remain behind; for the point of swearing an oath, was surely to show absolute trust.

As for Inga, she did not care where she lived as long as she was with Ambrosius for she expected their lives and fortunes to be forever entwined. In the past few months though, the presence of a beautiful British widow at their fort had caused Inga some flutterings of doubt, for she observed how Ambrosius was drawn to the young woman. Inga and Ambrosius had sworn oaths to each other before many witnesses, but where the heart was concerned no outcome was ever certain. Wyrd had unveiled the dark-haired widow for Ambrosius and Inga did not believe that the hand of fate would stop there.

"There!" hissed Arturus suddenly, snapping Inga's wandering mind back to the task in hand and almost causing her to slip sideways off her mount.

Recovering her balance - and her composure - she looked ahead along the river to where Arturus was pointing and saw the Roman vessel at once. Raising an arm, he brought the small band to a halt.

"Keep quiet now," he ordered and Inga wondered, not for the first time how the older men obeyed this youth so readily. Yet she had to concede that Arturus was an impressive young man; so perhaps Dux was right to give him such responsibility.

"We should send a man to Dux," advised Inga.

"Not yet," said Arturus. "We're too few already, so let's wait till we have something useful to tell Dux. Our task is to follow and see what Florina does."

"Frigg knows where that foul bitch is going," muttered Inga. "We don't even know where this river leads."

"Well, so far it's taking us north," he told her. "If it carries on that way, the Lady Florina is going to end up a very long way from Portus Adurni."

The ship was making only slow progress, perhaps because the river was shallow in places but also because it was being rowed by far fewer men than it required. Hence Arturus and the others dismounted to walk their horses lest they ventured too close to the ship. For several hours they followed the vessel through the late afternoon until at dusk it came to a halt and moored up on the far bank of the river. Inga and Arturus edged closer to observe it from a stand of trees about fifty paces south of its mooring.

"What do we do now?" she hissed, crouching down beside the youth.

"We wait," he replied, "unless you want to go back to Dux."

"No," scoffed Inga, "because I want to find out what that lady's doing. But I still think we should send word to Ambrosius."

"We still don't know what she intends," argued Arturus. "Better to delay a little longer -and we're not in any danger here."

She sat down on the grass, feeling at once the familiar pressure of Ferox's head in the small of her back before he flopped down beside her. The beast had grown fat and lazy, she thought; though she could hardly complain since he had spent the winter recovering from wounds he sustained when defending her at the villa. Ferox was a dog bred for war, but just now the poor beast had no war to wage. Yet, in the company of Ambrosius Aurelianus she reckoned the animal would not have to wait too long before his next fight.

"I think they know we're here," she whispered.

"Probably," said Arturus. "They won't know how many of us there are, but even so, we should be on our guard."

"They might slip away during the night," murmured Inga.

"Only if they want to run aground," he said. "This river's neither broad nor deep and I doubt they know any more about its course than we do."

Though she nodded Inga could not help feeling ill at ease, perhaps because she did not care to be quite so close to Ambrosius' half-sister. The bitter memories of Florina's betrayal were still too fresh.

That night on the damp ground Inga slept very little, despite the warmth of Ferox's great flank to shield her from the cool breeze. It seemed she had only just dropped off into a deeper sleep when Arturus shook her awake.

"It's still dark," she groaned, peering up at the youth.

"Florina's on the move," he said and at once her eyes blinked open wide.

Leaping up, she peered upstream to find that the ship had gone. "Frigg's breast," she snarled. "I warned you..."

"I don't think she's been gone long," said Arturus. "And we can easily catch her; it's not as if they can go anywhere but the river."

She scowled back at him. "Good, because I don't want to lose her now."

Though it was still dark, Inga was impressed by Arturus' calm demeanour which certainly encouraged a sense of purpose among the men. With Arturus leading the way, the rest mounted and set off through the trees at a cautious walk. Inga, slow to mount her horse at any time was distracted by a low, rumbling growl from Ferox.

Bending low, she chastised the animal roundly: "Frigg take you, Ferox. This is no time to be stalking some prey."

By the time she set off, the others were at least a dozen yards ahead of her and disappearing into the night. A sudden shout caused her pull up and peer ahead into the gloom of the trees. Their assailants came at them fast: at least one dropped down from an overhanging branch but several others ran out from their shadowy hiding places. Gone was Arturus' calm confidence as he railed at their attackers and drew out his spatha. Inga, caught in two minds remained where she was with Ferox beside her, his bullish snout pointing towards the melée ahead.

It soon became clear to her that Arturus' scouting party was greatly outnumbered. If she rode to the aid of the others she risked being killed or captured – yet she could not abandon them. So, taking a few deep breaths to steady herself she reached down for the Hun bow slung beside her. Bequeathed to her by a young bucellarii, it had scarcely been used until late in the winter when her torn hands healed enough for her to try it out. So far she could hit a tree from about thirty paces… in daylight and… as long as the tree didn't move.

With a sigh, she reached out with trembling fingers to select a sleek shaft from her arrow bag and carefully raised it to the bow. Though she tried to remain still, her frayed nerves soon overwhelmed her and, before she had even taken aim she let the arrow fly. Gasping as it disappeared wild and high into the trees, she was relieved at least not to have struck one of her own comrades.

In the darkness she tried to keep her skittish mount still, hoping she would not be seen but the arrow's flight must have alerted several of Florina's men to her presence. One of them, having commandeered one of the horses began to ride in her direction and she knew that if she could make him out then he could see her well enough too.

Fumbling for another arrow she promptly dropped it and was snatching at a third as the soldier came straight at her.

"Frigg help me," she cried aloud and, without a moment's thought, she lodged a shaft, strained to draw back the bowstring and loosed the arrow in one flowing action. If she did it a hundred times, she knew that the result would be the same: an arrow veering away into the grey half-light. But just once... this once, Frigg must have guided her shaft and, at a range of barely ten yards it buried itself into the oncoming rider's shoulder. Though it hurled him from his borrowed horse, the arrow did not kill him. Angrily snapping off the offending shaft, he struggled to his feet and drew out his spatha. If he can still wield a sword, thought Inga then Frigg should have aimed for the other shoulder. He was close enough now for Inga to see his vengeful countenance as he walked towards her.

The poor fellow probably never saw the great black hound, but Ferox, needing no invitation to defend his mistress leapt at the wounded man's throat. Sadly the war dog was out of practice and it took him several bloody attempts before the soldier stopped screaming. Nevertheless, his tortured death had an immediate effect upon his comrades who took any mounts they had captured and fled after their ship.

When Inga reached Arturus and the others, she found them scattered among the trees and, for two of her comrades there was little she could do. As for Arturus, he nursed a bleeding head but, like the rest of the survivors his wound would not kill him.

"You were right, lady," he conceded bitterly. "I should have known she'd deceive us. Now we've lost two men and all our mounts save yours. We'll never keep up with her."

"You two," ordered Inga to the two men who appeared to have escaped any serious wounds. "Follow the ship on foot."

Though they hesitated before obeying her, a nod from Arturus sent them on their way. As they trudged off, one observed: "They've left a wounded one over here."

"Then finish the bastard off," ordered Arturus.

"No, wait," cried Inga. "Leave him to me."

It occurred to her that something might be learned from the captive but she had her doubts when she saw that he was no callow youth. An older, more experienced man was less likely to give much away.

"Tell me where your ship is going," she said.

There was no response from the prisoner.

"What does your lady plan to do?"

But the fellow simply gave a slight shake of the head and remained silent.

"Let me have a go at him, lady," urged one of her wounded comrades. "I'll soon make him talk."

Arturus and the other men gathered around the victim uncertain, she imagined how far she intended to take her questioning. Among those present, none had ever seen their lord's Saxon lady raise a hand against a prisoner. But harsh lessons in the past six months had taught her not to be too forgiving where prisoners were concerned and besides, the Saxon had a different interrogator in mind.

"Ferox," she called and the dog trotted to her at once, licking jaws still bloodied from his first kill.

Turning to the captive, she said softly: "All I have to do is tell this dog to attack you and it will. I suppose you heard your dead comrade's pitiful cries; such a savage way to die…"

"Hah," retorted the captive. "I shan't be able to tell you much with my throat all torn out."

"I didn't say anything about your throat," replied Inga. "Look at those teeth; he can shred the flesh on a man's arm, or leg… or anything. It might not kill you at once, but I can promise you that you'll feel pain and, in the end of course you'll bleed to death…"

White-faced, the prisoner shook his head. "Well, I'm still not telling you anything."

Perhaps the soldier thought that the Saxon girl with the faint scar lines upon her face was bluffing… Perhaps he expected her to call the dog off at the very last second – and she might have done so. But, over the winter she had spent a good deal of time trying to control the belligerent Ferox and now seemed the perfect occasion to test his progress.

"Ferox," breathed Inga, her eyes never leaving the soldier's pale face.

Beside her, Ferox shuffled forward, jaws slavering and barely under control.

"Seize," ordered Inga.

The soldier screamed in shock when Ferox leapt forward to clamp his teeth around the flesh of his forearm. But Inga was delighted for the dog had done very well, since the fellow's skin was scarcely broken.

"Move and he'll rip off your arm," she murmured. "Shout at me and he'll kill you… so I'll ask you a question and you'll answer… very calmly, so as not to alarm the beast… "

Though her eyes never left his, she knew from the rank odour that the prisoner had just pissed himself – which she decided was a promising start.

"Where is your lady, Florina taking the ship?" asked Inga.

The soldier's reply was croaked through dry lips, but his words were clear enough: "Up the river…"

"That much I know," said Inga. "But tell me where… exactly the ship is going."

For a moment he hesitated before replying: "Vindocladia."

Inga looked away for an instant to Arturus, a single thought in both their heads: what could Florina possibly hope to achieve at Vindocladia with one half-manned ship? But when Inga put her second question, the prisoner's whispered response sent a chill down her spine.

"Oh, shit," groaned Arturus.

And Inga, with tears in her eyes needed to pose no more questions.

"Let him go, Ferox," she said, senses numbed by what she had just learned.

When the animal, scaling new heights of obedience released its quarry, the soldier leapt to his feet.

"Don't-" she began, but too late for the moment the soldier darted away, Ferox was upon him, pulling him down by the arm and then tearing at his throat and ripping out bloody shreds of flesh.

"-run…" murmured Inga, with a sigh.

By the time she persuaded Ferox to stop mauling the prisoner, only the echo of his screams lingered among the trees. Inga felt powerless in every way - and still the dawn had not quite come.

"We have to tell Dux," cried Arturus. "You should go."

"No, I want to get after Florina," retorted Inga. "Send one of the wounded on my horse - and tell him to ride the animal into the ground."

Part Two: Vindocladia

5

Every night held fears for Lurotriga, widowed queen of the Durotriges. So often did sleep elude her that in the small hours she took to wandering the north rampart of the ruined burgus. Perhaps it was the cool air upon her face or the dark silence, broken only by a hunting owl or a scavenging animal. But whatever it was, it brought her a little peace of mind until dawn. Often she found one of her own people up there on guard who remembered her from past times; but not this night for Ambrosius had taken them all with him to the south coast. The nervous youths who patrolled the rampart now were still children in her eyes - little more than boys with sharpened sticks.

Lurotriga knew all about being thrust too young into the ruthless world of men. Less than fifteen years old when she wed the king of the Durotriges, she had not been ready for marriage… let alone a role of such high status. Though her husband had been a good young man, all her memories from that time were bitter. When the end came for him, it was sudden and brutal. All too soon she was a widow – part of the spoils to be haggled over by the treacherous men whose hands were still wet with her husband's blood.

When, a little later Ambrosius stumbled into her life, she prayed that he could lift her out of the pit of despair into which she had been cast by her husband's successor. And he did, but not in the way she hoped. The perfect outcome of a marriage to the powerful Roman Dux never happened. Despite his obvious attraction to her, Ambrosius refused to marry her because he was already pledged to another: the pagan Saxon, Inga.

Lurotriga struggled to understand why a Roman officer would make such a commitment to a barbarian slave. There was a certain raw beauty to her, so of course he would want her in his bed but surely not as a wife. Soon enough Lurotriga learned that his bond with Inga had been forged in adversity, but she held onto one thin strand of hope. Since Inga was not a Christian, in the eyes of the church and the law the Saxon girl could not truly be Ambrosius' wife. Yet, as the weeks passed by it seemed that no-one cared much about the Saxon's lack of faith. Patient and loyal, Lurotriga bided her time but her growing love for Ambrosius brought only a sense of desperation, until a passing remark by Ambrosius' sister Lucidia rekindled her hopes.

Lucidia mentioned their mother, Clutoriga and the name awoke a long-forgotten memory from Lurotriga's past. She must have been a child at the time but somewhere, some when... she had heard the name Clutoriga before. Knowing that Ambrosius was eager to learn more about his mother's kinfolk, she began to wonder if she might be able to discover something so priceless that it would demonstrate to him the true depth of her love and loyalty.

Using an intermediary - a Christian monk - she had set in motion a search for anyone with information about

Clutoriga. But it was now more than two weeks since she had heard from the cleric and she came to believe that she was simply chasing ghosts. She was no fool and knew that she was becoming a sad and troubled woman, so lost in love that she would grasp even the devil's hand. If she stayed at the fort much longer, her resentment of Inga would grow to the point of hatred. All too soon their rivalry would become a festering sore at the very heart of Ambrosius' company; for even now, the other Saxon women shunned her and it would only get worse.

When Ambrosius suddenly departed again for the south coast and took Inga with him, Lurotriga felt utterly abandoned. How foolish she had been to think that she could ever break the iron chain that bound those two together. Only one path remained: she must leave; and, once the idea took root in her head she knew she must go before Ambrosius returned. Thus, as she gazed out over the fields to the north, she reflected that this would be the last night she would pace along that rampart. She would miss it… miss him; because though she was not in his bed, it helped her to know that he was close by.

Though she was widowed, she was still young and of high birth so she could hope for a noble marriage elsewhere – perhaps at the much-admired court of King Erbin of Dumnonia. A few of the Durotriges, she was sure would leave with her but not so many as to weaken Ambrosius' company – she owed him that much loyalty.

6

When Aurelius Varta surveyed the burgus in the fading light, he felt well-satisfied with what he had achieved in Ambrosius' absence. He smiled down upon the tired men who, after another exhausting day's toil were now replete with food and wine and determined to carouse until sunset. His gaze fell upon the wall of Ambrosius' chamber and he grinned, hoping that his Dux would be impressed to find that it had finally been repaired. True, any stonemason worth employing would be ashamed of the ugly patchwork of flint and chalk, but it would have to do for now.

To the south-west, the fires and torches of nearby Vindocladia fused with the dim red glow of the setting sun. It was not much of a town and it grew less impressive by the day, but the next nearest one, Durnovaria was miles away. With a pang of guilt Varta remembered that he had contributed a little to Vindocladia's decline by robbing some stone for their repairs from one of the many decaying buildings. At least it was in a good cause, he thought for the town could only benefit from the presence of a strong fort close by. He was confident now that the burgus could hold out for a long time should the wretched High King Vortigern decide to come after Ambrosius.

The very thought of Vortigern brought back harsh reminders of the winter – memories of a day of slaughter that would live with him forever. Varta, the Frank had almost died that day and he would never be the warrior he once was. With his ruined left leg, he could no longer charge into battle alongside his friend, Ambrosius as he had done since the two were callow youths. Thus it was that while Ambrosius went south to fight Scotti, Varta was left behind to oversee repairs.

Just as he was in danger of wallowing in his misfortune, his great comrade Aurelius Marianus Onnophris - or 'Onno', as the cheerful Egyptian was known - entered the chamber. Varta was glad of Onno's presence and indeed it was mainly thanks to the Alexandrian engineer that the repairs to the abandoned fort were progressing so well.

While his friend stood at the window overlooking the west wall and squinted at the sun's last rays, Varta poured him a cup of wine.

"Another day of labour done then," said Onno.

"A successful day though," added Varta, sensing that his friend seemed a little more weary than usual.

"I don't know," lamented Onno. "This place is still falling apart and by Christ, it'll take a lifetime to restore it. It might be quicker to knock it down and build a new one."

"Really," said Varta.

"Er, no," replied the Egyptian, with a rueful grin.

"You're usually the one who looks on the bright side," laughed Varta.

"Well, that's true enough, but there's so much still to do and so few of us to do it."

"I'm sure it'll all seem better when Dux returns," said Varta.

"I suppose, but I can't help wondering whether we could have found somewhere better than this crumbling relic of a burgus…"

"Well, my friend, there are few such places to be found," said Varta, handing the Egyptian his wine. "But at least there's always the drink to fall back on..."

Late into the evening, the pair commiserated with the dubious assistance of some truly terrible wine. Varta was not sure how long they were dozing before a soldier plodded up the treacherous steps to their chamber and rapped on the open door.

Varta woke with a start and glared at the soldier.

"There's a fellow at the south-west gate," said the soldier. "Says he has word from Dux."

"Word," cried Varta, "What, at this time of night. What does he say?"

"Nothing yet," the soldier replied. "He asked to talk to you."

"Did he ask for me by name then?" enquired Varta.

"No… just for 'the man in command.'"

"You've not let him in yet," said Onno, also now wide awake.

"No. Orders are not to open the gate to anyone at night unless they have the night word."

"Yes, I know; I gave you those orders," said Varta, with a nod of approval. "I suppose I'd better come down to the gate then."

"I can go," offered Onno.

Varta waved a dismissive hand at his comrade. "Pah, you need the rest more than me," he replied, "and I can still manage a few steps."

Whilst he could manage them, he took his spatha to lean on just in case. It wouldn't look good for the fort commander to be tumbling down the stair like some drunk.

As of that day, the south-west gate was in fact the only gate since they had just walled up the north-east one. It remained a sensitive subject with Onno for it was the weakest feature of the fort's defences and would be until they could replace a few more of the gate's rotten timbers.

Given the late hour, he wasted no time on pleasantries when he reached the gateway.

"This is Varta, the Frank," he announced. "Tell me who you are and what you want."

"I bring a message from Ambrosius Aurelianus," said the man, who sounded about as thrilled to be having the conversation as Varta was.

Yet Varta hesitated for a moment, surprised that any messenger from Ambrosius would answer so bluntly. He was not familiar with the fellow but then there were still some among the recent Durotriges recruits that he did not know.

"Open the gate just enough for the fellow to slip in," Varta ordered the gatekeepers, "but mind you keep your wits sharp."

The ancient timbers creaked and groaned as one of the heavy gates was hauled open to reveal a lone figure on foot. That puzzled Varta for, if the messenger had indeed come from Ambrosius he surely ought to have a horse. Yet the man appeared to be on his own, so the quickest way to get some answers was to have the fellow in.

"Come in, man," ordered Varta. "And tell me what's so urgent."

Two flickering torches struggled to illuminate the interior of the gateway as the stranger entered slowly through the narrow gap between the two great gates, carrying what appeared to be a heavy sack.

"What's that?" grumbled Varta crossly.

"All I need," said the messenger, letting his load drop to the ground.

"Well, give me your message then, fellow," urged Varta.

"I am sent to tell you that Ambrosius Aurelianus is dead."

In the deathly silence that followed, the words struck Varta like a blow to the heart. He gasped, unwilling to believe that Dux – the mighty Dux - could possibly be dead. Surely only an immortal could kill his brother in arms; so the messenger must be false. But hard upon that thought came the tramp of boots approaching the gate and in that instant Varta's spatha cut down the messenger.

"Shut the gates!" he roared. "Sound the alarm!"

Only when the gate refused to shut, did Varta remember the sack but, by then of course it was too late. As the two gatekeepers attempted to wrestle the heavy bundle clear, spears thrust between the gates again and again until both men fell and those outside forced their way in.

Varta bellowed for help as half a dozen spears lunged at him. Chopping aside shaft after shaft, he could only retreat into the adjacent courtyard where several of his comrades snatched up their weapons to join him. Like him, they wore no armour or mail shirts – a few had no boots on either. Even as they formed a ragged line with him, Varta knew they were too few against the numbers pouring through the gateway: a score, two score… too many…

Backing away, he sought a place where he could hope to mount a proper defence; but the fort was almost all open space and ramshackle wooden lean-tos. While he was glancing around for inspiration, a spear point caught him low below the belly. Not mortal, he reckoned, grunting with pain but not helpful either. He was falling back steadily with his young comrades when suddenly he thought of the yard outside the women's chambers. There was a low wall there which separated it from the main courtyard, so if they retreated to the women's quarters, they might just make a stand there.

Despite his wound, he felt a spark of confidence for he and his fellow soldiers were maintaining a strong line as they retreated across the burgus. He wondered where Onno was but, knowing the wily Egyptian he would be organising a swift counterattack to take their assailants in the rear. Since they held all the ramparts, his men should be able to rain down death upon the intruders. Except, with most of the exhausted men asleep in the yard it occurred to him that very few were actually up on the rampart. Glancing up at the fort's central tower, he could see no-one - nor was anyone hurling spears from atop the west wall.

The man to his left suddenly stumbled and dropped to his knees and, since Varta had been leaning upon his shoulder he too crashed down. In the ensuing tangle of bodies, he tried to rise but the hilt of a spatha clubbed him back down. Spear points glinted in the torchlight as he raised his sword to stab blindly upward. Rolling onto his side, he managed to stand but, when he sought for his comrades, none were close by. Alone and surrounded he parried several thrusts until one spear got through to carve a deep furrow down his right thigh.

"Not the other damned leg," he groaned.

But when he tried to take a step back, he staggered and realised that a river of his Frankish blood was pouring down onto the cobbles.

"Live long, Ambrosius," he murmured, as a dozen hungry spears reached out of the darkness in search of his heart.

7

The Saxon Wynflaed and her younger sister, Ishild had retired early to the women's chamber for neither was interested in spending the night with drunken youths. Wynflaed was missing her husband, Ulf and she knew that Ishild was pining for the handsome, young Arturus. Neither expected to sleep undisturbed for girls would no doubt be slinking in during the small hours, bringing with them the stale smell of wine and the scent of men. The third occupant of their narrow straw mattress was Lucidia, Ambrosius' sister who had grown close to Ishild over the months since their arrival in Britannia.

Wynflaed lay there contemplating a secret which not even her sister knew; though she did wonder sometimes whether Ishild, who usually noticed everything had guessed. It was unusual for Wynflaed to keep anything from her sister but she was still getting accustomed to the maternal changes she was feeling and decided that Ulf deserved to be the first to know.

Being so crowded together with the younger girls, Wynflaed found sleep impossible most nights and often listened to the sounds of the fort slowly settling down for the night. This evening was especially noisy so when she heard voices sound out across the yard, she was not surprised. It was not unknown for young, hot-blooded soldiers to get into a fight – especially if Ambrosius was away. Varta or Onno would soon tear a strip off their hides and she grinned at the thought of the culprits facing the wrath of Varta the Frank. Yet the shouting continued unabated and no reprimand came.

Since she was now wide awake, she got up from the straw to deliver a rebuke herself. She grinned in anticipation for nothing felt as good as treating young Britons to a glimpse of her savage Saxon temper. That, she thought would sober the rabble up soon enough. In getting up she disturbed her sister who rolled over and woke Lucidia.

"What," groaned the Roman girl.

"Just a quarrel that's gotten out of hand," grumbled Wynflaed, going to the chamber door.

But before she reached it, something slammed hard against it from the outside.

"I've had enough," snarled Wynflaed, wrenching open the door but stumbling backwards as a bloodied young soldier fell inside on top of her.

Ishild, still in her linen shift pushed aside the dead youth and hurried to help up her sister. The pair stood then in the doorway looking in disbelief at the chaos erupting in the yard outside. For a moment Wynflaed feared that the Saxons and Britons had fallen out again, until she remembered that Ulf had taken all the Saxons with him. In the darkness it was impossible to tell who was fighting whom so, flanked by Ishild and Lucidia Wynflaed took a hesitant step out of the door. When a spear thudded into the door post Lucidia screamed which caused other women, rudely awoken to cry out in alarm.

"Be still," ordered Wynflaed and at once the chamber fell silent for, with Inga away all looked to her for leadership.

"Dress yourself, sister," she told Ishild. "Then go and find out what's happening. The rest of you, pull some clothes on and have a blade close at hand."

Ishild dressed swiftly and flew out of the door while the others followed Wynflaed's instructions. Moments later, a white-faced Ishild was back, crying: "The fort's breached. It's breached."

All knew what those few, terse words meant for a woman: if an enemy took the fort, their lives might only be measured in moments.

"Vortigern," wailed Lucidia.

"Who else would it be?" snapped Wynflaed.

"Then we're lost," breathed Lucidia, clinging to Ishild in terror.

Only a handful of those in the room had witnessed the bloody struggle of the previous winter, but those few knew that Vortigern would give no mercy to the sworn men of Ambrosius - or their womenfolk…

"There are other women in the fort," said Lucidia.

Their chamber housed all the unmarried women as well as those, like Wynflaed, whose husbands had accompanied Dux south. But some married women lived with their children wherever space could be found. Other girls were still no doubt entwined with their lovers when the storm broke. Thus the womenfolk were scattered all over the burgus.

"We can't protect them all," said Wynflaed. "But we can hold here until Varta and the others throw them out of the fort."

"But, sister," hissed Ishild, "they already have the gateway and the courtyard…"

Despite Wynflaed's reassurance, panic gripped the women and several shrieked at the thought of what might be to come.

Wynflaed's deep voice shouted them all down: "I've enough to do here without a dozen empty-headed women screaming about my ears. All we can do is defend ourselves; so block the door with all we have."

But all they had did not amount to much of substance for they slept upon straw mattresses at best. The only item of furniture was a long table which they now dragged up against the door. On top they stacked the straw mattresses, though Wynflaed knew it would not be enough. At best it might frustrate their attackers and persuade them to seek easier prey elsewhere. But such thin hopes were dashed when, moments later, there was another crash against the door. The two Saxon sisters held their long knives out in front of them as they awaited the inevitable. A few others followed their belligerent lead but most, like Lucidia simply sat on the floor and sobbed.

The next impact splintered the door giving Wynflaed a glimpse of the impatient men outside. Very soon, eager axes made short work of the rest of door and two men stepped forward to clear away the mass of straw. Behind them waited many others, baying for blood; but Ishild darted forward through the straw-filled air and plunged her blade at the nearer of the two men. Her rash assault brought a groan of pain and a knife glistening with fresh blood; if their assailants got in now, they would be hot with anger.

An axe carved away some of the timber debris and several more men set their shoulders against the table. Ishild cried out to her sister for help, so Wynflaed took a pace forward but then hesitated. Only a few weeks before she would have leaped to Ishild's side but now the new life inside her entreated her to hold back.

Ishild's rebuke was scathing. "You can't protect the life of the unborn, Wynflaed," she screamed, "by doing nothing over there."

Wynflaed stared at her sister with a bitter smile; so Ishild had known all along, but kept silent. And she was probably right, but it was already too late for several men thrust back the table to squeeze past it. In the howling darkness, women who resisted were beaten or cut down - while Wynflaed stood transfixed. Ishild, refusing to take a backward step planted both feet to stand alongside two other young women. A spear lunged at Ishild's breast but she turned it deftly aside in triumph with her swift blade only to be punched to the floor by an angry fist.

When her assailant lifted her up and hurled her against the wall, Wynflaed could hold back no longer… for after all, blood was blood… Charging at Ishild's assailant, she ducked under the hand that tried to cuff her down. Thrusting her knife up under his chin, she met some resistance as the blade chewed through his flesh. A moment later she felt the blood dribble onto her hand and she stumbled aside as the soldier fell.

Dropping to the floor, she was at the mercy of her victim's comrade until Ishild snatched up the fallen man's spear and aimed a fierce lunge at his side. Passing under the lip of his rudimentary breastplate, the spear point must have carved a path to his heart for, in an instant he collapsed onto the upturned table.

Yelling like the Saxon warrior she always craved to be Wynflaed, though still crouching on the floor, was in fighting mood. When another soldier raised his axe to swing at Ishild, she reached up to deliver a mortal wound to his thigh. While the life pumped out of him, she stood up and pushed him aside, screaming from the doorway:

"Keep coming in and we'll drain the blood from your worthless bodies!"

After that no more ventured in and Wynflaed beseeched Frigg to send their opponents elsewhere. Then she saw the flare of torches being lit and understood what was coming next. Even as she backed away, two flaming brands were hurled in through the shattered entrance; one fell harmlessly on the table but the other landed upon a heap of straw-filled mattresses.

Flames scorched across the bedding in a wave of fire which sent burning wisps of straw spiralling all over the room. The women now faced a new terror – gone was their fear of rape and slaughter – for now they expected to be burned alive. Instinctively, all shrank back but to no avail for soon tendrils of smoke began to swirl around the chamber.

Ishild, seizing Wynflaed's arm dragged her down as the air was filled with glowing filaments of straw and ash. Acrid smoke stung Wynflaed's eyes as she wrapped her arms around Lucidia and her sister.

8

Onno jerked awake, instantly aware of raucous shouts reverberating around the yard below – another scrap, no doubt. It was always the same after a few drinks, but he might just castrate the troublemakers this time. Varta, he noted had not yet returned so perhaps the Frank was cracking a few heads among the culprits.

With a sigh, he started to pull on his boots when his comrade, Aurelius Xallas burst into the watch chamber.

"Arm yourself," cried the warrior from Baetica. "We're under attack – and they're already inside."

"No," gasped Onno. "Where's Varta?"

"Right in the shit by the sound of it," snapped the Spaniard.

Seizing his axe, Onno made to leave but Xallas stopped him. "I said 'arm yourself', my friend. You'll need all you've got. Trust me, it'll be worth it if you want to last the night."

"Come on then, give me a hand," urged Onno, snatching up his mail shirt.

Though it did not take long for Xallas to help him don his mail and strap on his breastplate, Onno knew that the longer he delayed, the more of his inexperienced young comrades might be killed.

"I'll make for the gate," he said, as the pair hurtled out of the door and began to descend the long flight of steps to the courtyard two at a time.

Before Xallas could reply, two armed men appeared at the foot of the steps and began to climb up.

Eyeing his friend's axe, Xallas said: "Yours, I think, Onno."

For a big man the Egyptian was as nimble as a stoat and he descended the steps fast. At the sight of the burly figure hurtling down towards them, the soldiers stopped half way up open-mouthed. Onno despatched them as if he were swatting at troublesome flies rather than carving through flesh. Nor did he pause at the bottom of the steps but carried straight on to the gateway. At once he saw that he had come too late for the way was blocked by a tight wedge of men crowding into the fort.

"To arms!" he cried. "Every man to arms - stand fast here with me."

In vain he sought a glimpse of Varta as he attempted, with Xallas beside him to gather enough men to drive back the invaders. Axe whirling, he tried to hew a path to the gate to stop the incursion, but there was such a press of men coming in that their sharp spears compelled him to fall back.

"If we can just get to Varta we can toss these devils out between us," raged Xallas.

Onno was no man to foster false hopes so, gripping his friend's arm he cried: "It's too late, Xallas. The fort's lost – and Varta… Varta's gone…"

"No, the Frank will fight to the end," insisted Xallas, shaking free from his comrade's grasp. "We just have to find him."

But Onno hauled the protesting Xallas away across the wide yard. "All we can do, my friend, is save as many of the rest as we can…"

70

Even then Xallas hesitated, consumed by impotent rage until he was forced to accept that Onno was right.

Clapping his comrade on the shoulder, Onno said: "Aye, my friend, come then, let's make Dux proud of his sworn warriors."

Around the two battle-hardened bucellarii others began to gather – most with a spatha or spear in their hands but uncertain which way to turn in the deadly confusion. These were the youths, thought Onno who had only volunteered in the past few weeks - raw recruits who would now be blooded long before they were ready. Ill-equipped and unprepared, they would pay a heavy price in blood… but they were all he had.

"Come, lads," Onno bellowed above the clamour. "The fort's taken, but our folk may still be saved. We'll go for the women and gather others up as we go." But he wondered how many even heard his cheerless words which were all but drowned out by the clamour. Ambrosius would expect his bucellarii to do better than that. Onno might not be able to train them now, or arm them any better but at the very least he could put some steel into their young hearts.

"By God!" he roared. "You're the bucellarii of Dux Ambrosius Aurelianus and you're going to act like it. You've drunk his wine and fornicated with women under his roof; so now you can damn well fight to keep them alive – or die trying!"

"Stay together," barked Xallas, as Onno led them out of the yard. "Do as you're told and you might just live till dawn."

Onno thought it unlikely that any of them would but he was determined to give the poor bastards something useful to do before they were hacked to pieces. Breaking out of the stable yard was easy enough, but forcing a path to the women's chamber through a growing mass of fighting men would take a heavy toll of the young recruits. The moment they entered the main courtyard of the burgus, the youths saw for the first time by the flickering torchlight that they were hopelessly outnumbered.

"In God's name, don't stop!" bellowed Onno, as he darted forward knowing all they had in their favour was that first moment of impact. After that, it would all go very swiftly to hell.

Still seething at the knowledge that Varta the Frank must have fallen, Onno turned his rage upon his opponents. He caught a glimpse of a pale, frightened face seconds before his axe cleaved it in two. Not for an instant was his weapon still and its blade reaped victim upon victim while Xallas worked his heavy spear with lethal skill. Working together, the two men cut a great gash in the tightly-packed ranks of their enemies.

If they could convince their attackers that the fort was defended by a horde of experienced warriors, there was a slim chance they might break and flee. At first their efforts bore fruit as several men fell back in disarray before the brutal onslaught. But, as Onno feared the effect did not last long for this was the army of Vortigern. Only the High King of Britannia could possibly have raised such a large fighting force to attack Ambrosius. And Vortigern was a seasoned commander who would very soon rally his scattered forces.

Onno's idea of rescuing the women was all very laudable but it ignored the simple fact that, since they had walled up the north gate there was only one way out of the fort which was the gateway now held by Vortigern. Thus as he led the men across the main courtyard, the Egyptian set his mind to the task of finding another way out of the burgus.

"I'll go straight to the women's chamber," he told Xallas. "You take a couple to fetch the Lady Lurotriga."

"You mean that lady," said Xallas, gesturing across the yard to where the lady in question was encircled by an unruly throng.

"God's truth," snarled Onno. "Take half a dozen with you and make haste, or it'll too late."

Xallas nodded and started to choose a few of the terrified youths around him.

"I'll wait for you here," said Onno, "and do you see that hoist we used yesterday to raise the stones?"

"Aye," gasped Xallas, eyeing the ever-growing horde sweeping into the yard behind them.

"Fetch me the rope on it," ordered Onno.

Without wasting any more time questioning Onno, Xallas set off with his six men.

"The lady - and the rope, my friend," Onno called after him.

While Xallas darted away across the yard, Onno glanced over his shoulder towards the women's chamber and was appalled to discover that a cluster of men had already broken through the door.

"By Christ, hold on girls," he muttered to himself. "Just a little longer, Wynflaed – keep safe a little bit longer..."

He dared not go to the aid of the women until he covered the retreat of Xallas and his comrades when they struggled back through the fierce crowd of Britons. But before Xallas even reached Lurotriga, a sudden bright glare burst from the doorway of the women's chamber.

"Oh, shit!" exclaimed Onno, seeing that the small courtyard outside the fiery entrance was crowded with men and the fire would only draw more.

With more men flooding in all the time, Onno's small force was now almost surrounded. But with retreat impossible, they would just have to hold their ground until Xallas could fight his way to them with Lady Lurotriga – and Onno prayed, the rope.

Wielding his axe in the front rank, Onno set about his opponents with unbridled fury, while another frantic look at the women's quarters told him that time was running out. To save Dux's sister, along with Wynflaed and all the rest, he would have to abandon Xallas and Lurotriga. Onno knew how fond Ambrosius was of the latter, but one British noblewoman was not worth the lives of all the other women in the fort - unless of course, Xallas had managed to get the rope...

9

Lurotriga was leaning over the parapet of the north rampart when the cries of alarm first disturbed the night's peace. Turning to peer into the dark courtyard below, she glimpsed several spectral figures locked in the savage embrace of combat. Wide-eyed, the young recruits manning the rampart watched the slaughter with her and several turned to her for orders since none had fought in a battle before.

"We don't know what to do, lady," they cried. "What should we do?"

Though Lurotriga was no soldier, even she could see that the garrison was under dire threat. Her youths would be far more use down in the yard than looking on from the rampart, but it appeared that the yard was already almost overrun. She was certain that Varta and the other bucellarii would try to protect the women at all cost so, if her young guards were to go anywhere, it should be there.

Taking out the knife which experience had taught her to carry with her at all times, she summoned the young men from the rampart.

"Come, we must go down there," she told them, with a show of confidence she did not feel. "I trust those spears you bear are not just for decoration."

While the apprehensive youths dithered, Lurotriga seized a flaming torch from the wall and led the way down the steps to the courtyard. They were furthest from the gate which had been breached so, she reasoned they should be able to make it across the yard to the women's chamber. But it was one thing to gaze down upon chaos from above and quite another to wade through the belly of it. They had scarcely taken half a dozen steps before the youth beside her was cut down by an axe blade which arced down upon him out of the darkness.

Her impulsive action would most likely result in the untrained young men around her being butchered like pigs. Screaming somehow helped her to release the terror which threatened to trap her in its fierce, uncompromising grasp. Courage, she told herself brandishing her knife wildly about her until a hand seized her wrist. In that instant all her calm demeanour evaporated into one irresistible thought: she would never see Ambrosius again.

"Peace, lady. Stop struggling," cried a voice close by – a voice she seemed to remember.

Gulping in deep breaths, Lurotriga forced her eyes wide to stare at the man whose hand was locked upon her arm. When she realised it was Ambrosius' trusted comrade, Xallas, she shuddered with relief and clung to him. Letting him steer her away, she stumbled over a fallen body while another of the young soldiers seeking to protect her succumbed to a spear thrust.

Surrounded by the others, she was shepherded across the yard where the uncertain flicker of torches cast an array of ever-moving shadows. Fighting their way across the cobbles, the small knot of warriors around her was harried without mercy and several more spear thrusts struck home. Just ahead of her came a cry from a wounded youth trying in vain to stay on his feet. Lurotriga blinked in shock when he slid down and was trampled, screaming under the boots of his own comrades. And, all the while Xallas walked beside her to shield her with his own body.

Suddenly Onno was there too and, despite her determination to keep calm she cried out as her small escort was absorbed into a larger band of soldiers. Even so, when she looked into their faces all she saw was her own fear staring back at her – until Onno took command.

Snatching the rope Xallas was carrying, he roared at his men: "Those bastards are burning out our women. So let's do something about it."

Peering across the smoke-filled yard through smarting, half-closed eyes Lurotriga saw the fire-scorched doorway of the women's quarters surrounded by men. It surely offered no hope of respite but, ahead of her the Egyptian raised his axe and plunged into the midst of their enemies, scattering them with the ferocity of his assault. And, God preserve them the youths followed him into the bloody mêlée and a host of men fell before them until finally Xallas pushed her towards the flaming doorway.

Onno had crashed through before her, sending shards of smouldering timber in all directions. Propelled inside by Xallas, Lurotriga gasped when a hot splinter sliced across her cheek. In the close, choking interior the fire was thrashed out while the spears of Xallas and several of the youths defended the doorway.

Even from the far side of the smoky room, Lurotriga felt the steely glare of hostility from the Saxon pair, Wynflaed and Ishild, though they spoke not a word to her. What did it matter now, she thought when all of them were doomed to perish there, trapped in that smoke-choked room. Her rescue was surely the hollowest of reprieves for, even if they broke out the fort's gateway was too far away and impossible to break through.

Despite their mortal predicament, she thought Onno looked far less concerned than she was so she squeezed over to him through the press of bodies.

"We have to surrender," she cried.

"There'll be no surrender," snapped Ishild.

"But they will slaughter us all," insisted Lurotriga.

Wynflaed seized her by the arm and cried: "Vortigern will kill us all anyway - it's what he's come here for: revenge."

"Peace," said Onno, his voice already hoarse. "Stop your bickering. We're not surrendering so get ready to move, all of you - and keep a blade in your hand if you have one."

Lurotriga was about to point out the obvious: that there was no way out of the room when she realised that Onno had sent some of his men to toil in the far corner of the chamber. In the gloomy haze she saw that they were hacking a hole with their axes in the chalk of the back wall while several others were chopping at the roof timbers.

"I can't see where all this gets us," she cried in despair.

"Outside," was his terse response. "These lads only finished rebuilding this section of wall yesterday. We had to use lumps of chalk in with the flints; so trust me, lady, we can get through it."

"But there's a massive ditch outside," she hissed at him. "And it's very deep. You're offering these women only false hope... It's impossible, Onno."

"Impossible, lady," replied the Egyptian, with a dark grin. "Not for the finest engineer in all Alexandria, it's not…"

While the doorway was being relentlessly assaulted by wave after wave of Vortigern's soldiers, the outer wall was soon breached and the women began to scramble over the shattered chalk blocks and sharp flints. There was a mighty crash as a roof timber dropped down and was then manhandled out through the wall. When Onno thrust Lurotriga to the gap, she glanced back to see Xallas and the others being forced back into the chamber by the fresh soldiers being sent against them.

"Make haste, lady," urged Onno, "In God's name, make haste."

Another roof timber was brought down as she passed through the gap in the wall and wandered alongside it in the dark like a lost child. Then she cursed like a foul-mouthed soldier as she tore her knee on a protruding flint. Next moment, she was shoved roughly aside by Onno and two youths bearing another long length of timber. Several more grim figures surged past her and then another bundled into her as she heard the chamber roof collapse with a crash that echoed across the fields. A cloud of ash and chalk dust enveloped her as Xallas thudded into her and knocked her forward to the edge of the black ditch. Just as she seemed certain to plunge head first into it, he caught one of her arms to haul her back.

"Come, lady," he whispered.

She clasped his strong hand knowing it was her only hope of survival and the pair staggered after the others. As her eyes adjusted a little more to the night, she glimpsed the line of shadows moving ahead of her but flinched when she saw how they were supposed to cross the deep inner ditch. Each woman had to scramble across a makeshift bridge comprising three roof timbers; but, since the joists were too short to span the entire breadth they first had to slide down several feet of earth bank to where Onno waited to help them.

Though Xallas pushed Lurotriga forward, her first instinct was to hang back and protest that she could not possibly make the crossing. But then she saw the Saxon sisters doing so below her and she found her courage once more. Moreover, since many of the women were local Durotriges like her, she had a duty to give them a strong lead. Thus, when Xallas held out his hand to help her down to Onno, she brushed it aside and jumped down. Bravery almost proved her undoing because on landing she skidded further down the bank and, had Onno not caught her would have plunged down onto the forest of sharpened stakes that she knew lay below.

"Bold not rash, lady," Onno murmured in her ear, as she heaved in several deep breaths to bolster her failing nerve.

"You'd better go on across," he said.

"No," she argued. "Get the others across first; then you can start leading them over the last two ditches."

"That would be better," he acknowledged, "but you should still go before me."

With a brusque shake of the head, she replied: "If we're to move fast, the women will need encouragement. I'll come at the end with Xallas."

"Very well," he conceded and set off across the beam with the rope Xallas had given him now coiled over his shoulder.

Ushering the next woman forward Lurotriga could sense, even in the dark how nervous she was – and by God, she should be. Crossing the deepest ditch in the small hours of the night and trying to do it in silence was a tall order for anyone. Though brimming with admiration for their courage, she knew it was all taking far too long for they still had to negotiate the shallower ditches and cross the fields to Vindocladia. Even then, they would have to hide out until Ambrosius returned – which might not be for days...

Soon enough Vortigern would work out where the survivors from the fort had gone. True, the smoke and debris in the women's chamber would delay discovery of their escape route for a while, but then the angry High King would send men in pursuit. The thought prompted her to peer back towards the still-smoking hole in the fort wall, for any sign that their flight had been discovered.

She was relieved when Xallas joined her, until he warned: "Get these last few across fast, lady - we've little time left."

There were only two girls left to cross: Dux's sister Lucidia and a younger Briton – one of the few that Lurotriga did not know. Scarcely more than a child, she was rooted to the brink of the ditch. Even when Xallas offered to carry her over, she shrank away from the tall warrior in fear. Lucidia had waited with the young lass, perhaps anticipating that she might need to help the trembling girl across.

"Come on, girl," pleaded Xallas, as gently as he could, but he could not persuade the terrified girl to cross.

Instead he helped Lucidia to mount the timber bridge, while the young girl clung to Lurotriga's arm.

"Off you go," she whispered to Lucidia. "We'll be close behind you."

Wynflaed and Ishild waited at the far end of the crossing. Some, like young Ishild wore courage like a skin but for Lucidia, of a similar age such resolve did not come so easily. Yet the two very different young women were friends and Lurotriga had no doubt that the Saxon would take Lucidia's hand the moment she was close enough to her.

"Make haste now," Xallas hissed when Lucidia was safely across.

But the last girl was still shaking as Lurotriga led her to the bridge.

"In God's name, they're almost upon us," urged Xallas.

"I can't do it, lady," whispered the girl. "I just can't do it…"

"Just crawl," ordered Lurotriga, hardening her tone. "You can crawl, I suppose. Upon your scrawny knees - and crawl damned fast, unless you want to die."

Stung by Lurotriga's scolding words, the terrified girl set off across the wooden supports only to pause half way across. Lurotriga held her breath hoping that, having seen all the others cross the lass would not baulk at it now. Encouraged by Ishild ahead of her and Lurotriga behind, the girl at last plucked up enough nerve to set off again but, at that moment there was a shout from above them and a spear flew past the girl's shoulder to disappear into the ditch.

Perhaps the blade tore the young girl's arm or the shock of it startled her but, whatever the reason she lost her grip on the timber beams. In an instant she slid off the bridge eluding the flailing hands of both Ishild and Lurotriga. The drop was perhaps only ten feet but a mortal scream told them how the girl had landed.

Lurotriga shouldered the heavy weight of regret and lowered herself swiftly onto her haunches, wincing as her bleeding knee cracked the end of the timber. Ahead, she saw Ishild facing her across the chasm and began to wriggle towards her as fast as she could. Usually Lurotriga moved with grace and poise – and she knew it - but this was different. This was a visceral task where she had just seen that a single lapse of attention could kill. Trying to shut the girl's death from her mind, she concentrated on sliding her legs forward and taking as penance the splinters that clawed at her flesh.

Coming face to face with Ishild at the far end of the bridge, she was met by a curt Saxon nod of respect. But when the girl backed away to allow her off the beam, a second spear thudded into the wood just behind her feet. The timber shuddered and Lurotriga's right foot slipped off it. Sliding sideways, she scrabbled for a handhold but found none. Her fingers clawed in vain at the bare earth on the edge of the ditch. As she muttered a final prayer, all she could think of was the young girl plummeting to her death.

10

Worried that he had not heard from Inga and Arturus, Ambrosius was relieved when, just before dawn a breathless rider arrived at his camp beside the estuary. But relief turned to apprehension when he recognised the exhausted horse lathered in sweat. It was Inga's mount and, for a moment Ambrosius knew despair.

"Your lady," he shouted at the messenger. "Is she…"

"No, Dux, Lady Inga is well," replied the horseman. "But…"

"But?"

"I bring the most terrible news, Dux…"

And when he delivered his dire message, Ambrosius could scarcely believe what the rider was telling him. A twisting knot of guilt tightened in his belly as he recalled how undermanned he had left the burgus at Vindocladia. At the time he thought it a justified risk; but now… now it seemed the greatest folly imaginable. The unexpected arrival of Florina in league with a host of Scotti raiders had been worrying enough; but the notion that Vortigern himself was involved went far beyond his worst fears.

It was clear enough to him now that the role Vortigern intended for Florina and the Scotti was simply one of distraction. Their attacks would delay Ambrosius in the south long enough to allow Vortigern to besiege the fort in his absence. All Ambrosius could do now was ride hard for Vindocladia and pray that Varta, Onno and the others could hold the crumbling burgus until he returned.

His wounded men could not travel fast, so he would be forced to leave them behind to follow on more slowly. But the seven captured Scotti presented a more difficult problem, for they would need to be guarded and he could spare no men for that. Desperate to leave with all speed, he considered executing all of them on the spot. There would certainly have been no shortage of volunteers among Argetrus' Britons to carry out such a sentence. Yet… he had given his word to the surrendering Scotti so, shorthanded though he was he would have to take them with him. He consoled himself that, once he joined Arturus he would have a few more fighting men at his side.

When he roared the command to strike camp, there was only a trace of dawn upon the horizon. His startled bucellarii captains scrambled to obey: gathering up their arms, marshalling the younger men and running to fetch their horses. Leaving only the wounded at the camp, Ambrosius set off at a dangerously fast pace. Though they only had to follow the river, it would have been all too easy for a horse to stumble in the poor light and break a leg – and Ambrosius had no more mounts to spare than men. Even so he rode on as if death was hunting him down… but of course, it was not for death lay in wait ahead of him.

They had travelled several miles when a thin finger of light crept skywards to taunt Ambrosius with the knowledge that if Vortigern planned to attack at dawn, he and his bucellarii would arrive too late. Yet what else could he do but race against the rising sun, as he scoured the tree-lined riverbank for Arturus' small band. They would be on foot so he expected to overtake them at any moment; but in the end his horsemen very nearly rode them down where the track disappeared into a stand of trees.

At the mere sight of Inga, Ambrosius' spirits soared and, reining in his horse he vaulted down from it to sweep her up into his arms.

"You're safe," he breathed. "I feared you might have been taken by Florina."

"Aye, I'm safe," she murmured, "but we're all that's left. She indicated two bloody corpses sprawled on the river bank where the first rays of dawn danced upon their broken bodies.

As Ambrosius clasped Arturus' hand, he said: "Tell me what happened here."

"I sent our two fittest men on ahead to overtake the ship," replied the youth bitterly. "I thought they could warn our comrades at the fort, but it seems that Florina is not so easy to outwit."

"You risked half your number," grumbled Ambrosius, lamenting the loss of men who would at least have swelled his company a little more.

"I had to warn our friends," explained Arturus. "Your sister, Lucidia... and Ishild... I thought I must do something, Dux."

"Aye," agreed Ambrosius. "It's always hard to do nothing, lad."

Ambrosius understood that it was the bright-eyed Saxon, Ishild who was at the forefront of Arturus' thoughts. They both knew that if Vortigern captured Ishild and Lucidia, he would be revenged upon the pair for what they had done to his son, Catigern in the winter. Indeed this was all about revenge for the humiliating defeat Ambrosius, with only a handful of fighting men had inflicted upon the High King of Britannia. Two of Vortigern's sons had been killed and, from that moment on Vortigern had pursued Ambrosius with all the considerable resources he possessed.

"All the same, next time I give you six men to command," said Ambrosius, "try not to get most of the poor bastards killed."

It was a harsh indictment of the young warrior's leadership but the reprimand, though necessary, grieved Ambrosius. Arturus was like a younger brother to him and a few moments later he embraced the youth to soften the rebuke.

"You only did what I'd have done at your age," he conceded. "So... where's the ship now?"

"I fear it must be close to Vindocladia, Dux," replied the distraught youth.

"And we only have fifteen men," observed Inga.

"Aye, the fight against the Scotti cost us dear," admitted Ambrosius. "These are the only fit men; the wounded will follow when they can."

"Yet," Inga hesitated. "You've brought prisoners with you..."

She made a fair point for, without Arturus' half dozen men to join him Ambrosius could spare no-one to watch the prisoners. He must either kill them, or release them. If he let them go they would make for the southern shore to steal a boat to get home. Even if they gave him their word to keep the peace, he could not trust them. Such barbarous thieves who plundered homes, raped women and stole away boys could hardly be expected to keep their word. Yet, despite all his misgivings he did not want their blood upon his hands.

When he explained to the Scotti that he was cutting them loose on foot without any weapons, they seemed to understand well enough but the response of their giant leader was unexpected.

"You're a great war leader," said the Scot.

"Thank you," said Ambrosius, cutting the bonds that encircled the captive's wrists. "Now go back – in peace – to where you came from."

"You demand nothing more of us," said the Scot.

"No," replied Ambrosius. "Only that you keep your word, be glad of your freedom and go. If you don't, I'll hunt you down and decorate my spatha with your entrails."

It was a bold boast; but an empty one and everyone knew it.

Pausing only to help Inga onto a horse, Ambrosius mounted his own and was about to leave when the Scotti leader called out to him.

"We're a long way from home," said the Scot. "And you need men. We could fight for you."

"No," snapped Ambrosius.

"You don't trust us…"

"To trust your word is one thing," replied Ambrosius, "but to trust you enough to have you at my back is very, very different."

Without further delay he urged his horse forward and left the disgruntled Scotti beside the river.

"Our pace will be too fast for you," he told Inga, when she rode up alongside him. "But I'll leave you two men."

"No you won't," she replied. "You'll need every one of them – and I have Ferox…"

With a taut smile, he nodded and reached out to clasp her hand for an instant before galloping away.

Though only his most accomplished riders could keep up with him, he was determined to pursue Florina's ship with all speed. When he saw the familiar outline of an ancient hill fort on the skyline to the north, he was encouraged to learn just how close they were now to Vindocladia. If Florina was only just arriving, he might yet forestall Vortigern's attack – except… he caught a trace of smoke in the air.

11

A wise woman once told Lurotriga that death sometimes came as a welcome relief; and hours earlier, as she stared out over the fort's rampart she thought the old crone might well be right. But, when her desperate fingers lost their grip on the wooden beam Lurotriga knew that she wanted to live. She wanted to live very much so she snatched at the pale hand snaking down towards her and clung on to life with every stubborn fibre of her body.

Looking up, she gasped to see Ishild staring down at her - Ishild, who hated her. The young Saxon, grunting with the effort of supporting her reached down with her other hand to seize Lurotriga's wrist. Even so the Briton felt herself sinking further and knew that Ishild was sliding down with her. It was time to accept her fate for the Saxon must let go, or they would both be impaled upon the sharpened stakes that had already claimed one victim.

"Let me go," she hissed.

"I'll not let you fall now, Briton," cried Ishild, "when I've spent so much effort catching you."

So, to her surprise Ishild held her fast until moments later Xallas came to their rescue.

As he hauled both women up and onto the bank, Lurotriga gasped at Ishild: "I thought you'd just…"

"Let you die," whispered Ishild, thrusting her face an inch from Lurotriga's. "Oh, I would have; but I think Inga would rather kill you herself…"

Crushed by her saviour's bitter words, Lurotriga let the Saxon go on with Wynflaed and waited while Xallas pulled on each beam to send them tumbling down into the ditch. Up ahead she could just make out a line of dark figures crossing the two shallower ditches. It struck her that, if she could barely see anyone there was every chance they might also be hidden from their pursuers. A sudden blaze of light dashed that hope and, looking back at the fort she saw flames curling over the wooden ramparts to send slender darts of fire showering up into the sky. The fugitives might not be fully illuminated but Vortigern would see exactly where they were going.

Onno, now atop the outer ditch was using his rope to haul some of the women up the short slope, while a few of the younger girls scrambled up on hands and knees. Urging Lurotriga to run, Xallas took her hand and his powerful strides enabled him to pull her up and over both ditches only a few yards behind Wynflaed, Ishild and Lucidia.

The Saxon pair, she noticed were very protective of Lucidia, so there was clearly a strong bond there. But she too kept an eye on the girl, knowing that Ambrosius would want her to. Though the Saxons did not trust her, Lurotriga was past caring about that; all that mattered now was keeping all the women safe and together.

Having divided up their charges into two smaller groups, Onno and Xallas led a column each across the fields towards the town with the young soldiers arrayed to protect their flanks. Once Vindocladia boasted gates and a paved entrance through its timber rampart, but now that part of the town lay in ruins and both gates and rampart must have disappeared long ago. Only a cobbled street remained which passed right through the ailing settlement down to the river ford. The two bucellarii led the exhausted refugees along it, hoping to find refuge in one of the many deserted buildings.

The mantle of command had fallen upon Onno's shoulders and, when Lurotriga joined him she could tell from his demeanour that the responsibility was weighing heavily upon him.

"If we don't get off the streets, lady they'll find us at once," he told her. "We have to find empty properties to hide in - however ruined they might be. I'll take one party with me to the west of the town while Xallas goes east. If some are... discovered then at least not all will be taken in the hours before dawn."

"And when dawn comes, we..." said Lurotriga.

Onno paused, perhaps deciding how much to tell her. "Once our pursuers grow weary of their task," he said, "we'll make for the ford and get across the river before dawn."

It all sounded very simple, she thought as Onno gave a final wave to Xallas and led his group, including Lurotriga, Lucidia and the two Saxons deeper into the town. They hurried past a row of dilapidated buildings which, in a different age would have housed shops selling food and other goods to the people of Vindocladia. Such fine places were long ago abandoned and it was there that Onno hoped they could hide out.

Before they could even begin searching for a sanctuary, they heard horses clattering along the cobbled way they had just left. It could only be Vortigern's men thundering into the town after them and Lurotriga was grateful for Onno's decision to leave the main thoroughfare. They were still by no means safe but, as the street narrowed a little they sought refuge in the half-ruined houses.

"This one," hissed Onno, darting to his left to force entry into a dark hulk of a building.

But within the first few moments Lurotriga knew that Onno had chosen badly for the place was so damaged that a roof fall blocked their way inside. Before they could look elsewhere, they heard several horsemen cantering along the street.

"Get down," ordered Onno.

It was all they could do: crouch down in silence, praying that their God had not deserted them. There they remained for some time, their backs aching and legs growing ever more cramped, until at last all the riders moved on. Some nervous chatter started up among the youngest girls whose relief was almost tangible. It was also premature for raucous voices soon announced the arrival of many more soldiers, no doubt emboldened by their victory at the fort. And the real devils, thought Lurotriga would be those who came searching on foot – those who craved blood, plunder or women...

She caught a glimpse of flickering torches as men began to break down doors and drag folk out from the ramshackle hovels they called home. Nor was it just those who had fled from the burning fort who were to feel the High King's wrath. At first the fugitives, cowering in their hiding place did not understand what was happening until they recognised the familiar stench they hoped to have left behind at the burgus.

When the first torch was hurled into their fragile refuge, Lurotriga was one of many who squealed in terror. Others fell upon their knees in the rubble to pray, while some sat clasping hands as the heat intensified all around them. Men were tossing torches into every building, regardless of who occupied it and a tinder-dry June ensured that fire soon began to rip through the town.

Lurotriga shivered when the crackle of dry timbers nearby heralded the fire's approach. Very soon flames raging out of control would force them to flee into the chaos outside though they would find no respite there. Tears filled her eyes as she realised that their very presence had brought fire and sword down upon all the town's unfortunate inhabitants. When the hot air was so stifling they could endure it no longer, Onno announced that they must abandon the house. But just then the rotten door of their hiding place was smashed apart and Lurotriga knew that he had left it too late. For Onno's unlucky charges there would be no easy way out.

Some of the girls screamed and Lurotriga could not blame them for, scarcely a few hours earlier these young girls had been flirting with raw recruits – many of whom were already dead. With a mighty roar, Onno crashed through the doorway, axe in hand. Half a dozen snarling youths followed his lead while the rest waited a few moments and then saw the women safely out.

Once outside, Lurotriga discovered that hell had come to Vindocladia, for Vortigern's quest for vengeance had set the entire town ablaze. Onno's ragged column emerged into a firestorm where houses were reduced to piles of scorched rubble and ash while a strengthening north wind drove the flames south towards the river. The terrified women were engulfed in a whirlwind of hot embers which seared their hands, hair and clothing. Though Onno tried his best to keep them together as they stumbled along the debris-littered street, several wandered away crying out in pain as their skin burned. Despite Onno's bellowed commands, Lurotriga could see that the women's morale was shattered. Several joined the bewildered townsfolk who fled along the streets in uncomprehending despair.

Poor Onno, used to fighting alongside his fellow bucellarii could offer no solace to the panic-stricken women. Instead it was Wynflaed who cajoled and bullied them into a closely-packed group when all they wanted to do was scatter before the shards of fire. Whether out of fear or respect, the Saxon convinced them to listen once more to Onno.

"We must make for the river now!" he shouted.

But Lurotriga's attention was elsewhere for she had suddenly realised that Dux's sister was not with the others. Staring about her in alarm, she screamed at Wynflaed: "I can't see Lucidia."

"Shit of the Nile," groaned Onno, desperate to escape the wild fury in the street.

"I'll find her," cried Ishild.

"I'll come with you," said Wynflaed at once.

"By Christ, no," protested Onno. "I need you with the other women, Wynflaed. All I do is frighten the poor souls; but they believe in you."

Lurotriga, seeing that Wynflaed was set to argue said: "I'll go with Ishild."

"I don't need your help," snapped Ishild.

"But Lucidia might," insisted Lurotriga, "so I'm coming."

"But you…" Onno stared at her in horror and she knew very well why: he dared not lose both her and Lucidia.

"Give us two good youths," cried Lurotriga, "and we'll bring Lucidia back for you."

All knew that further delay would be a death sentence, so Onno gave a curt nod.

"Go then, both of you - but keep together. We'll cross the river at the ford and wait for you on the south bank."

Wynflaed gave her younger sister a swift embrace before glaring at Lurotriga and despatching her with the words: "Don't come back without them."

12

By the time Onno had chosen two youths to accompany them, the fleet-footed Ishild was darting away with Lurotriga in her wake. Onno might fear for them, but he could hardly endanger the whole company - even for the sake of Dux's sister. As he watched Ishild and Lurotriga disappear into the swirling mass of flame and shadow, he knew that Wynflaed's eyes were also following her sister. Though misery was etched upon the Saxon's smoke-streaked face, he found a shared understanding in her eyes. If any of the three young women were lost, Inga and Ambrosius would never forgive them – nor would they forgive themselves.

"Come," he told Wynflaed and led out the remaining women with the young soldiers once more flanking them. He nodded with approval to see that Wynflaed, with blade in hand at once dropped back to the rear to encourage the very youngest girls for whom the flight was a never-ending nightmare. What a woman, he thought with unbridled admiration. That Saxon bastard, Ulf was a lucky man indeed to have such a formidable wife.

It was then that he heard several screams; not the woeful cries of many in distress, but the shrill voices of individuals who knew they were about to die. Though he shut his mind to them it was a reminder that, despite the horrors they had faced so far they had nonetheless been fortunate. But well before they reached the river, their good fortune ran out.

As they were creeping along a narrow lane, a house wall collapsed just ahead of them spewing lumps of stone and smoking timbers across their path. Veering to his right, Onno contrived to avoid the falling debris and the rest followed his lead until roof tiles began to cascade down upon them, smashing into jagged fragments as they skidded across the cobbles.

"By Christ!" he roared, when a piece flew past his head, cutting his cheek.

Though it jarred him for a moment, he carried on unaware that several others were far worse off than he was.

"Onno!" yelled Wynflaed and her tone told the Egyptian what he would see when he stopped to look back.

The tiles had sliced through the group, killing outright one of his most promising young soldiers while one of the women had sustained a deep cut that Wynflaed was struggling to bind up. Onno was still endeavouring to absorb yet another senseless casualty when a further blow came.

Hurrying towards them were a woman and child, faces distorted by fear which warned him that soldiers must be very close behind. Waving the fleeing pair past, he raised his axe and called out to his remaining soldiers. Even he was shocked to discover that there were only five of them left, but his heart swelled with pride to see them hold their spears at the ready. Arrayed in a tight half-circle they prepared to protect the women who were still binding up their wounds with torn-off strips of clothing. But Onno knew in his heart that he could no longer defend them all.

"Wynflaed," he said. "When you're done, get them all further down the lane – the lads too – and head for the river." Then he added: "Don't wait for me – just get across the ford any way you can."

"But we need you with us," cried Wynflaed, the strain telling in her voice.

"I'm just going to slow them down a bit," he replied, forcing a grin.

Wynflaed wasted no words trying to persuade him against his decision, but gave him a broad smile. "Stay alive, Onno," she said, "Because… we need you."

The moment she set off with the rest of the group, Onno observed several armed men at the top of the alley. Shouldering his axe, he began to trudge up towards them for he was confident about taking on three of the bastards. But the closer he got, the less he liked the odds for it turned out that there were rather more than three. Still… it was too late now to turn and run; besides, he had promised to buy Wynflaed some time.

When they were less than twenty yards away, however, Onno's face cracked into a sly grin as he inspected his adversaries. Hands and clothes stained with the blood of their victims, they exuded a wild confidence – no doubt enhanced by more than a little of Vindocladia's finest wine – known to his comrades as horse piss. If this lot ever possessed shields, they had long ago discarded them and their spears were held loose in their hands as if they expected not to need them.

They were sniggering at him and they laughed even harder when he broke into a run. Pumping his weary legs, Onno charged straight into their midst and their amusement ended when he punched the head of his axe into the leading soldier's chest. The drunken fellow dropped like wounded ox, groaning while the rest came to a shocked halt, which gave Onno a vital moment to sweep his axe across them. One, his weapon half-raised watched as the axe blade snapped off his spear point. Another lost his hand altogether along with his spear and stumbled away screaming. A third, distracted by his comrade's plight, delayed his lunge just long enough to receive the back swing of Onno's weapon across his throat.

Well pleased with his first encounter, Onno took a menacing pace forward keen to press home his initial advantage. As he hoped, his brutal assault had sobered up the survivors and they backed away hastily. If their courage returned he prayed that the torn bodies of their fallen comrades would provide a sharp reminder of his prowess.

While they hesitated, Onno retreated back down the lane to where the roof fall had half-blocked it and decided to make his next stand there in the narrow passage. Glancing up, the Egyptian glimpsed through the smoke-laden sky, the first glimmer of dawn, but it was not a welcome sight. At least darkness offered some hope of concealment, but in daylight it would be a different matter.

A second band of Vortigern's soldiers had joined the first and all were now moving with measured step towards him. He doubted these men would make the same crass mistakes as their comrades and sure enough they came at him hard. But he had chosen his position well and only two at a time could drive their spears at him. All the same, he was tiring while they could take turns to try and disembowel him.

When he could barely fend off their persistent spear thrusts, he growled out an anguished prayer and it seemed that God was listening. Divine intervention came like a roll of thunder in the form of a collapsing building. His opponents looked up in horror and tried to scramble away as an entire house seemed destined to fall upon them. All save one were buried; but that one contrived to ram his spear at Onno and the Egyptian cursed as it struck home. Within a few moments though, he decided the wound would not kill him and set off after Wynflaed and the others.

13

Hurrying after Ishild, Lurotriga prayed that the young Saxon knew where Lucidia had gone. After twenty yards or so, Ishild cried out: "I think see her. I see her."

Falling behind, Lurotriga yelled at her to slow down but the strong-willed Saxon forged ahead, replying over her shoulder: "Keep up - if you can."

Even the two young spearmen Onno had sent with them struggled to overtake Ishild and the streets were becoming ever more dangerous. More folk were out – no doubt plucked from slumber when Vortigern's tempest of fire overwhelmed their homes. Some were carved aside like dogs and sent screaming to their deaths by the rabid soldiers; while others simply dropped to their knees in stunned supplication and never rose up again.

Without the two armed youths beside her, Lurotriga knew she could not have survived for even a few minutes. Once, with her eyes fixed upon Ishild the Briton was bundled aside by a clutch of fleeing, terror-stricken women and only remained standing because one of her guards seized her arm. By then she was aching for breath for she had never run so far, nor so fast since she was a child. Just when she thought she could not take another step, Ishild came to an abrupt halt.

Amid a chaos of tumbling stonework and eye-chafing smoke, two men grappled with a sobbing Lucidia. One slapped her across the face as the other tore at her clothing until Ishild jabbed her avenging knife into his exposed side

– once, twice, three times or more into the lower ribcage before his comrade hurled Ishild aside. By then Lurotriga arrived and her escort's lunging spears despatched Vortigern's scavengers. Though the two wounded men cried out for mercy, there was none to be given that night.

Ishild, though bleeding from a cut to the head wrapped her friend, Lucidia in a tight embrace. But it was plain that Dux's wild-eyed sister was deep in the grip of despair.

"You're safe," Lurotriga assured her, though of course that was a lie – and a poor one – for none of them was safe.

Though Lurotriga wept with relief that they found the girl, their pursuit had taken them almost to the western outskirts of Vindocladia. Now, to reach the ford they would have to retrace their steps through the burning shell of the town. She was exhausted and even Ishild's face was pale and drawn. A glimpse at the sky told her that dawn was beckoning and the morning light would only bring even greater dangers.

While they caught their breath and Ishild did her best to calm Lucidia, the soldiers patrolled the street, peering nervously down nearby alleys. After a few more moments Ishild looked across to meet Lurotriga's eyes and the Briton nodded in silent agreement: it was time to move.

Lurotriga led the way with one of the soldiers, while his comrade followed behind the two younger girls. As they stumbled past blackened stonework and smouldering timbers, they coughed and choked under the heavy pall of smoke. Passing a battered caupona which they had frequented several times in the past, Lurotriga wept to see the owner split open like a carcass of beef. With a groan she recognised his wife beside him, her tunic half-torn away and throat hewn through. She had been a kind woman, Lurotriga recalled... and they had brought down mortal destruction upon her.

Ishild, she observed kept a comforting arm around Lucidia's waist and steered her away from the corpses. The care and affection Ishild displayed towards her friend forced Lurotriga to reconsider her opinion of the fierce Saxon.

Emerging at last onto one of the streets which led down to the river, Lurotriga was relieved to recognise where she was, but the ford still lay much further east and they were not the only ones making for it. Many folk were already in headlong flight and every moment more darted out of the damaged buildings to join them.

She saw few of Vortigern's soldiers among them and prayed that, having chased the escapees from the fort for several long hours the soldiers had given up the pursuit. From what she could see some had taken to looting - or worse, so she expected very few of them to be guarding the ford. Ahead of them the first rays of the sun glinted on the dark waters of the River Sturr and, as they toiled along the bank she was relieved that they encountered no armed men at all.

All the time she was staring ahead to the ford and searching for a glimpse of any of her companions, especially the tall Onno. But the crossing was choked by townsfolk desperate to escape Vortigern's retribution. Dozens were gathering on the north bank as they waited for those ahead to enter the water. But Lurotriga welcomed the crowds for the three women would surely be far safer in such a large group.

"Look out for Onno and the others," she cried to her companions, prompting a sniff from Lucidia.

"We already are," growled Ishild with a roll of Saxon eyes, causing Lurotriga to reflect that it was very hard work to like the girl.

In the half-light they struggled to pick out any of their comrades so they simply pressed on to the ford in blind hope. Just as they were about to join the throng massing by the riverbank, a low murmuring began which soon turned into a great groan of misery. Only when folk began to cry out and scatter in all directions, did Lurotriga see a column of Vortigern's horsemen thundering into the mass of people by the river.

It was only a dozen or so riders but their sudden charge prompted some folk to rush out into the deeper water beside the ford where most sank beneath the surface. Others, in their panic abandoned any attempt to cross and instead fled further east along the north bank. Even the seemingly fearless Ishild blanched at the sight of the mounted men and for Lucidia, it was too much to bear.

"He's here!" cried Lucidia, as Ishild hauled her faster along the riverbank. "Vortigern's here."

"Wait," shouted Lurotriga, slowing to a halt. "We'll never cross the ford with those riders there."

"We can't protect you against so many warriors, lady," gasped the anxious youth beside her.

"We have to get to Wynflaed and Onno," declared Ishild, trying to pull Lucidia away once more.

But Lurotriga gripped the young Saxon by the shoulders, looked her in the eye and said: "We won't find them."

"What then?" demanded Ishild, tearing away from her grasp. "There's nowhere else to go."

"We'll go into the river here," murmured Lurotriga.

"But it's too deep," protested Lucidia.

"She's right," said Ishild. "We've just seen folk drowning…"

"We'll keep to the shallows," Lurotriga told them. "The reeds are not tall, but if any one comes too close, we crouch down lower in the water."

Like Ishild and Lucidia, the two young recruits looked doubtful and Lurotriga suspected they were far from confident in the water. They would need persuading, so she looked to Ishild.

"Just because I say it," she insisted. "It doesn't make it a bad idea."

For a moment Ishild said nothing but then she replied: "You're right; it's our best chance."

Though Lurotriga favoured the Saxon with a smile, it was not returned.

Ishild, having approved their course of action led the way as they scrambled over the river bank. They found a place where the earth had been eroded enough to allow them to slide into the river. But just for a moment they all paused at the water's edge, as if perched upon a precipice. Fearing Lucidia might lose her nerve Lurotriga slithered down the muddy bank and into the water, gasping at the chill it sent through her. One by one, the others joined her: first Ishild and the leading soldier and then Lucidia, helped down by the last man.

"If we creep along towards the ford," said Lurotriga, "as soon as our feet find the river bed, we can make our way across."

Though she tried to make it sound easy, they all knew that the instant they were observed, the riders would be upon them. The distance across the river was short but even at the ford they would have to wade through waist-high water. Their feet squelched and slipped in the muddy river margin as they moved along parallel to the bank. Then watching from the dubious cover of the thin, bankside foliage the five refugees witnessed a new horror unfold as the mounted men rode into the ford and cut down anyone in their path.

Lurotriga thought her eyes could weep no more, but the ferocity of the assault brought yet more tears. "Why are they doing this?" she murmured.

"Revenge," whispered Ishild from close behind her. "Revenge - plain and simple. See the horseman on the river bank – with the grey, fur-lined cloak – that's him."

"Vortigern," breathed Lurotriga, who had never seen the High King before.

Lucidia cried: "He shan't take me - not again; not this time…"

"Hush, my dear," said Ishild, clinging tight to her friend. "I'll never let him take you."

Shivering with cold, the small group crawled through the water on hands and knees until the ford lay only a dozen or so yards away.

"Lady," gasped one of the soldiers, pointing downstream.

"Is that… a ship?" breathed Ishild.

107

Lurotriga stared at the vessel which, though it was some distance away beyond the ford was gliding slowly towards them.

"It could be my brother," hissed Lucidia, with a spark of hope in her eyes. "It could be Ambrosius."

"Can't tell yet, lady," said the soldier beside her.

"We should move out further from the bank now," said Lurotriga, "it's a little shallower here."

So they waded out into the stream a few yards, attention fixed upon the oncoming ship. But before they could make out what the vessel was, they were distracted by shouts from the bank. Several of the riders had spotted them and were plunging their horses back into the river to cut them off.

"The stream will take us towards the ford," cried Lurotriga, who pushed herself further out into the river, gambling that the current would carry her to the ford before she drowned. But as soon as she could no longer feel the stony river bed beneath her feet, courage deserted her. She began to flounder and soon slipped under the water; but the young soldier with her had followed her out and swiftly grasped a flailing arm to raise her up. As the river swirled around her, she saw Ishild and Lucidia clinging together two yards behind her; but by then she could feel the ford beneath her boots.

"Come on," she urged. "It's shallower here - we can cross this damned river now."

Though the pace of the current did take Ishild and Lucidia towards the ford, Vortigern's riders were driving through the water towards them.

"The ship," cried Lurotriga in desperation, for the craft had now stopped on the far bank only a dozen yards from them. "Make for the ship."

Gathering the others to her once more, she guided them to where they could just stand with their heads above water. The ship gave them a chance of escape but, to her astonishment Lucidia shrank away from the vessel.

"No," cried the girl. "Don't go to that ship - it's Ambrosius' ship!"

Lurotriga, unaware that Ambrosius even had a ship was utterly confused because, if it was his ship then surely they should take refuge there. Besides, hesitation now would kill them all and they were only yards from the vessel.

"Get me those women!" bawled a voice from the bank, as both Lurotriga and Ishild tried to take hold of Lucidia's arms.

"Go on, lady," said the brave youth beside Lurotriga as he turned to confront the nearest of the horsemen.

"No!" shrieked Lurotriga, for it was an unequal struggle and though the youth's spear struck home, he was soon carved down by a spatha blade.

Ishild and Lurotriga locked eyes once again in a silent pledge to gain some time for Lucidia to reach the ship.

"Help the lady to the ship," Lurotriga ordered the remaining soldier, while she and her unlikely ally stood with their knives out, side by side, up to their armpits in muddy water as several horsemen surged towards them.

Lurotriga could only admire Ishild who fought like a cornered animal. Stabbing up with her knife, she screamed abuse until a blow from a spear haft cracked against her temple and one of the horsemen plucked her dripping from the water and tossed her limp body over his mount. Snarling at the riders who now encircled her, Lurotriga risked a glance towards the ship and was relieved to see that the young soldier had taken the reluctant Lucidia to the vessel's side. Once there, he waded on ahead and called to those aboard for help.

Willing Lucidia to move faster, Lurotriga saw her stop as if transfixed in the waist-deep water. While her young guardian was helped aboard, Lucidia stared white-faced at a tall, dark-haired woman at the ship's prow who beckoned her on.

Trapped between two horsemen, Lurotriga was pulled up screaming by the riders. Twisting and writhing between their mounts, she was hauled towards the north bank. When she looked back, Lucidia was still motionless in the water. Even as the struggling Lurotriga willed the girl to make haste, her eyes were drawn to the woman on the ship. With a careless flick of her hand she condemned Lucidia's loyal young soldier to be hacked down upon her deck.

Finally, Lucidia began to back away but Vortigern's riders were almost upon her. With Lurotriga shrieking at her to flee, Lucidia looked about for another way of escape and found only one.

As they carried Lurotriga to the river bank, she no longer offered any resistance. Away to the east, a small noisy crowd was putting up a fight; perhaps Wynflaed, Onno and Xallas were among them but, in truth she did not care anymore. Hanging limp in the grasp of her captors, she felt numb; her spirit broken by the sight of Lucidia slicing a blade across her own throat before being borne away in the blood-reddened stream.

14

With the breaking dawn Ambrosius at last spotted Florina's ship ahead, slowing as it approached the ford. But the vessel no longer mattered for beyond it the world-weary town of Vindocladia, shrouded in a billowing cloud of smoke was burning to the ground. Struggling to make sense of what he saw, he could only think that Vortigern, thwarted in an attempt to storm the burgus had turned his vengeful rage upon the local townspeople. He was appalled to see corpses floating downstream towards him, some still staining the water with their blood.

Though he feared for his comrades at the fort, it had not occurred to him that the town itself – hardly a centre of wealth or power – would come under such savage attack. It was a cruel act, even for Vortigern and this time Ambrosius resolved that the High King would pay for it with his life. But first, he must ensure that Florina did not add to the chaos.

"On me!" he roared, urging his horse towards the ship, which was now moored up in the deeper water just before the ford.

With every yard covered, another horror was exposed as men fled past them and white-faced women too – some with children howling at their breasts. As soon as Ambrosius' horsemen were observed, there was a flurry of movement on the ship's deck. Standing still as a marble sculpture - aye, and just as cold - Florina glowered at her half-brother. When she turned away, it was only to dispatch men along the river bank to halt his charge.

Drawing out his spatha Ambrosius met the straggling band of Romans just before the ford. Though they were armed with spear and axe, Florina's foot soldiers – deprived of their valiant leader, Stavelus – were no match for the bucellarii and this time there would be no mercy. In a breath their fragile line was ridden down and shredded, leaving only a bloody tangle of torn bodies to weep yet more blood into the river.

Surging on, Ambrosius saw several mounted men in the ford savaging those trying to flee across the river. He plunged off the bank into the water to confront them and, though his company was small each man was a formidable warrior fired by what he had seen. The bucellarii struck the stunned horsemen so hard that none escaped slaughter.

As Ambrosius approached the far bank, he was astonished to see scarcely twenty yards north of the river a cluster of men and women fighting for their lives on foot. In a daze, he scanned the beleaguered group for Varta, but of course the tall Frank was not there. None of his men would be there for his experienced warriors would not have left the burgus to take on Vortigern in the open. Then he caught sight of Onno and cried out in despair for he knew at once that the burgus had fallen.

A glance behind told him he had lost several of his men, but he was encouraged to see Ulf, Arturus and Rocca still following close with several of the Britons, including the brave Argetrus.

"Close up!" he cried, urging his mount up onto the north bank of the river where many of Vortigern's foot soldiers were frantically turning around to face Ambrosius' horsemen.

He saw that Onno and his comrades were doing their best to shield a group of women in their midst, but he could not see Lucidia among them. Then his heart almost stopped when he realised that Lurotriga was not there either.

"We must get to Onno," he bellowed at his comrades, his throat suddenly dry from alarm. "Make haste!"

Abandoning all care, he slashed aside the first man in his path and launched himself into the thick press of Vortigern's warriors. The wedge of mounted horsemen crashed through their opponents' line, cutting down any man who stood in their path. Their brutal momentum propelled them right through the king's ranks. Some, still intent upon capturing the women never saw death coming as they were speared down from behind.

The merciless charge killed scores but more important, it destroyed the will of Vortigern's men. War was more often about willpower than numbers and the High King's soldiers simply broke ranks and fled. In doing so, however, they were merely following the lead of their commander who was already abandoning the field.

When Ambrosius reached Onno and his comrades, they sank exhausted to their knees. Dismounting, Ambrosius rested a gentle hand upon the Egyptian's shoulder. There were perhaps a score of women screened by a dozen or so youths led by Onno and Xallas. They had worked a miracle, but several carried wounds and Onno's mail shirt, he noticed was torn and bloodstained on one side.

"You're hurt," said Ambrosius, but Onno waved aside his concern.

"But what of all the others?" cried Ambrosius.

Onno gave only a weary shake of the head in response.

"So many lost," murmured Ambrosius. "And Varta?" he pleaded, only to receive another desolate gesture of regret.

"Lucidia," he breathed, but by then Onno could make no answer.

He did not dare ask of Lurotriga – indeed he refrained from uttering any more names, for he saw too much misery in Onno's eyes.

Wynflaed was sobbing in the arms of Ulf when Arturus dropped from his horse to kneel beside Onno, crying: "Ishild, where's Ishild?" But poor Onno could not tell him that either.

Ambrosius wanted to reach out to them or join them, as they knelt weeping on the ground; but instead he steeled himself to turn his attention back to the field of slaughter. Far to the north a ragged crowd of soldiers were making their escape, while elsewhere some of his own men were exacting a savage retribution upon those they captured. He might have stopped it with a word or gesture but he did not, for he shared his soldier's rage – and he had other work to do.

However dread the outcome he must discover the fate of his loved ones: Lucidia and Lurotriga. Some women might have been taken as hostages but to be certain he would have to begin the bloody business of accounting for all those who had perished. Nor was it a task he could delay lest someone was lying injured and in need of their help.

115

The ship, he noted was still moored beyond the ford but appeared abandoned now.

Consumed by anger, he cursed aloud: "That bitch, Florina is at the heart of this."

Then he saw the dog Ferox crossing the river and, with a shudder his rage turned to fear because Inga was not with the animal. And it never, ever left her side…

"Arturus, Argetrus – get after Vortigern," he shouted. "Follow him and try to find out if he has any prisoners."

Leaving Xallas, Ulf and the wounded Onno to oversee the final acts of carnage, he told Rocca: "I have to find Inga."

Remounting, the pair set off back across the ford but now unveiled anxiety drove Ambrosius to inspect the body of every woman that floated there. Though he did not find those he loved, the experience did nothing to lessen his anguish. They tracked back eastwards along the south bank and when Rocca, who was ahead of him cried out in alarm he feared the worst. But it was not Inga that Rocca discovered.

The sight of his sister's pale corpse, with a ragged wound across the neck and shrouded in her blood-stained clothing, almost broke Ambrosius. Yet he knew better than most that when death stalked a field, it struck down one and spared another as it pleased. Though he might swear to avenge Lucidia, it would not restore the colour to her cheeks nor fill the dark chasm of loss in his heart.

15

With Ferox loping along beside her, Inga followed Ambrosius' bucellarii along the riverside track, hoping at any moment to catch a glimpse of Florina's ship. Soon she tasted smoke on the breeze but that was not all the west wind carried for, by the time she rounded a sharp bend in the winding river she could hear voices crying out in distress. Thin shrouds of smoke drifted across her path but they could not obscure the dark fate of fire-torn Vindocladia.

When she did catch sight of Florina's vessel only a few yards beyond the ford, it did not seem to matter anymore; for now Inga sought only Ambrosius. Slowing her horse to a walk, she stared across the river where a maelstrom of warriors fought for control of the north bank. She had little doubt that her Dux would be among them.

Before she even reached the ford, she picked her way through a trail of shattered Roman bodies which told the bloody tale of Ambrosius' swift passing. While she was trying to discourage a sniffing Ferox from investigating the corpses, she only belatedly noticed that three horsemen were blocking her path. A single glance told her that these were not men of Ambrosius' company which meant they must be Vortigern's.

With a bitter sigh, she recognised the feral hunger in their eyes. Finding a girl alone on the south bank, while all others were busy elsewhere must have truly lifted their spirits. And just as Inga thought that her situation could deteriorate no further, she heard the strident tones of Florina telling the soldiers that Inga was a Saxon whore who must be taken alive on Vortigern's orders.

It was enough to chill Inga's heart – far better to die she decided than face the High King's slow vengeance. So she fled, attempting to slip between two of the mounted men but, as she drove her horse forward they closed in around her and several more men leapt down from the ship to cut off her retreat. A rider drew alongside and reached across to snatch her rein, while a soldier on foot seized hold of her leg. The outraged Ferox charged at the latter, slamming him into Inga's mare which bolted in panic with Inga barely clinging to its mane. When she cried out to Ferox, Inga's appeal brought a savage bark followed only by a single yelp. The dog's abrupt silence terrified her for, if Ferox was dead then so, very likely was she.

In vain, she struggled to control the horse which was carrying her away to the south of the river with Vortigern's frustrated riders in pursuit. At last she persuaded the frightened animal to slow down with gentle, soothing words and coaxed the horse back towards the river. If she could just find Ferox she might be able to evade her pursuers, cross the open meadow and return to the ford. Her hopes were crushed when the mare stepped into a hole and crashed down, sending Inga head first onto the ground.

Dazed by the fall, she saw the nervous horse get up, apparently unhurt and trot away from her. Feeling bruised but no worse, she got clumsily to her feet in time to discover a cordon of soldiers blocking her way to the river. Though she retreated from them, she knew they would overtake her in moments. Sometimes the patchy smoke hid her from view, but she was scouring a path through the young green reeds and grasses that any child could follow.

She had heard Ferox go down, so she was on her own. Her legs were tiring fast and if she carried on running there would be not a trace of fight left in her. So, making for the nearest stand of trees she selected a thick trunk to lean her back against and drew out her long knife. Staring down at the weapon her first thought was that it was not much of a blade; but it was all she had.

When her pursuers emerged into the clearing they were only a few yards from her and her fighting spirit all but evaporated at once for there were at least seven or eight of them. Knowing she could not escape, Inga was pleased to have a weapon in her hand as she accepted what wyrd decreed. She would make them work hard though to take her life; and she would make Frigg proud.

"I'll cut the first man to touch me," she warned, her eyes following their every movement.

Of course there were so many that she would be lucky to wound even one of them, but she prayed that Frigg would reward her bold intent and guide her hand. A rustling in the scrub behind her suggested there were even more of them than she thought. As one darted forward to seize her knife hand, a piece of dry twig cracked behind her and her assailant paused to peer beyond her into the trees.

He did not see the branch until it struck him full in the face, smashing nose, jaw and much more - if his scream was any measure of the damage. A large hand hauled Inga around to the other side of the tree where she found herself staring into the face of the giant Scotti warrior. A tremor of raw fear threatened to turn her bowels to water until his stern countenance turned into a broad grin and he thrust her to the ground.

"Stay there," he told her.

Perhaps her pursuers, enraged by the brutal assault on their comrade believed that the blow the Scot delivered with his torn branch was only a clumsy, if effective piece of luck. Hence they moved towards him and, when he took a pace backwards they pursued him whooping as if hunting a boar. Too late, they noticed several other figures creeping out of the trees around them.

It seemed to Inga that her rescuers matched Vortigern's men in numbers, yet Ambrosius had left the Scotti with no weapons. Nonetheless each Scot was, she observed armed with a length of rough timber which they wielded like men possessed. One by one Vortigern's men were taken down and the rest fled while the triumphant Scotti roared with laughter.

The tall leader bent to offer his bloodied hand to Inga and she accepted it with good grace. Though she had no idea what they intended to do with her, she supposed they had no intention of killing her – at least not yet.

"Tell me your name," Inga asked their leader.

"Lugaid," replied her rescuer. "And you're Ambrosius' woman, Inga."

She nodded. "You were following Ambrosius."

"We can't walk back to our homes," he grumbled. "And at least your lord didn't kill us -as many folk around here would."

Inga laid a hand upon the Scot's arm. "Ambrosius rewards loyalty above all else, Lugaid. I think he might trust you a little more now."

Bending down to select a weapon from one of the dead men, Lugaid nodded and said: "We have weapons now; perhaps I don't offer him my service twice."

His comrades retrieved the remaining weapons and anything else of value that the fallen soldiers possessed.

"Come," she said, striding away back towards the river but, when her rescuers showed no inclination to follow she stopped. "Come on," she urged. "You may have weapons now, but you still can't walk home. So we need to find Ambrosius."

"You might," said Lugaid, "but what will your Ambrosius give us that we don't have?"

"A safe place to lay your heads," she said, "while he thinks again about your offer."

Without waiting for a reply, she set off again and this time neither looked back nor slowed down. Whatever the Scotti chose to do, she still needed to find Ambrosius. She could not, however, resist a satisfied smile when she heard the tramp of boots closing up behind her.

Only when she reached the river bank once more and observed the carnage there, did her newfound confidence begin to drain away once more. First she scoured the bank and the ground near the ford for Ferox, but could not find him. Then, for a moment she simply watched transfixed as the ill-used bodies floated past her. Some were carved open, others unmarked but all moved her to tears. Once or twice she glimpsed a face she knew from the burgus and had to look away.

Lugaid trudged to a halt beside her but said nothing.

"This is what you do too," she said. "You kill men, rape women and steal their children away."

When her barb drew no response from the tall, impassive Scot, she relented a little. "All are the same," she conceded. "Scotti, Saxon, Briton… and Roman too…"

"And your Dux Ambrosius," asked Lugaid. "Is he not the same?"

It was a fair question about the man she had given herself to, life and soul. "Aye perhaps he is," she replied. "He can be brutal when he has to be, but I think he still believes in the rule of law…"

"Hah!" retorted Lugaid. "Then he must be the only poor beggar who does, lady."

Without another word she left him to continue along the river bank where several survivors were beginning to emerge, huddled in small, shivering groups. Only a day ago many of these folk would have been toiling in the fields north of the river below Ambrosius' burgus. Others, their faces now scarred and blackened by smoke worked in the town. One, a young girl she recognised from somewhere they frequented, wore an ugly slash across her cheek. When Inga bent to lay a gentle hand upon the girl's shoulder she shied away in fear.

The clamour of fighting on the north bank had ceased and Florina's ship was deserted. At the ford, blood-soaked bodies littered both banks and some lay still with only the water caressing them in death. Though others still lived, it was plain that some would never work again. Inga sat down weeping and it was Lugaid who lifted her to her feet again and pointed to Ambrosius who was crouched upon his knees further along the river.

When she screamed his name Ambrosius looked up, despair etched upon his face. She raced to him, almost stumbling into the water in her blind haste to reach him. He rose at once and the two hurled themselves together in a savage embrace.

"Thank God," he murmured, holding her so tight she thought he might crush the life out of her.

As he held her fast, her tear-filled eyes lighted upon two bucellarii, Onno and Xallas sitting on the river shore with other exhausted survivors. But there were very many that she could not see there...

"Lucidia is gone," she breathed and felt Ambrosius tremble in her arms. She had never known him do that before and it told her that her man, her invincible warrior was broken. After that she said no more about those they loved for she would learn soon enough who had perished. For a few more precious moments they held each other until she felt Ambrosius stiffen and he pushed her away. He had noticed Lugaid and the other Scotti coming up behind her and at once drew out his spatha.

"You savages," he roared at them. "Your cowardly allies may have fled, but you'll pay for your part in their treachery."

Onno, Germanus, Rocca and others, hearing Ambrosius' angry shouts struggled to their feet and crossed from the north bank to join him, but Inga thrust herself between the two ranks.

"No!" she cried. "They saved me, Ambrosius. They slaughtered Vortigern's men when I was as good as dead..."

Ambrosius looked into her eyes and hesitated; then glared at Lugaid. "But these men were part of it all," he told

123

her. "They helped Vortigern destroy our fort, the town and kill so many…"

"They fought you, but they clearly played no part in taking the fort," she replied, "and, when you freed them they offered to serve you."

"But-"

She cut her lover short. "Even when you refused their service, they risked their own lives to save me. They didn't have to, Ambrosius… We have enough folk to bury – and more than enough enemies."

Sheathing his sword, he signalled Onno and the others to do the same and walked towards the tall Scot. The latter met him halfway and the two men exchanged words. Inga could not hear what was said but it ended with Lugaid settling down on his knees with his fellow Scotti. Tears rolled down her cheeks when Ambrosius lifted Lugaid and embraced him, for that was the Ambrosius she believed in.

The submission of the Scotti was not greeted with any enthusiasm by most of the Britons and she heard an ugly murmur of dissent among them. Clearly Ambrosius heard it too for he led the Scotti towards the hostile Britons and, addressing them directly he announced: "These men have sworn to serve me – as have you."

"But they're ruthless, thieving barbarians," protested one of the Britons.

"Perhaps they are," conceded Ambrosius, "but now they are my ruthless, thieving barbarians."

"But-"

"You know that I welcome all men and women to my camp until they give me a reason not to. All are accepted here: Romans, Britons, Saxons – and now Scotti. If any man disagrees then he breaks his oath to me."

Inga could not help smiling when he added: "We surely have enough enemies already; what we need now is more allies. Remember that."

Few could argue against that for their numbers had been drastically reduced and now they lacked even a safe place to live. Inga saw the pain and despair in Ambrosius' eyes as he took charge and began to fling orders at his startled and weary company.

"Inga and Wynflaed will make sure the wounded are cared for – Xallas, my friend, they'll need your help. Germanus and Rocca, organise all the fit men to stand guard; let's be sure we're not taken by surprise again."

"You think he'll come straight back," Inga said.

"I'm still alive, so I'm guessing he'll want to finish me – or what was the point of all this?"

16

"How's your wound, Onno?" enquired Ambrosius.

"Pah, a scratch, Dux," replied the Egyptian. "Thank the lord for mail shirts."

"Aye," agreed Ambrosius. "Come then, my friend. Let's do what we must."

Ambrosius strode off up the slope towards the ruined burgus with Onno beside him. Between the two men no words were needed for the last thing either wanted was to exchange lame expressions of sympathy. For Ambrosius, an ocean of well-meant words could never mitigate the catastrophe that had befallen them - nor wash away his own guilt. His decisions and, most of all his absence had determined the fate of those he left behind. But he did not regret his actions for, at the time he had done what he thought best; though of course he would regret the outcome forever.

After the brutal events of the winter, the struggle with Vortigern had been inevitable but Ambrosius had known from the start that it was a fight he could not win without allies. He hoped to have more time to win over those much-needed allies, but now all that had changed. The clever Vortigern had outmanoeuvred him and the surprise attack had dealt his cause a near-fatal blow. Few rulers in the south west would now want to throw in their lot with a vanquished Roman renegade. His belated return might have driven Vortigern away for the time being, but it could not disguise the savage losses his company had sustained.

So, while Onno accompanied him without a word Ambrosius contemplated what he must do next. When they stopped outside the splintered gates of the burgus to survey the carnage there, Ambrosius hesitated to enter. He knew what he would find for he was no stranger to the aftermath of a siege, but it troubled him more than ever before. Nevertheless, a commander must bear witness to the sacrifice of his fallen men - and women. These folk lying here, still and grey had bought the escape of their comrades with their life blood. And there was one, among them all that Ambrosius had to see one last time.

They discovered his old friend, Varta buried under a heap of other bodies. Young, barely-trained youths who had stood at his shoulder to the end now lay entwined in death with their opponents. Ambrosius knew that the Frank had never really recovered from the grievous wound he suffered in the winter but, as ever Varta had given all in the service of his Dux. Though the great warrior had fallen, it was the death that Varta always desired: to fight and die with sword in hand. It was the best any soldier could hope for and an aspiration that the two men had shared since their first meeting as boys.

"By Christ," murmured Ambrosius, "neither of us ever expected to live beyond twenty years. I always thought I'd be the first to go – and I reckon he did too..."

It was the custom among the bucellarii for a fallen man's favoured weapon to be bequeathed to a comrade. Ambrosius smiled at the thought that, in Varta's case the weapon could only be his great Frankish spatha. He half-expected that the valuable sword would have been stripped from his dead comrade, but the weapon was hidden under the many corpses piled over his body.

Turning to Onno, he asked: "Did you ever hear Varta say who should have his spatha?"

With a shake of the head, Onno replied: "No, Dux, he never said a word about it – because we all knew who it must go to…"

"Germanus, perhaps," mused Ambrosius. "He could use it well enough."

"Pah, Varta never cared much for Germanus – as you well know, Dux. In any case the Burgundian prefers his axe. It's yours, Dux; Varta's spatha could only ever be held by you."

"I'm careless with swords," muttered Ambrosius. "I had a similar blade once but lost it last year in Gallia… You hold onto it for now, Onno."

"As you wish," agreed Onno, shouldering the weapon. "But you should take his body."

"No, others will see to the dead."

"But… he was like a brother to you," murmured Onno.

"Aye, and Lucidia was a sister to me," growled Ambrosius. Then he softened his tone. "Both are beyond my help now, my friend and we must look to those who still live. We must do what leaders do: plan, prepare and rebuild."

"This burgus is well beyond repair now, Dux," advised Onno gently.

"I know," replied Ambrosius, pointing further up the slope. "We're going to rebuild up there."

"The old hill fort of the ancients," scoffed Onno. "That's worse than this ruin. The timber ramparts are long gone - we'd have to build new ones and it's even bigger than the fort. We simply don't have the men, Dux..."

"I think we've got a whole town of men – or what's left of them," replied Ambrosius. "Those folk down there can't live in the funeral pyre of Vindocladia and we have a debt to repay to them. So, we need enough space to house them and the safest place is the old hill fort. If they have to rebuild their homes anyway, they'll be more secure up there."

Ambrosius knew the Egyptian all too well and, after his initial surprise wore off Onno's practical mind would set about the daunting task of refortifying the long abandoned hill to accommodate the survivors of both the burgus and the town.

And so it proved for, after a few moments' quiet contemplation, Onno said: "I suppose... there is a spring up there so, plenty of water. But it'll take a very long time, Dux."

"Well, it's your task to speed it up, Onno. I'll hammer out an agreement with the town magistrate - if he's still alive. As soon as the dead are buried, I want you to get started. While you solve that modest problem, I have to find a way to defeat Vortigern and Florina."

Onno gave a shrug. "All we have left is a handful of bucellarii and a few dozen young men who are scared shitless."

"And our new Scotti friends..."

"Oh, good Christ yes," groaned Onno. "Let's not forget those thieving bastards..."

Ambrosius never found the town magistrate, but persuading the surviving town elders to move to the hill fort proved much easier than he expected. Perhaps he should not have been surprised since Vindocladia was a smoking heap of charred timber and rubble. Faced with the stark choice of a blackened wasteland or the hill, the survivors chose the latter.

Within hours of being given the task by Ambrosius, Onno had men working on a primitive rampart of wooden stakes driven into the inner raised bank of the fort. It would be weeks before Onno would be able to bring any sort of order to the encampment within the stockade. Huts, gates, storehouses – all would need to be constructed from scratch and the defensive ditches would have to be deepened and perhaps new ones dug. The fresh water spring would have to be fenced and controlled, or it would quickly become a stinking morass of mud and shit.

Ambrosius had no illusions about the scale of the task he had given his Egyptian comrade for the list of his labours was endless. Yet when he observed Onno he saw a man at peace in the world he loved: a world of building anew and creating hope for the future, far removed from the destruction that lay all around him.

For Ambrosius, the way ahead was less straightforward and his concerns were mounting by the hour. No trace had yet been found of Lurotriga or Ishild, as well as perhaps half a dozen other women and girls. Nor had Arturus and Argetrus yet returned from their pursuit of Vortigern, which led Ambrosius to imagine that the young pair had succumbed to all manner of dire fates.

In the late afternoon he witnessed the establishment of a new burial ground overlooking the river where all the dead, whatever their origin were buried. By the time Varta and Lucidia were interred along with all the others, Ambrosius was in the blackest of moods and even Inga's presence could not heal the loss he felt. All that kept him sane was the thought of driving Varta's spatha – which he finally accepted from Onno - through the rotten heart of Vortigern, if only he could get close enough to do it.

Part Three: Kinfolk

17

Arturus and Argetrus did not return to Vindocladia until very late in the evening and when they arrived at the makeshift camp on the hill, they brought dire news. The two young men had tracked Vortigern for miles, expecting that at any moment the High King would call a halt to reform his ragged army and turn back to attack Ambrosius once more. But he did not; instead he pushed on northwards.

During the afternoon Arturus rode ahead of Vortigern's company and then watched from concealment as it passed him by. He could see that stumbling along, close behind the High King, were perhaps as many as ten women prisoners bound together in a ragged line. Among them he had no difficulty in recognising, even from a distance the tall, dark-haired British noblewoman, Lurotriga and of course his own Saxon lover, Ishild.

While Arturus was scouting ahead, Argetrus managed to infiltrate the ranks of Vortigern's weary foot soldiers at the rear of the straggling column. As he shared in their ribald humour and nodded at their grumbling complaints, he learned that the army was retreating to Vortigern's stronghold in the land of Ercing, very far to the north of Vindocladia.

For many of those camped at the hill fort, the news that Vortigern had truly gone away brought a welcome relief. On the morrow they would construct their new shelters and ramparts without fear of an attack. But for Ambrosius, any fleeting respite they had gained offered only an illusion of safety. Thus, as the new camp settled down for its first night in peace Ambrosius sat alone by a crackling campfire.

What he craved more than anything was to have Inga beside him, but she was tending Ferox who she had finally discovered, after several hours of searching in the burned-out shell of Vindocladia. A vicious head wound appeared to explain the animal's disappearance; he must have been wandering all day in the ruins seeking in vain the familiar scent of Inga. Ambrosius had long ago come to accept the bond between the war dog and his unlikely mistress; it would take a braver man than he to get between Inga and that damned hound.

Onno and his other close comrades would willingly have remained with him but he sent them all away, knowing what great deeds they had already accomplished that day. Some bore wounds and others were needed elsewhere, such as Aurelius Molinus Caralla who could celebrate the survival of his young wife, Carina - one of the few to escape the ordeal at the burgus unscathed.

Ulf, by contrast had to offer solace to the distressed Wynflaed, who would forever reproach herself for the capture of her sister. Both knew that a flame had been kindled in Wynflaed's heart that would only be extinguished when she found Ishild. Indeed, had it not been for Ulf's intervention, the furious Saxon would have ridden straight off to try to rescue her sister.

Ambrosius felt her pain all too keenly, for he was obliged to acknowledge that he too had lost someone he loved – and not just his dear sister, Lucidia. His distress at the loss of Lurotriga was only matched by the joy he felt that she still lived. Though he loved Inga, he could not deny that whenever he was with Lurotriga he felt a fire of passion between them – and he knew that others saw it too. Such a problem would have to be resolved but for now, all his efforts were focussed on trying to free her – along with the other hostages.

At first he wondered why Vortigern had spared the women at all. After all, he had slaughtered many others without any compunction, so he could easily have executed them at once. He might have simply wanted more slaves but Ambrosius decided that there was another motive entirely. The only explanation that made sense to Ambrosius both of Vortigern's retreat and his seizure of so many women, was that he was sending Ambrosius a challenge: 'I have your women; come and get them if you dare.'

Goading Ambrosius to pursue him was, of course an invitation to a trap - that much was certain. But it mattered little, since Ambrosius did not in any case have the resources to mount a rescue attempt. He certainly did not have enough men to storm any sort of fortress. When, the following dawn Wynflaed and Ulf came to persuade him to follow the High King, he told them he could not.

"We have to get Ishild back," insisted Wynflaed. "She's fought for you for months and asked for nothing in return. You have to try to free her – as you freed Inga last winter."

Arturus too begged Ambrosius to lead the men in pursuit of Vortigern and his plea was followed by one from Argetrus; for Lurotriga was the widowed queen of his people, the Durotriges. The young Briton was quick to point out that many of his folk had perished in the defence of Ambrosius' burgus.

God knew that Ambrosius was seething with frustration that he could not do what his loyal friends asked; but his anger could not change what was. So, he did what every honest leader should do: he told them the stark truth. Whatever he, or they wanted to do could not be done without more men.

Throughout that day the mood at the hill fort was tense and squabbles broke out at the slightest provocation – sometimes with no provocation at all. At every turn the divisions within his company were brutally exposed and the sight of so many at odds with each other only depressed Ambrosius more. Fearing he might lash out at those he loved, he withdrew to his tent for the rest of the day and left the running of the camp to Onno and Inga.

There was only one matter on his mind: how he might raise an army that could defeat the powerful Vortigern. He knew only one man who might possibly help: King Erbin of Dumnonia. But though Erbin seemed a good man and well-disposed towards Ambrosius, he was no fool and only a fool would risk the safety of his own kingdom and people by choosing Ambrosius over Vortigern.

For many hours Ambrosius brooded alone until, late in the day a stranger came searching for him. The fellow was dressed in the shabbiest of robes and stank like a privy, though he claimed to be a Christian monk. Despite his initial temptation to toss the beggar out on his head, Ambrosius hesitated. The Lord, he recalled had a habit of favouring lowly men, so perhaps it was just conceivable that this ugly brute might be an envoy of God. With a great show of reluctance, Ambrosius agreed to see him – briefly. After a short while, he reckoned he would be able to send the man away with a clear conscience to annoy someone else.

When the monk began his introduction, Ambrosius scarcely paid any attention until he heard the words: 'Lady Lurotriga' and then Ambrosius listened very carefully indeed.

"Tell me what you know of the lady - and be sure you speak the truth, monk," he warned, "Or be prepared to meet your God sooner than you expect."

"Can I sit?" enquired the monk. "I've been walking all day."

With a scowl, Ambrosius nodded. "Very well, but get on with it – and you can start by telling me your name."

"I am Father Gobban," replied the monk.

"Gobban – an unusual name," observed Ambrosius.

"Scotti," murmured the monk, prompting a groan from his host.

"I spent some years in what you Romans might call Hibernia," he continued, "though I was born not so far from here. I was a soldier once but in Hibernia I found my way to God and-"

"Get on with your tale, monk," ordered Ambrosius. "You were a soldier - for whom?"

"A local nobleman with high ambitions," replied Gobban, looking Ambrosius in the eye. "And like many such men, his pride destroyed him."

Irritated by the veiled criticism, Ambrosius told him: "The only reason I'm sitting anywhere near your reeking carcase, is that you claim to know Lady Lurotriga. So, tell me now how you know her, or you'll be thrown out on your head."

Accepting the rebuke with good grace, Father Gobban began: "I've known the lady since she was a child."

"Describe her," said Ambrosius.

For an instant a smile lit Father Gobban's lined face. "Dark hair, brown eyes and moves with the grace of a queen," he said. "And… she is loved by all who know her."

Ambrosius gave dismissive grunt at that. "Not quite by all, monk…"

"Then they don't know her well enough," replied Father Gobban.

His remark caused Ambrosius to pause and reflect for a moment about the ruffian cleric, before he urged him to explain why he had come.

"A few weeks ago, the lady came to see me in Vindocladia," said Father Gobban. "I was surprised because she'd not reached out to me at all before that – though she knew that I was there."

"What did she want to see you about?"

"Well… you."

"Me."

"Or I suppose I should say, your mother, Clutoriga-" Gobban stopped, unable to speak with the point of Ambrosius' knife at his throat.

"Choose your next words with care, monk," growled Ambrosius, withdrawing the blade an inch or two, "especially if they include my mother's name again."

"Lady Lurotriga thought she remembered your mother's name from her childhood," explained Father Gobban. "And, knowing how much you wanted to discover any living kinfolk, she told me to find out anything I could about your mother…"

Sheathing his knife, Ambrosius said nothing, while he absorbed this new information about Lurotriga.

"She only wished to help you," added the monk.

Still Ambrosius remained silent, puzzled by Lurotriga's intervention in his family's affairs. Though he was certain that she did genuinely want to help him, he also suspected that she would use any knowledge she gained to draw him closer to her. Yet, for that he could hardly blame her…

"Very well, monk," he said finally. "So what did you discover?"

"I discovered a woman who remembered Clutoriga very well," said Father Gobban.

Ambrosius held up a hand to stop the monk for a moment as he wrestled with the shocking revelation that he really might learn more about his mother.

"Where is this woman?" he demanded.

"I can take you to her, if you wish."

"Who is she?"

"She goes by the name of Marac."

"I never heard my mother mention that name," said Ambrosius, though of course Clutoriga had never mentioned anyone from her past. "She had some connection to my mother."

"She would not tell me what, but I sensed that they were close – old friends perhaps," replied Father Gobban. "But if I take you to her, she will tell you what she knows."

"Yet she would not tell you…"

"I fear she didn't trust me."

"I don't trust you either. So, tell me where she is and I'll have her brought here; I give you my word that she'll not be harmed."

"She will not come," said Father Gobban. "She shuns all folk, living a solitary life in a desolate place which she refuses to leave. If you want to learn what she knows, you'll have to go to her."

"Aye, because that's exactly what I need to do just now," grumbled Ambrosius, "make a journey to see some crazed woman, when I've more than enough trouble just holding this fractured company together."

"Perhaps it's what you do need," suggested the monk. "Some time to reflect and seek God's guidance. I think-"

"Your thoughts are of no importance to me, monk; but… go and get yourself fed – and, for the love of God, washed - before I see you again."

"Will you-"

"Go," ordered Ambrosius. "I'll think upon what you've told me."

But he did not think long upon it, for he suspected that the scruffy man of God was right: he did need to take a step back from the abyss which lay before him. Even if the

139

woman knew nothing at all about his mother, it was an excuse to take some time away from the camp and consider how he might deal with Vortigern. In the meantime, the conflict in his camp could not be allowed to continue unchecked or it would destroy them all. He needed to give them all a purpose; and it seemed that rebuilding the hill fort was not enough.

More than anything else, his people needed to know that he had not forgotten, nor abandoned the captured women. It was time to stir the pot… so he summoned his bucellarii captains: Germanus, Xallas, Ulf, Rocca and Caralla. Before the burgus was attacked the five men had, with Varta been preparing the new Durotriges recruits – some of whom had since been killed during the assault and subsequent retreat to the river.

"I'll be away from camp for two or three days," he announced. "Rocca will be coming with me and, while we're gone the rest of you must continue to train the men we have left. Recruit more if you can. Onno will have enough to do with the work on the fort."

"The youths are beaten men, Dux," grumbled Germanus.

"If they're still alive," retorted Ambrosius, "then they're far from beaten. They've fought and survived – that's how a soldier's steel is forged. So make them feel that strength – make them believe in it."

Caralla, he singled out for a special task because he had been trained as a cataphract - a mounted warrior. Cataphracts were not just any horse soldiers but heavily-armoured cavalry. Indeed, if they were employed in sufficient numbers cataphracts could turn a battle with one charge and Ambrosius wanted Caralla to train a great many of them.

"Choose the best horsemen," he told him. "Train as many as we have mounts for. Teach them to do what you can do – or at least close to it. I want a company of riders whose appearance alone will strike fear into every foot soldier's heart."

"We have few mounts, Dux," replied Caralla, "but I'll do what I can."

"Good. The rest of you, train them hard. If we're to take on Vortigern, every man of ours must be worth three of theirs. Enlist the help of Argetrus – he'll know how to get the best out of the Durotriges."

"You're going somewhere then, Dux," said Germanus.

"Rocca and I will be seeking out new allies," replied Ambrosius. "You have three days to put back together our broken army. And I want everyone else at work: men, women, children – all. They're either working up here on rebuilding the fort or they're training, or making spears and anything else we need. Three days – that's all you'll have."

"Yes, Dux," agreed his comrades and all save Rocca left him with a renewed vigour in their step.

"Rocca," murmured Ambrosius, "tell the monk we're going on a journey…"

18

It was a sparkling new morning but the sunshine did little to brighten Inga's thunderous countenance. Since she had been with Ferox all night, Ambrosius had not yet told her that he was about to leave and, the moment he saw her he knew that someone else had already done so. The dark expression on her face threatened a daunting conversation ahead.

"I hope poor old Ferox is recovering," Ambrosius said cheerfully.

Ignoring his remark, Inga demanded: "Why are you leaving us – and why am I the last to know?"

"I have to find allies – you already know that."

"You're going off with that shit-stirring God peddler," declared Inga.

With a sigh, Ambrosius began to wonder how much Inga already knew of his plans.

"Father Gobban knows something about my mother," he explained, attempting to remain calm in the face of the Saxon's onslaught. "And you know she was the reason I decided to come here in the first place."

"I thought you came here to escape from Rome and carve out a new home with your comrades and… those who love you."

Her eyes flared brilliant blue in the early morning sunlight as he reached out to take her hand. "Of course I did," he told her. "And I could have gone anywhere in Britannia; but here I hoped to find some trace of my roots."

Inga clutched his hand, wringing it with her trembling fingers. "We sit upon the very edge of the keenest blade and yet you would leave us... to prise out a few kinfolk who'll be strangers to you. When they look at you, Ambrosius they won't see family; they'll just see a Roman."

"We must have allies to defeat Vortigern," he insisted. "Perhaps among my own kin I can find such allies."

"And what if they prove to be enemies rather than allies," countered Inga.

"Then I'll go to King Erbin and ask-"

"But you already said he won't help you," said Inga.

"Well, perhaps I can change his mind..."

"I can't see how," she retorted. "Nothing's changed for the better - and we need you here."

"No, you don't," he said. "While I'm away, my comrades will prepare the men to fight Vortigern."

"Prepare the boys, you mean - and what if Vortigern comes back while you're gone?"

"He won't," declared Ambrosius. "Arturus watched him ride north almost to Caer Baddan. He won't turn back now; he wants me to come to him."

"But... if you're not here, someone must keep the peace."

He heard the desperation in her voice but had little consolation to offer her.

"You will do that very well – with Onno and Ulf. You three can keep these people together much better than I can."

"And instead you're putting your life into the hands of this wretched monk, Gobban who smells like a turd and looks even worse."

143

"If Lurotriga trusted him, so must I."

"Ah, Lurotriga…" Inga ground the name out as she let fall Ambrosius' hand. "How that widow meddles in our lives even when she's not here…"

"She was trying to find my kin."

"She was trying to get you between her legs," cried Inga.

For a few moments, a wretched silence stretched out between them before Inga said: "So, if you must go then I should go with you."

"I need you here," he told her. "Everyone here knows that you're my lady and that you speak for me. Folk respect you."

Her expression softened at his words and he saw with relief that the Saxon storm had passed. Curling her arms around him, she crushed her breast against his.

"I am your lady," she whispered, "and ever will be. And… I know we've both had cause to be grateful to Lurotriga in the past months, but I won't share you with her – or any other woman."

Gently, Ambrosius released himself from her fierce embrace. "I'm always with you," he said, "even when I'm many miles away."

After a final embrace, he mounted his horse and walked it over to where Rocca and Father Gobban were waiting.

"Ah, women," sighed Father Gobban, "always a source of trouble - especially Saxons..."

Fixing the monk with a stern glare, Ambrosius growled: "Speak ill of my lady again and I'll cut out your tongue."

With a gulp, Father Gobban fell silent and led the way without further comment. The monk had told him it was a day's ride away but, when Ambrosius saw the sluggish speed at which the monk set off he began to doubt that.

"Ride on, man," urged Ambrosius. "Every moment I'm not in my camp is a time of danger for my people. You're not riding a mule; so make more haste, if you please."

"I find it painful to ride any faster," complained Gobban. "I'll get sores…"

"Well, if you don't ride faster," said Ambrosius, "I'll beat your arse with the flat of my spatha, which I'd say will give you more discomfort than a few sores."

Father Gobban stared at Ambrosius in disbelief, but finding no humour in the Roman's eyes, he nudged his horse from a gentle trot to a brisk canter.

"Thank you, Father," said Ambrosius, with a grin at Rocca. "Now perhaps we'll arrive in half the time."

Father Gobban led them across the river onto the south bank and followed its course for many miles across the terrain which Ambrosius and Rocca had traversed in such blind haste only the day before. In places the monk abandoned the river side track to cut away on what Ambrosius assumed was a more direct path. He found his way with the confidence of a man who knew the area well. For the first time, Ambrosius began to wonder whether the monk might possess a rather wider and more useful knowledge than he had first given him credit for.

At the pace dictated by Ambrosius, their journey did not take a day but only a few hours and he was pleased to see the river widen out to the familiar broad estuary with

Iron Hill in the distance. But Father Gobban pulled up long before the estuary and pointed to a crossing place in the river.

"The river Sturr is affected by tides," he explained, "but, as you can see it's shallow enough here. There's always been a ford, though not so many folk are here to use it in these Godless times."

After they splashed through the ford, Father Gobban led them north where the ground rose gently at first but then turned steeper towards the top of what became a considerable climb. While they rested their tired horses at the summit, Ambrosius looked across towards Iron Hill beyond the settlement where he defeated Florina and the Scotti only a couple of days before. Looking across to the bluff where the Scotti made their brave defence, he felt regret for the loss of so many lives that day. But swiftly he cast such thoughts aside, for he was a soldier and a soldier who dwelt on regrets was only half a soldier.

"Is this where we're to meet her?" he asked Father Gobban.

"You and I must go the last part on foot," replied the monk. "I'll take you down to her, but she will want to see you alone."

"Sweet Christ," groaned Ambrosius. "I'm tired of this peevish old woman already."

Leaving Rocca with their mounts, he followed Father Gobban to the edge of the hillside where a deep scar ran along the eastern edge and ended as a sheer cliff. At first he thought there could be no way down there but Father Gobban surprised him for the monk's agile feet seemed to dance over the rocks and crags. Abruptly, his guide sat down on a large stone beyond which Ambrosius saw only a narrow rock ledge.

"This is as far as I go," Father Gobban told him. "At the end of this path, you'll find Marac's... home."

With a shrug Ambrosius, anxious to waste no more time strolled onto the short track which, on closer inspection he realised was quite skilfully paved. At the end there was only a small gap in front of him and, for a moment he stood there shaking his head. He was visiting an old woman who lived in a cave... this was surely a fool's errand.

"Come in," invited a stern voice from within. "I'm not shouting to you out there."

He squeezed through the constricted entrance into a rank-smelling chamber which, at some distant point in the past must have been hewn out of the cliff face. Whatever low expectations he had of Marac's dwelling, the interior of the cavern fell far short of them. It was a simple cavity in the rock face with a few old furs lining several patches of the wall and a scattering of worn out rushes underfoot. The only effect of the latter appeared to be its pungent contribution to the unpleasant odour which pervaded the entire place.

Marac's appearance seemed only to reinforce his dire impression of her home, for she sat upright in a chair which was wholly out of place since there was no other item of furniture – or indeed space for any. Yet, despite the manifest poverty of her surroundings her stiff, unyielding bearing revealed a woman once steeped in pride. Here was someone of status he decided, who had not always lived in such a squalid little hole.

He attempted a smile which proved to be a mistake for it only caused her frown to deepen.

"You're Marac," he said.

"If I'm not, you've wasted your journey, Ambrosius Aurelianus. Now, tell me what you want with me. I tire of you already - as I do all men of war."

Before he could reply, she continued: "I don't know why I agreed to see you at all. I always regret taking advice from that fool of a monk. I know who you are, Roman – and what you are: the son of Aurelius Honorius Magnus. What a thoroughgoing shit of a man he is and so, I imagine are you."

"You knew my-"

"I knew your wretch of a father, yes – and he's a smear of bloody ambition upon God's earth…"

"You didn't much like Magnus then," ventured Ambrosius.

"Don't play with me, boy," snarled Marac and, despite her diminutive stature there was something he found truly compelling about her.

Simply staring into her eyes made him feel small, like some raw recruit who hardly knew one end of a spear from the other. He couldn't explain it but he felt almost weak in her presence and that was not a feeling Ambrosius experienced very often – or one he enjoyed.

"So, you knew Magnus," he said, stumbling out his words like a drooling idiot. "And my mother, Clutoriga."

"I knew them both and I had put both behind me - until that great lump of a monk came asking questions. I know him of old and I've never trusted him; but he said he was your man now."

"He isn't," Ambrosius managed to interject before she continued her complaint.

"False Gods," she cried. "I thought so – the evil little dog. He came here, claiming to be your man – and the Lady Lurotriga's man. By God's breath, the bastard claimed to be every man's servant. He came asking about Clutoriga… but she's long gone now."

"Yes, Clutoriga," said Ambrosius, alert at once. "She was my mother…"

"I've gathered that much. But I knew Clutoriga long before that," said Marac, her voice somehow smaller. "It was a long time ago; why do you come here asking about her now?"

"She's my mother..."

"So you've said, but after so many years…"

"I've only been in Britannia a few months," he said.

"Even a few months in this God-forsaken land is too long," lamented Marac,

"I'm starting to understand that," said Ambrosius.

"But tell me…" she asked, her eyes sparkling just for an instant. "Tell me, do you know if she is still alive?"

"No, she's not," he replied.

His blunt reply seemed to crush the life from her. It was as if she aged ten years in that moment. Gone was the haughty and formidable countenance; and, in its stead her lined features were suffused with a pitiful sadness.

"You knew her well," he said softly.

She nodded, with a tear glinting in the corner of her eye. "I did... a long time ago. So, she's dead. But, if that's true, why do you trouble her soul with questions? God knows, no-one cared much about her in life, so…"

149

Her voice faltered as her mouth fell open with lips trembling and Ambrosius suddenly felt deeply sorry for her.

"Why don't you tell me what you already know of your mother," she suggested.

It was a harder question than his host probably imagined, for all Ambrosius knew about his mother was what she revealed to him on the day he left home – the day he abandoned her. In the depth of her despair, she had blurted out that she had been sold to his father, Magnus in Durnovaria. There, she was bedded and married. Magnus was a widower who already had three children, including two sons from his first marriage to a woman with excellent social connections in Gallia. The children Clutoriga later bore him, Ambrosius and Lucidia, were thus of little consequence to him at all.

All Clutoriga ever revealed to her son about her past were the few morsels he tore from her when she was at her lowest ebb and Ambrosius - worthless pisspot of a son that he was – had left her there. To save himself from his cruel father, he had abandoned his mother and sister. Even now, many years later Ambrosius felt his fury rise at his father's callous treatment of Clutoriga. But it was not a righteous anger; only one that was born entirely out of guilt.

The story his mother told him was a mere fragment but now, before him was the answer to his prayers: a woman who actually knew his mother.

"How did you know her?" he asked.

"Clutoriga was my daughter," she confided, "so, I suppose that makes you my grandson - not that it'll bring either of us much joy…"

In that moment he was obliged to utterly revise his opinion of Marac, for he assumed that she had encountered Clutoriga as a procurer of young whores. It had never occurred to him that he might be interrogating his own grandmother.

"Tell me about her," he said. "What she was like before she met my father… where she came from. All she ever told me was that she was a slave and a… whore."

"A slave, no – and she was never a whore." Marac spat the denial at him with such venom he thought she might leap up to scratch out his eyes.

"She was no whore," repeated his grandmother, her voice softening, "nor even a slave before your Roman father took her away."

After a long pause, Ambrosius said: "Nothing you tell me about my father can shock me."

"I hope he's dead too," she said.

He nodded.

"Good," she said. "I hope he died a very slow and painful death."

"Slow and painful enough," said Ambrosius.

She seemed to collect herself again, as if setting aside a great weight.

"How distant it all seems," she began. "It was a time of which I have only bitter memories, Ambrosius. Our world was no longer Roman – if it ever had been; imperial magistrates and military men were faced with the choice of fleeing with nothing or staying here in the hope that their prospects might improve. At first, your father chose the latter path and remained at Durnovaria, despite its slow decline.

"Why do you think he stayed?" asked Ambrosius.

"Greed," scoffed Marac. "Britannia, though stripped of its legions was still a wealthy place and a few, ambitious men saw fortunes to be made in the growing chaos. Some were Romans, but there were many other men too – men deluded by dreams of power - who sought to gain supremacy among their own people. The Durotriges, the Dobunni, the Atrebates, the Dumnonii and all the rest… those were just the Roman names for the old tribes of this land. Believe me, it was not a time for the faint-hearted…"

"But none of that explains why my father wanted your daughter," said Ambrosius, confused.

"You mean aside from her great beauty and her kind heart." Marac's tone was bitter, and her expression desolate. "It was my doing," she said. "I gave her to him."

"You…"

"He found out who she was, of course; and no doubt he thought that by marrying her he might enhance his position and perhaps even carve out a kingdom for himself."

"Who she was…" murmured Ambrosius.

Marac's sudden laugh unnerved him – a harsh, raking cackle of mirth.

"You don't know," she cried. "I thought that's why you came here… but you don't even know."

Ambrosius' eyes narrowed as he said: "Well, you'd best tell me then *grandmother*."

With a sigh, she looked away as she began to explain. "My fool of a husband, a magistrate had the blood of Dobunni royalty in him-"

"Dobunni?" queried Ambrosius.

"The people of the land far to the north of here in places that some folk now seem to call Caer Gloui or Caer Ceri," explained Marac.

Ambrosius nodded for he had heard of several such independent lands to the north.

"So," continued Marac, "my husband, like others before and since, declared himself a king. He then tried to take control not only of the Dobunni lands but those long disputed with the Durotriges to the south and the Atrebates to the east."

She paused, frowning at the memory. "What monstrous ambitions you men entertain. He was not the man to accomplish such a task; and, when he failed his many rivals hacked him to pieces on a barren hillside on the eastern frontier with the Atrebates. I fled with Clutoriga, our only child to seek sanctuary among the Durotriges - first in Vindocladia, then Durnovaria. My husband's reckless folly haunted us for years and even here, we were not safe. Many tried to find us but I hid my daughter well, knowing that her blood would attract a score of suitors.

"Perhaps, as the years passed I became careless and lulled into thinking we were safe; but some folk have a scent for royal blood. I don't know how it happened but we were discovered in Durnovaria. So I took a desperate gamble in the hope of saving my daughter's life: I asked a Roman officer for his protection."

"Magnus," murmured Ambrosius, who knew all too well the terrible outcome of the story. "Sorry; pray continue… if you please."

"For a month, your father did protect us – both of us - until he turned me out on the streets. But he kept Clutoriga and I soon learned that he had married her as part of an attempt to seize control of the Dobunni lands for himself. Like all you Romans, he believed that conquest was the only way to succeed. But, though he had Clutoriga's royal claim a few trained soldiers and a little coin, his bid for power came to nought. Before he knew it, he was forced out of Britannia altogether. I knew he took my daughter with him but, until these past days I never heard her name again."

"When Father Gobban came asking about her," said Ambrosius.

"Aye and now you know the story of your poor mother," she replied and added, with grim countenance: "Look about you and see how far this Dobunni queen has fallen."

"It's a shock," he told her. "To discover that the mother I've always known as a slave was once a princess of the Dobunni people..."

"Princess might be overdoing it," said Marac, "but she certainly had a trickle of royalty in her – as of course must you – amid the taint of Rome…"

"Are there any others of our kin?" he asked.

"Scores at one time," she replied, "but several were slaughtered with my husband and then later the great sickness killed many. Now, perhaps a few remain; distant in every sense. I advise you not to seek them out."

A knowing smile played across his lips and he said: "You think they might be upset if a new heir came to light."

"I doubt they would even believe you are an heir. So much has changed – it's over thirty years since I fled from… Caer Gloui. New men, I suppose, have power there now."

"What about the kings of Dumnonia," he said. "How does King Erbin fit into all this?"

"Erbin has none of our blood upon his hands," she said.

"You're my grandmother; you shouldn't be living in this squalor," he said. "Come back to Vindocladia with me."

"You have a splendid palace, I suppose," said Marac.

"Not exactly..."

"I've heard what happened at Vindocladia," she said. "Local folk keep me well-informed, so I know you have almost nothing – and no-one, Ambrosius. Forgive me then if I don't choose to share your poverty and would rather live out my days here."

"But I could protect you."

"We both know that's an idle boast," she said. "You can't even protect what you have... Come and see me again when you can... perhaps if you become king of the Dobunni."

"I don't want to be a king."

"So you say," said Marac. "But when did God ever care about what we want. Do you pray, Ambrosius?"

"I pray," he replied wearily.

"Well, if I were you, I'd pray a great deal more."

19

"Where now, Dux?" asked Rocca when Ambrosius returned from his visit to Marac.

Ambrosius was far from certain what his next step should be because what Marac had told him was forcing him to reflect upon his place in the long-troubled land of Britannia. He had a sense that this was a moment of decision which might set him on a path that he would follow for the rest of his days. It could be the path to success, or oblivion...

In one respect, Marac's claims changed nothing; for he still needed to free the hostages and did not have the men to do it. Unless it was somehow God's will that Vortigern was retreating northwards towards Caer Gloui and Caer Ceri which, if Marac was to be believed was exactly where Ambrosius' distant roots lay. But he had enough problems already without embarking on some wild quest to inherit a kingdom. And who would even support him since no-one had even heard of him. Before he could even contemplate rekindling some lost claim to the lands of the Dobunni people, he still had to defeat Vortigern once and for all.

So, either Marac's revelations were simply God's way of extending a guiding hand to help him or, they were the tortured ravings of a bitter old woman that the devil was using to seduce him into a dark world.

"Dux," prompted Rocca, breaking into his thoughts.

He needed at the very least to verify what Marac had told him and he could think of only one way he might do so.

"I think we should go to see King Erbin," he told Rocca.

"We've seen him before, Dux," remarked Rocca glumly.

"Aye," said Ambrosius, "but that was… before…"

"Before our defeat, Dux," said Rocca.

"No, before today…"

Dumnonia was a large kingdom and despite some hard riding, much to the discomfort of Father Gobban, it took them two days to track down the royal court at Isca in the south of the kingdom. The welcome Ambrosius received was cool to say the least and very different from his only previous meeting with the young king. On that occasion the two men made an agreement as if they were equals but, after the destruction of Vindocladia and Ambrosius' burgus by Vortigern, King Erbin was clearly in a less generous mood. Ambrosius started to wonder whether he was just wasting two more precious days.

"You promised much, Ambrosius," grumbled Erbin, "yet you've achieved nothing – God's breath, less than nothing."

"I defeated the Scotti-"

"Aye – and now I'm told that, instead of cutting the all devils' throats you hired some of the survivors for yourself."

"As I'm sure you already know," said Ambrosius. "I have too few men to turn away volunteers – whoever they are."

"More fool you then because they'll cut your throat, rape your women and-"

"Forget the Scotti," interrupted Ambrosius, unwilling to concede authority to the king. "They'll keep their oaths. We've more pressing matters to discuss."

"I don't want to discuss any 'matters' with you," replied Erbin testily.

"I've a proposal for you," said Ambrosius.

Erbin, scratching at his thin, youthful beard gave a weary sigh. "Your last proposal didn't work very well so, just give it up, Ambrosius," he counselled. "Vortigern is a most difficult opponent. You've tried, but you've failed; so perhaps it's time you went back to your crumbling old empire."

"Vortigern still needs to be put down," insisted Ambrosius, fixing the king with a determined stare.

"That's not a proposal," scoffed Erbin. "That's you talking though your balls. He's just crushed you; your fort's in ruins, your town's been fired and you've lost half your fighting men. He's still the High King and you, Roman are dead meat. You're finished here."

Ambrosius gave a mischievous chuckle. "Finished? Why no, I've hardly begun."

"Listen to me," said Erbin. "I like you and I might even trust you; but you've no place here. Just accept that and leave. You can still save yourself and some of those dear to you. I'll even give you safe passage back to Gallia in one of my ships."

"I'm not leaving," replied Ambrosius, "for I'm more certain than ever that my fate is bound up with that of Britannia."

"Britannia," retorted Erbin. "There is no Britannia. That was just a name bestowed upon us by Romans. Well Rome is long gone and so is Britannia. Believe me: we don't need Romans to slaughter us because we're very good at killing each other on our own. There's not been a Roman soldier in these parts for generations, Ambrosius so you have no place here."

Ambrosius nodded. "A few days ago, I was beginning to think that too."

Erbin gave a sympathetic shake of the head. "I don't doubt your abilities and I suspect there's not a warrior to match you anywhere in this land. But, like me others will question what right an outcast from the empire has to interfere here at all – let alone challenge Vortigern."

"It's true that I came here as an outcast, but perhaps I've found a reason to stay," declared Ambrosius, "because my mother was born here."

Erbin could not hide a smile. "Rumour has, my friend that your mother was a slave," he said, "so she was a British slave. I can't see that impressing anyone."

It was time, thought Ambrosius to drop the pebble in the pond. "My mother's name," he said softly, "was Clutoriga."

"Clutoriga," murmured Erbin, his genial countenance freezing just for an instant.

"Aye, Clutoriga… a name you seem to know."

For a few moments Erbin seemed unable, or perhaps unwilling to reply but when he did, his voice was charged with emotion. "You're telling me that the Dobunni heiress, Clutoriga was your mother."

"I am."

"Well, I don't believe you – and I'm disappointed that a man I respect would try to peddle such an obvious deception."

"But is it a deception-"

"It's nonsense," stormed Erbin, for the mention of Clutoriga's name seemed to have disturbed him greatly.

"My grandmother, Lady Marac told me…" said Ambrosius.

Erbin winced, muttering: "Lady Marac is long dead…"

"No, I assure you she's not."

"Marac's dead," repeated Erbin. "My own father told me that years ago."

"Aye, I'm sure he did to protect the noble lady from those who would have hunted her daughter down simply for the blood that ran through her. But, only two days ago I spoke to Lady Marac at some length…"

Erbin fell silent, chewing his bottom lip until it began to bleed before finally he murmured: "I would need proof…"

"That Clutoriga was my mother is certain," replied Ambrosius. "That she was a Dobunni heiress, you have just confirmed…"

Erbin did not bother to argue further. "Very well, Clutoriga did carry her father's blood line, Ambrosius; but it's a long time ago and others rule in those parts now…"

"Aye, and how well are those rulers doing?" enquired Ambrosius.

Erbin shrugged. "They're beset on all sides – Catuvellauni in the east, Atrebates to the south and so on. I'm told Caer Gloui is all but ruined now. So, good luck if you want to rule the Dobunni."

"I'm not a man who wishes to rule anyone," said Ambrosius, "but it seems the Dobunni may be my people."

"I thought you made the Durotriges your 'people'," said Erbin, "before you got so many of them slaughtered..."

Ignoring the jibe, Ambrosius continued: "Vortigern does nothing to end these land disputes. Our best men are squandered year after year to feed the ambition of a few wealthy men. And all the while new enemies seek to carve off some of this land's bounty: Saxons, Scotti and, God knows almost anyone. Someone needs to hold it all together... to make it strong enough to survive."

"Which is what the High King is there to do," argued Erbin.

"But either he cannot, or he will not do so," replied Ambrosius. "Yet you continue to support the lying, thieving old bastard."

"Because you're right," retorted Erbin. "Someone has to do what the rest of us don't want to do – keep some order, punish our enemies... and there's no-one else but Vortigern to do it."

"But he exploits our differences and does nothing to stop those, like the Saxons or the Scotti who seek to plunder homes and seize land. As long as he's paid tribute in coin or slaves, the High King doesn't care who it is that pays him."

"He's not the only ruler to bring in Saxon foederati, Ambrosius – everyone has," protested Erbin. "And how can you complain about Saxons when your own lady is a heathen Saxon."

"Some Saxons want to live in peace," said Ambrosius, "but there are others who don't – and in the east their numbers are steadily growing."

"I don't care what happens in the east," cried Erbin.

"Because already Vortigern holds little influence there at all; and mark me, he can't protect you from the scourge that's coming."

"You know nothing about any of this," charged Erbin.

"What I know is that between Vortigern and I there can be no peace," declared Ambrosius. "Thus, one of us will emerge the victor and the other will fall. You, Erbin, need to decide – as do all rulers – which of us you want to act as your shield, because I can promise you that very soon, you're going to need one."

"Are you threatening me?" laughed Erbin.

"No, I'm offering you another alliance," replied Ambrosius, with a smile. "I shall defeat and kill Vortigern; so, you need to choose which side you want to be on after that's happened. If you choose me, then I expect you to send fighting men to join me against the High King."

For the first time Erbin's affable expression clouded, for Ambrosius' sudden blunt ultimatum required him to make an enemy either of Ambrosius, or Vortigern. On Ambrosius' part, it was a desperate gamble since Erbin might simply capture or kill him now where he sat. But for the Dumnonian king it was not a straightforward choice because, though Ambrosius had few men he was young and strong, while Vortigern's most effective years undoubtedly lay far behind him.

Ambrosius was hoping that Erbin would simply supply him with a detachment of armed men so that, if the attempt to bring down the High King failed he could deny any direct involvement. Ambrosius understood Erbin's position for if Vortigern did survive then any man who had been part of the conspiracy against him could expect severe retribution. Whereas Ambrosius, already Vortigern's sworn enemy had nothing to lose by trying to kill him.

"This is not a matter I can decide alone," blustered Erbin. "I must consult my noblemen – for it's their men whose blood would be spilled in such a war."

"You have a week," said Ambrosius. "By then I'll be on my way north to Caer Gloui to seek Vortigern and… more allies. If your men make haste, they may catch me up."

"But you don't have the men," insisted Erbin.

"Nor did I last winter," said Ambrosius, "But by the end, two of Vortigern's sons lay dead and the High King fled with the few men he had left. We fight to protect our own and Vortigern has taken some of our own hostage. Think well upon your decision, King Erbin – for you have less than a week to consider it."

When Ambrosius stood up before the king stirred from his throne, there was a murmur of disquiet in the chamber but Ambrosius rarely made futile gestures of show. He wanted all those present to know that he was King Erbin's equal, not his subordinate. At once Rocca scrambled to his feet and hauled Father Gobban up with him to follow Ambrosius as he swept from the royal chamber.

Acutely aware that he had used up several priceless days by seeking out King Erbin, Ambrosius lost no time in setting off back to Vindocladia and only stopped overnight to rest the horses. But he did not regret his hasty visit to Isca for the Dumnonian ruler's reaction convinced Ambrosius that what Marac had told him was indeed true. Even so it was a shock to have it confirmed that, by blood he was half-British.

When he thought of all the wriggling coils of fate which had carried him from distant Rome to Vindocladia, he was certain that the hand of God must have played a part. Perhaps the Lord had brought him all those hundreds of miles to take down a corrupt High King – unless He envisaged an even greater destiny for Ambrosius...

The tasks that lay ahead would be difficult so, whatever brought him this far - whether it was God, fate or just his own wits - he must continue to trust in it. Vortigern must not learn of his blood descent too soon, lest he took measures to undermine Ambrosius before he even arrived in Dobunni territory. He doubted that Erbin would tell Vortigern for he expected that the Dumnonian king would eventually join him. Of course, if he was wrong about that then he was doomed.

As the three riders cantered along the old Roman road from Isca to Durnovaria, Ambrosius considered who else knew his secret and shouted across to Rocca: "How much did you hear at Isca?"

"Enough," said Rocca, prompting Ambrosius to chuckle to himself for the North African was ever sparse with words – unlike their other companion.

"Are you truly intending to pursue Vortigern and go to Caer Gloui?" gasped Father Gobban.

Ambrosius frowned at the unkempt figure who rode beside him with all the grace of a sack of flour. "It seems

164

you listen well – for a priest. Yes, I'll be going north with all the men I can muster – and you'll be coming with me."

"Me?" cried Father Gobban, aghast. "But I can't help you. I can't fight - I'm a man of God."

"Then you can lead the prayers for my men, father," replied Ambrosius. "It'll give them great comfort but, if I were you I'd leave the Saxons to themselves…"

With a long glance at the monk, he added: "And you may be a man of God but, if you reveal what you know about me to another living soul, you'll be a very dead man of God…"

20

Inga was still incensed with Ambrosius when he left the hill fort and, over the ensuing days her resentment only deepened. However he justified his absence, it was plain to her that he had abandoned them to pursue a futile quest conceived by Lurotriga for one purpose alone. It was just as well that lady was not in the camp, thought Inga because over this they would surely have come to blows. At the burgus Ambrosius contrived to keep the two women apart as far as he could; but that only infuriated Inga even more. She wanted her rival to see and hear her displeasure – aye, and feel the heat of it too.

If she was honest, what hurt her most about Ambrosius' abrupt departure was that he had not taken her with him. It felt like a betrayal for, if the journey was so important to him then surely he would want the woman he loved to share it. Unless of course she was not the woman he loved…

In her lover's absence, Inga's doubts festered away until they were all she thought about, distracting her by day and keeping her awake at night. No-one else seemed to understand her feelings and, when she complained to Onno whose opinion she always respected she found little comfort in his response.

"I took an oath to Ambrosius," the Egyptian told her. "I swore to put my life in his hands without question. I didn't swear to be loyal until I disagreed with him. What was it that you swore to do, Inga?"

She should have expected little else from Ambrosius' closest bucellarii for they would never think of questioning their precious leader. But even when she consulted other women, she received a similarly blunt response. Even Caralla's wife, Carina, who had no knowledge of Ambrosius before she married his horse master refused to condemn him.

"But you expect him to come back," she said.

"Well, yes I know he'll come back," replied Inga.

Carina offered a dismissive shrug and said: "Then perhaps you should just be pleased that he does; for there are many women here who'll never see their menfolk again..."

"But he should be here now," Inga insisted.

"I don't see what he could do here now that others aren't already doing," enquired Carina, "except warm your bed. Onno runs the camp and sees to our needs; others train the men and protect us. Perhaps Dux is doing what he needs to do."

"Trailing the myth of his dead mother," groaned Inga.

"Or perhaps," suggested Carina, "trying to find more men…"

Even Inga's fellow Saxon and closest friend, Wynflaed gave her complaint short shrift.

"So, great surprise," she scoffed. "Your man has left in search of his mother; but all men revere their mothers. They may lie with us and declare their undying love but if their mothers pull on that cord to claim them back…"

"But-"

"Enough of your peevish whining, girl," grumbled the Saxon. "The man's lost his sister - the last of his close kin, so he reaches out for word of others. And we are so few, Inga that if Ambrosius is seeking allies among his kin – or anyone else - to help us then I for one am with him."

Taken aback by the vehemence of Wynflaed's defence of Ambrosius, Inga returned to her tent chastened but still restless. It was all very well for Wynflaed and Carina to condemn her; but they both had their men with them while she did not. Since the onset of winter last year, she had spent almost every day with Ambrosius and now she ached for him to be with her. Even she realised that she was overwrought – so perhaps she was going down with the fever which had afflicted several others in the hilltop camp.

The next day, she threw herself into the work of the camp and joined the tireless Wynflaed in caring for the wounded. If her friend could work so hard while she carried her child then Inga should be able to do even more. Working did make her feel better and she realised that her annoyance with Ambrosius had caused her to neglect the very duties he would expect his lady to carry out: setting an example to all the women, consoling some, counselling others and, if necessary punishing one or two. While she had been berating Ambrosius for shirking his responsibilities, she had been guilty of exactly that fault.

Thus, fired with a new determination she laboured from dawn to dusk and perhaps she did too much for, when she and Wynflaed were walking back to their tents in the evening Inga suddenly folded at the knees and slumped to the ground.

Having revived her and helped her back to her tent, Wynflaed hovered there, looking both puzzled and anxious.

"This is not like you, Inga. You're always so strong – stronger than any woman here."

"These past days have been hard for us all," replied Inga. "But I think I'm just missing him, that's all."

Wynflaed's face was still etched with concern. "You're very pale," she said. "You have no fever, but you look ill."

"A little sickness, but that's nothing."

Wynflaed greeted that admission with a sly grimace. "I wonder, dear Inga whether you might have caught my… condition," she murmured.

The two young women exchanged a glance. "No," said Inga.

"It might help to explain how you've been feeling."

"No."

"But-"

"If you're my true friend then say nothing of this to anyone – not even Ulf; and certainly not Ambrosius when he returns."

"But it would be a cause for great joy, for hope…"

"I am not with child; so say nothing. Swear it, Wynflaed."

"Very well," agreed Wynflaed, "I'll hold my tongue until you tell me otherwise - or your… affliction improves."

§§§

It was several more days before Ambrosius returned to the hill fort and when he did, only Rocca and the unwelcome monk were with him. Though she wept to see him back safe, she was disappointed that he did not bring the allies he had promised, nor had he recruited any more men. Others, she observed shared her dismay.

Nevertheless, Ambrosius appeared undaunted – indeed he seemed much more confident than before he left. He began to discuss with his closest bucellarii how they might overcome the High King and rescue the hostages. But it seemed to Inga that Ambrosius had only one plan which was to ride out with every man he could muster and hope that others would join him as he made his way northwards to confront Vortigern. It did not seem to her that a campaign based solely upon hope was very likely to succeed.

Of course, she wanted the captives to be freed and it pleased her to observe that Wynflaed was much heartened by Ambrosius' fresh commitment to releasing her sister, Ishild. Yet, dark thoughts continued to besiege Inga and she could not banish the idea that Ambrosius was driven, not by a desire to free all the women but just one of them.

Though she knew he had given her no specific cause to be jealous, suspicion still gnawed away at her as she lay beside him that night, unable to settle to sleep. He too was restless, no doubt weighed down by his responsibilities and, when she felt him sit up she could not help but give voice to her concerns.

"Why do you care so much about Lurotriga?" she asked him.

"Please, not that again," he murmured. "You know why: she's helped us a great deal – by Christ, both of us owe our very lives to her. That's reason enough."

"It's more than that," said Inga.

"You know that I would try to free any hostage," he declared, "as I came for you last winter."

"But that was different," she retorted. "We were lovers..." But then she drew slowly away from him and breathed: "Unless it isn't so different... and you've bedded her too..."

"No, I haven't!"

"But you want to," she cried.

"You're my lady," he insisted. "The only lady I need..."

But Inga turned away from him for words alone could not extinguish the jealous fire that still glowed deep within her.

Part Four: War

21

The ancient settlement of Caer Ceri lay a few miles north of the heavily-forested high ground where Ambrosius halted his modest army for the night. Though half of his forty men travelled on foot, they had made good speed thus far: more than ninety miles in just four days. Nevertheless, the column was dangerously stretched out at times because it included two wagons laden with weapons and food. For the most part the old imperial roads served them well, but on several occasions both wagons had been mired up to their axles in mud. Now, after another punishing day's journey every member of his company was exhausted, sore and hungry. But above all, they were desperately uncertain about what lay ahead of them.

The first two days passed so quickly that they reached the border town of Caer Baddan full of hope but the town magistrates, unimpressed by Ambrosius' claim to sovereignty over the Dobunni, refused to provide any men at arms to fight against Vortigern. Ambrosius was not surprised for Argetrus had already told him that the Durotriges, Dumnonii and Dobunni all dwelt around Caer Baddan in a fragile, uneasy stand-off. Given the tensions the magistrates laboured to keep in check, he could not blame them for their caution.

When he learned that the High King had only left for Caer Ceri three days earlier, Ambrosius was puzzled. Vortigern should have been many miles ahead of him by now even if he travelled slowly; so Ambrosius decided that his quarry's sluggish progress could only be a deliberate ploy. He was lingering in the hope of drawing Ambrosius into a reckless pursuit. When the Caer Baddan magistrates remarked upon the string of hostages that Vortigern took with him, it seemed to confirm Ambrosius' suspicions. He had no doubt that the hostages were being dangled in front of him on the wily old king's instructions. At least it seemed likely that the captives were still alive, but he had no intention of taking any precipitate action. With so few men, he might get just one chance and he must ensure that he did not waste it.

The old imperial road that ran north to Caer Ceri was as good as any Ambrosius had used since his arrival in Britannia. His two wagons were thus able to move a little faster - provided the oxen could be coaxed into action. Though they passed some small farmsteads and saw a few workers toiling in the fields, Ambrosius observed that much land which might once have been cultivated was left untilled. Thus swathes of scrubland, heath and open woodland flanked the road. Perhaps the plague some years ago and the recent famine had caused the decline, but he sensed that this land had lain unused for much longer than that.

After another long day his company neared Caer Ceri at dusk with his foot soldiers close to exhaustion. According to Argetrus Caer Ceri, which some remembered as the old Roman town of Corinium, was once the heartland of the Dobunni people. All Ambrosius could see was how small and poor the town looked now with its shabby buildings clustered around what appeared to be an ancient amphitheatre. Unless in the half-light he was mistaken, the latter had been fortified in places which gave it a strange and decidedly un-Roman appearance. Since darkness was fast descending and he was uncertain of the welcome he might receive there, he decided to make camp outside the town.

At dawn the next day he found some high ground from which to scan the road they had taken from the south. If King Erbin was coming to join him that was where he would come from; but, despite the drying weather no distant haze of dust signalled the approach of an army. Ambrosius had given him just a week – perhaps he should have given him longer. Thus, by the time he approached the gates of Caer Ceri he was forced to accept that if he was going to defeat Vortigern, he would have to do it alone. He had promised his comrades they would have allies, but Erbin was his last hope and he began to question whether he could still rely upon those already with him.

As the men trudged along in silence behind him to the gates of Caer Ceri, the sight of the ramshackle settlement would have done little to cheer them. Though it was clear that it had once been a great town, it was now much-ruined. The original town walls had fallen into disrepair and most folk appeared to be living in the numerous timber buildings which sprawled around the newly-fortified amphitheatre. Yet Ambrosius found some grounds for optimism because, though small the settlement seemed a well-ordered place. Not only that but the faces of those who watched their arrival, wore expressions of interest or expectation rather than fear. He sensed that whoever commanded here might be more sympathetic to his cause than those he had encountered so far.

The gates were opened in a hospitable manner and, from the moment Ambrosius was welcomed by the ruler of Caer Ceri he felt at ease. The magistrate, Cadrullan was a soldier and so his greeting felt like that of one battling warrior to another. Though Cadrullan dutifully passed on word of Vortigern's progress as others had before, he added a warning of his own.

"You'd be well-advised, Lord Ambrosius," he said, "to be wary of the High King."

Ambrosius, amused to be referred to as a lord wondered whether it was possible for him to be any more distrustful of the High King than he already was.

"If you don't care much for Vortigern," said Ambrosius, "then perhaps you should join us against him."

Cadrullan laughed. "If it was just me, then I would," he replied, "for I've no love for the pompous old king. But Caer Ceri is protected by so few that I dare not squander my soldiers' lives in a quarrel that can't be won. We have battles enough of our own, Ambrosius against the folk on our eastern frontier. And... you don't have anywhere near enough men to defeat the High King; but you must know that."

"Aye," agreed Ambrosius, "but I can't abandon the women he's taken hostage - assuming they're still alive."

"Oh, they are," Cadrullan assured him, "or at least they were when he was here two days ago. But I think your feud runs deeper than that; he told me you killed two of his sons."

"One I killed, though I tried to spare him; the other, a brute called Catigern was killed by someone sworn to me – so I suppose, it's true enough."

Cadrullan regarded him carefully for a moment before saying: "Vortigern has another son, Pascent…"

With a sigh, Ambrosius replied: "Well, I've no particular wish to kill him too..."

"Nor should you," advised Cadrullan, "for he and his father are by no means close. Not close at all…"

"I'll bear that in mind," said Ambrosius.

"I think Vortigern intends to draw you beyond Caer Gloui into his own domain of Ercing."

"Tell me about Caer Gloui," said Ambrosius, keen to understand the nature of the town he hoped to claim as his own - if he lived long enough.

"There's not much to tell," replied Cadrullan. "Like this place, it was ravaged by plague years ago and never recovered. Some folk have made a home there but, as you'll see its walls are no longer manned. I expect you'll find its great gates hanging wide open with long grass taking over what's left of the streets. It's not the town it once was, Ambrosius."

"Who rules there now?"

"There's nothing left to rule," lamented Cadrullan. "Vortigern claims sovereignty over it, along with most other places hereabouts; but when it was ravaged and plundered by raiders, he was far away."

"Does the name Clutoriga seem familiar to you?" he asked Cadrullan abruptly.

At once Cadrullan studied Ambrosius closely. "It's a name the Dobunni people still mourn," he said.

"They mourn it," probed Ambrosius.

Cadrullan seemed to hesitate before answering but Ambrosius saw that he had gained the magistrate's interest. "It was Clutoriga's father who single-handedly destroyed this whole area. There were many to mourn..."

"Clutoriga was my mother," said Ambrosius.

Cadrullan grimaced. "I like to think that I'm well-informed, Ambrosius but I'll admit I'd not heard that."

"Erbin of Dumnonia knows, but few others; I felt I owed it to the leaders of the Dobunni to tell them first."

"You'll forgive me if I'm a little... uncertain about your claim," said Cadrullan.

"My grandmother, Lady Marac could confirm it – if confirmation were required..."

"By God, Marac - that's a name many here might recall, though I fear not very favourably. If you expect folk to welcome you with open arms and bend the knee, you'll be disappointed. Thanks to Marac's husband - and his forebears - we've been at war with neighbouring peoples for generations – among them the Durotriges, many of whom are in your army. Such a force might be seen by the Dobunni as an army of invasion..."

Ambrosius smiled. "My army has many faces - including Durotriges; but also Romans, Saxons and Scotti, so why not Dobunni too. I intend to refortify Caer Gloui when I've defeated the High King so perhaps that will offer a safe haven to some of the Dobunni."

"Hah! When you've defeated him," laughed Cadrullan. "He's aware that you're coming; you do know that, I suppose."

"I do," said Ambrosius.

"When you're deep in Ercing, he'll employ every man he has to ambush you - probably in one of the many forested valleys there. And when he's trapped you he'll kill you all."

Ambrosius grinned. "Aye, I've fought him before – and I've also fought in forests before."

"But you're hopelessly outnumbered," cried Cadrullan.

"My men are worth three of his…"

"Even if they were…"

"Tell me," said Ambrosius, "if King Erbin were to bring up an army from Dumnonia – would you let it pass unhindered?"

"But he has no reason to do that," said Cadrullan.

"He does - because I asked him to…"

"As long as Erbin did not lay waste our fields, we'd allow him safe passage," agreed Cadrullan. "But he won't come. He's promised aid to us in the past but never once sent any."

"I believe he will come," said Ambrosius, "because King Erbin, like you does not want to be on the side of the loser in this great struggle."

Cadrullan smiled. "Well that's true enough so, if God should choose to keep you alive perhaps we'll speak again."

Though Cadrullan was not prepared to risk his own soldiers in battle, he did replenish their supplies with fresh food and provided half a dozen men to guide Ambrosius into Vortigern's territory. Ambrosius could take scant encouragement from anything Cadrullan had told him, but among his men he attempted to radiate confidence. But despite his efforts, the morale of the company began to deteriorate the moment they left the safety of Caer Ceri.

Cadrullan proved right about the condition of Caer Gloui - the old imperial town of Glevum - for its gates were indeed lying open. When Ambrosius' army passed through the gaunt shell of the town and crossed the great river Sabrina into Ercing, it felt as if they had crossed more than just a bridge. Far from home and with little hope of reinforcements, their fears and doubts began to trouble them.

Ambrosius shared their concerns especially when he glanced at Inga riding alongside him. Of course, he never intended to take her with him; it was all Wynflaed's doing. She insisted upon joining the search for her sister, Ishild; and naturally Inga was not about to allow her friend to go alone.

Despite Ambrosius' protests, Wynflaed's husband Ulf accepted his wife's decision with little argument. As he told Ambrosius: "To stop her, I'd have to beat her senseless and how can I do that to the mother of my son. She's a fiery spirit driven on by revenge; and it's a fire she must quench, Dux before she gives birth to our child."

"Thank you for that, Ulf," Ambrosius grumbled. "But I tell you: if my Inga was in the same way as Wynflaed, I'd not allow her to come."

As they rode deeper into Ercing, Ambrosius recalled Ulf's rueful grin. "Arguing with a woman, Dux is just about the most foolish thing a man can do. You might as well try to push water back up a waterfall. Women always win – even when we think they haven't..."

So Inga went with him and her presence twisted tighter the knot of fear growing steadily in his breast. Nor did the sight of Inga's wounded war dog, trotting along beside her, alleviate Ambrosius' concern for if they were heavily outnumbered, even Ferox might not be able to save his mistress. Ever since he confided to Inga that he was heir to the royal house of the Dobunni, she had been cooler towards him. He suspected that her resentment stemmed solely from the role Lurotriga played in the discovery of his lineage. Mention of the British woman's name alone was enough to make Inga scowl.

As they rode deeper into hostile territory, tensions began to arise amongst the men; most obviously when brawls broke out around the campfires - often between Saxons and Britons, or between the Scotti and almost anyone else. Some squabbles were to be expected for these were fighting men who had not yet fought together. They had no bond of shared struggle to draw upon and careless banter quickly turned to insult and injury. His chief bucellarii, such as Germanus and Rocca easily quelled such little storms but Ambrosius knew that the longer their journey lasted and the more perilous it became, the more fractious his men would become.

The land they passed through looked poor and even where he noticed iron workings in forest clearings, they seemed to be long-abandoned. As they drew closer to the realm of Vortigern, Ambrosius sent out more scouts – often employing Cadrullan's men along with several of his own. It would have been folly to lead his column blind into the steep, dark valleys which seemed to flow one after another. The bright green foliage of early summer would provide perfect cover for an ambush and even more so once his guides steered them off the old road and onto a narrower track leading ever westwards towards Vortigern's hilltop stronghold – or so they told Ambrosius.

On the rougher track, his wagons struggled and for the first time he considered leaving them behind. When his scouts reported movement in the trees, both ahead and behind he felt even more ill at ease. As Cadrullan had reminded him, Vortigern knew they were coming and he had the means to destroy them utterly. So in the first large clearing they came to, Ambrosius halted the column and drew the wagons together into a defensive camp with the horses corralled between them. His men, having cut stakes to drive into the earth around the perimeter were arrayed in a cordon around the wagons.

Praying that he had not strayed too close to Vortigern's main army, Ambrosius decided he must locate the High King before he proceeded any further. Thus, having ensured the camp was as well defended as it could be he left the reliable Ulf in command and ventured into the forest on foot taking only Lugaid, Arturus and two of Cadrullan's guides with him.

As they moved carefully through the trees, only silence greeted them – no bird calls, nor the sound of small animals scratching at the forest floor. That told him they were not alone as they worked their way westwards, keeping to the north side of the track. Any man they encountered there was likely to serve Vortigern.

181

After a while, Ambrosius whispered to Arturus: "Either there's no-one here, or more likely they know this patch of ground well enough not to be found. We'll go back and search to the east of the camp – just to be certain."

His concern was that Vortigern might have posted a small force to their rear and, if he had there would be no escape for Ambrosius when the High King attacked. The landscape of trees through which they passed to the east gradually gave way to sparsely-wooded scrub land and at that point Ambrosius decided that they could make their way back down through the forest to the track. As soon as they reached it, a dozen or more men emerged from the trees on the south side of the track. In moments Ambrosius' small band was surrounded and trapped.

22

Sitting with her back pressed against one of the wagon wheels, Inga stared at Wynflaed's haggard face, grey with exhaustion. She could only clasp her friend's hand in the hope that a little sympathy might revive her.

"So, here we find ourselves in this wretched forest, surrounded by enemies," she said.

Squeezing her hand, Wynflaed replied: "I had to come – for Ishild's sake, no matter how it ends. And… if I said I was sorry I dragged you here with me, it would be a lie."

For both women the past days had been gruelling, though for very different reasons. Wynflaed was feeling every last bruise she had acquired from travelling in one of the supply wagons.

"I should have ridden like you," she groaned.

"Then your arse would be purple like mine," replied Inga, only belatedly remembering that the monk was lolling close by. When she glanced across at Father Gobban, she saw he was awake and his heavy eyebrows were raised.

"If I offend you, then don't stray so close," snapped Inga, but the monk made no reply.

Wynflaed shook her head. "I should be straining at the leash to get to my sister, but I feel so weak."

"It'll pass," soothed Inga, "And this is our path now, for good or ill; so… we keep our knife blades sharp and rely on Frigg."

By contrast with her friend, Inga's distress was being played out entirely in her own head. When, in Vindocladia

183

Wynflaed suggested that Inga too might be with child, she dismissed the notion out of hand. But with every day that passed she was forced to acknowledge that her friend was probably right. It was hardly surprising, she thought since the winter months at the desolate Villa Magna had offered very few means of entertainment. She should have noticed the signs herself for she had witnessed them often enough at the brothel in Verona.

Riding every day beside Ambrosius, she longed to tell him she was carrying his child but always the joy she wanted to feel was overshadowed by darker thoughts. Any child she bore to him would, in the eyes of his precious Christian church be a bastard. When he was a soldier and she a freed slave, it did not seem to matter very much; but now... all was changed with the revelation that he was of royal blood.

She feared Ambrosius would cast her aside to ensure a legitimate heir to his bloodline and she could not shake off the suspicion that he was only undertaking this perilous venture to rescue the woman he truly wanted to marry. Lurotriga was a noblewoman and the widow of a Durotriges king - and she was also a woman that he already lusted for. Such a union would also bring peace between the Dobunni and Durotriges; whereas union with Inga, the heathen Saxon offered only more conflict.

Wynflaed, no doubt sensing her disquiet reached across to lay her palm against Inga's cheek. "We must draw strength from each other," she said.

"I should tell Ambrosius about the child," muttered Inga.

"You should have done so before," hissed Wynflaed, glancing around in case the cleric had overheard. "But you can't now – not here. He's got enough demons filling his head without you putting another one there. Nothing must distract him from the fight to come, Inga. Nothing – else we're all dead…"

Inga nodded. "I know."

"There'll be time enough to tell him after," said Wynflaed. "And… if there is no after then it won't matter, will it?"

Ferox, lying at their feet suddenly lifted his head, opened an eye and sniffed the air. Well-versed now in interpreting the animal's behaviour, Inga sprang to her feet and peered over the row of stakes towards the forest which was scarcely twenty yards away. A moment later the war dog leapt up and, with a low growl began to pace along the palisade in front of the two women. Then he stopped with his snout pointed at the flimsy fence line.

Others too were moving: Germanus was stalking along the wooden barrier with his axe resting upon his shoulder. Caralla, with spear in hand went to his horse and rallied his fellow riders to join him. The two Saxon women exchanged a worried glance and then crouched down on all fours under the wagon.

Inga, her throat suddenly dry croaked out a command: "Guard, Ferox, guard."

The truculent beast slunk back from the palisade to lean his head against his mistress' shoulder. With the stench of the animal's vile breath only inches from her, Inga fought the urge to deliver up the sparse meal she had eaten a few hours earlier.

185

When a spear thudded into the wooden side of the wagon only a foot above Wynflaed's head, even the stoic Saxon gave a yelp. Both gasped as another spear buried its point between the two women. Lying down flat on their bellies, their fingers were tightly entwined to give each other strength while, in their other hand each held a naked blade. Ferox stood in front of them, teeth bared to rip to shreds any man who ventured too close.

Those first attackers, emerging from the trees at a trot looked confident as they hurled more spears into the camp. Others followed them to hammer their axes into the meagre timbers. More and more men slid out from between the trees and thrust their spears clean through the fence in the hope of wounding or killing the defenders.

That moment Inga considered for the first time what she would do if their menfolk were all killed and Vortigern's warriors took her. She would do anything to avoid becoming his prisoner for, like Wynflaed she had travelled that brutal road before. She thought back to Vindocladia and the despair that must have persuaded Lucidia to take her own life. But that was not a path she could follow when she had Ambrosius' child, still tiny inside her belly.

Very soon the attacks were coming from all sides and Inga could not see how the fragile barrier could possibly keep them all out. As she feared, it was not long before hostile axes pierced the stockade and half a dozen warriors burst in. But Ulf and Rocca were ready for the incursion, having formed up a rank of closely-packed warriors with their shields overlapping. Stepping forward as one they hurled back their opponents and closed the breach.

When another small band broke through the stakes, it was Caralla's young riders who surged forward to slam into their opponents with such force that Vortigern's warriors were obliged to fall back or be trampled under the savage hooves. Caralla led his horsemen out through the newly-forced gap to pursue the attackers across the clearing, hacking down man after fleeing man. But once their opponents disappeared into the trees, they had no choice but to retreat to the stockade.

Surveying the damage, Inga saw that the perimeter needed repair in several places. Worse still, though the encounter seemed to pass in only a few moments two of their own men lay dead and another was badly wounded.

"Breath of God," groaned Xallas, "we can't take such losses every time they attack."

"Aye, that's why they're doing it," said Ulf, "to bleed us a few men at a time..."

"That's no way to fight," said Germanus, his dignity clearly affronted.

"It's what we'd do in their place," Ulf pointed out.

"And we'd better get used to it," said Xallas, "because they'll just keep coming. Vortigern can afford to lose as many men as it takes."

"Dux should be here fighting," complained Germanus, "not chasing shadows in the forest. By Gunnar's beard, this is where the fight is."

"Dux will come," said Ulf, in a tone that suggested Germanus should keep any further thoughts to himself.

Once the rudimentary palisade was mended, the defenders could only stand ready to meet the next assault. Some did so in tense silence, but Inga heard others muttering prayers to the Christian God, while she invoked the aid of the goddess, Frigg – both for herself and her unborn child.

The time spent waiting passed slowly and Inga's head was just starting to nod when a thunderous roar announced the next onslaught. It followed the same pattern as before: thrown spears followed by an attack on foot which strove to hack apart or remove stakes from the defensive line. Once again, Caralla sallied forth but this time Vortigern had left some of his men among the trees and, as their comrades retreated they launched spears at the mounted men, wounding two. The horsemen, since they could not enter the woods could only withdraw once again; and this time their efforts did not halt the attack.

More warriors just kept coming, forcing more breaches where ragged lines of men fought to hold their ground. When an attacker fell, another eagerly took his place and yet more stakes were chopped aside. As the Saxon women stood with their knives pointed at the enemy and the bullish Ferox snarling in front of them, Inga regretted not telling Ambrosius her secret.

23

At first Ambrosius was genuinely baffled, for the men facing them made no attempt to attack nor even said a word. They merely stood in two impassive ranks that formed a circle around his small band. Though he was confident that, with Lugaid and Arturus beside him he could break out of the ring of soldiers, he was less certain about Cadrullan's two men.

After a few more moments' thought, he concluded that these men must be carrying out Vortigern's explicit instructions – after all, the High King would not want some insignificant spear man to deny him the pleasure of killing Ambrosius himself. So, the longer he remained there, the more certain he was that Vortigern would soon arrive with even more men.

"We need to break out," he murmured to Arturus, who gave an almost imperceptible nod in response.

Ambrosius took a pace forward and Arturus and the others followed his lead. It brought no reaction of any sort. No man ordered him to stop nor even scowled and none drew his spatha or made any threatening gesture with his spear.

Confounded, Ambrosius took another step and then a third until he was scarcely a yard from one of the surrounding men. Whatever else these fellows were, they were certainly disciplined; but when he took another pace and raised his hand to ease the soldier aside, the man's hand came up fast to press back against his chest.

189

"Wait," instructed the soldier.

"No," replied Ambrosius, staring down at the hand upon his chest.

In that moment he decided that, if the fellow did not remove his restraining hand then he would draw his spatha; knowing that when he did so blood was certain to be spilled. And of course, the most likely outcome of that would be death for him and all his comrades. Ambrosius was about to reach for his sword when his opponent glanced away towards several horsemen who were approaching up the track. As the riders drew closer, Ambrosius saw that Vortigern was not among them and so, intrigued he drew his comrades back to await their arrival.

When the strangers dismounted, the surrounding circle opened up to allow one of them to pass through and when he was standing in front of Ambrosius, he waved his men aside.

"Ambrosius Aurelianus, I believe," he said, with a broad smile.

"So you know me," said Ambrosius, his hand still resting, albeit loosely upon his sword hilt.

The stranger gave a rueful shake of the head. "Oh, I've heard all about you - tall, powerful looking warrior, with a mane of unruly, reddish hair who looks like a devil – or so they told me."

"Who told you?" enquired Ambrosius.

"Quite a number of my father's men remember you very well after their encounter with you last year at Villa Magna."

At last, Ambrosius understood. "You're Vortigern's son, Pascent."

"Aye, the one you haven't killed yet," said Pascent.

"Give me time," replied Ambrosius. "I might get around to it especially if you hold me here much longer."

"I apologise," said Pascent, offering Ambrosius his arm in greeting. "But I needed to speak to you before my father got a chance to kill you."

Ambrosius clasped the other man's arm with good grace, but said: "I need to re-join my men; they're camped further up this track."

"I know where they are," said Pascent. "And any time now my father's men will attack them-"

"All the more reason for me to get back to them now," argued Ambrosius.

"Of course," agreed Pascent, "but perhaps we should talk first."

"We have talked," said Ambrosius.

Warlike cries sounded out in the distance and, though muted by the forest all heard them well enough.

"Come," Ambrosius told his comrades, turning to go.

"Wait!" cried Pascent. "Your men are only being attacked by a small force but, if you leave without talking to me you'll soon walk into my father's entire army and he'll kill you all."

"And you care what happens to me," said Ambrosius.

"Come," asked Pascent, drawing Ambrosius away from the others. "Hear me for a few more moments only – that's all I ask – and I'll offer you a chance to save many lives."

"You'd best choose your few words well then," urged Ambrosius.

"The track you're taking will lead you to the River Gwy."

191

"That's what my guides tell me," agreed Ambrosius.

"Where the track meets the river there are shallows where you can cross – and that's where my father plans to attack you."

"I don't need you to tell me it's an obvious place for an ambush," replied Ambrosius. "I've heard enough."

But Pascent caught his arm and continued: "It's not just an ambush, it's a trap. He'll be on the west bank and those who are attacking your camp now will stay behind you so that, at the river they can come at you from the rear. You'll be in the river and there will be no way out. Your men will be drowned, or slaughtered."

"Your father told you all this," said Ambrosius.

"I have men in his camp," said Pascent.

"So you don't trust your own father."

"That much should be clear, Ambrosius; indeed, I can't recall a man I dislike more than my father. But I've never had enough men to overthrow him - until now. Between us, we might just be able to do it."

Cadrullan had told Ambrosius about the disaffected Pascent but still he was wary of trusting a man – a complete stranger – whose father was his mortal enemy.

The clamour of fighting to the west suddenly petered out and he fixed Pascent with a cold stare. "I swear, if your task was to keep me from that fight, I'll kill you."

"You know very well that your camp would not be overwhelmed so quickly," Pascent told him. "Your men will have seen off the first attack, but there will be others."

"How many men can you bring to this fight?" asked Ambrosius.

"Fifty."

"Horsed, or on foot?"

"On foot," said Pascent, adding: "This is mostly poor terrain for horses."

"And your father's strength…"

"After the last mauling you gave him, about two hundred," said Pascent.

"He did far more damage to us than we to him," conceded Ambrosius. "So, even between us we don't have anywhere near enough. We'd both lose scores of men – and still we might fail. For me, there's no choice but to carry on but I can't see why you would take such a mortal risk."

"Ercing," replied Pascent. "I've controlled it in my father's name and he's rarely been anywhere near it - until now. And it seems that he intends to stay close by and rule it; I'd rather he didn't…"

Another decision on a knife's edge, thought Ambrosius.

"I assume you have a proposal," he said.

"A simple strategy: on the morrow you continue along the track but divide your force and send your horsemen back to me. I'll guide them through the forest to where they can safely cross the river Gwy further upstream and sweep my father's main force from the west bank of the river. Also, when he attacks you at the river I'll bring up my fifty warriors to prevent you from being surrounded. If you can fight your way across the Gwy then it will be my father who'll be trapped between you and your riders."

Ambrosius hardly dared to contemplate the numerous risks that such a plan would have.

"You're asking me to hazard the lives of all my men on your word that you'll come to my aid," he said.

"I am," replied Pascent, "but all their lives will certainly be lost if you don't accept my help."

"I promise nothing," said Ambrosius. "But I'll discuss your proposal with my trusted comrades."

"So, how will I know whether you agree?"

"You'll know because I'll send my horsemen to you with that youth over there," said Ambrosius, pointing to Arturus.

Pascent appeared to consider for a moment and then nodded. "Very well, but don't wait too long, Ambrosius…"

The son of Vortigern was obliged to raise his voice for Ambrosius was striding away, taking his comrades with him along the track back towards his camp. Even as he did so, he heard the unwelcome sound of further fighting and broke into a run. His great, long strides ate up the yards and only the fleet Arturus could match his pace. Gasping for breath, they approached the camp together and Ambrosius flinched at the sight of Vortigern's men forcing their way inside at several places.

Where his few bucellarii stood, the line held firm but in other places he could see that resistance was beginning to crumble. Fear and desperation showed in the youthful faces of his less experienced men, as the enemy spear points drove them back. In the midst of all, he saw Inga cowering with Wynflaed while Ferox savaged one of their assailants.

With a howl of fury, Ambrosius charged into the rear of his adversaries, sweeping his spatha across the back of the first man he encountered before carving a ribbon of blood beneath his throat. A spear thrust from Arturus ripped open the belly of another, while a third turned to flee only to be clubbed down by Lugaid. Arturus, who had remained subdued since the loss of Ishild laid into some of her captors with grim enthusiasm.

As Pascent had predicted, the second assault was short-lived and not long after the arrival of Ambrosius, Vortigern's men melted away into the forest once more. Having ordered his men to cut fresh stakes to replace those broken and to embed loose ones more firmly, Ambrosius sought out Inga. Everything he knew about her told him that she would want to be standing in the defensive line, hurling their foes backwards with arrow upon arrow from her bow; yet there she was, on her knees.

Lifting her to her feet, he cried: "What ails you?" and hugged her trembling body close.

"We were under attack," murmured Inga, "so Wynflaed and I... we kept our heads down."

"And you were right," he said approvingly, though still surprised for he had never seen either Saxon shrink from a fight. Wynflaed had some cause since she was carrying Ulf's child so perhaps Inga was simply remaining close to her friend.

He was still holding Inga, enjoying the feel of her against him when he noticed Father Gobban lying under one of the wagons with his hands over his head. Though churchmen were not usually known for their fighting prowess, he had expected the monk to at least remain on his feet and give encouragement to others. Gobban seemed agile enough and always carried a staff which Ambrosius assumed was not there just for decoration. Before the next skirmish, he resolved to have a few well-chosen words with the cleric.

Though the light remained good for several more hours, Ambrosius ordered fires to be built both within and outside the encampment. Now that he knew how close and numerous his enemies were, he could take no chances and posted guards within a few yards of each other around the whole perimeter.

Later Ambrosius sat around a fire with his closest comrades and laid out what, according to Pascent would unfold the next day; and to these trusted men he always gave the stark truth. They were hopelessly outnumbered and, if Pascent was to be believed they would face simultaneous attacks from both front and rear when they attempted to cross the River Gwy.

Such a two-pronged assault would destroy them so, as Ambrosius saw it they had three choices. They could abandon the hostages and withdraw, hoping to escape with their lives back to Caer Gloui. Another option was to ignore Pascent and fight on their own; if he was lying or exaggerating Vortigern's numbers, they might still win. Finally, they could put their faith in the word of a stranger – and not just any stranger, but the son of their enemy.

It was possible that Pascent's offer was merely a ploy by Vortigern to weaken Ambrosius' small army even further. If they accepted Pascent's offer of help, it would mean dividing their force and losing the support of their horsemen for some hours, which might prove fatal.

"I say we ignore this Pascent fellow," said Germanus, who was never shy to express a blunt opinion. "We should just take Vortigern head on. We've stormed across rivers before and survived. If we keep the horses we can ride across."

"But what if Vortigern's numbers force back our horsemen at the river and slow the crossing," said Ulf, "and then we are taken from behind…"

"That's the point of Pascent's plan," said Ambrosius. "If our horsemen can cross further up the river then they can strike Vortigern's flank with real impact."

"If you can trust Pascent," added Xallas.

"Was he at Vindocladia," asked Ulf, "or the fort?"

"I don't think he was, no."

Ulf nodded. "That's good."

"You can't trust any man who seeks to kill his father," muttered Germanus.

Xallas coughed, making Ambrosius smile despite the seriousness of their position.

"You may recall, Germanus," said Ambrosius quietly, "that I sought to kill my father -and I would have, if his daughter hadn't killed him first."

While the discussion continued all evening, Inga sat beside Ambrosius and said nothing. But, when silence eventually fell around the fire Ambrosius turned to her.

"What do you think, Inga?" he asked.

Germanus rolled his eyes at the notion that a woman could have anything worthwhile to say about war; and Ambrosius could see that even Inga was a little startled to be asked her opinion, but she was his lady and respected by all.

"I ask you because when we fight at the river tomorrow," he said, "you and Wynflaed will be with the wagons. If we are attacked in the rear, you will face the very worst of it; so, you should have your say."

"Well, I've not met Pascent but we came here to take back the hostages and you always said we couldn't do it without allies; yet, we have none. So, I think we've no choice but to accept Pascent's offer."

When Ambrosius saw several of his bucellarii nodding their agreement, he concluded: "When I spoke to Pascent, I looked into his eyes and saw no deception there; so I do believe his offer of support is given in good faith and thus... we will accept his help. At dawn we'll strike camp and, while I take the men and wagons down the track to the river Arturus will lead the mounted men, with Caralla to meet Pascent. Arturus, if Pascent gives you any cause for doubt then you must ride back at once to join us at the river."

Catching Arturus' eye, he saw that the youth was surprised that it was he, not Caralla whom Ambrosius charged with responsibility for the mounted warriors. Others noticed too and Germanus interrupted at once: "Caralla should lead, Dux – or I could go; Arturus is too young."

Biting back his annoyance at Germanus' persistent interference, Ambrosius replied: "If this Pascent fellow is to be believed, it will be hard going just to fight our way across the river. We'll need you with us, Germanus. Arturus and Caralla will do well together. Now, all of you: go to rest and prepare for battle tomorrow – and, if any man has need of a priest that's why Father Gobban is here."

Later when he retired with Inga, they found the monk arguing with Wynflaed which only a very brave or foolish man would have attempted.

"Keep your God-peddling nose out of my life," snarled Wynflaed.

"Trouble?" asked Ambrosius, as Father Gobban scuttled away.

A still-incensed Wynflaed glared at him briefly before softening her expression. "I don't like that monk," she grumbled. "My son's not yet born and already that dog threatens to drown him."

Ambrosius smiled. "I think he was offering to baptise the child."

"My son will be a Saxon warrior like his father," declared Wynflaed. "Our gods will watch over him and he's not going to be washed in Christ's water."

"As you wish," said Ambrosius. "I'm sure Father Gobban won't trouble you again."

Though he was a Christian, Ambrosius had rubbed shoulders with many folk from all over the empire and soon learned the quickest way to persuade a man to break an oath was to start questioning his faith. Every man – or woman – had to find their own faith wherever they could. Yet, he reflected even faith could be seduced for, in his case nothing had muddied the clear waters of his faith more than his love for the Saxon Inga.

When he first declared his feelings for her, he had in mind that a Christian marriage would follow; but she made it plain that she would not give up her faith. Thus, though they exchanged oaths before all their comrades, in the eyes of many Britons Inga was not truly his wife. If they survived the present ordeal he might have to resolve the troubling uncertainty of their union but just now, as they prepared to fight for their very lives it was the least of his concerns. This night, they must be lovers again and pay no heed to what the morrow might bring.

24

Long before dawn, Ambrosius rose to visit his sentries around the camp and was relieved to find none had anything to report. Soon after, he watched Arturus and Caralla rouse from uneasy sleep the youths who would ride with them into battle. Though still very young, Arturus was an excellent horseman and Ambrosius believed he was natural leader whose raw courage would inspire the others, some of whom were even younger than he was. But, for all his admirable spirit, he lacked experience which only Caralla could provide. No-one fought better on a horse than Caralla but he was not comfortable in command. Hence, when Ambrosius took him aside to ask him if he would serve under Arturus, Caralla was visibly relieved and swore to give the youth every support.

By the time Ambrosius despatched the company of mounted warriors back along the track, the sun had risen but its bright rays struggled to penetrate far into the forest. When, a little later the main column set off, it was arrayed to combat an ambush. Ambrosius was in the vanguard with Rocca, followed by the two supply wagons in the centre and Germanus and Xallas commanding the rear. Ulf protected their right flank with his Saxons while Lugaid's Scotti prowled along the left. All were alert for the slightest hint of enemy presence.

There was nothing more Ambrosius could do except wait for the inevitable; because, sooner or later an assault must come. He could only pray that he was right to trust the Briton, Pascent. Yet, for all his doubts they descended to the river Gwy without incident and continued upstream along the river bank until they reached the shallows Pascent had mentioned. If the latter was right, the High King would strike the moment Ambrosius tried to cross the river. He smiled to see Rocca trudging back towards him having attempted the river crossing. Though his tunic was soaked through and the dark wet skin of his legs glistened in the morning sunshine, there was a broad grin on the North African's face.

"It's sound, Dux," he reported. "The water flows fast, but it's shallow enough."

"We shan't be running across though," observed Ambrosius, who had seen the squat Rocca wading at times up to his waist. "I can't see any movement on the other side."

"No," replied Rocca, spreading his hands. "But as you can see, Dux beyond the narrow valley floor it's thick forest over there. Vortigern could have a thousand men in those trees and we'd not see them."

With a rueful nod, Ambrosius replied: "Let's pray it's not a thousand. But, there's no advantage in delay - so, let's get everyone ready."

"You're still sure you want to leave the women with the Scotti," enquired Ulf.

"I am. They've protected Inga before so I think they'll be willing to do it again."

"Aye," acknowledged the Saxon, "but the few young Britons you've left with them don't seem convinced. We Saxons should stay in their place."

"No. I can't afford to lose you and your comrades from the main attack," said Ambrosius. "By God, I can't afford to leave any man – yet, I must. Your Saxons have fought with me several times, but the Scotti haven't – better they stay behind."

A glance at the wagons revealed Inga, smiling at him and blowing a kiss. Knowing how nervous she seemed at first light, he loved her for the brave effort she was making. With her Hun bow clutched tight in her right hand, his tall, fair Saxon lady looked utterly magnificent and he saluted her with a wave of his arm.

When he returned to scanning the far bank, Ambrosius tried to judge how swiftly Vortigern would be able to deploy his men from the forest. The moment he set foot in the river, their foes would race out from the tree cover. Spear throwers would come first – perhaps some with slingshots too. He prayed that Vortigern had no archers, but that was by no means certain. Then Vortigern's best soldiers would attack with spatha, spear and axe; by God, there would be a lot of blood in the River Gwy.

The bawling voices of his captains, Rocca, Ulf and the others, echoed along the valley as they cajoled their comrades to form up in good order. Those who had never seen a pitched battle before - let alone fought in one – would be terrified and so they should be. He saw a few kneeling in prayer and hoped they were praying for good fortune. He had learned in the opening moments of his first battle that, without luck a soldier's life could be measured in seconds rather than hours.

Even if one generous piece of luck ensured that he survived the initial lunge of spears, he would always need more and, in the end of course, good fortune always ran out. If you slipped on a patch of blood, you died; if you tripped on a corpse beneath your feet, you died; if you swung your spatha too wildly and overbalanced, you died. Luck then, and a little help from God was all that kept any soldier alive – and Ambrosius knew he had been luckier than most.

Glancing at a shivering youth beside him, he noticed the lad's legs were wet before he'd set foot into the water. The young eyes that stared back at him were dulled by shame so Ambrosius clapped a reassuring hand upon the raw soldier's shoulder.

"If you're going to piss yourself, lad," he murmured, "then there's no better place to do it than a river. Now, don't think about it – just worry about keeping that shield up."

His show of support garnered a nervous smile from the recruit and Ambrosius prayed he would make it through the day. His first encounter would pass in a blur but, assuming he was not speared before he entered the water and survived the first exchange of blows, the youth might have a chance…

Next moment he felt, rather than saw Rocca and Germanus flank him which told him that his men were ready - or at least as ready as they would ever be. Was he ready… to win, or lose all? He thought so, for he had waited long enough for this reckoning. Now, as he slowly drew out his spatha – Varta's splendid, well-honed blade - Ambrosius the man stepped back to allow the soldier to take control.

As he surveyed the terrain on the far bank of the river for one last time, the command to advance was on his lips when scores of men rushed out of the woodland, weapons at the ready and shields held high. He was astonished that his opponent, in his eagerness was prepared to sacrifice the element of surprise. Vortigern's desperation was laid bare for he was willing to risk an assault before his enemy was even crossing the river. The tactic brought a wry smile to Ambrosius' face, for an over-eager opponent was always welcome.

While the High King had skirmished against Ambrosius last winter in the narrow passages of Villa Magna and at the dog end of the fight at Vindocladia, he had never faced Ambrosius in open battle. The field of war was an arena where the soldier, Ambrosius Aurelianus dominated. When he looked across the River Gwy now, he did not see an invincible enemy host racing towards him; he saw scores of men about to die by his hand.

Stepping forward to ensure that his voice carried to all his men, he bellowed: "Advance to the water's edge!"

Answering his command were the familiar shouts of: "Dux, dux, dux!"

"Shields high," he cried, as the ranks of men strode towards the river.

Vortigern's men were still about thirty yards short of the river, so Ambrosius shouted: "Halt!" and waited where his boots were gently caressed by the stream.

Their opponents charged on into the river and thus surrendered another advantage: their momentum. The instant they surged into the water they could no longer run and, when they reached the middle they could only wade –

as Ambrosius had observed earlier. If Vortigern had any sense he would have allowed Ambrosius to end up exactly where his own soldiers were – treading water and using up half their strength simply to reach their the far bank.

"Spears!" roared Ambrosius, launching a deadly volley of throwing spears into the High King's massed soldiers.

As Vortigern's attack faltered, another more ragged raft of spears delivered more carnage to the front ranks. Men began to fall back in panic even as their comrades were wading into the river to join them.

Leaping into the water, Ambrosius cried: "Attack, attack!"

First into the river were the bucellarii and the Saxons, eyes gleaming at the dire predicament of their enemies. With Germanus and Rocca beside him, Ambrosius drove into the chaotic centre of Vortigern's line and all but cut it in two. Ulf's Saxons made equally impressive inroads into the Britons on the right flank, forcing them back so that many slid down into the river where Ambrosius' young, barely-trained spear men butchered them where they floundered.

Ambrosius had one eye on the battle and another on the flat strip of land beyond the river where the mounted Vortigern, surrounded by many more men was flinging out orders. No doubt trying to recover from his disastrous start, he was bringing up slingers and more spear throwers. Though Ambrosius held a slim advantage, it would soon disappear if he did not press it home.

"Advance!" he roared yet again and pumped his legs as fast as he could to power through the deeper water.

Knowing that Ambrosius would be the focus of Vortigern's spear throwers, Rocca was matching his speed to stay close enough to offer some protection with his shield. Vortigern's men were still in disarray with some advancing while others tried to escape the merciless onslaught of the bucellarii and Saxons.

Having battered his way beyond the middle of the river, Ambrosius did not stop and, when he felt the water become shallower again he increased his pace. If Vortigern's men had a moment to think, they would stand and fight but he gave them no time. Then the missiles arced towards him from the far bank and, more than once he felt the rap of a stone striking his shield before deflecting away behind him. Spears, thrown with venom plunged into the water beside him or clattered against his shield and, all the while the clamour from Vortigern's men grew louder as more joined the fray.

Still driving hard for the far bank, Ambrosius was only yards from dry land; but his opponents were quickly forming up again, their morale no doubt bolstered by the arrival of fresh men. Their aim was to stop the bucellarii getting across and one of the tallest among them, sun flashing on his axe blade made straight for Ambrosius.

No doubt the fellow expected his first strike to knock Ambrosius off his feet, but he was disappointed for the Roman barely flinched as he parried the blow with his spatha. By the time his adversary was raising his weapon for a second swing, Ambrosius' spatha was slashing under the arms bearing the axe. Sinews sliced open, the warrior shuddered and nerveless fingers let fall his weapon. Before he could draw out his knife, Ambrosius plunged his spatha blade clean through the old mail shirt he wore.

Only with difficulty did Ambrosius wrench his spatha free from the falling soldier before another one reached him. But he was ready – just – to carve aside the fellow's shield. His new opponent, shield hanging in pieces could not stop Ambrosius' savage cut at his head. Ignoring the splashes of blood upon his cheek, Ambrosius swept his stricken enemy aside and stepped forward out of the water and onto firm ground. He fought with cold, barely-controlled fury knowing that anything less would get him and many others killed. He might die anyway – for that was the soldier's lot – but if he was to fall, he was damned certain he would go down fighting.

Though Vortigern's men had withdrawn from the river in the face of the brutal assault of Ambrosius, Rocca and Germanus, elsewhere along the line all was not going so well. Permitting himself a glance along the river, Ambrosius took in the scene with precision: on both flanks his less experienced men were being wrestled backwards. He might have reached the bank but, if he was not careful he would be encircled.

One thing was certain: if he retreated now, not only would he fail to cross the river but he would not live out the day.

"Germanus, right flank!" he bellowed. "Rocca, take the left."

With his two most formidable warriors fighting their way to the flanks, Ambrosius drove on, his spatha and battered shield smeared with blood. When a spear thrust grazed his thigh, he twisted sideways to crash his shield boss into the spear-bearer's face. The lump of iron struck with a satisfying crack and his opponent crumpled down onto the river bank.

Moving forward again, his foot slipped on the ground made greasy by the mingling blood and water. Stumbling, he half-parried a spatha aimed at his head and, though it had no mortal power when it struck his helmet the blow sent him reeling off-balance. Staggering backwards, he contrived to stay on his feet and bought some time by stabbing his assailant in the upper leg. He was lucky for the dark dribble of blood from the wound soon became a torrent and the fellow collapsed in a puddle of reddening water.

Suddenly there were no men directly ahead of him and he glimpsed Rocca driving forward on his left. Unless he had fallen, the mighty Germanus would be doing the same on the right flank, while at his back the young survivors of the first charge were roaring like wild men. Stern-faced, Ambrosius pressed forward again and was rewarded by the sight of Vortigern's frontline soldiers in retreat once more. This time they were running, scurrying away across the strip of low-lying land to flee up the slope and into the trees.

At once Ambrosius called a halt to assess the condition of his men. Though exhausted, their bloodied faces shone with exhilaration for they had survived the crossing and believed the hard part was done. He knew that it was not and was appalled to find that he had lost a quarter of his men.

"Dux," cried Rocca. "The wagons!"

Ambrosius swivelled around to stare back across the Gwy where a horde of warriors was surging along the riverside track towards his rear-guard... towards Inga...

A single shouted command rang out from the forest and Ambrosius slowly turned his back upon Inga and the Scotti. The arrival of his warriors on the east bank had persuaded the High King that the moment had come to send in all his forces and finish the struggle. Once more, men surged out from the trees shouting their war cries as they hurtled down towards the river. Ambrosius' survivors scarcely had time to take a breath and form up with their shields together before the great enemy wave enveloped them.

"Steady," roared Ambrosius. "Hold your lines."

Easy to say, but near impossible to do... for at the moment of impact, though every man knew what was coming the shuddering collision of men and steel was always a shock. When the Britons crashed into them with axe, spear and sword, the impetus of the charge drove even Ambrosius back into the water. Spear points thrust with brutal force aimed to prise open tiny gaps in the wall of shields. For some, the blunt encounter was a mortal one as a spear pierced their groin, or upper leg. A bad wound was a death sentence for you would certainly fall. At best you might drop to one knee but even then other spears would hunt down your flesh. A mail coat might delay the inevitable, but not for long. And, once you were down your comrades could not protect you without endangering themselves and those alongside them.

Pascent had been right about his father's tactics, but he should be there by now; for that was the arrangement. If he and Arturus did not come soon then the dire outcome he predicted would happen all too swiftly. In vain Ambrosius stared upstream for a glimpse of riders' helms flashing in the midday sun, but saw none.

If Pascent had no intention of keeping his word... if Arturus did not come, then the day was already lost.

25

Though Inga beamed a broad smile at Ambrosius as he left to cross the river, beneath the loving gesture lay a trough of worries - and fear of imminent death was only one of them. Watching Ambrosius, her heart was flooded by a strange brew of emotions.

As always, there was pure lust at the sight of his straight-backed, muscled figure which reminded her of the previous night... when so little time was wasted in slumber. She blushed at the memory of his gentle touch but it was not enough that Ambrosius wanted her in his bed. There was another who would readily take her place there: a woman for whom he had dragged them across western Britannia. Inga wanted more for, whatever it took she was determined that her son should be accepted as Ambrosius' heir. And, lurking beneath her unquestioned love was a darker desire, festering away deep in her Saxon soul: a black, consuming guilt. Guilt that she was bitterly jealous of Lurotriga and guilt, that she never ever wanted Ambrosius to set the beautiful widow free.

Thus, as she watched him battle his way across the river, Inga was drowning in that guilt – and it almost killed her. The first spear narrowly missed her head and flew on past her to thud into the ground behind the wagon. With a gasp of shock, she spun around to see armed men under Vortigern's banner racing along the river bank towards her.

In that moment so close to death, a new resolve seized her and fired her with passion and pride. To wish ill of

Lurotriga was shameful and beneath her; she must win Ambrosius by shining in a manner that her rival could never equal. She would fight like the bucellarii and impress her lover in the one arena that mattered most to him: the fight. Let her raw courage persuade Ambrosius that he could never ever cast her aside.

Tearing her gaze from the seething mass of bodies advancing towards her, Inga stared down at the Hun bow in her hands – as if noticing it for the first time. In the shock of the attack, she had quite forgotten it but now she felt the reassuring curve of wood and sinew in her hand. Just for an instant she recalled the brave young Hun archer, Uldar who once owned it. Then with a deep breath, she climbed up onto the wagon while the warlike Scotti, with blood-chilling cries charged at the Britons in the hope of stopping them before they reached the wagons.

To her dismay, it was the heavily-outnumbered Scotti who were driven backwards with two of their number hacked apart in moments by a frenzy of blades. At once she picked up one of the arrows she had laid out earlier on the wagon. Had their opponents noticed her, she wondered as she set the first arrow to her bow and strained to pull back upon it.

Studying the mass of men spread out before her, she swiftly chose her victim: a tall, bearded warrior with a great shock of hair – hair as black as death. Letting fly, she watched her arrow dart fast and true to strike the Briton in the throat and hurl him backwards. For a moment or two his dying body, head lolling to and fro was borne up by the press of men around him until finally it slipped down and was lost from sight.

As Vortigern's men continued their advance, she chose another sleek shaft – this time not bothering to aim but directing it at a great clutch of warriors. It was bound to kill one of them, she decided. It didn't and instead, to her annoyance simply deflected off an iron helm. But a third arrow followed it and brought down an opponent as Inga warmed to her work. She was reaching for another arrow when the first stone rapped against the wagon and tore out a splinter of wood.

"Watch yourself up there," cried Wynflaed in alarm, as more stones flew past.

Inga grinned down at her friend and loosed another arrow, aiming at one of those who seemed to be leading the assault upon the Scotti. Another shaft followed and another, but the slingers were finding their range and getting closer. Worse still about half a dozen Britons, no doubt tiring of the Saxon archer, charged at the wagon and put their shoulders to it. Others joined them and soon the wagon was being lifted off the ground and Inga was flung backwards off it.

As she fell, Inga begged Frigg to keep her safe so perhaps the goddess intended her to drop into the arms of Father Gobban. The monk staggered as he caught her but Inga was surprised by the strength she felt in his arms as he set her down gently upon the ground behind the wagon.

Moments later, the whole wagon was tipped over and, though Inga seized Wynflaed's arm to haul her back a wheel struck her friend's head. Escaping with only a few bruises, Inga bent down to drag Wynflaed further back with Father Gobban.

214

"It's nothing," bawled the scowling Wynflaed. "I'm still alive."

"You're still complaining at least," retorted Inga, "but you've a cut."

"Leave it," snapped Wynflaed, brushing away the smear of blood in her hair. "It matters little now."

Despite her friend's protests, Inga propped Wynflaed up against the upturned wagon and examined her wound until satisfied that the cut was indeed only a slight one.

Close by, Ferox was snarling and snorting, lunging at their assailants until Inga pulled him away. "You'll get yourself killed," she scolded.

"He's got something in his mouth," groaned Wynflaed.

Peering closer, Inga murmured: "I think it's a... finger..."

"Oh, Frigg," muttered Wynflaed. "I hope it's one of theirs..."

Above them Vortigern's men were attempting to clamber over the wagon to get at them while several youths prodded with hopeful spears to force them back. Lugaid and the Scotti drew closer to the wagon to help keep them at bay with their bloodied axes.

Inga and Wynflaed, as stubbornly defiant as ever stood up and began to hurl a bitter torrent of abuse at the men of Vortigern. Raging contempt was all Inga had left for she could see that, with up to a hundred men around them their plight was utterly hopeless.

Lugaid squeezed through the press towards her. "We have to try to get you two away," he said. "For, if you are lost..."

"Get us away?" cried Inga, watching the Britons close in upon the diminishing ring of spears and shields. "Not us, Lugaid… we're Saxons – and there's nowhere else to go…"

"Frigg's teeth," shouted Wynflaed, pointing further down the valley to where more fighting men were coming fast along the bank.

"Not more…" groaned Inga. "We already face enough to kill us ten times over."

"No, wait," cried Lugaid. "That's Pascent's banner – and by God, I see him! He's making good on his promise – at last."

Though Inga did not know Pascent she reckoned that, if his bearing and fine breastplate were anything to go by he would be a formidable ally. Thus, once more hope swelled in her breast for he was at the head of at least two score of warriors – perhaps even the fifty he had promised Ambrosius. They surged along the river bank until their cries alerted Vortigern's men, who were forced to turn and face their new adversaries.

The grinning wild man beside Inga roared his approval and all around her the youthful warriors drew fresh determination from the timely arrival of their allies. But, even as Pascent launched his assault upon his father's men, Inga thought something looked wrong. Her brief flourish of hope turned to disbelief as she watched as some of Pascent's men stop their forward charge and turn instead upon their own comrades. In moments, Pascent's impressive company disintegrated.

Inga heard shouts for Pascent, while others roared the name of Vortigern but many more on both sides cried out: 'Traitor.' Perhaps the prospect of fighting against

Vortigern's soldiers – some of whom they must have known – was too much for many of Pascent's men. But, whatever the reason, the result was that Pascent's small army swiftly fragmented into a dozen savage mêlées. One moment Vortigern's warriors encircling the wagon were plagued by doubt, the next they were grinning with relief and set to finally press home their attack.

"Do you have any arrows left?" Wynflaed asked her.

"I don't know," replied Inga, giving a start as a spear thudded into the wagon, splitting a timber.

She ransacked the contents of the wagon which had been tossed out when it overturned and retrieved her arrow bag. Looking inside, she murmured: "Four left. Might as well use them, I suppose."

With a smile, Inga embraced the young woman with whom, in a few short months she had shared so much. To her surprise it was Father Gobban who had retrieved her bow.

"May Frigg guide your arrows," breathed Wynflaed.

"God will send them into the black hearts of their best warriors," declared Father Gobban with uncharacteristic zeal.

Inga stared at them both, grim-faced. "When I'm dead," she said, "don't forget to feed the dog…"

Then, clutching bow and arrow bag she said: "Father Gobban, make yourself useful and help me up onto the wagon."

"But-"

"Just do it – and don't stop to mumble one of your miserable prayers."

She sucked aired into her lungs as if for the very last time for she knew that, once the monk hoisted her up she would not have long. Even so, when she clambered up there on the wagon and confronted the terrible truth of their plight it stole that breath from her lungs. All around them even unto the river margins, Vortigern's men were pressing in upon them. From above the carnage was all too real, bringing tears unbidden to her eyes. So much death… and for nothing…

Assailed by stark cries of war and the all too familiar stench of blood, sweat and shit, she looked down upon the men of their ever-dwindling ranks who stood shield against shield with their opponents. To her right Lugaid and his few warriors fought like demons but to her left the line was held, not by a handful of grizzled warriors but by a dozen or more young men. They were hardly trained, but how they fought – and how they bled…

She could not help but glance across the river for one last look at her lover still waging war against Vortigern himself. If only he could defeat the High King and return to help them… but she saw that he was being driven back into the river and the very thought of him falling chilled her soul. She was still staring at Ambrosius when a spear slammed into the boards of the wagon next to her right foot. Shaken, she looked again at the sea of hostile faces beyond the wagon.

Below her, Lugaid roared up cheerfully: "Lady Inga. Remember you're an eagle, not a damned pigeon."

All she had was four arrows, so she had to make them count. Suddenly Pascent's shining helmet caught her eye and she saw that he still had perhaps a score of men with him. They were surrounded and doomed of course, because their erstwhile comrades were stabbing and hacking at them with a fury they could not long endure - unless perhaps someone could help clear a path for them to the wagons.

Decision made, Inga wasted no more time and laid an arrow to her bow. Taking aim, she found the perfect target – a near-stationary one: a tall, muscled warrior laying into Pascent with his mighty axe. Only as she let fly did it occur to her that if she missed, her arrow would almost certainly strike Pascent himself.

"Pascent!" she screamed, but gasped with relief when saw that she had hit her mark. The arrow struck the warrior in the back and he stooped to his knees. For an instant her victim reached out in vain to his comrades nearby and she felt a pang of regret; but there was no pleasant way to fight for your life.

Once she had attracted Pascent's attention, he guessed at once what she was trying to do. While he dragged his men towards the wagon, Inga readied another arrow and picked out a spear man who was turning to block Pascent's progress. The distance was short and her arrow flew true, punching into the fellow's neck to pluck him aside and allow Pascent's men to step over him, drawing ever closer to the defenders at the wagon.

As Inga put the last arrow to her bow, she saw that Pascent was close and shouted down to Lugaid to be ready to let him through, but the Scot had seen what was happening and bellowed up at her: "We know."

Selecting her final target she took careful aim, though at such close range even she could not miss. Just as she released the shaft, a stone from a slinger scored across the side of her head and felled her like a storm-damaged oak. Dropping down hard onto one knee, she cried out in pain but gave a grunt of satisfaction when her arrow struck her victim in the shoulder. It distracted him enough for Pascent to drive his spatha into the warrior's groin.

By then Inga was feeling dizzy and crouched there for a few moments, intrigued by the blood trickling down her cheek. Dazed, she was vaguely aware of Lugaid and his comrades surging out to shield Pascent's men as they joined the ring of men around the wagon.

Between them, Gobban and Wynflaed pulled Inga down from the wagon. Ferox, no doubt smelling the blood proceeded to lick at her wound until Pascent arrived to push him away.

"I thank you, lady," he cried before returning to the fight.

It was Father Gobban who bent down with Wynflaed to tend to her wound. They sat her on the bare earth while her Saxon friend bound up her head with a strip from Gobban's filthy robe.

"Frigg's bones, that hurts," wept Inga.

"It should," groaned Wynflaed. "The stone cut deep so it'll leave yet another mark on that scarred head of yours."

"It matters little now, for this is where our venture ends," murmured Inga.

"Have more faith, lady," entreated Father Gobban. "The Lord God will-"

"Your God should keep out of Frigg's way," she said. "Frigg's our only hope now..."

"Unless..." Despite Wynflaed's protests, she scrambled to her feet and lurched towards Pascent.

Gripping his arm, she hissed: "Our horsemen… are they still coming?"

With a downcast countenance, Pascent replied: "I fear, lady that my guides were among the traitors and led them too deep into the forest. They will be lost…"

"So be it then," cried Inga and, picking up a spear from the ground she used it to help her clamber onto the overturned wagon. When Father Gobban tried to dissuade her, she favoured him with a particularly harrowing glare.

"But Inga," warned Wynflaed. "You've no arrows!"

When the monk declared: "That girl doesn't know when to give up." Inga smiled to hear her friend's reply: "That girl is Inga – and she's all Saxon…"

Inga, determined that her last shrill words would soar above the clamour of the encircling throng, raised her voice.

"Know this, you dogs," she screamed aloud. "Even if you kill us all, many of you will fall too… and any who survive, my lord Ambrosius will slaughter and leave your bloated, rot-blackened flesh to feed the crows!"

Perhaps the Britons' advance faltered a little as her words rang out across the green Gwy valley and perhaps even Ambrosius heard them on the far bank of the river. Yet she knew that their foe's hesitation would last only moments and then, in the shuddering chaos of battle she would fall and the son she carried would never be born.

26

So soon after dawn, the sun shed only a glimmer of light upon the forest track, but Arturus was relieved to find Pascent exactly where he had promised to be. Without delay, the British leader sent them on their way with two of his men to guide them through the heavily-wooded valleys to the north-west and on down to the river Gwy. For the first time since he left Vindocladia, Arturus dared to believe that the destruction of Vortigern and the rescue of Ishild had begun. Ever since her capture, he had been dogged by a dread fear that she might be killed at any moment – before he even had a chance to save her. But now at least he had hope.

As they moved swiftly through the forest, he was glad of Pascent's guides for he found it hard to discern a clear track. Very soon his riders were spread out in a long, straggling line which prompted Caralla, with a nod to Arturus to drop back along the column and ensure that no man lost touch with his comrades. Arturus, glad to have an experienced horseman at the rear took the opportunity to ride up alongside one of the guides.

"How much further to the river?" he enquired.

"Not far," replied the guide, before riding on ahead again to join his comrade at the front.

Staring back along the strung-out line of horseman, Arturus caught a reassuring glimpse of Caralla through the trees but when he turned his eyes ahead once more, he could not immediately locate their guides. Just there the forest was especially dense so he darted forward to catch them up knowing they could not be far away. Still he could not see them so he pulled up to look for their tracks to follow; but the ground, hard and stony showed no hoofmarks.

Only when his comrades began to close up around him, did Arturus realise that their guides had deliberately abandoned them. He was still staring around at the green cloak of woodland, when Caralla rode forward to join him and guessed at once what had happened.

"There's only one reason they would do that," murmured Arturus.

"Aye, it seems that Lord Pascent doesn't intend to be our ally after all," said Caralla, glum-faced.

"So, where in God's name have they left us," groaned Arturus.

"Far away, I should think from where they said they'd take us."

"But we don't know this forest at all," whispered Arturus. "I can't see how we'll ever find Dux and the others."

Glancing at his comrades, now crowded around their leaders he saw in their eyes the growing anxiety he felt - until Caralla reached across to lay a gentle hand upon his arm.

"Stay calm, young Arturus," he murmured, with a reassuring smile. "It's not the first time I've had to find my way through a damned forest. And it's a bright morning, so at least we know which way is east."

"But we don't know how far they've led us astray," said Arturus.

With a shake of the head, Caralla replied: "I've been keeping an eye on where we're heading. They've taken us north, I think – as Pascent claimed they would – but I suspect too far north. As long as we head west and try to keep moving downhill we should still reach the river."

"Perhaps, but the guides were supposed to take us straight to the crossing point," argued Arturus.

"So," replied Caralla, with a shrug of his powerful shoulders, "we'll just have to follow the river till we find a place to cross."

"But it's not just we who are betrayed," said Arturus. "And, if Pascent's not going to help Dux then he's probably going to attack him. We have to warn them."

"Better make haste then," urged Caralla, setting off at once to forge a path in a westerly direction through the trees.

"Stay alert," Arturus warned the others. "And keep the rider in front of you in sight all the time." Wise words, he thought. Pity he hadn't done so himself earlier.

After a short while, the terrain began to slope away to the west, which offered Arturus some encouragement – perhaps the river was not so far away after all. But just as he wanted to increase their pace, Caralla abruptly pulled up.

"What's wrong?" demanded Arturus, eager to carry on.

"The trees are thicker ahead," observed Caralla, "so before we go down into the valley, we should try to get a better idea of where the river lies - unless you want to ride down into the wrong valley."

As he spoke, he was eyeing the tall oak beside them and Arturus, understanding the inference at once, said: "I'll go up myself."

"You're sure," said Caralla.

Arturus gave him a grim smile. "I've always been good at climbing."

"Don't care whether you're good at it," said Caralla, "as long as you're quick."

"Well, at least I'll be closer to God," muttered Arturus.

"Not if you fall," remarked Caralla.

In response, Arturus leapt up onto the tree and proceeded to climb as fast as he could; but half way up, with his arm muscles complaining he regretted having volunteered. His determination to prove himself a worthy leader had rather got the better of him. But he could hardly turn back now so he carried on, slowing with every yard as he struggled to locate handholds on the oak's rough bark.

Exhausted, he clambered ever higher until he emerged above several other treetops close by. Though terrified he might lose his balance and plummet to the ground at any moment, he could not deny that his lofty position afforded him an excellent view. Almost at once he located the broad, curving swathe that the Gwy valley carved through the woodland. Though he could not see down to the river itself, he was encouraged to find that they were not so far from it.

Descending the great oak proved rather faster than the climb up, though it cost him several patches of skin torn from his raw hands. Dropping with relief the last few feet to the ground, he wheezed: "We've only a short distance to go. We'll reach the river very soon."

Despite his newfound optimism, navigating the forest still proved difficult because the densely-packed trees often forced them to turn aside from their intended path. But, as their descent grew steeper, so Arturus' hopes soared.

Leading them down the slope with gathering pace, his momentum carried him onto a ribbon of open ground beyond which, he was certain lay the river.

Before he even glimpsed the river Gwy however, Arturus was obliged to haul mercilessly upon his rein since the promising strip of ground ended in a sheer precipice. As his terrified horse skidded to a halt, it almost slid over the edge of the cliff. Instead it managed to stop but the experience left both horse and rider trembling. Fearing his comrades would crash down into him, Arturus shouted up a warning and mercifully all were able to slow down safely.

Arturus then dismounted and went to the brink of the overhang and to stare down at the river. It was perhaps only thirty feet below – close enough to hear the flowing water, but far enough to have killed them all. And it might as well be a hundred feet for he could see no way down.

While the riders were still and silent, Arturus heard another sound drifting up from the river: the distant, but unmistakable clamour of men clattering into one another in the din of battle.

"It's started," he breathed, peering over the edge into the gorge. But a slight bend in the river prevented him from seeing where the conflict was taking place. It might be the sound of Dux crossing the river in triumph, or the helpless cries of the bucellarii being cut down by the faithless Pascent. Arturus had to get there… and instinctively he looked to Caralla for guidance.

"South," suggested Caralla. "If we ride south, we might cut across a narrow valley that can take us down to the river."

"Might," groaned Arturus.

226

"It's our best chance," said Caralla, "and at least we'll be riding towards the fight, not further away from it."

Arturus nodded, though he thought it would take too long... and they would arrive too late. In his blind haste, Arturus led them back up the slope hard, driving his mount to the limit of its endurance until he crested the rise, then he slowed a little to calm himself while he waited for the rest to catch up.

"Take care with that poor animal, Arturus," warned Caralla, "else he'll fall under you when you need him most."

"I know," said Arturus, acknowledging the fault. "Lead on, Caralla... lead on."

As they explored further south, they discovered a narrow stream which appeared to run down towards the Gwy.

"What do you think?" asked Arturus.

"I think it's steeper than the last route you tried, so it'll most likely kill us all before we even get to the river," said Caralla, grinning for the first time that morning. "But... it's our best chance. So, let's try."

Arturus surged down alongside the stream with the others in close pursuit and very soon he could hear the river Gwy again When the stream dropped down even more steeply, he followed its course without hesitation for, if they did not get to Dux soon they might as well all be dead anyway. Abruptly the stream plunged almost vertically for several feet and then cut through the bank of the river Gwy. Arturus leapt his horse the last yard, landed on a patch of muddy ground and wrestled his mount to a skidding standstill at the river's edge.

Elated, he stared ahead along the river and saw just downstream a series of fast-flowing rapids. And in an instant his hopes were dashed once more.

"Oh shit," he muttered. "We can't cross here."

"No," agreed Caralla, reining in his horse to join him on the river bank. "Not unless you want to lose half the men and mounts. The water swirling around those rocks might be too deep anyway."

"But we have to cross the river," cried Arturus. "For the love of Christ, our friends are dying, Caralla."

"We'll just have to follow the river and cross further down," replied Caralla simply.

"But there might be more sheer cliffs at the river's edge to stop us riding any further," argued Arturus.

Caralla nodded. "There might be," he conceded. "But then – and only then – do we take our chances in the water."

Fighting down his anger and frustration, Arturus followed Caralla along the Gwy's east bank. It was hard not be impressed by his comrade's horsemanship as he negotiated at speed every dip and bank in their path. Arturus, once he cast aside his fears about what might go wrong, saw that Caralla was right.

As they rounded the long, gentle curve in the river, the cries of battle sounded ever closer and soon the whole chaotic scene was laid out before them. On the east bank, their comrades around the wagons were cut off and surrounded by an overwhelming force. But on the opposite bank, Ambrosius and the bucellarii were being driven back yard by yard into the churning waters of the Gwy. What Arturus saw was not just defeat, it was annihilation.

Caralla pointed to the stretch of river below the rapids. "We could cross there," he said. "If you still want to cross…"

For that was the mortal decision Arturus now had to make, for he commanded a force too small to divide. So, either he could cross to the west bank and go to Ambrosius' aid, or ride straight along the east bank to save Inga, Wynflaed and her unborn child. Only one thing was certain: he could not do both.

27

Ambrosius could never truly decide whether it was a gift or a curse to be able to see a battle unfold around him in all its grisly detail, even as he slashed his spatha across an opponent's chest. He wasn't born with it but somehow had learned it, perhaps because in the white heat of battle he was able to rein in his fury just enough to think. However he acquired it, the skill had always served him well. The ability to absorb the whole scope of a fighting arena and make sense of its bloody chaos, had more than once had kept him – and others – alive. Yet, this time he was not sure that it could help him.

As they contested the river crossing, his men were being driven inexorably backwards and he knew that, if he allowed that to continue it would not be long before every last one of them succumbed to a mortal wound and fell into the shallow water. Yet, if they tried to retreat the same fate awaited them only much quicker for they would be swallowed up and cut to pieces in moments.

A spatha carved down at him but he took the blow easily upon his shield and then crashed its iron boss back at the culprit. Some of his soldiers looked in bad shape: several carried wounds, while others were still bewildered by their first experience of battle. All stood upon trembling legs that ached from the colossal effort they had already expended and yet they were still outnumbered by more than two to one.

Ambrosius knew that numbers did not always bring victory – if only he knew how many more Vortigern was holding in reserve. On the few occasions he dared to lower his shield, he peered beyond the High King's front ranks and realised that there were almost no men held back. The heavy casualties Vortigern suffered in the initial struggle for the river must have taken him by surprise. Now, since he had committed half his army against Ambrosius' small rear-guard on the east bank, Vortigern was forced to take a risk. In a desperate gamble to destroy what was left of Ambrosius' main force, he had thrown all his warriors into the fight.

There was every chance that Vortigern's gamble would succeed if Ambrosius' dwindling army continued to fall back, bleeding men with every yard they conceded. Evading yet another thrusting spear, Ambrosius decided he must unleash the only powerful weapon he had left: his bucellarii. Earlier he had deployed them individually among the ranks to stiffen the resolve of the younger men and now his captains must work together with him.

"Close up!" he bellowed, hoping that Xallas, Germanus and Rocca, having served with him for years would know what was coming. They knew his mind in battle almost as well as he did; but he prayed that others would find the nerve to drive forward with them. Even now his few bucellarii would be forging the rest of his army into a tight, steel wedge of bristling spears and blood-painted axes. They needed to be close enough to draw strength from their comrades for he would ask them to do the unthinkable: to charge into the midst of an overwhelming host. Their advance would certainly fail and they would be slaughtered to a man, but at least they would not be cut down like dogs as they fled the field.

At the very moment of decision, a shrill cry from behind him on the east bank drove a blade of ice through his heart; for it was Inga's voice he heard and he knew what it meant. Swivelling around to seek her out, he swallowed hard when he saw her down on her knees atop one of the wagons, clearly hurt. Next moment, she slid away and was lost.

"Dux!"

The warning roar came from Germanus, as he blocked a spear lunging at Ambrosius' groin. Though Inga's fall had distracted him for only a moment, it would have been fatal had it not been for Germanus' vigilance. From his dark pit of despair, Ambrosius launched into his new adversary with rapid, savage blows that all but eviscerated him. Then, thrusting aside all thought of Inga's loss, he gave the command.

"Forward!" he roared and his heart sang to hear the answering shouts of: "Dux, dux, dux!" led by his handful of bucellarii.

The first step forward was always the hardest but, with grim determination Ambrosius willed his weary legs to move and he took a long pace forward to slam his shield into the first warrior he encountered. Forcing his opponent back, he took a second step then a third as he bludgeoned his sword hilt into a startled face.

Together Ambrosius' men trudged forward, the bucellarii moving as one with their Dux and cajoling the others to keep up. To his left Rocca and Xallas led, with heavy spears in hand thrusting and jabbing back their

232

opponents; while on his right the whirling axes of Germanus and Ulf split shields and shattered bones. All maintained the steady pace set by Ambrosius as he drove forward in the centre, his shield boss cracking against a breastplate, or sometimes a helmet, while his spatha sought flesh to lay bare to the bone.

Vortigern, like any experienced general would soon despatch men from the congested centre to the flanks to surround the smaller force. It was the best tactic to counter the assault but, as long as Ambrosius kept moving it would fail. Thus when bodies fell, he did not stop but trampled over them careless of the brave limbs he crushed beneath his boots. The fighting wedge must grind onward though Ambrosius knew that, with every yard they covered his men were falling one by one.

An arm reached up from the ground beneath him to stab a broken, but defiant spear up at his legs. Even as he hacked down at the determined hand, he felt the wound in his thigh. Stifling a grunt of pain, he prayed that God had further use for him else he would swiftly bleed to death. Once he managed another good stride, he knew the wound would not kill him and thus buried the pain.

His losses were terrible, but Vortigern's were far greater and he soon noticed that the ranks ahead of him were beginning edge backwards even before he reached them. A closer look told him why: Vortigern was scarcely a dozen yards away and his royal body guards were breaking from the battle line to form a protective screen around him. Such men had not earned their high status without showing great mettle and skill, but if Ambrosius could kill Vortigern then the struggle would end there.

Legs aching and lungs bursting, he quickened his pace and headed directly towards the cluster of formidable warriors defending the High King. Beside him were two young warriors that he remembered from the fight beneath Iron Hill. The pair had shown courage beyond all his expectations and when he attacked the royal guards they were still by his side.

When he hammered his spatha against the first shield he reached, the warrior rocked back half a pace, but stood firm. These men were Vortigern's personal retinue and would not be easy to defeat. A sudden spear thrust caught the rim of Ambrosius' shield and twisted him round a little. For an instant, there was a gap between shields and another spear lanced through it. The lightly-armoured youth on his right hand took the razor-sharp point in his belly and it ripped him open. The moment the lad dropped to his knees, Ambrosius' line was breached. On such moments whole battles could turn and Ambrosius stepped swiftly to the right to fill the chasm left by the fallen soldier – but it was too late.

One by one his exhausted men staggered to a halt and, attacked from all sides their tight wedge was shattered in just a few torrid moments. Some of Vortigern's men who had just been swept aside at the river were now emboldened to return to the fight.

"On me!" shouted Ambrosius, wielding his shield like a weapon to smash aside anyone who dared close upon him.

Next moment he found the gritty Rocca beside him and a glance to his rear told him that Ulf and Germanus were hauling the younger men into a defensive circle. But of course such a circle could never hold against such numbers and they were gradually pressed back into each other. His bold gambit had failed and, once the fragile ring was pierced it would all be over.

"No man takes a pace back," cried Ambrosius, hoping his voice did not betray his despair.

His bucellarii tried to rally their comrades with the familiar cry of: "Dux, dux, dux!"

But the other voices that joined the call were hoarse, or half-hearted. Throats were dry and lungs devoid of breath to fight, let alone squander upon a forlorn battle-cry. Only Germanus continued to spew out a string of insults at his opponents for the truculent Burgundian would meet a fitting end if he was reviling his enemies with his very last breath.

On Ambrosius' right Vortigern's warriors pressed harder, forcing gaps between the battered shields and soon only the formidable Saxon, Ulf was keeping them at bay. When an axe blade chopped clean through his shield and bit into his shoulder, the whole battle line seemed to shiver. Several nearby backed away, seized by panic. When a fellow Saxon stepped across to protect the wounded Ulf, he was impaled by two spears at once.

To Ambrosius' astonishment Ulf, still on his feet tossed away his splintered shield and swung his great axe in ever wilder arcs of fury. Several fell to his savage blade before it became lodged deep in a dying man's breast. Unable to free his weapon, Ulf went down under a welter of vengeful blows; a spear sank into his groin and another skewered his leg before an axe finally cut through his neck.

Seeing the mighty Saxon fall, Ambrosius wanted to rail at the heavens for allowing such a bitter blow; yet he had no breath left to roar his distress. Ulf was more than just a loyal warrior; he was a friend who inspired his comrades to great deeds. If Ulf was dead then no-one could survive such an onslaught. Ambrosius could only pray that when he fell, he too would die such a death. So he brandished Varta's great spatha, though only rage now powered his arm for strength in muscle and sinew was long ago expended.

From all around him the yelling of Vortigern's men grew louder as they sensed they were on the cusp of a great victory – God rot their miserable souls…

Yet at the very moment of their triumph, Ambrosius noticed something amiss in the ranks of High King's army. In their rabid cries, so wild and urgent he detected an edge of fear. Only then did he hear the low thunder of hooves and, darting a glance to his right he saw to the north what was causing panic among his foes. Horsemen – his horsemen - were sweeping along the west bank towards them – and at their head, outpacing all the rest rode Arturus.

The mounted men crashed into the left flank of Vortigern's army, killing dozens in the first moment of impact. Cutting a great gash through the enemy ranks, they left in their wake only a trail of blood and shattered bodies. Vortigern bellowed frantic orders to his fleeing soldiers and might perhaps have persuaded them to reform their line, had they not been struck by a second wave of riders led by the mighty Caralla. The latter, finding a brace of twitching bodies impaled upon his spear discarded it to draw out his spatha. Then, hacking down to left and right, he let no man in his path survive.

It was a charge that Ambrosius – and probably every other man there - would remember for all their days. But he knew that, despite his weariness there was still work to be done so he roused his survivors for one final, and he prayed decisive assault upon Vortigern. Men who, only moments earlier had been committing their souls to God, had been granted a reprieve. So now, spurred on by the sight of their mounted comrades butchering the High King's royal guards they went onto the attack.

"Break them now, lads," cried Ambrosius. "Else we'll be fighting these bastards again tomorrow."

So they pursued the fleeing men, some of whom were already wounded and they cut down any man they caught. Though some discarded their blood-smeared weapons, no-one was spared. It was a time, Ambrosius judged for blood, not mercy and his exhausted men killed until the ground about them was blood-soaked and littered with dead. Arturus and the other horsemen in their turn slaughtered every man who did not escape into the trees.

Stumbling across to greet Arturus, Ambrosius reached up a bloodied hand to grasp that of his young comrade.

"Did you get him?" his rough voice rasped out the question. "Did you kill Vortigern?"

"No, Dux," confessed Arturus. "He escaped with a few others into the forest."

Ambrosius released his hold upon the youth and sank to his knees, crushed; they had won the battle, but lost the prize. Vortigern would scuttle away to his nearby hilltop fortress, which Ambrosius did not have the men to assault, and there the High King could kill the hostages at his leisure.

Yet, despite his bitter disappointment Ambrosius knew that he and his men owed their survival to Arturus and Caralla. Still on his knees, gasping for breath and suddenly aware again of the ugly gash in his thigh, he said to Arturus: "I will never forget the service you've done me today."

"Aye," replied Arturus bitterly, "nor will you ever forgive me..."

When Ambrosius looked up in confusion, Arturus pointed back to the east bank. "I had to choose, Dux between saving you and saving Inga; because I couldn't do both..."

Ambrosius stared back across the Gwy to see Vortigern's men devouring the last remnant of his rear guard. They must have seen what befell their comrades moments earlier; so they would leave no-one – man or woman - alive.

Arturus' riders were scattered across the plain and only a few heard his frantic commands as he turned his bloodied mount back to cross the river.

"Bucellarii!" cried Ambrosius, but it was more of an anguished croak than a call to arms.

Barely able to stand, Ambrosius willed himself to break into a shambling run on legs that promised to fold under him at any time. Rocca, Xallas and Germanus trotted after him for, as he knew they would follow him into the jaws of hell – and that was where he was going. Inga might already be dead, but he would not abandon her even in death.

28

When the end came, it happened so fast there was scarcely time for Inga to snatch a last breath. One moment she was standing beside Wynflaed with Ferox growling in front of them and the next the wagons, which had provided such vital protection were crashed aside. At once two youths who had worked their spears tirelessly to defend the Saxons, were utterly exposed. Though they tried to fight on, they were quickly overwhelmed by a host of spears.

Inga and Wynflaed, knives in hand stood shoulder to shoulder while Ferox protected Inga's their flank.

"For Frigg," declared Inga, for both young women were wild-eyed with outrage to see so many of their brave young warriors succumb to blows from axe and sword.

Somehow Lugaid's booming voice, like thunder from the gods gave the survivors the will to carry on. "Stay close by me," he barked.

But to the tiny band of defenders dwindling fast, defeat was certain. Though Pascent still battled on bravely, only half a dozen of his men remained. Fighting alongside them were several youths who had made the journey from Vindocladia together. And, of the fierce Scotti warriors who had sworn oaths to Ambrosius, just Lugaid and two others were still standing.

"Keep low," Father Gobban advised the women. "Then you may be buried under other bodies."

"Saxons don't cower like God-peddlers," retorted Wynflaed and the women fired the monk such a look of pure contempt that he shrugged and thrust out his ash staff to help keep Vortigern's spear men at bay for a few moments more – until an axe blow shortened its length by a half.

One of the Scotti stumbled back into the women and then another coughed a mouthful of blood over their desolate faces. Both women screamed as the spear points ventured ever closer until the ring of bloodied men was carved open. Lugaid was struck down trying to shield the women with his large frame. A spear lunged at Wynflaed's breast but the Scot pulled her down with him to the ground.

Inga was left standing a little apart with only Ferox between her and oblivion. With her knife gripped tightly lest a mortal blow should wrench it free and leave her in death with no weapon in hand, she stood tall, screaming: "Dux, dux, dux!"

Several pursued her and, with faces twisted in anger cursed her for the evil Saxon whore she was. Levelling their spears, they planted their feet wider apart for balance and drove their spears at her.

None found Inga's breast for, in a blur Ferox leapt up and took each spear point in his massive flank. His momentum took him into two of the soldiers and his weight felled them both in a tangle of blood and spear shafts. Though one scrambled backwards to escape, his comrade remained pinned under the great war dog whose jaws were clamped firmly around his neck. Ferox gave a last shudder and lay still as the spreading pool of his blood began to blacken the earth.

In the wake of the dog's final, if futile service another warrior rushed forward to finish Inga with his axe. Having prepared herself for death several times over, she did not move but took a deep breath and looked her nemesis in the eye, for a quick death was all she desired now.

When he hesitated, she shouted: "Make it swift, or may Frigg haunt you in the afterlife."

With a sullen shake of the head he brought down the axe but Father Gobban, who had been knocked to the ground drove his broken staff up into the warrior's groin. The axe swing missed her completely as her assailant bent over double and released his weapon. Seizing the unexpected reprieve, Inga stabbed her knife into the side of his throat and left it there, protruding like a grossly misshapen item of neck jewellery.

To her astonishment, the blade struck no vital place and the warrior tried to rise up again. As she opened her mouth to deliver another withering threat of divine retribution, a spatha cut her opponent down. Bewildered, she looked about her to find scores of men driving away their assailants. Dozens of Vortigern's men were caught unawares and slaughtered there on the east bank of the Gwy and at once Inga sought Ambrosius, knowing that her salvation could only be his work.

She stumbled along the river bank, scanning the valley floor but when she saw him she stood in shock, for he and his bucellarii were still coming back across the river and they moved like corpses.

A hand found hers and she was suddenly wrapped in Wynflaed's embrace. "We're not dead," breathed her friend.

"I thought Ambrosius had saved us," murmured Inga, burying her head in Wynflaed's breast. "But… it was Frigg – as ever, it was Frigg."

In truth Inga knew that the goddess had been given a measure of help by Father Gobban and… poor Ferox. When she released Wynflaed and looked around again, she saw banners everywhere – some she remembered from Caer Ceri, but others she did not know at all.

In a daze she stared back towards the broken wagons where so many bodies lay, bloodied and still; but then smiled to see that Lugaid had survived the final onslaught - and Pascent too appeared almost unscathed amid the carnage. Father Gobban, for whom she had now to concede a grudging respect, was gathering several of the younger warriors together to tend to their wounds.

Suddenly a familiar figure stood before her, beaming and at last she understood who had saved them.

"Lady Inga," he said, "are you alright?"

With a weary shake of the head, she replied: "Alright, no; but I am alive."

"Alive will do," he said gravely, "for I fear most are not so fortunate."

"You came, Cadrullan," she said, "though you told Ambrosius you would not…"

He shrugged. "And I would not… could not, have come," he replied. "But I was persuaded by this man."

His companion stepped forward and said: "You can only be Inga, the Saxon."

"This is King Erbin of Dumnonia," announced Cadrullan. "And without him, you would most certainly all be dead."

Inga stared open-mouthed at the young king, about whom she had heard so much from Ambrosius and could not think what to say.

In the end all she could manage was: "Oh, Frigg, oh shit… he always said you'd come…"

29

Ambrosius, saw Erbin's banners flying as he trudged back across the river but cursed the king for leaving his arrival too late for, when he reached the bloodied ground by the wagons he thought no-one could possibly have survived. Though his eyes sought Inga, he prayed he would not find that beautiful body amid the ugly slaughter. Everywhere he looked, he wept to see the faces of those he had brought there to die.

When Inga cried out his name, he looked up to see her with Erbin and Cadrullan and thanked God for her deliverance. He stumbled over to her with every intention of sweeping her up into his arms, but he was so exhausted he almost dropped her and the pair tumbled to the ground at King Erbin's feet.

"More bruises," complained Inga.

"I thought you were lost," he murmured, burying his head in her blood-streaked fair hair.

"And I you," she said.

When they finally drew apart, there was blood on Inga's tunic.

"You're bleeding. Sit down there," she ordered.

"It's not so bad."

"I'll bind it up for you," she said.

In truth he was glad to sit, even though he knew it could only be for a moment. Cadrullan and Erbin squatted down beside him and Ambrosius regarded the latter with mixed emotions for though he had arrived late, his coming had undoubtedly saved Inga, Wynflaed and the others.

"Don't say it," warned Erbin, "because I have only to look at the river banks to see that I delayed too long. But… if you had only waited a little longer."

"There was no sign, or word of your coming," grumbled Ambrosius. "Every hour I waited, I lost more men; Vortigern would have destroyed us all in the forest."

"But you've defeated him now," said Cadrullan. "His power's destroyed."

With a bitter shake of the head, Ambrosius replied: "Aye, I've routed him – but at too great a cost – and he still lives, still has our hostages at his mercy and will be safe now inside his fortress."

"But you've crushed the High King's army - that's no small achievement," insisted Erbin. "And such deeds often require great sacrifice."

"I've always hated leaders who talk of sacrifice without partaking of it," said Ambrosius. "I brought people here to free their womenfolk, yet even all this bloodshed has not bought us their freedom."

"We'll start to see the dead taken care of," said King Erbin, getting up and taking Cadrullan with him.

Ambrosius gave a nod of acknowledgement, but his mind was elsewhere, remembering those who had fought and fallen. When he thought of Ulf, he glanced across at Wynflaed who was sitting on a patch of dry ground further from the river. One look told him that she knew husband's fate. No-one had informed her yet, but she knew; because, if Ulf was still alive he would have been there with her now. Words of comfort from others might help her healing later, but in the raw wake of death, nothing he said could make any difference.

"Ferox saved me again," Inga told him, as she started to bind his thigh with a strip torn from her tunic. "But this time it... killed him."

"Aye," he said, grateful once more for the beast's courage. The life of Ferox the dog was of little value compared to the life of a man or woman, but then a dog was never just a dog... Inga would surely take the loss of the brutal but faithful Ferox very hard.

"I fear I also owe a debt to the monk," she added, with a wry smile.

"Father Gobban," scoffed Ambrosius, in disbelief. "I thought he'd still be hiding under the wagon."

"Well, since the wagon was toppled over he had to move," explained Inga. "And, though I'd never have believed it, he fought well with his staff and... saved me at the end."

Ambrosius grinned, quietly pleased that he had found at least some reason to elevate his low opinion of the monk.

"If you keep tearing strips off your clothes," he observed, "you'll have nothing left to cover you."

It would be so easy, he thought just to sit with her and put aside all else. But to do so would be to dishonour those who would never again embrace their loved ones. He owed it to them to see the task through to the end and he could not let slip the advantage that had been won at so great a cost in blood. So, though he ached in body and spirit, he left others to grieve and went to find his captains.

Neither Arturus nor Rocca had received a wound worth mentioning so he ordered them to recruit a dozen or so fit men from Erbin or Cadrullan and scour the forested slopes to the north-west. He needed to ensure that none of Vortigern's men were hiding there in ambush. Since Pascent knew exactly where his father's fortress lay, Ambrosius told him to accompany them.

"I need to know how many men your father can still muster," he said. "And I need to know how strong his fortress is because, one way or another I need to get men into that place."

Pascent, perhaps accepting that his knowledge would be vital in what was to come, agreed without protest.

Having despatched them, Ambrosius turned his attention back to his tardy allies. If he was honest, even he had given up all hope of Dumnonian support so the intervention of Erbin and Cadrullan at the river crossing had taken him by surprise. But, as Cadrullan explained Erbin had only been a day behind Ambrosius at Caer Ceri where he found that Cadrullan, already sympathetic to the Roman's cause, needed very little persuasion to join him.

"We followed you as quickly as we could," declared Erbin. "I am only sorry we did not get here sooner."

"Well, you're here now," conceded Ambrosius. "But, let's be clear: Vortigern's army is all but destroyed, but he will believe that he only has to sit in his fortress and wait for us to leave. Now, I've no intention of doing that but I need to know that you are both in this fight to the bitter end."

"What do you want from us?" asked Erbin.

"Vortigern can't fight another pitched battle," replied Ambrosius. "But, even with your men I doubt we'll take his fortress by storm without more heavy losses. Your presence alone though might be enough to convince Vortigern that he can't win."

"Then we'll stay," agreed Erbin and offered his hand which Ambrosius clasped willingly.

"I have men scouting through the forest," said Ambrosius. "As soon as we know it's safe, we'll move everyone up closer to the fort. But first, we have heroes to bury and prayers to say for them."

Indeed there were many to bury – more, he suspected than his comrades ever imagined. He wondered whether Wynflaed, for example would have been so desperate to free her sister, if she had known from the outset that the price would be the life of her husband.

Ulf's death had shaken him too, especially since every last one of the Saxon warriors who had sworn oaths to him the previous winter had also perished. The Scotti too had been all but annihilated at the wagons for only two remained. Ambrosius had to accept that his sworn men would no longer be an alliance of Britons, Romans, Saxons and Scotti; because, for the most part only Britons were left now.

While the wounded were tended to, graves were dug on the higher ground across the river Gwy and the battered bodies were prepared for death. Some of the Saxons, according to Wynflaed would have preferred their bodies to be burned; but, in the circumstances she accepted that they must be buried. With a lover's care, she cleaned Ulf's wounds and then polished his bloodied sword and helm until they shone before placing them with him in his grave. The dead were buried with fine words and prayers, according to their faith and Ambrosius was grateful that a man of God – albeit a somewhat flawed one - was present to oversee the Christian burials.

For the rest of the day the mood in the camp remained solemn while the weary survivors took what rest they could. For Ambrosius, however, there was no respite and he went to each one of his own men to give them thanks for what they had done that day. Even to rescue Lurotriga, Ishild and the other women, he could never have justified such a terrible death toll. But their venture was not just about hostages, or even the mortal threat Vortigern posed to all those of Ambrosius' affinity; for Ambrosius was working upon a greater task.

Vortigern's corrupt rule only served to keep the different British tribes at each other's throats and, elsewhere in the empire Ambrosius had seen for himself the results of such weakness. Franks, Burgundians, Saxons and many others had encroached upon the empire's once impenetrable northern frontier and spilled into the fertile lands to the south. The Britons did not yet know it, but they would soon face the same incursions and, if they were still squabbling among themselves then the Saxons and others would sweep them aside. That was the struggle that Ambrosius was fighting and destroying the power of the High King was just the beginning. King Erbin and Cadrullan saw that, which is why they had joined Ambrosius.

In the evening the valley was illuminated by dozens of small camp fires and around one of them Ambrosius sat discussing his next move with King Erbin, Cadrullan and his most trusted bucellarii. It was late when Arturus and Pascent returned with the last of the scouts to report that

Vortigern's fleeing men had either melted away in the forest or followed their commander into his fort.

"It's high on the hilltop where there was once an ancient fort, Dux," explained Arturus.

"And it's shut up tight," added Pascent. "Though its ramparts are sparsely manned, you'll not take it by storm without losing half Erbin's men."

Since Erbin had far more armed men there beside the river Gwy than the other leaders, he could determine the outcome of their campaign if he wished. Yet Ambrosius sensed that, despite Erbin's undoubted rank the Dumnonian king was reluctant to take the lead in the destruction of Vortigern.

"So you could get us in," said Ambrosius.

"Perhaps," said Pascent. "There is a weakness, but my father is well aware of it and he'll have it closely guarded."

Ambrosius nodded. "I'm sure we'll think of something," he replied, because indeed he already had.

"He may have lost many men," Erbin pointed out, "but he's still dangerous."

"He's a wily opponent," advised Cadrullan. "And most untrustworthy."

For several long hours they argued about what could be done but eventually Ambrosius decided that the rolling discussion had gone on long enough; it was time to make decisions.

"We're agreed, I think," he began, "that we can't undertake a long siege of Vortigern's fort. Not only do we have little food, but I imagine that no-one amongst us is keen to be absent from our homelands for too long. So, whatever we decide must bring a swift end to this struggle."

"I don't see how we can though," argued Cadrullan. "The High King can't break out, but he can just sit up there in his fortress on his bony arse and wait for us to leave."

"And let's not forget he still has the hostages," said Pascent.

"I haven't forgotten," growled Ambrosius.

"He'll threaten to kill them," said Pascent. "If he hasn't already done so."

"No, I suspect they're still alive," said Erbin, "for once they're dead he has nothing left to bargain with."

"What could we trade for them anyway?" asked Pascent "All he'll want is his freedom – and if we give him that, we're all dead men."

"No, we can't let him go," protested Cadrullan. "He still has allies - and his reach is long."

"He's right," agreed Erbin. "If we release him, we'll have sacrificed many lives for nothing."

"I've no intention of letting him leave this place alive," declared Ambrosius. "He deserves no mercy."

"But how then can we release those hostages," asked Cadrullan simply.

There was an awkward silence before Inga spoke up for the first time: "Know this, Britons if you let your High King go free, I'll put two arrows in the devil before he's taken half a dozen steps from his gate – whatever you promise him."

Ambrosius closed his hand upon hers and felt the tension there for, as ever Inga spoke from the heart. She was no doubt remembering poor Lucidia and all the others who had perished because of Vortigern.

"Let me make it clear," he said. "I won't be leaving here without both the hostages and Vortigern's head."

Ambrosius had always known that, even if he defeated Vortigern the High King might retain the hostages, so this was not the first time he had given some thought to the matter.

"We have to talk to him," he said, "and, while we're talking we'll find a way to get a handful of our men into that fortress."

"It looks formidable enough to me," grumbled Cadrullan.

"Believe me," said Ambrosius, looking to Pascent, "every fortress has a weakness."

"I told Ambrosius earlier that there might be a way in," said Pascent.

"One other thing," said Ambrosius. "There's another snake to be reckoned with in this pit - my half-sister, Florina."

"She doesn't matter," said Erbin, "for surely a woman wouldn't go against the High King."

Ambrosius could barely suppress his bitter laugh. "My friends, this is a woman who has killed her own father and brother," replied Ambrosius. "I can assure you that she fears no-one and she will sacrifice anyone to save herself."

"So, where does all this leave us?" asked Erbin.

"First, we move up closer to the fort then we offer to talk to Vortigern," said Ambrosius. "And, while we discuss terms we prepare to destroy him."

Part Five: Fate

30

The rain began to fall in the early hours, steadily at first but torrential by dawn so that Ambrosius' weary soldiers were thoroughly and miserably soaked. Water pooled briefly around some of the freshly-covered graves before trickling down muddily towards the river. The low-lying ground by the riverside, already churned up by the fighting, fast became a quagmire which they were obliged to cross before they could move their camp up the slope closer to Vortigern's fort. Hoping the summer rain would pass quickly, Ambrosius waited all morning but by noon it seemed that the weather had set in for the day.

"God favours the High King," grumbled Erbin. "While we sit here rusting in our mail shirts, he and his men stay dry."

"There are places we could shelter," observed Pascent. "Several large caves on the higher ground – and they're not far from my father's fort."

"They're safe?" said Ambrosius.

"Safe enough," said Pascent.

"Very well," said Ambrosius. "The longer we stay here, the more it nurtures our enemy's hope. We need to press him hard; so, let's go up to the caves."

Although the lower slope was not especially steep and the woodland by no means dense, the ground itself was

253

treacherous and such slow going that they quickly decided to abandon the wagons by the river and walk the horses up. Once they reached the higher slopes, the tree cover was thicker and Pascent's men were able to find usable tracks to follow. But by the time they reached the caves, it was late afternoon and Ambrosius regretted the loss of a whole day – time which Vortigern would no doubt have used to strengthen his defences.

Though the caves provided some respite from the rain, now a persistent drizzle rather than a downpour, they could not accommodate even half of the men. Nevertheless, even those left outside were able to benefit from the generous leaf canopy that the trees provided.

Even before their camp was properly established, Ambrosius despatched Rocca and Cadrullan as envoys to Vortigern.

"Take half a dozen men and all our banners," he told them. "Offer him the chance to discuss terms of surrender."

The moment they left, he too set off with Pascent, Arturus and several of his bucellarii to discover for himself the nature of the trapped High King's eyrie. It took only minutes to ride the short distance from the caves to the base of the rugged slope upon which the fort stood.

"It's an ancient site – a relic of Rome's early attempts to seize this land," said Pascent with a look to Ambrosius.

"Don't blame me," said Ambrosius. "I wasn't around then."

"On its sunlit side," explained Pascent, "the fort stands on sheer cliffs while, where the sun sets it's protected by a high ridge of rock. Only on this flank, facing the rising sun is the slope less steep and thus, as you see there is a gate and a wooden rampart either side of it. So, even there, a frontal assault would be difficult and costly in lives."

"Aye, lives we can't afford to lose" agreed Ambrosius. "But you suggested there was another way in."

"At this end the rock barrier falls away into a steep valley," explained Pascent. "But, for a short distance the slope is not so steep; so to strengthen the defensive line there's a timber palisade."

"So that's our way in," said Ambrosius.

"Come and see," said Pascent.

"Is it far?" asked Ambrosius, for he had to admit that he was tired and the damp was making his leg wound ache. He was also aware that the light was failing and he still had much to do.

Pascent led them up into the valley where they could observe most of the timber rampart from the cover of trees.

"It looks strong enough," grumbled Ambrosius.

With a grin, Pascent replied: "It does, but in truth it's in a parlous state. My father last repaired it many years ago and he's rarely been here since. I know a place where a handful of men could force their way in unnoticed…"

"Then there's that great tower in the centre," said Ambrosius, pointing towards the fort's interior.

"That's in better condition," said Pascent, "and that'll be where he's holding your women."

Only a day ago, Ambrosius would have been wary of trusting a son of Vortigern; but Pascent, despite the divisions among his own men had risked all come to their aid and such a man demanded his trust.

"When we get back to the caves," said Ambrosius, "I want you to tell my bucellarii all you know about the fort – and that weak point. While we occupy Vortigern with negotiation, you'll prepare to take them into the fort."

"Me," said Pascent.

"No-one better," smiled Ambrosius.

When they returned to the camp, Ambrosius marvelled – as he always did - how the men had managed to light fires in such damp conditions. But seeing them huddled together, with the rain showing no sign of abating he knew that, if he delayed there too long their morale would be eroded swiftly.

Just before dusk, three riders approached the caves – peace envoys it appeared from Vortigern, for they were certainly no warriors and one wore the vestments of a priest. When they pulled up, they found Ambrosius, Pascent, Erbin and Cadrullan standing before them.

"Are you ready to discuss the High King's surrender?" enquired Ambrosius.

It was the priest who answered. "The High King orders King Erbin of Dumnonia to hand over the traitor, Ambrosius Aurelianus at dawn tomorrow and then leave his lands at once… on pain of death."

Erbin stepped forward. "I am King Erbin," he announced, "but I do not command here, priest. You must address your words to Lord Ambrosius."

The messengers exchanged a look of confusion. "But…" began the priest.

"Continue," growled Ambrosius.

This prompted a whispered discussion between the three men until finally the priest spoke out again. "The

High King orders the traitor, Ambrosius Aurelianus to surrender himself at dawn tomorrow."

"In return for what?" asked Ambrosius.

"For nothing," replied the priest, his tone sharp and impatient.

"Then my answer is no."

The priest, clearly expecting such a response offered a thin smile. "If you refuse then the High King will execute the hostages taken from your fort."

While the exchange was continuing, many of the men as well as Inga and Wynflaed had crept away from their campfires to hear what was being said.

"You approve of that, priest," said Ambrosius. "Executing women."

"You're a murdering renegade," declared the priest, "and Lord Vortigern does not negotiate with such men – nor should he."

"I thought negotiation was exactly what we were doing," replied Ambrosius.

"You must surrender at dawn and King Erbin must leave," announced the priest once more.

Ambrosius felt the tight grip of a hand on his arm. "No, do not go," whispered Inga. "He'll just kill you as well as all the women."

"I'll only surrender," Ambrosius told the priest, "if your turd of a master releases all the hostages."

Again it seemed that the priest was well prepared for a variety of outcomes, for he replied without the slightest hesitation. "The High King will consider that but only if King Erbin removes all his men to the east bank of the Gwy."

Ambrosius felt Inga's scarred fingers digging deeper into his arm. "No," she pleaded.

"Agreed," answered Ambrosius, "provided a dozen men can remain to protect the hostages once they're released."

"This is madness," gasped Inga.

"Be still," Ambrosius ordered her.

But even King Erbin enquired softly: "I trust you're certain this is how you want it to be, my friend."

In reply, Ambrosius looked the king in the eye and gave a solemn nod.

"God will decide…" muttered Father Gobban.

"No," said Ambrosius. "I will decide; and God will judge me for it…"

Turning back to the envoys, he said: "Priest, you have your answer. I'll be outside your gate at dawn; pray ensure that your master… understands the terms: King Erbin will withdraw his army; all hostages must be released unharmed to the dozen men waiting to escort them home. In return, I shall enter the fort."

"That is acceptable to the High King," confirmed the priest and, without another word he turned his mount around and rode away with his two companions into the gloom of the forest.

"That was foolish," Inga hissed at him.

"We'll talk about it later," Ambrosius told her. He was dismissing her and she knew it, but she was not ready to comply so easily.

"I want to talk now," she insisted, eyes fierce in the firelight.

"I have others I must speak to first," said Ambrosius. "Wynflaed, take her back to the cave and make sure she stays there."

Sending her away was made all the harder by the look of bitter resentment on her face. He hated doing it but he really did need to speak urgently with several others for he had very little time to flesh out a plan with his bucellarii. Thinking about the sworn men of whom he was about to ask yet another sacrifice brought a lump to his throat. He had left Italia with ten of them but now only five remained. Since he had left Onno at Vindocladia, there were just four to send out yet again to do his bidding and shed their blood for him. Those four deserved all his attention to give them the best possible chance of success... and survival. So, on this one occasion even Inga would have to wait a little.

§§§

It was much later when Ambrosius joined Inga in a dark corner of one of the larger caves. Wynflaed was with her but, when Ambrosius arrived the newly-widowed Saxon left to sleep elsewhere. When he lay down beside Inga and folded her in his arms, her whole body was stiff and unyielding. Even hours after he had sent her away, she was still angry with him and twisted away to avoid facing him.

"I had to make plans," he murmured, kissing the back of her neck.

"Aye - plans to get yourself killed," she retorted.

"Plans to finish this whole sorry tale, my love," he told her. "And with the least cost in lives that I can manage..."

"By sacrificing yourself," she said.

"It won't come to that."

259

"I know you, Ambrosius," she whispered. "You never go into anything without being prepared to die."

He sighed. "And that's how a soldier must enter every struggle," he said. "If I don't bring Vortigern down then we'll never have a life for ourselves – you and I will have no future."

"Do we have a future?" she asked him and he heard the words catch in her throat. "We both know that you're risking all to free Lurotriga. Perhaps your future lies with her – a British noblewoman that you could marry her in your precious Christ church…"

"But it's you I've sworn my life to," he insisted. "I owe a great debt to Lurotriga, but I love only you."

It was a lie, of course for he loved them both; but he had no intention of admitting that to Inga.

"I'm with child," she murmured.

For a moment he thought he had misheard her hesitant words. "Did you say…?"

"Aye."

"Then that is the best news I've heard for a very long time," he said, hugging her to him as she wept.

"I thought…"

"You thought I would abandon you to marry Lurotriga," he hissed.

"I had doubts… because, whatever you say I know you care deeply for her."

"I care what happens to her," he said, "but you and I will have children together – among them many sons, I'm sure of it."

She turned round to embrace him. "Yet you're about to put yourself at grave risk once again."

"Wynflaed has lost Ulf," he said, "but she never begged him not to fight…"

"She knows, as I do that wyrd made it so… and she is pleased for Ulf that he died the death of a great warrior."

"And thus it is for me," he told her. "If God decides that it is my day to die then I too will want to die with sword in hand."

"But Wynflaed and Ulf had years together," she protested. "We've had but a few short months…"

"Whether we have years, or just a few hours," he told her, "both your faith and mine decree that we shouldn't waste that time…"

31

It was still dark when Arturus clasped Ambrosius by the arm to bid him farewell, not knowing whether he would ever see his lord again. He felt a deep honour to be counted one of the eight men Ambrosius sent in to breach the fort. With him rode the four bucellarii, along with their guide, Pascent and the two surviving Scotti: Lugaid and his younger brother Donnan. Where Lugaid was tall and muscular, Donnan was small and agile; but Arturus knew nothing of the youth except what Inga had confided after the furious fight at the river. Donnan was eager to strike – too eager, she judged – but swift as a devil with his blade.

If all went to plan, just before dawn they would break through what Pascent assured them was a thoroughly rotten, timber stockade. After entering the camp, they would then stay out of sight until Ambrosius needed them. The moment Ambrosius set foot inside the gate the hidden warriors would rush out to join him. Between them, they would take control of the gateway to let in Cadrullan's escort which would give them a score of highly effective fighting men to capture the fort.

All depended, of course on Vortigern keeping his word to release the hostages. If he did not then it would be bloody and they might all perish there in the High King's stronghold. To be sure, it would make a grand and heroic story for telling around campfires, but Arturus doubted he would be alive to recount it.

As they rode slowly through the forest, alert to every sound Arturus' hand rested nervously upon the hilt of his spatha. It was a weapon he was using more and more, rather than the spear his father had trained him to wield. Over the winter months Varta had given him some lessons, though there would be no more of those now.

Arturus was still lingering in the past when Pascent came to an abrupt halt and they all dismounted – or, more accurately seven dismounted and Donnan fell to the ground with a loud thump. Though Lugaid chided him mercilessly, Arturus reckoned the young inexperienced rider had done well to stay on his horse for so long. His fall at least amused the others and served to break the tension amongst them.

"We leave the mounts here," whispered Pascent. "And keep quiet now for, up here a fart sounds clear as a hawk's cry."

"I'll be sure to listen out for that," said Lugaid, with a grin.

"Come, friends," urged Rocca. "We don't have long."

They followed Pascent in single file with Germanus, as ever at the front. The Burgundian though was not particularly well-suited to clandestine work, thought Arturus. Hacking a man to pieces with his great axe perhaps, but not creeping around in the half-light to evade discovery.

Following in Germanus' footsteps were Rocca, Caralla and the two Scotti with Arturus and Xallas at the end of the line. There were worse men to fight alongside, reflected Arturus but, of them all he most admired Xallas. It was not just the warrior's exceptional skill with any sort of blade, but his whole demeanour and especially his stoic acceptance of even the most hopeless situations. Aside from Ambrosius, Arturus had never encountered anyone as calm in battle as Xallas.

For a time the small group followed the gentle slope uphill in broken woodland while Arturus tried not to embarrass himself by tripping over some protruding root or stepping into a half-hidden burrow in the ground. When the trees thinned out almost to nothing, the incline grew ever steeper and their pace slowed appreciably. At one point Arturus stopped, thinking he heard the howl of a wolf.

"Did you hear that?" he whispered to Xallas. "I think it might be a wolf."

"Or a hawk farting," chuckled Lugaid.

"It was a wolf," confirmed the man from Baetica. "But what of it, lad?"

"Oh, just wondering," murmured Arturus.

"Well, wonder in silence," scolded Xallas.

Arturus nodded, feeling foolish. Though he was young, Dux had given him much responsibility and he had earned a little respect at least from his more experienced comrades. But sometimes, he still acted like the youngest...

The final climb to the fort was even steeper and they trod with great care, knowing how close they must be to the nearest of Vortigern's sentries. After another twenty yards or so, Pascent stopped to gather the rest around him.

"This will do," he told them, in a low voice. "It's far enough from the gate that no-one should notice us."

"I'll take my axe to the palisade," offered Germanus.

"No," replied Pascent. "You'll just make a noise. Some of the posts are so rotten we can just pull out a few to get in."

"As you wish," grumbled Germanus.

Rocca pointed to the eastern skyline now rimmed with light. "Dux will soon be at the gate."

Xallas nodded. "Time we went in."

"Let me go first," said Pascent and at once he slid away into the darkness while the rest waited with weapons drawn. Arturus heard nothing and was surprised when the Briton returned only a few moments later.

"That was fast," said Rocca.

Pascent grinned. "I said the timbers were rotten… but have a care because, if you fall over someone you'd better be ready to silence him at once."

Creeping through the gap created by Pascent, they began to search for places to hide themselves. To make concealment easier, they split into two bands with Arturus accompanying Xallas and the two Scotti. Though in the half-light his eyes could discern little, a noxious stench in his nostrils told him that the latrine was close by. Low voices sounded from across the open yard towards the tower; the fort was waking up.

Ahead of them was the dull red glow of a struggling camp fire and, behind its feeble light a dark shape loomed up which could only be the great wooden tower. Xallas was moving forward with more purpose, no doubt seeking an outhouse of some kind. Arturus soon made out a row of them to his right, lying hard against the rock barrier which protected the upper end of the fort. As a hiding place they might have been perfect except they were too far from the main gate where Dux would need his warriors.

Xallas carried on ahead past the tower and, as Arturus neared it he noticed several spluttering torches at its base.

The sight of the great edifice unsettled him a little for he suspected that his beloved Ishild must be in there somewhere. Once the thought occurred to him, he could not banish her image from his head. Thus, while Xallas continued on past the tower, Arturus lingered close to the entrance. For a few moments – perhaps even longer - he stood there feeling Ishild's presence… so close to him.

When he looked around, he could no longer see his comrades and, for an instant he knew blind panic. Then calming himself, he tried to remember Pascent's description of the fort's layout. Beside the tower lay several more outhouses but only a yard beyond it was the mortal drop of the dread cliff face. So, assuming that Xallas and his comrades had not hurled themselves over the nearby precipice, they must be in one of the lean-to sheds.

Arturus muttered a curse as he realised that, since dawn was already on its way he might now be spotted. He must carry on walking, he told himself as if he belonged there. Except that, when he reached the row of low huts he just stood like a fool, uncertain which one his friends had chosen. Just as the nearest door swung open to reveal Pascent beckoning him inside, a shout came from behind him.

"You!"

Arturus spun around to find he was facing a dishevelled fellow who, from his soiled apron had the look of a cook.

"Give me a hand to get this fire going," ordered the stranger, poking at the tired embers in what Arturus suspected was part of the fellow's daily ritual.

His delay in responding to such a simple request must have made Arturus look guilty for the cook regarded him with sudden suspicion. Arturus decided that stupidity might be his best defence.

"What shall I do then?" he said, speaking slowly.

"Christ's Holy Mother, another fool of a southerner," groaned the cook. "Help me fetch some more logs – if you can manage that."

Arturus dutifully followed him to the outhouses, one of which had a stack of logs piled against its wall.

"You take some logs while I…"

When the cook wrenched open the outhouse door, he no doubt expected to find the supplies he needed but instead he discovered three armed men crammed inside. Arturus reached for his spatha to club down the cook, but felt the point of a spear at his back.

32

Leaving Inga was never easy, but this time Ambrosius found it even harder knowing that, despite his assurances she still doubted him. He felt it in their tense parting embrace and saw her fears reflected in the eyes of Wynflaed too. There was a close bond between the young Saxon women, born of shared dangers and nurtured by love and loss. So Wynflaed's stern glare might as well have come from Inga herself.

Yet he could not dwell upon it for he had hostages to free and, one way or another a feud to settle with Vortigern. Cadrullan's men were waiting for him outside the cave and, by their stern demeanour he could tell that they were ready to meet whatever trouble might arise. His favourable impression of Cadrullan, when they first met at Caer Ceri had only been enhanced as he began to know the man better.

When they set off, he glanced back at Inga to savour his last glimpse of her with a bloodied band of cloth around her head. He saw a warrior who wore her battle scars with pride; yet she was not a soldier… but the mother of his children, which is why he insisted that she, Wynflaed and the monk awaited his return in the safety of the cave.

King Erbin had already set off, as agreed to lead the rest of the fighting men back across the river Gwy. Though Ambrosius regretted sending away his most formidable ally, he was determined to do whatever was necessary to persuade Vortigern to release the hostages. Until he did,

Ambrosius' hands were tied and any assault upon the fortress, though it might topple Vortigern would almost certainly condemn the captives to death. If the worst happened and the High King refused to free Lurotriga and the others then the outcome would rest upon the keen edge of a spatha... with all the uncertainties that would bring.

Looking over his shoulder to the east, Ambrosius slowed up a little until he saw dawn's light creeping across the slopes below the fort. Unlike his bucellarii, he did not need to conceal his approach and rode directly there with Cadrullan's company following a few yards behind him. When he arrived at the gate, he found it shut firmly against him and the rampart above and either side of it well-manned with spear men. They stood impassive as he halted below them to dismount.

As he expected, Vortigern kept him waiting for with proud overbearing rulers such fatuous tricks were commonplace. Nor was it the High King who appeared first upon the rampart above him, but the tall figure of his half-sister, Florina.

"Welcome, brother," she said, with a smile that carried all the warmth of a steel blade.

Yet her gaunt appearance belied her confident manner for she looked but a shadow of the woman he met the previous year in Gallia. How formidable she had seemed then; but now, scarcely six months later she was a shrivelled husk of a woman, embittered by failure. And, in that one stark moment, Ambrosius knew that negotiation would fail because he saw the truth in the cold eyes of his half-sister. Even if he made an agreement with Vortigern, she would never surrender and, if she were to fall the murderess would ensure that she took with her to the grave as many other souls as possible.

Since he made no reply to her and she said nothing more, both waited in stony silence for the High King to make the dramatic entrance he clearly coveted. But still Vortigern did not appear and, with every second of delay Ambrosius' feeling of unease grew until two soldiers stepped up to the rampart and tossed a bloody corpse over it. Shocked, Ambrosius bent down to examine the body and recognised at once a woman from the Vindocladia burgus. She was the widow of one who perished during Vortigern's night assault and now she must join her brave husband in the afterlife. Ambrosius silently added one more to the mounting tally of those he had failed to protect.

When he looked up, Florina's gleaming eyes told him that she had played some part in the grotesque demonstration of power. Vortigern at last strolled to the rampart and leaned upon the parapet to bask in the meagre dawn sunshine.

"You agreed to release the hostages," said Ambrosius, his words carved from ice.

"And I've released one," said Vortigern.

"Unharmed, was the agreement," replied Ambrosius, his gaze drawn back to the torn body at his feet.

"Other hostages will be released – unharmed - if you surrender yourself now," said Vortigern.

"That was not what was agreed…"

But Ambrosius faltered as another woman was brought up onto the rampart and stood shivering with fear beside Florina.

"If you release them-" began Ambrosius but he stopped, open-mouthed as Florina dragged a knife across the struggling woman's throat. Bright blood sprayed in a looping arc as the second woman's body tumbled over the rampart and came to rest beside her fellow captive.

"I agree," shouted Ambrosius, fighting to control his anger.

"Ambrosius," protested Cadrullan, but Ambrosius waved his objection aside.

Whilst he always considered it possible that he might have to enter the fort to persuade Vortigern to free the last few hostages, he had not expected such butchery. Clearly he had underestimated Vortigern's desperation, or the influence of his brutal half-sister.

"I want no more dead hostages," snarled Ambrosius, approaching the gate which had been opened for him.

Just inside Vortigern stood in silence waiting for Ambrosius to walk in, but for a few moments, he stopped in the gateway so that the gate could not be closed upon him. Now all would depend upon his bucellarii who would make haste to join him at the gate. But before any fighting broke out he needed to learn at the very least exactly where the remaining hostages were being held. So he stood there, on the fort's threshold and drew out his spatha – not in haste, but in a calm measured gesture.

"Unless I see the other prisoners alive – now - I'll leave," he declared. "If you kill another hostage then I shall return with King Erbin's army, which is just across the River Gwy and destroy this fortress with you inside."

It was not an empty threat and Vortigern knew it; if he pushed Ambrosius too far, King Erbin did have the power to annihilate him. Even at this late stage, negotiation still offered him something better than a bloody death. If the High King felt under any sort of duress, he did not show it; indeed he smiled as he waved an arm and pointed to the lofty wooden tower at the heart of his fortress.

"Bring them out!" he shouted.

There on a wooden platform atop the tower, Ambrosius saw the small group of women. By her stature and bearing, he picked out Lurotriga at once and prayed that his face did not betray the deluge of relief he felt. She was alive; they were alive. So he stepped inside the gateway, though he did not yet sheathe his spatha even when several of Vortigern's men approached him, with spears raised.

"Release them now," he entreated Vortigern. "You have me; you no longer need them."

But Vortigern looked away from Ambrosius and instead called to Cadrullan outside the gates.

"Your services are longer required," he told the Briton. "Go back to Caer Ceri while you can, for you'll not command there much longer."

Since Cadrullan had agreed beforehand that whatever happened he would remain, Ambrosius was not surprised when Cadrullan delivered a withering response.

"You have no power over Caer Ceri, old man. I'll just wait here until you release your captives which a man of honour must do. If you do not, then I'll see your entrails torn out by your own dogs…"

Though he welcomed Cadrullan's brave words, Ambrosius' mind was distracted by another concern entirely for, by now his bucellarii should have intervened. They should already have swept aside some of Vortigern's

272

soldiers and captured the gateway to allow Cadrullan's men inside. He had staked his life and those of the hostages upon his most loyal warriors but they had not come to his aid.

It was Vortigern who helped him to understand why.

"You look disappointed," he told Ambrosius. "Perhaps you were expecting a little more... help to arrive."

Ambrosius made no reply but his worried eyes scoured the enclosure for any sign of his bucellarii.

"I fear that your four comrades have been detained," said Vortigern, enjoying his moment of triumph.

But the High King's words did not have quite the devastating effect he intended for that one word: 'four' gave Ambrosius a flicker of hope, because it meant that Vortigern had captured only half of those he sent into the fort. Even so, it was another blow because, though the main task of the bucellarii was to seize the gate, Ambrosius had made it clear that, if the hostages had not been released then half his men should attempt a rescue. But now, if only one half of the breaching party remained they would have to decide whether to help Ambrosius, or to free the hostages.

While Ambrosius was considering what to do next, he noticed Florina speak in a low voice to Vortigern. The latter glanced across at Ambrosius before giving her a curt nod. At once Florina hurried down from the rampart and set off towards the tower with half a dozen of Vortigern's soldiers in her wake. Ambrosius, chilled by Florina's grim expression feared for the hostages but he was powerless to stop her.

"Surrender your spatha, Roman," ordered Vortigern, "or the women will die while you watch."

33

After watching Ambrosius and Cadrullan ride away, Inga remained outside the cave entrance for some time. Only when a ribbon of pearl trimmed the eastern sky, did she exchange a knowing look with Wynflaed and stand up.

"We're going for a short ride," she told Father Gobban.

"A ride," said the startled monk. "But there are enemies all around us."

"I'm feeling queasy," said Wynflaed, "with the child and I think a short ride will… settle me." She rubbed her hand over her belly, allowing it to linger between her legs until the monk darted his eyes away.

"And she can't go alone," added Inga.

Had the distracted Father Gobban remembered how much Wynflaed disliked sitting on the back of a horse, he might have challenged the women a little more. But, with a sigh he nodded sagely as if drawing upon his wide experience of women carrying a child and made no protest.

"Don't stray too far from the cave though," he warned. "And keep well way from the fort."

"Of course," replied Inga, fighting back the urge to grin as the pair slipped away to their horses which were saddled in case a swift departure was needed.

It was Wynflaed's suggestion to go to the fort and, at first Inga tried to deter her friend, because putting them both in harm's way seemed only likely to make Ambrosius' task even more difficult. Wynflaed, however, was

275

determined that, having lost her husband she would not lose her sister as well.

"Tell me this," she said to Inga, "Do you trust Vortigern to simply hand over the hostages?"

To that, there was only one response Inga could possibly give. Besides if Wynflaed thought she could save Ishild, she would go with or without Inga. Her friend also mentioned in passing that, if Inga was there when the hostages were released then she could witness for herself exactly how fondly Ambrosius greeted Lurotriga. So, though she had no idea what they would do when they reached the fort, Inga agreed. And, since it would be folly to enter the wolf's lair unarmed, she took her bow and the few salvaged arrows she had with her.

The pair made slow progress through the forest, partly because neither was an accomplished rider but also because they were attempting to follow the tracks left earlier by the bucellarii. It was thus almost dawn when they traversed the lightly-forested slope to the northwest and came upon the tethered horses left by their comrades.

"It can't be far now," said Inga, as she dismounted – as clumsily as ever. "But it's already near dawn and I hear no sound of fighting."

"Perhaps that's good," said Wynflaed.

"Or we've come too late," murmured Inga, her face a mask of concern.

"They should be releasing the hostages now," said Wynflaed.

With a shrug, Inga shouldered her bow and arrow bag and they set off after the bucellarii whose footprints were easy enough to see after all the rain. As they climbed to the higher ground, an earth bank obscured the fort's rampart and gate from view so they were obliged to scramble up it to see what was happening. Outside the gate, they saw no sign of either Ambrosius or the hostages, though Cadrullan was still waiting outside with his dozen horsemen.

Wynflaed suddenly gasped and pressed her hand hard upon Inga's arm.

Staring at the two bloodied corpses on the ground beneath the rampart, Inga whispered: "I see them…"

"One of them could be Ishild," groaned Wynflaed.

"We can do nothing here," said Inga, pulling Wynflaed back down the bank.

For a moment they sat, bewildered on the damp ground at the bottom of the bank.

"If the hostages have been killed… and yet Ambrosius has gone in," muttered Inga, unwilling to contemplate what that meant.

"What can we do?" cried Wynflaed.

The two weeping friends embraced because, for each of them their darkest fears had just been raked over and exposed to the dawn light.

"We have to get in there," said Inga abruptly.

"Aye," agreed Wynflaed. "For good or ill, we have to know what's happened."

So they set off along the incline in search of the damaged section of palisade where their comrades had broken through. But, even when they found the breach they hesitated and squatted out of sight to stare blankly at the ripped out timbers. Somehow, entering the fort seemed an irrevocable step and in the brightening dawn they were almost certain to be discovered.

With a sigh, Inga leaned forward to peer through the gap and stare across at the high wooden tower on the far side of the fort. She could see no guards but nor could she see what was happening at the gate, so she stepped through the palisade and crawled across the open ground for several yards on hands and knees.

The moment she saw the gateway, her hand flew to her mouth for Ambrosius there, with his sword drawn but utterly alone.

"They're going to kill him," she murmured. "His comrades are supposed to be there…"

Wynflaed, having followed her in, lay down on the muddy ground beside her. "We can't go down there, my friend," she warned. "Don't even think of it; we'd just become hostages too, or worse - and we both have another reason to live…"

"But-"

"Look at the tower," said Wynflaed. "See, at the top – the hostages are there..."

And she saw that Wynflaed was right: they were there, being herded together like animals by several armed guards.

"We can't risk going to the gate, but we could try to get to the women," said Wynflaed.

"But Ambrosius-"

"Look at him," hissed Wynflaed, gripping her friend's hand. "He's trapped and you can't help him, Inga. He can't free the hostages but perhaps we can. We're so close, and I'm not leaving Ishild again..."

Inga was still contemplating whether she could take out several of the spear men at the gate when Wynflaed abruptly got up and ran towards the tower, keeping low.

"Frigg's heart," growled Inga, for now she must abandon either her friend or her doomed lover. Muttering Saxon oaths under her breath, she begged Frigg to keep her hidden from sight as she scurried across the stretch of open ground to join Wynflaed about halfway to the tower.

"What now?" gasped the breathless Inga, as she flung herself down flat behind a low stone wall which bordered the small courtyard around the tower.

"We go in," replied Wynflaed.

Steeling herself to carry on, Inga followed her companion over the wall and the pair crept to the tower. Hugging the great timbers at its base, they scanned the enclosure for any soldiers and found two standing by a row of storehouses about thirty feet away. If the two Saxons moved too much they might catch the guards' attention, thought Inga.

Glancing down to the gate, she was surprised to find Florina and a clutch of soldiers stalking towards the tower.

"That Roman bitch is coming," she snarled.

"Then we have to get to the hostages before she does," urged Wynflaed, "But the two soldiers will surely see us."

"There must be a few women in the fort," said Inga. "If we just walk in as if we're supposed to be there... Just pretend you're a-"

"-Whore, I suppose," groaned Wynflaed.

"Florina's on her way," argued Inga, unsheathing her knife. "We can't stay here."

Wynflaed nodded and they set off at once around the back of the tower to find its entrance. Only one guard was posted there but he looked so astonished to see the two women that Inga decided that perhaps there were no whores at the fort after all. It mattered little because, before he could raise his spear in protest Inga grasped him by the hand and pulled him through the doorway.

"I haven't seen you two before," he said.

"Nor ever again, woman killer," replied Wynflaed, plunging her blade into his throat.

As Inga let the body slump to the floor, she hissed: "We could have just knocked him out..."

"Come on," urged Wynflaed, already on her way up the wooden stair. "He and his fellows killed at least two of the hostages – and Ulf," snapped her friend. "Don't waste your pity upon them."

Though they hurried up the first two flights of steps, both women soon began to flag and were obliged to stop and catch their breath.

"So many landings," gasped Inga.

"There must be five, or six; but it doesn't matter how many because… we can't stay here," wheezed Wynflaed.

Her friend's concern was swiftly confirmed when they heard the strident and all too familiar voice of Florina announcing her arrival at the tower. In moments she would have found the dead guard and would be climbing the stair with only retribution on her mind. The two Saxons prepared to continue their climb when the rhythmic thud of descending boots sounded above them.

34

"Lugaid," murmured Arturus, "can you smash the door timbers?"

"Aye, if I could get to them," replied the Scot.

Arturus could see that Lugaid was pressed hard against the rear of the shed which was solid rock. Had their positions been reversed, the powerful Scot might have prised the timbers apart with sheer brute strength but, as it was the four men were crammed so tightly that no-one could move.

It was unthinkable that they had been trapped in the tiny shed so easily by just a few soldiers with spears – and Arturus knew it was entirely his fault. They could see nothing outside their prison and heard very little.

"We have to do something," said Xallas, "I've never let Dux down before and I'm not going to now."

Cries of alarm sounded suddenly outside and, next moment the door was flung open to reveal the grinning face of Germanus.

"We saw you fools being taken," he scoffed. "We'll go to Dux; you get the hostages - they're in the tower." And with those few terse words, the Burgundian was off.

Arturus scrambled out in time to see him follow Pascent, Caralla and Rocca down towards the gate. But Arturus' eye was soon drawn to the rear of the tower where a group of Vortigern's soldiers, led by the Lady Florina was approaching the entrance. Quickly she cajoled them inside and Arturus realised that they must be going for the hostages.

A mere six months earlier he had been so grateful to Florina for rescuing him in the blood-soaked ruins of his home town in Gallia. He thought her an angel then but soon he came to know her as a she-devil whose cruelty knew no bounds. The very last place he wanted to see Florina was anywhere near his Ishild. Consumed by fear for the beautiful Saxon, he paused only long enough to retrieve his weapons from where they were piled outside the store before hurrying to the tower.

Legs still stiff from his cramped confinement, he hobbled the first few steps but it took only a few moments for him to reach the door. Just inside the entrance one of Vortigern's guards lay dead, which was a mystery to Arturus for Florina's men would have no reason to kill their own comrade. Despite the glow from a large brazier illuminating the foot of the stair, his eyes were slow to adjust to the gloomy interior.

Though he heard his comrades pounding across to the tower after him, he dared not wait for them but set off up the stair in pursuit. Perhaps her soldiers heard him crashing up for, on the first landing several men waited to lunge their spears at him.

The shocked Arturus hesitated but Xallas, coming up behind him did not. At once he thrust his spear up at their adversaries, but only when Lugaid intervened with his fearsome spiked club did their opponents begin to concede a step or two. While Lugaid bludgeoned aside one soldier and forced back another, Arturus and the agile Donnan darted past them and on up the steps. The youths left the older men to finish their bloody work but, at the next landing three more men awaited them.

Donnan hurled himself at them with a fierce Scotti yell but the reach of the spears was far greater than his long knife. The brave Scot was stabbed under the arm and sent tumbling back down the steps, where Arturus picked him up and took his arm to drag him back.

"You alright?" asked Arturus, as he retreated back down the steps with an arm round his comrade.

"Small scratch," grunted Donnan, with a wince that told a different tale.

When Lugaid saw them, he berated his brother: "You should be more careful – for I taught you better."

"We have to get up there," insisted Arturus. "We have to at least try... Xallas, you know what evil Florina can do."

With a heavy sigh, Xallas gave a reluctant nod and the anxious Arturus led the way back up the stair, expecting an attack at any moment. At each turn of the stair there was a small landing with a tiny chamber off it; so they were forced to stop and search there lest someone lurked in ambush. Some were empty, others contained only a bench, and two, a privy - for below them was the sheer cliff face which marked the southern flank of the fortress.

"God's breath, surely we're at the top now," gasped Lugaid. "I've lost track."

"Only the fourth stage," guessed Arturus, for he too had no idea.

On the next landing they were faced by more of Florina's men and, with Donnan wounded the brunt of the fighting was borne by Arturus and Lugaid, supported by timely spear thrusts from Xallas.

"There's too many of them," cried Xallas, as he narrowly evaded the point of a spear.

Even Arturus had to concede that they could not break through the determined wedge of warriors above them. Though he hacked with increasing rage at the forest of spears and Lugaid turned all his brutal fury upon them, the bucellarii could not prevail. With so many blocking their path, Arturus could not see how they could free the hostages without more help. His mind ran wild as he imagined what was happening to Ishild and the others held captive only a few feet above him.

A sudden roar from Lugaid dragged his attention back to the fight for Vortigern's men were on the offensive and descending the steps, urged on by Florina. With Lugaid bleeding from more than one spear thrust, all Xallas, Donnan and Arturus could do was try to protect the Scot from further harm as slowly, but inexorably they were driven back down the steps to the landing below.

Only then was Arturus forced to accept that, not only was Ishild beyond his help but his own life and those of his comrades were in the greatest peril too. While Donnan and Lugaid supported each other, Arturus and Xallas fended off the lunging spears of their pursuers as they were harried back all the way down to the ground floor.

At the foot of the steps Xallas bundled the two Scotti towards the entrance, while Arturus wielded his spatha with all the skill that Varta had attempted to drum into him over those chill winter months. As he held back two men he felt as if the great Frankish warrior was with him guiding his sword arm but, of course he was not. And no-one else was coming to help either; it was all up to him.

By the dim light of the brazier, he spied beside the stair a stack of sharpened timber stakes – perhaps once intended to repair the rotting perimeter rampart. In desperation he seized one of them and hurled it as hard as he could at the men above him on the steps. It flew all of two yards and then rolled back down to land at his feet. His feeble attempt provoked only mirth among his opponents for all he had done was reveal to them his weakness. Thus encouraged, they began to crowd in close towards him at the foot of the steps.

Lugaid must have observed his young comrade's desperation for, shrugging off Xallas' supporting arm he lurched across to pick up the timber post. Its weight must have been nothing to the giant Scot and he tossed it with the utmost venom at the nearest of the descending soldiers. Striking him on the chin, it knocked him down senseless and prompted his fellows to fall back a little.

With a groan, Lugaid lifted another stake and stabbed it up at the tight knot of men. It caught the knee of one whose leg buckled under him and sent him reeling down to land at Arturus' feet. The youth, in no mood to grant any quarter plunged his sword into the prostrate man's throat. Even so, in his anger Arturus almost missed his aim and ended up chopping through the side of his victim's neck; but the ugly outcome was the same.

When Lugaid tossed yet another piece of timber up the steps, the Britons were persuaded to retreat out of range. After that though, the Scot sank to his knees and Arturus saw the blood seeping from a raw wound beneath the tall man's ribs. Their only choice was to withdraw and pray that perhaps he and Xallas could defend the tower entrance more effectively than they could the stairs.

Staggering to help up the burly Lugaid, he caught the nearby brazier with his foot, tipping it over to scatter fiery coals over the rush-covered floor. Since the floor was damp, Arturus knew the coals would only smoulder a little but the rising smoke would act as perfect cover for him to escape to the doorway with Lugaid. When it then began to drift helpfully up the stair, the sound of men coughing gave Arturus a small dose of unexpected cheer.

Xallas clapped him on the shoulder. "Good lad," he said. "Now watch that doorway, while I bind up our Scotti friends. We're not done here yet."

Arturus grimaced as smoke began to emerge from the entrance, stinging his eyes. But a moment later his thoughts turned again to the love of his young life, stranded at the top of the tower. He was still thinking of her when a spear point lunged out of the entrance missing him by a hair's breadth. Angrily seizing the shaft with his left hand, he pulled on it so hard that its bearer was hauled out onto the point of his spatha. Though he despatched the man easily, he knew he had been lucky. In the swirling smoke he could not see his opponents coming and getting himself carelessly gutted by a spear would not help Ishild.

"Xallas!" he cried and, when his comrade finished binding up wounds he came to assist Arturus who was prodding the smoke-filled entrance with his newly-acquired spear. An occasional cry or grunt suggested he might have inflicted some sort of wound, but he was not foolish enough to think that he could hold out there for very long –

especially since his adversaries would be desperate to get some respite from the smoke.

"I thought it would have cleared by now," he told Xallas. "And Ishild's still in there..."

"Aye, and the others too," chided Xallas. "But we need more men, Arturus."

"There are no more men," retorted Arturus.

Xallas took his young comrade's arm. "If Dux takes the gate and can crush Vortigern-"

"If," cried Arturus. "If will get our women killed – and I don't think Florina intends to wait to find out whether Vortigern overcomes Ambrosius." For an instant he fell silent and stared at the smoke-filled doorway.

"Perhaps," he murmured, "in the confusion... perhaps one man... perhaps I could get up there."

"Not a chance," cautioned Xallas.

Arturus handed Xallas his spear. "I'll just take a look," he said and, drawing out his spatha he dashed into the murky interior of the tower.

35

On the third floor landing Inga and Wynflaed stopped, breathless and turned their anxious eyes upward to face whoever was coming down from the floor above. It was a lone soldier who appeared at the top of the next flight of steps and, seeing the two women came to a faltering halt.

"Who are you two then?" he enquired, giving them a crafty grin.

It was a look Inga knew all too well – the look men reserved for a girl they hoped might bestow on them more than just a fleeting smile. Inga, desperate to prevent him from calling out a warning, decided to play upon his hopes.

"We're here for you brave fellows," she said, employing the sultry voice she had perfected during her time in the Veronese brothel. It was a long time ago – though, she lamented not yet long enough.

"Why you carrying that bow then?" he asked, descending a few more steps.

A fair question, thought Inga as she struggled to think of an answer.

"It makes men look at her," Wynflaed blurted out.

Giving silent thanks to Frigg for her friend's inspiration, Inga moved up closer to the guard and, with skilful fingers began to stroke his thigh. When her efforts elicited a murmur of appreciation, Inga opened her blue eyes wide and the soldier fell right into them. Already regretting what she was about to do, she could only console herself that he was one of those holding her friends captive.

When she drove her knife hard up under his chin, blood bubbled out of the wound and dribbled down her hand onto her arm. Her victim gave no cry – indeed made no sound at all, aside from a miserable gurgling. Next moment Wynflaed stabbed him twice in the side, before Inga gently lowered the dying soldier onto the timber landing where his blood pooled briefly before trickling onto the step below.

"You can't kill a man more than once, Wynflaed," muttered Inga.

"Pity," grumbled her friend, before sheathing her bloodied blade with no trace of remorse.

Inga supposed that losing the one you loved changed you utterly; but she had no time to dwell upon their grisly deed for she could hear that Florina's escort had reached the landing just below them. The two Saxons hastened to climb the stair, hoping the corpse they left behind might encourage their pursuers to ascend with more caution.

A flood of sunlight on the stair above warned them that they were approaching the highest part of the tower. Creeping up the last flight of the stairs, they saw that two more steps would take them into the rooftop chamber. There they stopped to clasp hands briefly before Wynflaed drew out her knife once more and Inga, taking long, slow breaths put an arrow to her bow.

She was shaking for, without any idea how many guards would be in the chamber they would have only moments to subdue them before Florina arrived. Moving with all the stealth they could muster, they crossed the threshold onto the rooftop platform and found half a dozen hostages guarded by two soldiers, one of whom was soon staring, bewildered at Inga's arrow which had driven clean through his mail shirt.

His comrade, recovering quickly from his shock charged at Inga and his spear point might have found her breast, had Ishild not stretched out a foot to bring him down. Before he could get up, Wynflaed struck him hard with her knife. In her fury of wild, stabbing blows one, despite his struggling eventually pierced his throat and cut short his cries.

For a moment there was stunned silence among the hostages who included not only Ishild and Lurotriga, but two older women and a pair of young girls. Ishild looked in silent wonder at her sister, Wynflaed while Inga and Lurotriga shared a cool stare. Then, like a wall tumbling down, the captives ran to embrace their rescuers amid tears of relief and joy.

Lurotriga, though she nodded her thanks to the Saxon pair, said: "We're not free yet though."

"No," agreed Wynflaed. "And our cries of relief will bring Florina up all the faster…"

"Florina," growled Ishild.

"I hear them," said Inga, turning to face the steps. "Arm yourselves."

"Share out the soldiers' weapons," ordered Wynflaed.

With an arrow at her bow, Inga remained in the doorway and the instant the first soldier appeared at the bottom of the steps, she let fly. The arrow shaft flung him back against the timber wall, where he remained nailed like some prized hunting trophy.

As Inga hoped, the footsteps on the stair below came to an abrupt halt. When faced by a lone archer, caution was the best defence. So Florina would wait – but not for long – because soon she would send all her men at once, knowing the archer could kill only one.

"We can hold out," declared Ishild, as if daring anyone to argue.

Wynflaed gave her sister a grim smile. "We can try…" she conceded, but then glancing at Inga's bag, she asked: "How many more arrows do you have?"

"Six I think," replied Inga, "but I'll only get the chance to shoot one more."

Ishild retrieved one of the fallen spears but when Lurotriga picked up the other, Inga remarked: "That'll be a little heavy for you."

"I'll manage," replied Lurotriga, meeting the Saxon's scowl with a sardonic smile. The very air between the two seemed to crackle with jealous fire.

"Let her keep it," chided Ishild. "She's earned it."

Wynflaed laid a warning hand upon her friend's shoulder. "This is not the time for you two to be raking out each other's eyes," she murmured. "If we don't fight as one, they'll kill us all."

"They will anyway…" muttered Inga.

Though the stair was not broad, Inga did not believe that a brace of spears wielded by novices could possibly keep out the soldiers for more than a heartbeat. Yet, Ishild's fearless presence always gave her a little hope and besides, there were worse ways to go to Frigg…

Bow at the ready, Inga remained on the top step with Ishild and Lurotriga crouching just below her with spears braced against the stair. Lurotriga was so close to her that it would have been easy, thought Inga to slice her knife across the Briton's throat. While they waited, the shrill voice of Florina castigated her soldiers on the floor below until at last four soldiers shuffled into view at the bottom of the steps. One man stood in front, holding his great round shield out before him.

Having flung down the challenge, they waited for Inga to react but she knew that the moment she let fly, they would take the arrow on the shield and then rush the women. So she too waited, feeling the tension build as she considered where best to aim her shaft.

A sudden impatient shout from Florina startled Inga into despatching the arrow. Though the Hun bow was possible for a woman to draw, it was still powerful and, since the range was so short her arrow passed clean through the wood and leather of the shield, and struck the shield bearer's arm. His vain attempts to break the shaft and free himself caused him to drag the shield sideways and prevent his comrades from surging up the steps. Inga thus had time for a second arrow which caught one of the other soldiers in the shoulder.

"Chew on those," she screamed down at them. "Because I have many more left!"

With two of their number wounded, they retreated back out of sight and the women gave a gasp of relief. But it was short-lived for moments later, two more men appeared with shields raised and thundered up the steps towards them. Though Inga sent another shaft at them, it did not stop them and she backed away into the chamber with the other women.

36

Almost surrounded by spear men, Ambrosius was fighting for his life. He had but one simple thought: get to the gate and lift the heavy bar; but keeping Vortigern's spear men at bay required every last scrap of his attention. When he heard the warrior shouts from Rocca, Germanus and the others his spirits soared for, with his bucellarii beside him all things were still possible. Though there were only four of them, they immediately battered aside several of Vortigern's men.

"I fear the others are taken, Rocca," said Ambrosius, as he grasped his comrade's arm.

"Not any more, Dux," Rocca told him. "They've gone after the hostages."

While that was welcome news, Ambrosius knew that if he could not open the gate to let in Cadrullan's men then they were all doomed. And just now the way to the gate was blocked by a determined clutch of men, whose defence was so fierce that the bucellarii were being slowly driven even further from their goal.

"We need that damned gate open," declared Ambrosius.

"I think these bastards know that," said Rocca, grunting with satisfaction as he snapped a spear shaft with his spatha.

"Come on!" bellowed Ambrosius, taking a pace back towards the gate.

Rocca matched his stride and slammed his shield into an opponent's face. Gradually the five men, moving like a giant five-legged crab, crawled ever closer to the gate. More bodies pressed in upon them as Vortigern exhorted his soldiers to greater efforts for the High King knew that he could end all his troubles there at a stroke. Spear points punched at their shields while others thrust low seeking to slice into their legs. Only the grim, battle-hardened power of Ambrosius and Rocca enabled the tight formation to carve a slow and bloody path towards its objective.

"Germanus!" cried Ambrosius. "We'll clear the gatekeepers; you raise that bar – or, if you must hack the bastard timber apart with your axe!"

While Germanus shifted his position to come up on his right hand, Ambrosius swept his great spatha blade across the three opponents that faced them. Then, ramming the edge of his shield at one, he turned him enough to thrust the spatha into an exposed side. Germanus' axe split the shield of another and sent it clattering to the ground. Ambrosius slashed again and their adversaries fell back a yard to avoid the ranging sword blade.

One more time, Ambrosius told himself; one more time and they would be at the gate. And they might have been had not Pascent, behind Ambrosius taken a spear thrust in the calf which forced his companions to stop and rally around him. For an instant though, Germanus was within striking distance of the gate and smashed his axe down upon the bar. But, though the timber shaft was damaged it held and a fresh surge forward by Vortigern's men forced the bucellarii back once again.

With a curse of frustration Ambrosius saw that, if they did not breach the gate soon they would all, one by one succumb to a wound like Pascent's. The longer they remained huddled about their fallen comrade, the more likely it was they would die there with him. Though he never liked to divide his men – especially such a tiny group - he decided it was their only hope.

"Rocca, Caralla," he ordered, "stay with Pascent."

Then he rapped Germanus on the arm and together they broke out of the protective ring and surged towards the gate. It was about keeping going, he told himself – if you don't stop, you can't die. Cracking his iron shield boss into one man after another, his spatha never ceased its stabbing and chopping at his adversaries. His shield arm ached so much; he feared it might soon be torn off. Indeed Germanus abandoned his shield altogether and used both arms to cleave his great axe onto helms and through shields until the line before them simply disintegrated.

The ferocious pair, bruised, cut and bloodied, stepped over several squirming bodies to reach the gate where Germanus brought his heavy weapon down once again upon the bar. This time the timber split apart and the gates fell open. In an instant, willing hands from outside forced them wider and the two weary warriors turned to face Vortigern's men with Cadrullan's fresh men at their backs.

A glance across at the three comrades he had abandoned confirmed that they were paying the price for his success. He winced when he saw Pascent fall and then Caralla drop down to one knee with his shield over the pair of them. They were surrounded now with savage spears thrusting in at them from all sides. One of their assailants was wielding an axe and when, with successive blows he smashed Caralla's shield into several pieces, a bloody end seemed inevitable.

Even as Ambrosius, bolstered by his new allies fought his way towards the beleaguered trio, an axe struck Caralla a glancing blow on the helm. As the axe-bearer raised his weapon for a mortal blow, Rocca managed to stab at his thigh with a thrust of his spatha. Distracted for a moment, their assailant hesitated but then, seeing his wound appeared slight he lifted his axe again. He did not even notice Ambrosius until the Roman's savage spatha blade bit clean through his mail shirt to sever his shoulder joint. The deadly axe dropped from his trembling fingers as he cried out and crumpled to the ground. By then, Cadrullan's men were pushing forward to surround Ambrosius' wounded comrades.

Vortigern's warriors, who had fought well yet lost many comrades, were compelled to fall back. Indeed Ambrosius recognized that both sides needed a little respite. Though he was exhausted, his aim had not changed – could not change: he must defeat and kill Vortigern. Yet, with the fate of the hostages far from certain and Florina now at the tower, Vortigern's death might actually provoke his sister to further butchery. Ambrosius' thoughts became clouded by the idea that he might yet need to keep the High King alive.

First though, he had to overcome the enemy soldiers and, from their stern resistance thus far, he reckoned that alone would be far from easy. It had been a vain hope that, seeing the ranks of their enemy swell Vortigern's soldiers might just throw down their arms. It would hardly be the first time men deserted their lord – indeed, exactly that had happened the last time he fought Vortigern. But it would not be repeated this time, he decided. They might have retreated several yards towards the tower, but he could discern no trace of hesitation or uncertainty among them. These men were almost certainly Vortigern's royal guard - his finest warriors. Like his own bucellarii they would be oath-sworn to fight and, if necessary die beside their king.

When Cadrullan appeared beside him, Ambrosius clasped his hand in greeting.

"I wasn't sure whether I should try to get in through the north rampart where Pascent and the others did," said Cadrullan. "But then I thought how you might feel if you shed much blood to open the gate only to find me gone."

"A tough decision," agreed Ambrosius, "but I thank God you chose to stay. Now we have to get into that tower before my hellcat half-sister slaughters all the damned hostages."

"Simplest way: just charge them and break through their shields," suggested Cadrullan.

But Ambrosius was worried that, even with Cadrullan's men they were still outnumbered by about two to one. He doubted Vortigern's men would break and feared that his own men might be scattered in the charge and hacked to pieces one by one. So, despite the aching need for haste, Ambrosius replied with a shake of the head.

"Send a man to fetch King Erbin," he told Cadrullan. "We may yet need his help."

"Already done," said Cadrullan, "but I doubt Erbin will get back here in time."

"Only God knows," grumbled Ambrosius, aware that Vortigern's men were making ready to move against them once again. Their formidable-looking opponents clashed their weapons against their shields as they roared the accusation: 'Traitors!' They were still chanting as they began to advance and Ambrosius knew that such determined men who could only be beaten if their warrior spirit was broken. If he could stand toe to toe with them, shield against shield Ambrosius believed he might just do that – if only he possessed the time and the men to do it.

Already Pascent and the formidable Caralla were out of the fight, propped up against the rampart as they attempted to bind up each other's wounds. The rest of his small force formed a tight wall of shields, with Germanus and Rocca posted at either end. And Ambrosius, eyes fixed upon the advancing enemy, drew out his spatha once again and joined Cadrullan in the centre of the front rank. Men needed to see their leaders in the bloodiest, most dangerous place on the field; for only there could the enemy's will to fight be destroyed.

For a few moments Ambrosius watched Vortigern's soldiers run towards him then he lifted his shield higher and surrendered his soul into God's hands.

37

When Arturus dashed into the tower's smoke-filled interior, an apposite gobbet of advice leapt into his head: 'You move fast, youth," Varta had told him. "But so you should, else you'll be dog's meat.'

All winter, under Varta's guidance Arturus had laboured to practise swift, nimble movement and greater precision with his blade. Thus, from the moment he entered the tower he employed the one advantage he possessed in abundance: speed. In the stairwell he might as well have been fighting with his eyes shut - eyes streaming with tears induced by the troublesome smoke. Thus he kept moving, twisting and lunging blindly with his spatha. Though he saw no-one, he knew he must have wounded several – unless he had struck the same unlucky man three times…

Sooner or later though, if he did not escape from the ground floor he would be cut badly – or worse – unless of course, he choked to death first. There was a bright glow where the brazier had fallen against one of the timber walls and there the fire he expected to die out, seemed to be taking hold. The sight of it only doubled his concern, for it would hardly help the hostages if the whole tower went up in flames.

Then for a moment he stood still, gasping for breath as he tried to rein in his fear. The stair, he knew was opposite the fire so he headed away from the heat and was relieved when the toe of his boot collided with the bottom step. In the murky atmosphere he had to feel for each step and he only mounted two before tripping on the fallen body – which he had completely forgotten. Instinctively reaching out a hand to steady himself, his fingers slid on congealing blood.

Forcing himself on, he stumbled his way up to the next landing where he was reassured to discover that the smoke was a little thinner. Even so, when he tried to swallow his mouth had no spit; his throat was dry as straw and he found himself retching for air. Still wheezing badly, he began to climb the steps once more knowing that, higher up, there would be much clearer air – at least for now. The first few steps were hard, but the further he ascended the easier he found it to breathe and his natural confidence returned.

Having mounted several more floors, he became aware of Florina's voice raging above him and came to a halt. He and his comrades had accounted for several of her soldiers but how many more did she have, he wondered. He could only pray that she had not yet reached the hostages. As he stood thinking, he saw that the stair was acting like a flue – offering an escape route for the smoke – for it was rising up the steps below him.

"Make haste, you fool," he muttered, "or you'll never get back down again."

At the next landing, which he guessed could not be far from the top he paused and tried to distinguish the several voices he could now hear. Mostly, it was Florina haranguing her soldiers with ever more scathing abuse. But there was another - another woman – and a woman whose voice he knew very well… except, it couldn't be her… because Inga was back at the cave…

Arturus sighed in disbelief and then gave a rueful grin. Ambrosius might have told Inga to stay put, but you could always rely upon a Saxon to do whatever they damn well pleased. His grin faded as he tried to work out how and when Inga could have gotten there, for perhaps she was now a hostage herself.

Cursing all Saxons – save Ishild – he took a deep breath, gripped the hilt of his spatha more tightly and charged up to the next floor. To his surprise, a pair of wounded men was on their way down. Reacting fast, Arturus slashed his weapon across the pair of them. One took the brunt of it and fell but the other just groaned and hobbled away as Arturus pushed past him.

Clambering over the bleeding soldier, he stood at the foot of what appeared to be the last flight of steps. Above him, on the threshold of the highest chamber, he saw Florina. Dark against the sunlight, she stood with her back towards him with her attention fixed upon the chamber beyond, which Arturus could not see. He crept up the steps and could have thrust his spatha straight through her back there and then. God knew she would deserve every inch of steel that slid through her, yet the youth could not do it. Though she had committed the most terrible deeds, she had saved him once when no-one else cared to. Thus, he could not bring himself to kill her; for God, he decided must decide Lady Florina's fate.

Perhaps she sensed someone was there, only a few steps below her for suddenly she whipped around to face him. But her vicious glare could not prevent him from shouldering her aside to gain entry to the chamber and what he saw there would be forever burned in his memory. There were two armed men; one hauling a struggling Ishild across the floor towards the parapet, while the other wrestled with Inga. Two much younger girls cowered against the timber parapet, in the arms of Lurotriga and Wynflaed.

Seeing Arturus, Ishild found the courage to pull away from her captor and rake a knife across his face. In response, he darted his spear at her chest and she scrambled away, bleeding. Arturus, shuddering as he beheld the raw wound at his lover's breast was consumed with rage. Perhaps the nearer man saw the murderous look on Arturus' face, for he cast Inga aside and raised his spear. But Arturus, fired with the rage of the devil cracked aside the spear with his spatha before delivering several slashing mortal blows one after another. He then turned his attention towards the other soldier who had wounded Ishild. Seeing his comrade swept aside in a merciless spray of blood, the soldier seized Lurotriga and jabbed his knife against her throat. Arturus stopped midstride for he knew better than anyone how Ambrosius felt about the British noblewoman.

His opponent looked mightily relieved to have found some leverage and pressed the knife point harder at Lurotriga's neck.

"Drop the sword, boy…" he ordered.

Arturus remained still, his eyes focussed upon his opponent for he had seen that Inga was easing herself across the floor towards a fallen spear. Trying not to look at her lest he alerted his adversary to the danger, he held his nerve and waited – until something struck his back like a hammer. Of course, it wasn't a hammer, it was a spear thrust; and the point had punctured his worn, old mail shirt which meant that he had very little time to strike back.

"Remember me?" announced a voice from behind him, as the bearer of the spear shaped for another lunge.

Arturus did recall his assailant for it could only be the hapless soldier he had forced his way past on the stairs. Drawing upon all his speed, Arturus pivoted around to sweep the spear shaft aside with his spatha. This time he showed no mercy and hacked deep into his opponent's neck. He took no pleasure in delivering the fatal wound, because he knew that he too was badly hurt. Even that sudden, brief exertion made him feel faint and he dropped to his knees on the rough-hewn timber floor.

With a groan, he looked up to see Florina stepping towards him from the doorway, knife in hand.

38

Inga lay on the floor, one hand resting upon the discarded spear. As she glanced across at Arturus, her nervous fingers slid along the shaft, feeling the wet blood smeared there. Though the young warrior forced a smile, his ashen face betrayed his distress. Less than half a yard away from her, stood Lurotriga with her neck in the firm grasp of Florina's soldier. Inga slowed her breathing and waited. Any other time she would have struck the soldier down by now but the sight of his blade at the throat of her rival persuaded her to stay her hand.

The wounded Arturus glared at her, willing her to act and, when she did not he swung around and carved his spatha into his own assailant. It was a killing blow, but the effort brought the youth to his knees and, a moment later Florina crossed the threshold.

"Saxons don't hesitate," murmured Inga and, gripping the spear in both hands she reached up from the floor to ram the point as hard as she could between the legs of Lurotriga's captor. Whether the scream of the disembowelled man carried as far as the River Gwy, she did not know but it certainly sent Florina scurrying back down the stairs.

She felt no remorse for she had known such men all her life - men who killed, or threatened women – and they all deserved to feel the edge of her blade, even if it meant that Lurotriga still breathed.

Tears ran down Lurotriga's cheeks when she rested a gentle hand on Inga's shoulder in a gesture of reconciliation; but Inga shrugged off the hand and stepped away. The rebuff caught the eye of both Wynflaed and Ishild who frowned at their Saxon friend. Inga gave a shake of the head because the sisters were wrong; it was not spite that made her shun Lurotriga's gratitude, but guilt – guilt that she had not acted to save the Briton sooner.

"We have to get out of here," muttered Arturus, trying to rise up from the floor.

At once Wynflaed and Ishild scrambled to support him.

"You're bleeding," he said, looking up at Ishild.

"Pah, not as much as you," retorted Ishild, dismissing his concern. "And I've a lot more blood left too."

"We need to take off your mail," said Wynflaed, starting to lift the iron-sewn shirt.

"No," he said. "There's no time for that – I told you, we have to go."

"But you'll bleed to death," cried Ishild, crushing his hand in hers.

"We can't stay here, so just wrap something tight around me."

"Why have you come up alone?" asked Inga.

"Xallas is down at the door with Lugaid."

"But they should have come up with you," cried Wynflaed.

"It's… confused down there," he said, not wishing to acknowledge his rash behaviour. "The tower's on fire - you can smell the smoke even up here – and both the Scotti are wounded."

"So, we'd best go down now," said Inga, when Ishild had finished binding up the youth's wound.

"Yes," agreed the pale-faced Arturus. "But I fear a couple of you will have to help me."

"There must be more soldiers below with Florina," said Inga.

Arturus gave a sigh. "I'm not sure," he replied. "Perhaps one or two."

"We can't take you down between us and fight off more soldiers," declared Inga. "We'd never make it – not with the other women and the girls too... It's safer to wait here for others to come."

"Wait?" cried Lurotriga, who was peering over the parapet towards the gate. "Wait for what?"

"We'll wait for Ambrosius to get to us," snapped Inga.

But Lurotriga turned from the parapet with a solemn countenance. "However long we wait, he won't get to us," she said.

"You're wrong," declared Inga.

"See for yourself, Saxon," said Lurotriga. "He's outnumbered and his men are being driven back. He can't get to you, or me – now isn't that just a... disappointment for both of us..."

Striding across the platform, Inga pushed Lurotriga aside to gaze over the timber parapet. Though she hated to admit it, she had to concede that the Briton was right: Ambrosius was locked in a struggle that he did not have the men to win.

"Once Vortigern has killed Ambrosius," said Lurotriga, "wherever we hide, he'll hunt us down as he pleases."

Inga, crushed by the sight of her lover's army being ground down by Vortigern's greater numbers slumped over the timber rail and closed her eyes. Grief pierced her very soul, devouring the certainty that she and Ambrosius would be together for all time. For, as ever wyrd extinguished the feeble hopes of men and women. Cruel fate, having freed the beautiful courtesan from her comfortable Veronese brothel, now left her to die, heart-broken and scarred by battle on a bleak hilltop at the edge of the world.

"If we stay here," declared Wynflaed, "at the very least we'll burn to death. And I must try - at least try - to get Ulf's son out of this place!"

Wynflaed's plea hauled Inga back from the brink of despair as she remembered that Ambrosius too might yet have a son. Brushing aside her tears, she took one last look at Ambrosius before turning to face her comrades again. Wynflaed was right about the fire for her eyes were starting to sting a little and she could see wisps of smoke wafting up through the doorway and even between the floor timbers.

"I can't think why anyone would have been foolish enough to set fire to the damned tower in the first place," grumbled Inga. No-one replied but some instinct made her glance at Arturus where she found guilt emblazoned across the pallor of his cheeks.

She offered the youth a grim smile. "Wynflaed's right: we have to try to get out."

"Aye, and quickly," urged Arturus.

"No-one's arguing," said Ishild. "Come, Arturus I've bound up your wound, so now you and I can hold each other up."

But her attempt to lift him ended with both of them on the floor, grimacing with pain.

"Ishild, you go with your sister and I'll take Arturus," said Inga, picking up one of the spears to help her support his weight. She glanced then at the two older women and said: "You two can help each other."

"What about the girls?" asked Wynflaed.

"I've only a few cuts and bruises," said Lurotriga. "I'll walk with the girls."

A curt nod from Inga ended the discussion and she folded an arm around Arturus to help him to his feet. When he gasped, she cursed her foolishness and took the youth's other arm to avoid tearing his wound even further.

"Come," she said, offering him a smile of encouragement. "Lean on me."

Just as they were about to leave, a soldier appeared at the top of the stair and stood framed in the doorway. Next moment another came up behind him and Inga spied an ebullient Florina lingering just below them.

At once Arturus and Inga fell back and their companions retreated until they felt the timber rail of the parapet at their backs.

"So much for leaving," muttered Inga.

"Drop your weapons," ordered Florina, pushing forward.

But Inga gave a slow shake of the head. "That's not what we're going to do," she said.

"Good," replied Florina, pointing her knife at Inga. "Kill that one first."

Despite her unflinching response, Inga knew they were doomed. Wynflaed was weak, the pale Arturus was half-dead, Ishild was wounded, the older women were useless and Lurotriga had her arms wrapped around the two child hostages whose eyes were tight shut. So, whatever happened next none of them was capable of playing any part in it – which meant… she was on her own.

When one of the soldiers stepped over the gore-steeped corpse of his former comrade and took a pace towards her, Inga spread her feet wider and thrust the spear out before her. But the encounter lasted only a moment for the soldier, easily evading her clumsy lunge raked his own spear down the outside of her thigh. Wresting the weapon away from her, he tossed it across the chamber. Inga, stung by the pain in her leg invoked the goddess, Frigg and took out her knife to continue the fight. But only further humiliation followed when her opponent merely rapped her on the wrist to send the knife flying from her hand.

"Go on then," Florina urged. "Finish off the Saxon whore."

The soldier fixed the disarmed Inga with a grim stare, but did not immediately obey his mistress. "Are you certain, lady?" he asked. "Because the High King said…"

"The High King isn't up here," said Florina. "And that Saxon wretch would kill you in an instant, you fool. Just look at the bloody mess she made of your comrade!"

"But… we're supposed to be keeping the hostages alive," he ventured, glancing across to the other soldier by the door, who managed only a non-committal shrug.

"Yes," agreed Florina, struggling to contain her anger, "but she… she is not a hostage. She's a Saxon slave… and a whore…"

Still the soldier seemed reluctant, so Florina pushed past him and drew out her knife.

"Very well, leave her to me," she snarled. "We'll have no peace until all these Saxons are crow bait. You two watch the others - I trust you can manage that."

Florina strode towards Inga and was clearly savouring her moment of triumph until Lurotriga darted across the chamber to snatch up Inga's fallen knife.

"Too late," declared Florina, plunging her blade at Inga's breast.

As Lurotriga flew between the two women, Florina's knife tore into her and she in turn slashed at the Roman with the long Saxon blade. When the two women staggered apart, Inga could not tell at first whose hurt was the greater. But then Lurotriga reeled away to lean against the wooden rail of the parapet, before sliding down against it with dark blood already staining the left side of her tunic.

By contrast with the Briton, Florina had merely taken a cut on the forearm, from which a narrow ribbon of blood now dripped onto the floor. The wound was superficial and, once the Roman wiped away the blood the initial apprehension on her face turned to smug contentment. It was too much for Inga who darted forward to slam her fist into Florina's chin with such venom that the high-born Roman dropped, stunned onto the floor.

"That's how a Veronese whore fights!" she yelled, though her knuckles burned with pain.

Arturus, realising the soldiers' eyes were on the women used his remaining strength to slash his spatha across the guard at the door. Though his blade struck home, the soldier appeared far from finished until Wynflaed thrust her knife hard into his side.

The remaining guard who, a moment earlier had been so reluctant to murder Inga was enraged by the attack and turned his spear upon Arturus. Ishild, screaming her lover's name leapt upon the soldier's back and stabbed her Saxon blade at his shoulder. But the knife did not pierce his mail shirt; and worse still, it snagged in the iron rings to stop her lunging a second time. Though the soldier attempted to throw her off, the tenacious young Saxon would not be dislodged. Instead she raked his eyes with her fingers, digging her nails hard into the soft tissue there. Casting aside his spear, he tried to prise her from his back but Ishild persisted in her grim torture until blood dribbled down his cheeks and he screamed out in agony.

In their deadly embrace, the pair spiralled around the platform stumbling over the dazed Florina until the blinded man's hand chanced upon his knife hilt. In an instant he drew out the blade and stabbed with fury at the she-wolf clinging to his back. Several times Inga watched his knife flash in the sunlight as it cut into the girl's flesh and soon blood was seeping through Ishild's clothing.

Fearing for her young friend, Inga picked up a spear and thrust at the groaning soldier's belly. But she lacked the strength to wound him through his mail, so her lunge merely drove him back against the wooden rail of the parapet. Though the soldier fell backwards, he did not tip over the balustrade but slammed into it hard. The timber rail, perhaps rotten from age or weathering, gave a loud crack and snapped in two so that the guard and the Saxon, entwined together fell through it.

Rushing forward, Inga stretched out a hand to seize Ishild, but her fingers slid along the girl's blood-smeared arm. At the last moment, she managed to find Ishild's hand and the latter grasped it tight.

"I've got you!" screamed Inga, but in truth she had not... for she was bearing the weight of the soldier too and all that lay below them was the sheer cliff face.

Though white-faced from blood loss, Ishild was gasping with relief and Inga felt the girl's grip grow stronger. Ishild kicked her adversary loose, but as he fell he clutched at Ishild's leg with a flailing arm. It was just a slight tug on her ankle but it was enough to break her tenuous hold on Inga's hand.

Scrambling to the parapet to join Inga, Wynflaed could only wail at the sight of her young sister plummeting down from the precipice. A moment later Inga sank down onto her haunches, bloodied hands still stretched out beyond the broken spars of the rail. Though she stared down at the dark rocks below, she could no longer see Ishild. From behind her Inga heard Arturus' desolate groan of heartbreak and, for several long moments she could not move – for to do so would mean abandoning somehow the brave girl who lay down there, torn and broken...

No-one in the chamber spoke until a cold voice murmured: "One by one... you and all your friends will fall – just like she did..."

Inga whipped around and to face Florina who had recovered from the punch – though the fine Roman lady now bore an ugly cut upon her chin.

Lurotriga, still lying against the parapet reached up to hand Inga back her long knife and, with the familiar weapon in her hand the Saxon bared her teeth and told Florina: "This time, I'm armed."

"Come on then, slave," taunted Florina. "Let's see what you can do, apart from lie on your back with your legs wide."

Without waiting for Inga to move, Florina made a sudden lunge and, though Inga deflected the blade's first thrust, it was more by luck than skill.

"I think you've fought one battle too many..." breathed Florina, perhaps sensing an advantage.

Inga, still raging at the fate of young Ishild spat at her: "You sad, cold creature - you'll follow my Saxon friend over that cliff and she'll feast upon you in the afterlife."

"Vortigern will soon be here," warned Florina softly. "And when he comes, he'll have left your precious Ambrosius... headless in the field."

"Let's not wait," snarled Inga, hurling herself forward to thrust her knife at Florina's breast. But the Roman caught her wrist and slashed with her own blade. The cut on Inga's arm was slight but fuelled her growing fury. Wresting her knife hand free, she stabbed wildly at Florina's neck, slicing into flesh but, to her regret she severed nothing vital.

Florina, though bleeding slightly from the wound, stabbed again but only grazed Inga's shoulder. The Saxon's next thrust lanced into Florina's side but the Roman, grasping the hand that held the knife embedded there, slowly prised Inga's bloody fingers one by one from its hilt.

Unarmed, Inga was forced to take a pace back while Florina slowly inched out the blade from her own bleeding flesh to show that not enough damage had been inflicted.

"Soon be over," hissed Florina, now with a knife in each hand and a face twisted in hideous delight.

Inga focussed upon her opponent's dark, merciless eyes as she took a pace forward with both knives held out in front of her. Stepping back, Inga edged towards the damaged stretch of parapet determined that, if she perished she would take Florina with her. Following Inga step by step, Florina stood poised to strike but, as the Saxon braced herself to wrestle for her life, her adversary grunted as a shudder rippled through her from head to toe.

Open-mouthed in shock, Florina stared down at the razor sharp tip of a spatha that had crept an inch out of her belly. Like a new flower, opening for the first time a patch of crimson began to blossom across her stomach. Her knives clattered down onto the floor, but only when the Roman started to lean forward, did Inga see Lurotriga standing behind her. The Briton released her hold on the hilt of Arturus' spatha and let her victim fall.

Florina lay convulsing on the floor with blood pumping from her like a running stream but Inga was staring at the gaunt, bloodied figure of Lurotriga who took several faltering steps towards her before she sank down, gasping for breath. Standing over her, Inga was uncertain at first; but then she sat down and wrapped an arm around her, pressing her other hand against the Briton's wound from which a little blood still wept.

As both women were slowly enveloped by trails of smoke, Inga said: "You could have let her kill me."

"Why would I do that?" murmured Lurotriga.

"Because you love Ambrosius…"

"You think that matters anymore," replied Lurotriga, "if Vortigern is coming for both of us. In any case, I was leaving that night…"

"That night…"

"When Vortigern attacked the burgus," said Lurotriga.

"You were leaving…" breathed Inga.

"I would not be the cause of a rift among Ambrosius' sworn men – and now, it seems that my God favours you, Saxon; since you're carrying Ambrosius' child."

"You know," said Inga.

"She told me," said Lurotriga, indicating Wynflaed. "She was most… insistent that I should let no harm come to you…"

Inga felt like laughing at the grim folly of it all.

Lurotriga placed her blood-stained fingers against Inga's cheek "I would not have come between you. I swear it."

"No more time for words," said Inga briskly. "We still have to get out."

But Lurotriga just smiled and muttered: "I can't see how we're going to walk down all those steps now."

"I'll help you," said Inga.

"Will you take a look first to see how Ambrosius fares."

"I hardly dare," confessed Inga, but she rose and went to the east parapet, steeling herself for the worst – and it did not look good. Though Ambrosius was not dead yet, he was still hemmed in by Vortigern's men. And she could see that all the combatants were exhausted, as they fought each other to a standstill.

"If only he had just a few more men," groaned Lurotriga. "That coward Erbin should be here…"

Inga turned to stare at Lurotriga, suddenly alert to a forgotten possibility.

"There is a chance," she whispered. "Ambrosius could still break through…"

"But how?" mumbled Lurotriga. "Is your goddess Frigg going to fly down there and help him?"

"Aye," said Inga, "I think she is."

39

Vortigern seemed content to wear Ambrosius down by paring away men from his line until either he withdrew from the fort, or every last man was killed. At any point Ambrosius could pull his men back, and lead them out of the fort. Yet... there was a garland here to be won and it was not simply the release of a handful of hostages – however cherished they might be. There was a greater struggle taking place in the courtyard inside the gate - a battle for the beating heart of a land riven by conflict. These few men, crashing into each other on a desolate western hill, were fighting to decide who would lead Britannia - but it was a contest which everyone knew Ambrosius was steadily losing.

In the first savage encounter, which seemed an age ago both bands of men had bellowed their war cries and banged weapons against their shields as they hurtled into combat – but not now. Each man saved what little, precious strength remained for that one vital moment when he might need something more... perhaps to evade a deadly thrust.

As their numbers dwindled, men on both sides became ever more cautious; few would dart forward now and risk a mortal wound. Under the warm June sun, all were tiring fast; but in a battle of attrition, greater numbers mattered and Ambrosius did not have them. He was glad though that his remaining raw recruits from Vindocladia were miles away with King Erbin, for this was no place to learn how to fight. It was a place to die – and one by one, that's what his men were doing.

Once more the two battle-weary ranks of men trudged towards each other to resume their soul-sapping stalemate. Ambrosius set a slow pace, wondering how many on either side remembered, or even cared why they might be about to die. Most of Vortigern's men - like his and those of Cadrullan - were oath-sworn to fight and, if it came to it die. And of course, in such a struggle only death ever emerged the winner.

He glanced up at the high wooden tower ahead, seeking some sign that perhaps Arturus and the others had managed to free the hostages; but he saw none. What he did notice was smoke billowing up from the base of the tower, but there was no time to look more closely for the two lines were about to collide again.

As he shuffled forward in the rippling wave of shields, it seemed to him that the High King's soldiers were arrayed slightly differently. And, in that instant he knew... Vortigern must have assessed the numbers and this time, he intended to finish it. He appeared to have crammed every last man into his battle line making it three ranks deep in the centre. But, a few yards before the moment of impact men from the two rear ranks began to edge to left and right. If Ambrosius did nothing, they would overlap and curl around the ends of his shield line to surround his entire force.

He was still contemplating how to counter Vortigern's ploy, when an opponent's shield boss clattered into his with a resounding crack, Seconds later, he felt the point of a spear scrape across his mail shirt as he thrust his spatha with all the power he could muster. The shudder along his arm told him that his weapon had struck home, but he could not withdraw it. For a split second it was lodged in his adversary's midriff and the fellow's face told a mortal tale. With a savage twist, Ambrosius finally retrieved the spatha and released his gutted opponent. But such was the press of shields and bodies that his victim was held up, as were several other men with grievous wounds.

Only when the two ranks parted about a yard, did the dying fall for all to witness their last agony. Then the heaving ranks pounded into each other again: shield on bloodied shield and body slamming against body. Vortigern's men no longer held back and brought such brute strength and sinew to bear that it was clear they expected this attack to be their last.

In the bloody carnage at the heart of the struggle, no man gave quarter but, all too soon the flanks of Vortigern's long, thin battle line began to fold around Ambrosius' men in a grisly embrace. If he allowed his line to fragment into a mêlée of individual bouts, his cause was lost. Like the High King, he needed to change his tactics – and swiftly.

Vortigern's extended battle line was stretched almost to breaking point at its centre, leaving it vulnerable – but if Ambrosius delayed too long, the chance would be lost. With a dozen bucellarii at his back, he could have driven a wedge right through Vortigern's lines in a matter of moments. But his bucellarii were few now and he had never fought with Cadrullan's men before. While he did not question their bravery, they lacked the training and discipline of Roman soldiers.

319

"We must form a wedge!" he shouted at Cadrullan, who was still alongside him. "Pass the word!"

He thanked God that Rocca and Germanus were on the flanks, so at least the two experienced bucellarii could haul other men into the formation. But still… to break the will of their opponents such an assault would need to be sustained. Gulping in several deep breaths, he thrust aside the doubts that crept, as ever into every soldier's head and raised his spatha aloft.

"On me!" he roared and heard the deep guttural voices of both Rocca and Germanus shout out the rallying cry of: "Dux, dux, dux!"

Crashing his shield into his immediate opponent, Ambrosius pressed forward with Cadrullan. They battered the men facing them, using every ruse they knew to tip them off balance or turn them. A desperate spear thrust missed Ambrosius by inches as his great spatha chopped at a shoulder and then a helm – not once but several times, blow after blow. His spatha was wet with dark blood and flecks of it flew at his face as he carved aside another victim, but his sword arm felt leaden and he had scarcely gained two yards of ground. Worse still, Cadrullan was lagging a pace behind him and momentum was vital in driving a wedge through the enemy. Behind him he heard the two bucellarii bullying their comrades to greater effort but, in truth he really needed the pair of them with him at the sharp end of the wedge.

A stolen glance to the rear confirmed his worst fears: he was leaving his comrades behind and, though he had punched a hole clean through Vortigern's battle line, he would have to pull back now, or abandon the others.

"Hold here, Cadrullan!" he cried, dropping back beside the Briton. "We'll have to hold here."

But Cadrullan retorted: "Not if you want to win, lord."

"On, on!" roared Germanus. "Don't stop!"

But several enemy spear men saw Ambrosius fall back a pace and closed in upon him again, smelling a kill.

"Take your bucellarii and cut the head off the beast," declared Cadrullan. "It's our only hope."

Ambrosius, knowing the truth of it wasted no time in hollow argument. Both men knew that while he tried to reach Vortigern, Cadrullan and his men would most likely be slaughtered.

"Rocca, Germanus - on me!" he yelled and, without waiting for any acknowledgement he launched himself into the spear men ahead of him.

By the time he was battering aside British spears with his shield, the two bucellarii had bludgeoned their way closer to him. Rocca, with his spatha and Germanus, with his mighty axe cleared a gore-strewn path along Ambrosius' flanks so that soon the warriors had torn three gaps in their opponents' line. But no-one else would be following them for Cadrullan was already cajoling his handful of exhausted men into a small ring in a vain attempt to hold off the encircling force.

For Ambrosius there was only one objective: the cloaked figure of Vortigern who stood at the rear of his men, encouraging them to make ever greater effort. Grey hairs escaped from under the old man's helm and it was a troubled face that stared back at Ambrosius. All that lay between the two commanders were the soldiers clustered closely around the High King. These were the royal guard and every one would be a skilled and powerful warrior. Sure enough, their stubborn and relentless resistance brought the three bucellarii to an abrupt halt and, once their advance was halted they, like Cadrullan were exposed to attack from all sides.

Ambrosius was still endeavouring to hack his way towards Vortigern when, to his astonishment his immediate adversary appeared to throw himself to the ground. The moment Ambrosius spied an arrow in the soldier's back he was horrified for he knew its origin very well. A swift look up to the tower revealed a glimpse of fair Saxon hair and brought a bitter curse to his dry lips. He had believed she was safe yet here she was – here, in the bloody midst of it all...

So angry was he with Inga that he slaked his fury on the next man who faced him and then turned his spatha upon another. But before he could do so, that opponent too fell to the archer. This time Vortigern's men saw the arrow strike and it sent a shiver of doubt through their ranks. When Ambrosius glanced up again, the archer had gone but a shout from Germanus urged him forward.

For once, the Burgundian was right; if Inga had put herself at such great risk, he should not waste the advantage she had won for him. Some of Vortigern's soldiers were clearly rattled and darting looks behind them for a sight of the archer. It was of course the ideal moment to strike. Heedless of what was happening behind them, the three bucellarii found new resolve and surged forward. All that mattered now was reaching Vortigern – and they almost did. Ambrosius was only yards from his adversary, when

Vortigern began to retreat and his withdrawal signalled the beginning of the end of the battle.

"Hold the line here!" he bawled at his men, but they all knew what was happening. Their High King, their sworn lord was fleeing with only a core of the royal guard, leaving the rest to fight on and buy his escape with their blood. Several of his most loyal men tried to do just that; but a group of soldiers was like any other crowd: when faced with mortal danger, some would always run. And, though a few appeared determined to fight on their efforts were hampered by their fleeing comrades. A few even killed their own men if they came between them and Ambrosius.

Battering their way through the remnant of the royal guard, the three Romans cut down several diehard warriors before setting off in pursuit of Vortigern. When Ambrosius looked back, he was relieved to see that Cadrullan was still battling hard against the rump of Vortigern's increasingly demoralised men.

Vortigern himself was making for the tower and there the wily High King would try to barter the hostages for his miserable life. For what he had done at Vindocladia alone, Vortigern deserved to die and few would argue otherwise. But could Ambrosius bear to sacrifice Inga, Lurotriga or - God forbid – both, to ensure Vortigern's death? Worse still, the tower itself was on fire with, as far as he knew all the remaining hostages still inside.

A column of flame and smoke was spreading up one side of the tower but Ambrosius was relieved to see that it was still some way short of the higher floors. Vortigern and his men were at least a dozen yards ahead when they reached the foot of the tower and disappeared inside.

Casting aside his shield, Ambrosius tried to run faster though every straining muscle protested.

If Vortigern reached the top of the tower first the hostages, including Lurotriga and now Inga and her unborn child, would be at the mercy of the High King. Though Ambrosius prayed that Arturus and his comrades had rescued the women, a sick feeling in his belly told him they had not.

40

Lugaid worked his arm slowly to and fro, wincing as the movement pulled at his wounded ribs. Not for the first time, he was ruing the day he landed on the south coast with his Scotti comrades. Niall had promised him plunder with hardly any risk because he had made 'powerful allies' as he described them. Instead Lugaid and his little brother had barely escaped with their lives; they had won nothing, lost their boat, their freedom and now, all those who had sailed with them were gone too. True, Lugaid need not have sworn to follow Ambrosius but a beggar has few choices.

So here the two brothers were, both wounded and facing an enemy who outnumbered them - someone else's enemy... They should have stayed at home although, as Lugaid recalled with a grim smile home was a shithole too... And, in any case he had sworn to help Ambrosius and he intended to keep that oath. His damaged body had rested long enough, for there were still hostages to be freed and, it appeared no-one else left to free them. Struggling to his feet, he walked across to the tower entrance where Xallas was standing watch with his spear.

"Where's Arturus?" enquired Lugaid.

"He went to… have a look… inside…"

"The fool! You should've stopped him," said Lugaid.

"He just… ran in, before I could lay a hand on him."

"How long ago?"

"Too long," groaned Xallas.

"That young fool must think God sits upon his shoulder…" grumbled Lugaid, with a shake of the head.

"I should have known he'd risk all for that damned Saxon girl," said Xallas.

"Aye, you should have," agreed Lugaid.

"But… the longer I waited," explained Xallas, "I thought Dux would come any moment – but… he hasn't."

They couldn't just abandon the lovesick bastard, thought Lugaid. Dux would never forgive them; and, after all the blood spilled so far they had to get to the hostages if they could.

"We can't wait any longer…" said Lugaid. "Let's go in now."

Xallas grasped his arm. "You're both wounded."

Lugaid grinned. "Aye, but not real wounds, my friend, eh." Then he reached down to help up his brother. "Can you walk, Donnan?"

"Aye, I can," replied the younger man with a smile, "and hold a spear too."

Lugaid's dismissive grunt expressed some doubt but he picked up his monstrous spiked club and said: "Come on then; let's do it."

All the same, even he hesitated at the tower doorway where a near-continuous stream of smoke was now belching out.

"Best take a good long breath, my friends," he said, before stepping across the timber threshold.

Where before there had been only smoke, there was now a wall of heat from the flames coursing fiercely up the wooden frame opposite the stair. The Scot, ever one to find advantage in adversity was grateful that the fire would light his way up the stairs. There was no-one in sight - or at least no-one alive. They stepped over several charred corpses, one of which was so ravaged by fire that it spat and crackled at them as they passed. It was warning enough that they had little time left; indeed, Lugaid feared they had already waited too long. As for Ambrosius, if he did not come now then he need not come at all.

Climbing the stair in the heat and rising smoke was an onerous task even for a man of his strength. Though his wounds were not deep and were tightly bound up, he could still feel them and every flight of steps sapped his energy a little more. Soon he was panting for breath in the enclosed stairwell where little clean air remained. On each landing they searched the recesses, expecting to encounter some of Florina's men, but they found none.

"No-one…" Lugaid snarled at Xallas, before inhaling too much smoke and almost coughing up his lungs.

In part, his anger stemmed from his growing fear that Arturus had long since made his way to the top of the tower, faced Florina's half a dozen soldiers alone and been swiftly despatched. When they neared the final landing, the fleet-footed Xallas was three steps ahead of Lugaid though the Scot, worried what might await them at the top worked his aching legs harder to close up on his Roman comrade.

Following Xallas across the final threshold, he emerged into a chamber where the glaring sun drove spikes of light through dark swirls of acrid smoke. Even squinting through half-closed eyes, he could see it was a slaughterhouse; but he could not tell at first if anyone still lived. While Xallas bent down to examine Arturus, Lugaid picked his way towards Inga who was the one of the few who might know him. As he did so, two young girls shied away from him, whimpering in fear.

Inga's face was smeared with blood amid the smudges of smoke and the Saxon looked utterly spent, but she lifted her head to force a smile at him. Lugaid could see that the women had done all they could to bind up their wounds.

"You know the damned tower's on fire," he told Inga gently.

She nodded and murmured: "We thought about leaving, but we were all just too tired. Perhaps Ambrosius will be here soon…"

"Lugaid," called his brother, crouching by the wooden rail of the platform. "Look here!"

When Lugaid peered over the rail, he could see the fiercely-contested battle between Vortigern and Ambrosius only thirty yards from the tower.

"I think we're winning," suggested Donnan.

"Nobody's winning," growled Lugaid. "But it doesn't change what we have to do; which is to get these folk out of this tower – fast. At least we can take them somewhere safer till the battle's… decided."

He was about to turn away when he saw a small cluster of warriors around Vortigern break away from the main force and retreat towards the tower.

"Oh, shit…" he muttered.

Taking Inga by the shoulder, he said: "Lady, we must make all haste."

Their task, of course was impossible: Arturus couldn't walk unaided; and, while Inga and most of the other women could do so, Lurotriga would need to be carried. Even without the choking smoke and the prospect of being burned alive, they could not descend the steps fast enough to get out before Vortigern arrived.

With a weary sigh, Lugaid fell back upon optimism: perhaps the High King was simply fleeing the field and had no thought of venturing into the tower – especially since it was burning down. But the awkward truth could not be ignored: the tower contained Vortigern's one last hope of escaping Ambrosius alive.

Casting a forlorn look at Arturus and the wounded Lurotriga, Inga said: "It's not possible to get us out."

"It is," lied Lugaid, attempting to radiate some confidence. "Xallas can take the lead with you, Wynflaed and the two other women, then Donnan and Arturus can help each other down with the younger girls; and I'll be at the back with the wounded lady."

"Lurotriga," said Inga.

At once Xallas drew him aside. "You can't carry Lurotriga," he whispered, "not with your wounds."

Glancing down at his torso, Lugaid saw that blood had begun to seep through the bound cloth, but said merely: "I'll be fine," adding in a low voice. "You just take it slow and watch out at each landing, in case... Vortigern's coming up."

"Only a blind fool would come up now," scoffed Xallas.

Aye, Lugaid thought only a fool blinded by hate - or perhaps, love.

As was the way of Ambrosius' bucellarii, Xallas made no further argument but simply got on with his task. They made good progress down the first flight of steps but, after that they moved achingly slowly through the denser smoke and burgeoning heat. In Lugaid's arms, Lurotriga drifted in and out of consciousness. Sometimes she forgot who he was and wrestled to free herself from his tight grasp. When she did so, her struggle tore a little more at his wounds though, of course she did not know it.

On the fourth floor landing Xallas came to a halt and, though Lugaid desperately needed a rest he urged his comrade to continue.

"I thought I heard voices below," explained Xallas.

"All I can here is the crackle of burning wood," retorted Lugaid.

"I've good ears," argued Xallas, "and I tell you that men are on their way up!"

"It could be Ambrosius," said Inga.

"No," replied Lugaid. "Vortigern broke from the battle first."

"Frigg's dugs," muttered Inga. "Better give me a blade then."

Xallas gave a shake of the head. "You're in no condition to fight anyone, lady."

"Mind who you're ordering about," snapped Inga. "After all I've endured, I'm not just going to surrender."

"Peace," hissed Lugaid. "If we fight, we'll lose. They'll be heading up to the top as fast as they can. We'll just hide in the alcoves off each landing."

"If we're found, we're dead," Xallas pointed out. "And we can't all hide in one of them."

"Whatever we're doing, we'd better do it quick," said Inga.

"Inga, you and Wynflaed make for the next landing down," said Lugaid. "And... take my knife, just in case. But they'll be looking up, so stay out of sight and keep quiet… Go now, or they'll be at the landing before you."

That moment Lugaid felt a jolt of fear, knowing that he might just have despatched the woman Ambrosius loved into the arms of Vortigern.

"Xallas, you stay here, with the rest," he said. "I'll take Lurotriga back up to the floor above."

"But when Vortigern reaches the top and finds the chamber empty," said Xallas, "he'll come looking – and you'll be the closest to him."

But his words were wasted for Lugaid was already heading straight back up the stairs.

"Don't worry, lady," he told Lurotriga. "I'll look after you."

She gave a groan and replied softly: "So say all men; but all men lie…"

Lugaid did not bother to argue for they only just managed to conceal themselves before he heard the tramp of feet below which confirmed Xallas' suspicions. Moments later, a band of soldiers trudged up past them and he counted four. In the close stairwell, the sweat was dripping from him and the strain of bearing the woman for so long was beginning to take its toll.

Just as he was about to leave their hiding place, he heard a wheezing cough and stepped back as a fifth man laboured past. Lugaid knew that the hunched, cloaked figure could only be Vortigern. As soon as the High King reached the top floor and discovered the bodies of Florina and his guards, he would despatch his warriors down the steps to scour each landing. But Lugaid hesitated to move, wondering whether any more men were coming up behind

Vortigern. He was sure he had counted at least six fleeing to the tower and so far he had accounted for only five. But perhaps the sixth was posted at the entrance below… and, if he waited too long they would be captured in moments.

The heat was making him feel lightheaded and, before he knew it he was swaying back against the wall until an anxious gasp from Lurotriga jerked him back to his senses. Even so, his legs were trembling now as the slow blood loss also began to take effect.

"I've got you, lady," he murmured. But Lurotriga did not reply, perhaps knowing that his words were spoken to reassure him rather than her.

Listening hard for any further sound of approach, he staggered from the dim recess of the landing and started to descend. Eyes raw and streaming from the constant haze of smoke, he was struggling even to see where he put his feet. Halfway down to the next floor, he heard the tramp of boots coming up and he stopped on the stair. He was in no state to fight for his muscles were screaming from the strain of carrying Lurotriga. Turning to go back up to his hiding place, he heard Vortigern's men beginning to descend. So, now he could neither go up, nor down.

41

Ambrosius sprinted to the door of the great burning edifice but, when he felt the blast of heat from within he stopped dead.

"Sweet Christ!" groaned Rocca. "Surely no-one can still be alive in there, Dux."

"Vortigern must have thought so," said Ambrosius. "There's no sign of Xallas, or Arturus."

"Could they have saved the women and left?" asked Rocca.

Ambrosius gave a weary shake of the head, knowing that not long ago Inga had still been at the top of the tower.

"We'll be outnumbered in there," complained Germanus.

"Outnumbered," scoffed Rocca. "We'll be roasted alive first, you fool!"

Ambrosius thrust all misgivings aside for, if there was a chance in a thousand of getting the women out he had to take it.

Beside the tower stood a butt, brim-full of rainwater so, using his knife to cut a strip off the bottom of his tunic, Ambrosius dipped the cloth into the water. Making sure he soaked it through, he bound the dripping fabric around his face and mouth leaving only the eyes uncovered. His comrades needed no prompting to follow his lead.

"Remember: we've friends in there, as well as enemies," warned Ambrosius. "So, be damned careful who you kill…"

Then, after muttering a hasty prayer he filled his lungs with air, drew out his spatha and walked in through the fire-scorched doorway. After only a couple of paces, he was driven back by a jet of flame that seared up the tower's north-west corner. Though the stair opposite was not yet ablaze, crafty fingers of fire were creeping up onto the lower steps.

Keeping low and taking short, shallow breaths, Ambrosius began to climb the stair. Thudding onto the treads behind him, he heard the boots of his two comrades and very soon Germanus thundered right past him. It was a reminder, thought Ambrosius that, for all the Burgundian's annoying complaints his courage could never be questioned.

As the three pushed on faster, they were almost undone on the first floor landing when a spatha snaked out at them from the darkness of an alcove. Having abandoned their shields outside, they were all too vulnerable to the man Vortigern had left to slow them down. It was the eager Germanus who took the spatha in his side. In outrage the Burgundian, whose substantial mail shirt had most likely limited the blade's penetration pivoted fast and, with a single swing of his axe hacked off the outstretched arm along with the offending spatha. While his comrade examined the wound, Ambrosius put the bleeding soldier out of his whimpering misery.

"How bad?" he asked Germanus.

"Go on," urged Germanus, coughing from the smoke. "I'll come up slower and watch your backs."

Ambrosius gave his comrade a sympathetic tap on the shoulder knowing that for Germanus to surrender his place at their head, the wound must be serious. The incident persuaded him to proceed up the smoke-filled stairway with more caution, lest the High King had arranged any further surprises for them. Yet on the next landing they encountered no-one, which was as well for the smoke there seemed thicker still. Though the fire had not yet reached that far, some timbers were already scorched and smouldering. It would not take long for fire to engulf even such a tall tower, once the flames fed eagerly upon the dry timber of the stairwell.

On the third landing, two snarling figures rushed at them out of the drifting smoke but Ambrosius was ready this time and spun around to rake his spatha across his attacker's chest. To his astonishment the blade did not rip through flesh and bone but, instead rang against another steel edge. Rocca, following close behind him had thrust his spatha beneath Ambrosius' lethal sword. Only when he stopped to berate his comrade, did Ambrosius see his assailant's face.

"Inga," he gasped, seeing his spatha only kept from her breast by the thickness of Rocca's blade.

Putting up his weapon, Ambrosius pressed Inga to him. "I almost killed you," he cried. "By Christ, you should have stayed at the cave!"

"We didn't ask the Christ god what he thought," said a grim-faced Wynflaed, spluttering as she tried to say more. "And... if we hadn't come... the captives would all be long dead by now."

"Aye," he acknowledged, "and without your arrows, we'd not have broken Vortigern's men. But where are the other women?"

335

"Some are dead," wheezed Inga, still clinging to Ambrosius.

"Aye," growled Wynflaed. "My sister among them…"

"Ishild… dead," breathed Ambrosius.

Inga nodded. "And Arturus is badly hurt."

"And… Lurotriga," he said, for he had to know.

"She's still above with Lugaid," said Inga, "and she's hurt too… The fool took a blade trying to help me…"

"But where are they?" asked Ambrosius. "Surely only Vortigern is above us."

"They're hiding in the alcoves on the floors above - as we were," said Inga. "We let Vortigern pass by and then, when we were thinking of going down again… we heard you and thought you might be more of his men…"

Releasing his hold upon her, he said: "Germanus, take these women down while we fetch the others."

"I can stay and help," protested Inga.

"No," snapped Ambrosius. "I want you out of here before this damned tower falls down on top of you. Now go."

"I owe a blood debt to her!" declared Inga. "To Lurotriga…"

"But you owe a greater one to the child you carry," hissed Ambrosius. "So go. Germanus, get them all out of the tower."

While the wounded Burgundian herded the two Saxons and the two older women down the steps, Ambrosius and Rocca continued on up. Almost at once they met Xallas and the Scot, Donnan supporting Arturus with two terrified-looking girls cowering behind them.

"By God, it's good to see you, Dux," breathed Xallas, his voice hoarse.

Hearing the release of tension in his comrade's voice, Ambrosius clapped him on the back. "Well done, my friend. Where's Lugaid?"

"Floor above," coughed Xallas. "But Vortigern's up there somewhere too."

"I know," said Ambrosius. "And several with him."

"Five or six, I'd say."

"Keep following the others down as fast as you can," ordered Ambrosius.

Rocca pulled a face. "Germanus said we'd be outnumbered…"

"Don't tell him he was right," grumbled Ambrosius. "We'll never hear the end of it."

Eyes smarting, he led the way up but at the next landing there was a sudden roar as flames burst out onto the stair just below them.

"Make haste, Dux," urged Rocca, "or we'll be kindling."

Continuing up the steps, Ambrosius came face to face with the tall Scot, Lugaid clutching Lurotriga in his arms. The big man was tottering as if his legs were about to give way.

"They're right behind us," groaned Lugaid, stumbling down the stair as he tried to pass the widowed queen to Ambrosius.

Ambrosius caught Lurotriga as she fell, but only by letting the spatha fall from his hand. While the sword clattered down the steps, he just managed to keep his footing and, trembled with relief as he folded his arms around her. Lugaid too was falling and only Rocca's strong arms prevented him from crashing down onto the landing for the Scot looked exhausted.

A moment later two spear men thrust down at Ambrosius. One spear point grazed his mail shirt as he sought to shield Lurotriga. Rocca, hastily pushing Lugaid aside leapt up the steps to grasp one of the spear shafts. When he pulled hard upon it, the bearer overbalanced, and Rocca's spatha slashed across him as he fell forward. Though it cut the soldier only slightly, the North African followed it with a lunge of brute force that burst through mail and ruptured flesh - a wound from which no man could recover.

At first the remaining spear bearer retreated up the steps until, with others at his back he found the courage to drive his spear at Rocca again. Even so, the stocky bucellarius held his ground and then hacked clean through the haft before carving his sword across the face of his adversary.

Having driven back their pursuers – at least for a moment - Rocca helped Lugaid down while Ambrosius carried Lurotriga. But it was not long before they heard the familiar voice of Vortigern haranguing his men to pursue the fugitives. Despite the dangers all around him, Ambrosius struggled to tear his eyes from the young woman in his arms, for his heart was entreating him to hold onto her forever.

"You're badly hurt," he said, kissing her forehead.

"I'll live …" she murmured.

But not if we're caught, thought Ambrosius.

Though Rocca was helping Lugaid down each step, the Scot was all the while complaining: "I'm alright - I'm still good to fight."

"You don't look it," scoffed Rocca, bending down to retrieve Ambrosius' fallen spatha. "Dux," he said, as they reached the next landing. "You'd best have Varta's sword back – wouldn't want to lose that."

Ambrosius regarded the pale, smoke-grimed Lurotriga. "In case I need to use this spatha," he told her, "you'll have to walk while I support you on one arm."

She flashed him a grim smile, so he lowered her onto her feet before accepting the familiar blade from Rocca.

"They're close behind!" warned Rocca.

And of course they were, because their pursuers were unencumbered and were no more eager to burn to death than Ambrosius. Even if they paused to search the alcoves as they descended, the Britons were certain to overtake them. When they did, he would be powerless to fight them if he was still holding onto Lurotriga. So, at the next landing he stopped.

"This won't do," he told Rocca. "You must take Lady Lurotriga." And before either one could protest, he handed her over to his comrade. "Get her out safe," he ordered.

Not for an instant did Rocca hesitate but simply scooped up Lurotriga and set off down the steps. Ambrosius felt somehow liberated to know that both Inga and Lurotriga were on their way out of the tower and it allowed him to think more clearly. One thought stood out above all others: Vortigern could not be allowed to leave the tower alive. A glance down the stair well told him that the fire was surging up the tower towards them and, unless

Vortigern had decided to take a leap off the top he had to come down. Whatever else he was, Vortigern had proven many times that he was a survivor.

When Rocca went down, Lugaid lingered with Ambrosius.

"Follow Rocca down," Ambrosius ordered the Scot.

"Not a chance," argued Lugaid. "I leave here at your side, or not at all."

"A sworn man does as he's told."

"You can't stop them all on your own," declared Lugaid.

"You can't even lift a weapon," replied Ambrosius. "Just go and help Rocca with the lady."

But Lugaid, picking up a spear abandoned on the landing, said: "I can hold this little bastard well enough."

"Oh, come on then," agreed Ambrosius, too weary to argue. "We'll go down together."

Even so, he made sure that the wounded Lugaid went first while he, with eyes fixed ever upward behind him, felt for each step. As they descended, the heat in the stairwell intensified and he feared the bottom flights might now be impossible to pass through. The bewildering smoke combined with sudden eruptions of flame made it increasingly difficult to see in any direction and thus, despite Ambrosius' best efforts Vortigern and his three remaining soldiers still managed to take him by surprise.

They came charging down the steps – driven on, Ambrosius suspected by blind panic – and their momentum carried them crashing into him. Though he reacted swiftly enough to slice his spatha across the first man, he was then knocked down by the soldier's falling body. Locked together, the pair thudded into the blazing timber wall sending up a shower of sparks. Ambrosius felt the searing heat on his back as the flames, dancing nimbly from one timber to another came ever closer.

Heaving his dying victim aside, he managed to turn aside a spear thrust before burying his spatha into his new opponent's groin. Lugaid meanwhile was on the step below, thrusting his spear up against a third warrior of colossal size who had his eye fixed upon Ambrosius. While the Roman tried to wrestle free his spatha blade, the massive figure brought his axe down with every intention of hewing Ambrosius in two. Lugaid's next wicked lunge, however, caught their adversary high in the thigh and spoiled his aim. Thus the fearsome axe slammed into the charred timber by Ambrosius' head. Having tried in vain to free it, the soldier drew out a knife and hurled himself at Lugaid.

When the burly warrior tumbled past him, Ambrosius peered through the smoke to find Vortigern only two steps above him with sword in hand. The High King's haggard face wore a mask of fury and, seeing Ambrosius trapped against the wall he stabbed down wildly. With no time to bring up his spatha, Ambrosius was grateful that Vortigern's frantic thrust tore through smoke and little else.

While his opponent recovered his balance, Ambrosius retreated another few steps, more worried now about the fire than any threat from Vortigern. Searching for a glimpse of Lugaid, Ambrosius saw him several steps below, locked in a ferocious embrace with his massive opponent as they crashed their way down the stairs. Since neither man still appeared to possess a weapon, it would be a simple trial of strength which the badly-wounded Lugaid seemed certain to lose.

On the second floor landing, Vortigern caught up again with Ambrosius and the two bitter rivals faced each other amid the flames. Torn between trying to kill his old enemy and helping his new comrade, Lugaid Ambrosius attempted to do both. First he slashed at Vortigern to force him back and then jumped down a couple of steps to stab his sword with all the force he could muster through an exposed flank of Lugaid's opponent. Too late, the huge man half-turned in shock, but the blade of Varta the Frank was sharp enough to drive deep into the startled man's body – mortally deep.

"Get out - now!" Ambrosius yelled at Lugaid.

No sooner had he wrenched out his blade than he sensed movement behind him and spun around to see Vortigern on the step above. As the old man's blade arced down towards him, a sudden, explosive spurt of fire sent flame ripping through the steps below Ambrosius. He lurched down onto his knees and Vortigern's sword slid past his helm. Taking a hesitant step down, Ambrosius felt the scorched tread give way under his weight and, in trying to step off it he fell and tumbled further down into the dark fire.

For an instant he glimpsed Vortigern's flushed countenance above him before a torch of living fire shot up the centre of the stair between them. Shielding his face, Ambrosius looked up to see Vortigern enveloped in a fiery column, flapping his hands in vain at the flames which endeavoured to consume him. Any moment Ambrosius expected to hear a scream of agony, but none came. Instead

Vortigern, his cloak ablaze plummeted past him into a raging abyss where part of the stair had once been.

Vortigern was dead and Ambrosius could scarcely take in the suddenness of it. Only then did he realise that he and Lugaid were trapped. The Scot stood on the step just below him staring at the flaming void into which the High King had just plunged. Ambrosius tried to see how damaged the next set of steps was but the fire, ebbing and flowing before his eyes obscured his view.

"We'll have to jump!" cried Ambrosius.

But Lugaid's eyes were on the spot where Vortigern's body had fallen. "He's still alive!" shouted the Scot, as Ambrosius peered through the flames in disbelief at the smouldering, prostrate form of Vortigern, whose upper body was so horribly burned that he simply had to be dead.

Joining Lugaid on the next step down, he felt it give a little beneath their combined weight. A moment later a stab of pain lanced through his calf and, looking down he saw the blackened hand of Vortigern clutching a knife hilt. The High King's cackle of triumph might have unnerved him if he wasn't already facing imminent incineration. Yet, when all other emotions deserted you there was always anger – and it was raw anger that drove Ambrosius to punch his spatha down through his opponent's charred shoulder and into his blackened chest.

"Try surviving that!" he screamed.

Astounded by the madness he heard in his own marred voice, he seized hold of Lugaid and cried: "In God's name go now, my friend, or we'll be joining the High King!"

"Jump," gasped Lugaid.

The tread beneath their feet cracked alarmingly.

"God's breath," Ambrosius bellowed at him, "Just jump!"

"But it's a terrible death!" protested Lugaid.

"Aye," snarled Ambrosius, gripping the Scot by the arm. "But so are they all…"

Leaping out over the gap in the burning stair, he hauled the reluctant Scot with him and the pair landed in the midst of a devil's inferno on the first floor landing, before rolling on down several more burning treads of the last flight of steps. As soon as Ambrosius found his feet, he took the big Scot's arm and pulled him again, for timbers were cracking all around them.

Ambrosius' hair was being singed and his mail shirt felt like a thousand hot irons branding his skin. They blundered on down through the blazing corridor of fire until Lugaid was scarcely able to move.

"By Christ, you lazy bastard, you can fall down there from here!" exhorted Ambrosius.

And in the end they both did fall, tripping over charred boards and sliding on melting, unrecognisable flesh until they landed heavily on the ground floor. It was as if they had been hurled onto a bed of hot coals and Ambrosius' hands were blistered in seconds. He did not realise his hair was afire until a cloak was thrown over him to smother the flame and swiftly, Rocca and other comrades dragged the two men, gasping and retching out into the glorious sunshine.

42

By mid-afternoon, proud Vortigern's last refuge was stretched out in a broad swathe of smouldering ash and timber for, as the tower finally collapsed it spewed out fiery splinters of wood half way across the fort. Somewhere in the smoking heap, the bones of the High King were scattered. There would not be much left of the old devil, Ambrosius reflected for the crows to feed upon.

While the last embers of the tower still glowed, the combatants rested their weary bones and or had their wounds tended. Ambrosius was among the latter group, for much of his face and body was scarred by fire. Father Gobban seemed to take great pleasure in smearing an evil-smelling salve over the burns and, though Ambrosius had to concede that the ointment did ease his pain it also attracted flies faster than fresh cattle dung.

Cadrullan's battle-weary men had sustained heavy casualties as they fought the last remnant of Vortigern's royal army to a standstill. But in the last hour of the struggle, it was Erbin's late-arriving Dumnonian warriors, who finally vanquished the last of the High King's royal guard. A few perhaps fled, but most were not given the chance to do so.

Though the army upon which the power of Vortigern rested was no more, Ambrosius struggled to see much else that was worthy of celebration. His losses – and those of Cadrullan - were terrifying; and among the dead were Ishild and her sister's husband, Ulf. Indeed of all the Saxons that had joined his company the previous winter, only Wynflaed remained. Others, notably Arturus and Lurotriga would recover only very slowly from what they had endured. Arturus lost much blood that day, along with his youthful innocence; but he also sustained a far deeper wound from which Ambrosius sensed he might never recover: the death of his beloved Ishild.

When Ambrosius scoured the ravaged faces of those who had achieved such a costly victory, he began to doubt whether it had been worth it at all. Thus that evening, though surrounded by friends and allies he had seldom felt so alone. The men he always depended upon for guidance were all gone: first Marcellus in Gallia, then Varta and finally, Ulf. How he yearned for the wise company of such men now. Even Inga had deserted him, though he understood why she decided she must spend the night with the grieving Wynflaed. For that poor Saxon, life would be forever changed; with no husband and a child on the way, she lacked now even the loving support of her dear sister, Ishild.

That night their campfires burned bright on the high plateau where the shell of Vortigern's stronghold stood. Ambrosius shared a meagre feast with King Erbin, Cadrullan and the wounded Pascent as the four men wrestled with what must happen next. If they did not determine what power should replace Vortigern, then someone else would. Whenever such a man fell, others would vie to take his place – for that was the way of men. For once, Ambrosius found it a welcome distraction to turn his attention to such matters.

Pascent, Cadrullan and Erbin were all in agreement with Ambrosius that they had an opportunity to restore what Vortigern had distorted for his own benefit: a council of rulers across the land. Some, like Pascent and Erbin, might call themselves kings, while others such as Cadrullan desired to serve only as magistrates, or administrators. But all feared that Vortigern's demise would only encourage conflict among others.

According to Cadrullan and Erbin, there had in the recent past been border wars between the Dobunni and Durotriges, as well as with the Catuvellauni to the east and the Atrebates to the south. Added to those concerns was a growing Saxon influence in the east and all were agreed that they must establish a new High Council to determine the fate of their island.

Ambrosius, the soldier soon tired of political discussion. Having last year barely escaped death at the hands of Roman conspirators, he had no desire to become embroiled in the tribal disputes of Britannia. Nevertheless, to satisfy the other leaders he promised to think upon it overnight; but Ambrosius had other pressing matters to consider too. Clearly, whatever had happened in the chamber at the top of Vortigern's tower, it had wrought a change among the surviving women.

In particular Ambrosius felt strangely unsettled by the altered relationship between Inga and Lurotriga. The two women who, up to now had appeared to be sworn enemies seemed to have discovered a mutual – albeit rather steely – respect. Even Wynflaed, despite her trough of despair after the loss of both husband and sister was surprisingly civil to Lurotriga. For his part, he found it almost impossible to

347

disguise his feelings for her; but he knew both women too well to believe that the truce between them could be anything more than temporary.

When the fire darkened in the late evening, Ambrosius sought out Lurotriga who stirred from her sleep at his approach. Father Gobban, who had earlier been tending to her wounds had the good sense to scuttle away into the night.

"How's your wound?" Ambrosius asked her.

Lurotriga grimaced. "Father Gobban tells me it will heal well enough. What about your burns?"

He lay down beside her. "An inconvenience, that's all."

"And I suppose you… great men have decided our fate," she said.

"No," he replied and, when he reported to her what had been discussed between the four men she simply laughed.

"And where does my dear Ambrosius fit into this shiny new council of Britons?" she asked.

"Ambrosius doesn't know," he told her wearily. "And, with every hour that passes he cares even less about it."

"You must care!" she retorted, wincing as she did so. "Or they'll destroy you."

"They could destroy me now," he said. "I've scarcely any men left – and none of those are fit to fight."

"You must show that you care," she insisted. "If you do, they will support you – I'm sure of it."

"Perhaps," he conceded. "I think they want to make me the High King, but I'll not replace Vortigern."

"But you're not Vortigern – and you'd be a great king!" said Lurotriga.

"You know how I feel about petty kings who grow fat on their own importance," he said. "So, I refused the honour."

"But if it's not you, they'll just choose someone else."

"I'd rather they didn't choose anyone," he said. "Setting up one above all others will only cause trouble."

Lurotriga stared at him in thoughtful silence for a moment and then smiled. "You've already decided what you want, haven't you?"

"This land is not what I expected," he told her. "When I first came here, I thought Britannia was a broken land which I could help to mend and perhaps discover my mother's kin along the way. But I'm learning that it's not one land at all. It's a jumble of many different peoples who don't seem to get on very well together. Any High King would have an impossible task – and I don't want that. All I can do is try to create a safe place for those who wish to join me. I'll ask Erbin, Pascent and Cadrullan to accept my right to inherit Caer Gloui from my mother. I'll also swear to help defend the Dobunni lands of Caer Gloui and Caer Ceri."

"But what of my loyal Durotriges who have fought, bled and died for you?" asked Lurotriga.

"That's where you can play a part, because I want you to take charge at Vindocladia while I settle things here in the north."

"And why would I want to do that?" she asked.

"Because they're your people and will follow your lead."

"But I'm not a soldier…"

"I'll leave Argetrus and as many others as I can with you. With luck, Onno will have reinforced the hill fort there but it will need time to establish it. I owe the folk of Vindocladia that much."

"But you'll hate Caer Gloui - you've seen it: it's a wasteland of vermin and ruin."

"I'll rebuild it," he said.

"And you'll support Caer Ceri if the Catuvellauni or Atrebates attack it."

"Not just Caer Ceri," said Ambrosius. "Cadrullan tells me that there are many Dobunni farmsteads to the east which face constant attacks from the Catuvellauni. We'll see what we can do about that…"

"Always the soldier - but do you think your fellow leaders will accept your suggestions?"

"They will," he said. "Pascent and Cadrullan have already insisted on swearing oaths of allegiance to me."

"And Erbin?"

"He's a young king, feeling his way but he loses nothing by such an arrangement because he'll have me defending his eastern borders."

"Have you spoken about this to Inga?" she asked.

"No, not yet."

"Wynflaed told me that Inga is with child… and, while your lady and I lay bleeding together we had a long overdue, and… very frank, exchange of words about the only thing we have in common."

"Oh…" said Ambrosius, fearing the worst.

"I swore to her that I would never come between you two-"

"You didn't think I'd want a say in the matter," he said.

"To say what exactly, that you can't decide between us," said Lurotriga. "No, this is the only way… so I'll accept your suggestion that I go back to Vindocladia."

"While I take my Saxon lady to the wasteland of vermin and ruin," said Ambrosius.

"She will help you to heal your wasteland," said Lurotriga, "while I heal from my wounds."

"You'll recover from your wound, I'm sure of that."

"From one of them, perhaps," she replied, with a bitter smile.

Despite his burns, he clasped her hand in his. "I'll still see you often, for I'll need to show my face in Vindocladia."

"But, after tonight we will not be together again," she told him. "For I couldn't bear it and, I believe neither could you."

"Even seeing you…" he murmured.

"Then do not come often to Vindocladia," she said. "You may be sure that I'll look after your interests better than any other could. Now, you should go, for I imagine that Father Gobban is still lurking close by."

"Aye, I can smell the bastard," groaned Ambrosius.

"I'll send him to you when I no longer need his healing skills," she promised.

"Don't hurry to do so," he said, his hand lingering upon hers as he prepared to leave.

"Go to Inga," she told him. "She needs to be reassured…"

So he did and he found the Saxon sitting alone poking at a dying fire, whilst Wynflaed slept a few yards away with the young girls who had survived their ordeal at the tower.

For the second time that evening, Ambrosius explained to a woman he loved what would happen when they left the ruin of Vortigern's fortress.

"Our little company will never be the same," she said. "No longer an alliance of Britons, Saxons and Romans..."

"All things change, Inga and we must defend our eastern borderlands against any attack – whether from British rivals or... by Saxons."

"Ah yes, we Saxons are so dangerous," scoffed Inga. "Yet you owe everything to Ulf and his fellow Saxons; without their sacrifice, we'd all be dead by now, or enslaved."

"I know the debt I owe them," replied Ambrosius. "But many other Saxons are arriving in the east."

"But they're not threatening you," insisted Inga.

"Not yet perhaps, but in time they will... and they are heathens, condemned by God's church..."

"Aye, heathens, like me," she said.

"You're different," he said. "You're my lady - and soon will be the mother of my sons..."

"I'll not desert Frigg to worship your lonely, fickle God," declared Inga.

"We can talk about that later," he said, fearing her flushed cheeks might be the start of a burgeoning storm.

"You can talk about it forever, Ambrosius but you won't change my mind," she said, but then softened her tone. "I'm a daughter of Frigg – that's who I am and ever will be."

Ambrosius smiled and nodded for she had never pretended to be anything else.

A Note about Place Names

No accurate information exists about the names of places in fifth century Britain, but it is likely that a combination of Roman and British names existed side by side - at least for a time. The action takes place in south west Britain and in this book places are referred to as follows:

British	Roman	Modern
	Vindocladia	Lost town near Shapwick, in Dorset
	Durnovaria	Dorchester
Caer Baddan	Aquae Sulis	Bath
Caer Gloui	Glevum	Gloucester
Caer Ceri	Corinium	Cirencester
	Isca Dumnoniorum	Exeter
Iron Hill		Hengistbury Head
	Vectis	Isle of Wight
	Portus Adurni	Portchester

Historical Notes
The Fifth Century – Late Antiquity

The nature of evidence in this period, often referred to as Late Antiquity, is in a state of flux. For a long time history relied only upon a few written sources but, increasingly archaeology is leading the way in trying to make some sense both of the events and lifestyle of this period.

On an almost daily basis discoveries are made which are helping to shape our understanding of this period. Only recently in a British villa a mosaic was discovered which appears to have been laid down around the middle of the fifth century. This is a stunning piece of evidence which suggests that some elite folk at least maintained a comfortable villa lifestyle in a period when villas are usually reckoned to be well past their decline.

The traditional idea of a sudden "fall of the Roman Empire" in the fifth century is now largely discredited in favour of the view that the empire was constantly changing and evolving from the third century onwards. The fifth century therefore marks a period of further development in Britannia where the authority and structure of the Roman Empire no longer held sway and the individual peoples were asserting control once more over areas they had traditionally occupied. This meant that there were most likely tribal – or perhaps regional – disputes during both the fourth and fifth centuries.

In this book, set in the year 455 AD, Ambrosius has been in Britannia for scarcely six months and he is only just learning what it is like and how he can survive there.

Britannia c.450 AD

Anyone who puts forward any clear ideas about what Britannia was like at that time is seriously optimistic. The bottom line is that everything we think we know is open to argument; Britannia in the fifth century is a landscape of shifting sand. We have few written sources and among them, the only one that focusses on the period is the monk Gildas writing in the following century.

Gildas was not writing history; he was writing a long and bitter complaint about his own generation. Gildas tells us of the heroics of Ambrosius Aurelianus but only in fragments. He mentions Vortigern – very disparagingly – but we are still not entirely sure whether Vortigern was actually a person's name, or just a title. Nor do we know what the title, 'High King' actually meant. It could have been an honorary post, or the High King might have exerted great influence. Did he control parts, or all of what had been Roman Britain? We simply do not know.

The overwhelming impression is that the Britannia where my Ambrosius washes up is a divided land where the local population are still trying to carve out a new society amid the trappings and debris of the Roman Empire. The Saxon presence there has a longer history than some might think, mainly because it was the Roman custom to employ barbarian mercenaries [foederati] to defend parts of the empire. There is evidence that British tribes like the Catuvellauni employed Saxons against their own British enemies. Saxons were therefore gamekeepers who eventually turned poachers. They were most likely not that numerous in 455 AD but they still offered a potential threat to the native Britons.

People:
Ambrosius Aurelianus

This series centres upon Ambrosius Aurelianus - one of the few individuals mentioned by name in the history of Britain in the fifth century. Unfortunately, we know almost nothing about his life at all until he features in the struggle between Britons and Saxons. Gildas tells us about Ambrosius in his work: *On the Ruin of Britain*. To Gildas, writing a century later about a land much dominated by Saxons, Ambrosius was a heroic figure - in contrast with his successors.

We do not know for certain, but Ambrosius was most likely the son of a prominent Roman – whether in Britain or elsewhere is in doubt. What is clear is that he was involved in several major events in British history, but we are not sure how old he was when he first became prominent, nor exactly when any of those events occurred. Nor do we know where he was based, though there have been many attempts to suggest possibilities, often relying on dubious place name evidence. In this book Ambrosius moves to the south west of Britain because it is very likely that he was based somewhere in that area.

Arthur

Arthur, as portrayed in legends simply did not exist – at all, ever. But the exploits of the actual Ambrosius and the legendary Arthur have sometimes melded into a sort of hybrid person – who therefore also never existed. Some fictional stories actually link the two by blood, but I've tried to explore an alternative view that perhaps someone called Arthur might have existed, associated with Ambrosius, but not *the* leader of the British - at least not during the younger

356

days of Ambrosius. I've called this character Lucius Artorius – or 'Arturus' – but he and the whole notion are, of course pure invention on my part. The persistence over time of the Arthurian legend may suggest that some sort of Arthur did exist but probably not one we would recognise from any of the legends.

Vortigern

If you look up Vortigern on the internet, you'll find numerous references to him – all the product of the same tiny amount of knowledge we have about him. We know so little that it's perfectly possible to argue that someone of that name never existed. How can that be? Well, because the original sources are very few and all those recording any events of note in this period basically repeated earlier references. So for example, the Venerable Bede, a monk writing primarily in the eighth century used Gildas' work and other sources available to him but lost to us. He therefore copied a lot of what Gildas told us, but Gildas was not concerned with an accurate record of events or people.

Thus a flawed account was passed on from generation to generation with chroniclers and historians embellishing the story with snippets of information about what Vortigern did and about his possible sons: Vortimer, Catigern and Pascent. By Victorian times, this version of events and people had become established fact despite its uncertain origins.

According to Gildas, Vortigern was a greedy, brutal, rapist; but whether he was any of those things is very much open to question. My Vortigern is an ageing king with limited authority in his later years, trying to cling on to power in the face of a changing and fragmented Britain where Saxons were becoming more numerous – especially in the east and there was little coherence in the political map of the country.

In this book Vortigern is pursued to his fictional stronghold overlooking the Wye valley. Well, it's a possibility that he had a fort in that area but the evidence is thin. I have placed it at the hill fort of Little Doward and the caves nearby where Ambrosius spends the night are based on what is now called 'King Arthurs' Cave' – huge irony…

Pascent

Vortigern's son, Pascent appears to have existed – or at least as much as his father did and after Vortigern's death he ruled some of his father's lands – of which Ergyng might have been one. Much of what can be gleaned about Pascent comes from Welsh literature and is probably derived from oral tradition.

King Erbin of Dumnonia

Whilst I can say with some confidence that Dumnonia was a significant area of Britain in this period, I cannot be certain that Erbin was king of it. Again his origins lie in Welsh literature and if the dates given there are anything close to correct than he would have been a young king in 455AD.

The Tribes of Britain

When the Romans first imposed imperial rule on Britain in 43AD, they found a country riven by tribal rivalries. Often they used these differences to play off one tribe against another and in that way made their conquest easier. During Roman rule, many of these local administrative regions had boundaries based on the old tribal divisions. When Roman power diminished in the fourth century, it was the local tribal groups who picked up the slack.

The traditional notion that Rome abandoned a defenceless Britain to its fate in the year 410AD is about as fanciful as the legend of Arthur. There is evidence that the British were armed by the late fourth and early fifth centuries and, not only armed but fighting against each other. One notable set of tribal rivalries concerned the Catuvellauni in the Thames valley area who appeared to have border disputes with tribes around them, especially the Atrebates to the south and the Dobunni to the west. It is quite possible that the evidence of Saxons turning up far from the east coast in the early fifth century reveals that they were mercenaries hired by one tribe to fight against their British rivals. Into this mess, steps Ambrosius Aurelianus…

The Bucellarii

The word bucellarius means 'biscuit-eater' which suggests that these men were used to campaigning on hard-baked biscuit rations. Bucellarii were basically private soldiers hired by a prominent individual to protect them, their families and their property. In the late empire of Rome the creation of bucellarii was encouraged because, since they were funded by private citizens they cost Rome nothing. Usually they were numbered in hundreds, or even thousands but the bucellarii in this story are a small group – the remnant of a larger force. It was usual to swear an oath to the emperor, but also one to their employer – in this instance, Ambrosius. They were usually very well-equipped and recruited from virtually anywhere in the empire, or even beyond - as in Ambrosius' elite, fictional bucellarii.

By the sixth century these elite cavalry units reigned supreme and one can see how they might have developed over several centuries into something approaching medieval knights. The idea of an individual gathering support on a personal basis - by oaths sworn to him - rather than because of some office that he held, underpinned the history of the next millennium. It is also the bedrock of my stories about Ambrosius.

Places:
Britannia and the Empire

By 455 AD Britannia was no longer a part of the Roman Empire. By then, it was not the only part of the empire where Rome had lost control: most of Spain, modern day Brittany and much of North Africa, for example, were already ruled by others. The difference with Britannia, of course was that its isolation was emphasised by the fact that it was an island and, though it was still subject to barbarian influences that process was a great deal slower and rather less genocidal than traditional history would have us believe.

It is quite possible to argue – as I have in this book – that there was no such entity as 'Britannia' in the fifth century. It became increasingly fragmented during that century and was not united again for another five hundred years or so. Hence the power after Vortigern lay with the individual tribal rulers.

Towns & Place Names

During the Roman administration of Britain, many towns developed as part of the economic and political landscape. By the late fourth and certainly into the fifth century, towns were in decline. Some survived longer than others; some adapted to changed circumstances better, but most shrank to a shadow of their former glory. Perhaps there was a large community of hovels and lean-tos amid the decaying stonework of many towns – but we simply don't know.

Hence Ambrosius finds Vindocladia – once the hub of a major road network - in a state of disrepair. You would struggle to find it at all now in modern Dorset – the most likely site is the tiny village of Shapwick. What happens to the town in this book is wholly fictional.

For other towns mentioned in the story I have used the names Caer Ceri (Cirencester), Caer Baddan (Bath) and Caer Gloui (Gloucester) though it is impossible in the absence of written sources to know for certain what contemporaries called these places – indeed any places.

Roman Cirencester was a major British town but by the mid-fifth century it had shrunk to include only the area around the old Roman amphitheatre – as described in the book - and Gloucester may well have been abandoned at that time as I have suggested.

Names are a headache for the reason mentioned already – the almost total absence of written records for the fifth century. With river names I've used what I think is a reasonable version of the name – as in Gwy (Wye) and Sturr (Stour). Much of the early action takes place at what is now Hengistbury Head in Dorset at the estuary of the River

Stour. In ancient times there was a major port there but it is likely that by late Roman times it was hardly used, though – as described – there was a 'gravel hard' or landing place there for ships and also some iron smelting. The latter activity persuaded me to give it the fictional, but highly appropriate name of Iron Hill.

It is tempting to view Roman Britain as a land of villas and towns, but of course there were many farms, small holdings and hamlets - as there always are. Hence, because villas and towns appear to have declined, we should not assume that other settlements necessarily changed much in post-Roman Britain. As ever in this period, many simple dwellings were constructed of wood or other substances which leave much less trace than stone.

Forts & Hill Forts

Ambrosius turns up at the start of the book in a ruined Roman burgus near Vindocladia built in the fourth century. This was a real burgus and archaeology has revealed some information about it - though I have almost certainly taken a few liberties. Only a few hundred yards from the burgus is – as described – an ancient hill fort now known as Badbury Rings, which does show evidence, like many other hill forts of the south west of re-occupation in the fifth century.

About the Author

Derek was born in Hampshire in England but spent his teenage years in Auckland, New Zealand, where he still has strong family ties. For many years he taught history in a secondary school but took early retirement to concentrate on his writing. Derek is interested in a wide range of themes and writes action-packed historical fiction.

Derek's debut historical novel, **Feud** is set in the period of the Wars of the Roses and is the first of a series, entitled **Rebels & Brothers** which follows the fortunes of the fictional Elder family up to 1471.

A follow-on series, **The Craft of Kings,** takes the story to 1485. The last book in the series, **Crown of Fear** is due to be published in 2021.

This book is the third of **The Last of the Romans series,** set in the fifth century and focussing on the shadowy historical figure of Ambrosius Aurelianus.

Books:

The *Rebels and Brothers* series [in order]:
Feud
A Traitor's Fate
Kingdom of Rebels
The Last Shroud

The *Craft of Kings* series:
Scars From The Past
The Blood of Princes
Echoes of Treason
Shadow of Doubt, a novella
Crown of Fear [to be published in December 2021]

The *Last of the Romans* series:
*The Last of the Romans
Britannia: World's End
New Dawn, a short novella
Death At the Feet of Venus – a short story
Land of Fire

* also available in audio format

To find out more about Derek's books, or to contact him, you can go to his website: www.derekbirks.com

Printed in Great Britain
by Amazon

11390770R00210